# NEVER UNTIL NOW

# NEVER UNTIL NOW

JOANNE McLAUGHLIN

Digital ISBN: 978-1-7325852-0-1
Print ISBN: 978-1-7325852-1-8
Cover art by: Dawné Dominique, DusktilDawn Designs
Author photo by: Jessica Griffin, Philadelphia Media Network

To Catherine McLaughlin (1929-2016),
my first fan and toughest critic,
from the alien spawn who misses her.

I am forever indebted to my friends,
beta readers, and amazing sources of inspiration, chief among them Rhonda Dickey, Gwen Florio, Kevin M. Smith and Cheryl Squadrito, editor Lynn M. Ross, and page/website designer Amy Junod Placentra. Many thanks to cover artist Dawné Dominique of DusktilDawn Designs and photographer Jessica Griffin of Philadelphia Media Network, as well as to Tony Merlo, who listened when that's what was needed.

*Chapter One*

# SWITZERLAND, NOVEMBER 2011

All my senses are on fire. I am aflame with a poison that burns from within. Pain tears at my limbs, rips through my ears and nose and eyes. I face east purposely, to speed awareness of the dawn, to own the anguish and embrace the irrevocable truth that no antidote exists for this venom inside me.

I squint through the rays of freshly risen sun that infiltrate my corner of the railway station, just enough to observe the platform across from this bench I dropped onto uncomfortably an hour ago. Recorded announcements in French and German herald the train's arrival for no one but me, given the hour and the isolated locale. Brakes shriek, wheels spark against steel; cars slow to a stop on the far track. I have mere minutes to board. I can make it if I hurry. I drag considerable baggage behind me, hoist it up two steps; wrestle it into an empty compartment and onto the seat next to me. I close the door and hope for quiet, some calm, finally. I must sleep. I've been awake for days.

A conductor slides the compartment door open. "*Bonjour*," he says, but does not look up from the scanner he holds. "*Billet, se vous plait. Fahrkarte, bitte.*"

I have no ticket. If I play this right, I'll have no need for one.

"*Bonjour, monsieur*. My French is not the best," I lie, in a fatigue-roughened timbre that sounds sultry even to me. "My German is worse. English, please?" I brush a finger across the back of his hand. He raises his eyes to me, shocked by the contact yet not displeased by it.

"*Pouvez-vous m'aider?*" I whisper, seeking his assistance, thumbing the skin of his soft, not-quite-middle-aged knuckles, conveying my message in a manner he feels more than hears. "*Je m'appelle Chloe*. Your name is Paul, yes?"

He glances down at his nametag uncertainly, swallows hard, his Adam's apple pronounced against the pale skin of his neck. "I can help you, yes, miss. *Un billet simple*, that is to say, one-way to Zurich? It is the terminus of this trip, perhaps a three-hour journey, with many connecting routes possible."

"*Oui,* Zurich," I say, lifting his hand to my lips, "but I don't want to buy a ticket, and I don't want to show you my passport. No one need know but us, *mon amour*."

Pupils dilate in his watery blue eyes. He fixes on my mouth and every place I put it, watches as I suck on each finger, as I run my tongue along his thumb then tease the graying blond hair on his forearm. He witnesses the moment at which my teeth sink into his wrist, just a shallow wound, a little taste, just enough to ignite his desire, to ensure he remains in my thrall through this trip. My green eyes flash in his, the red wig I wear reflects back at me. He stares, not fully believing what he sees, not fully comprehending anything beyond a longing that I continue. Were I not so exhausted, I might put a little more into this seduction, maybe take him in my hand to reward him, pleasure him for his service, isn't that what I've been taught? This morning, he is destined to be shortchanged, poor man.

A moan distracts us both. I ease away from Paul's vein, thank him, press a fierce kiss to his lips, nibble a bit until he opens them to taste my tongue as it glides suggestively along his before I bid him *au revoir*. "You should take a minute to compose yourself," I urge, pointing to his obvious erection. He inhales raggedly, adjusts his trousers, backs out of the compartment into the corridor, turns in the direction he came, oblivious to everything but the memory of my touch.

The man lying on the seat beside me, hemorrhaging, has escaped Paul's notice. I lower the door's privacy shade and reach over Will to tug the cord on the window blind, to shut out the sunlight that wants to seep in.

Energized by the familiar scents of spilled blood and sexual arousal, my companion shifts awake, struggles to sit. "Juliette, who is Chloe?" Will licks my cheek like a big sloppy puppy, leans in and reaches for me, his own stiffening cock guiding him like a compass needle pointing north.

"Somebody I knew a long, long time ago." Who's to say it isn't true?

Will pulls me onto his lap, settles his head against my shoulder, dozes off again, amazingly serene for a man who should by rights be dead. My eyelids flutter closed. I long for some of his peace, and to be, instead, in Jackson's arms.

* * * *

His fever startles me awake. We are two hours into our trip, and I am saturated with Will's sweat. I feel it through the leather of my jacket, which sticks to him even as I try to maneuver away from his chest. The heat rising from him is stifling, makes me want to retch. He has lost so much blood; I have overindulged my new appetites. Fresh air beckons, rushing against the side of the train, but I dare not open the window, dare not experiment here with the before-noon sun's new potential for toasting my epidermis.

Like him, I am wearier, weaker, as if a tap has been turned and I am draining, drop-by-drop, from this self I call Chloe Hart into some other receptacle. Perhaps back into my original self, Clothilde Juliette de la Coeur, princess of the rock-and-roll realm, spawn of the now-departed Emilie and Sebastian de la Coeur, musical monarchs of the Court of Cruelty—my parents, the vampires. Their progressive-rock band sang of medieval torture and misery, and also of those opiates of the people, religion and love and hope.

Correction: They *still* sing about torture, et cetera. Sebastian and Emilie are not dead, not truly, reports of her cancer fueling their suicides notwithstanding. These days, the world sees them as a couple of second-rate Swedish musicians fronting a Court of Cruelty tribute band, Matins and Vespers, though Lord knows that's not all they're involved in. Illegal commerce in weapons and organs, human trafficking maybe, I wouldn't put anything past their rechristened selves, Katarina and Teppan Nilsson. Well within their power to arrange, if not participate in directly, were the deaths of one art gallery owner and four women who carried my father's dead babies.

I'll give them the benefit of the doubt regarding two victims of a tour bus bombed at Castle de la Coeur, the family fortress. As for their abducted-and-assaulted only daughter, the less said about her, the better. I am an accident of birth, apparently, a freak of nature even by vampire standards. Inexplicably begotten, misbegotten nonetheless. The responsibility for me lies squarely with them, as do the lies they have told me all my life.

Just thinking about Teppan Nilsson, the arrogant blond Adonis my father now styles himself as, makes me shudder. I am here because of my vain, impetuous sire; here in a rail car with a virtual stranger whose survival much longer is hardly assured. I should never have gone to Edinburgh, should never have listened to Teppan. Ought not to have allowed what occurred in that hotel room, or, rather, what did not occur. Either version seems a perversion.

No, wait, that lets me off the hook. I asked for this, didn't I? *Such a coward, Chloe. You demanded a share in your vampire birthright. You got what you wanted.*

So what am I running from except my own bad choices? Even intoxicated by the blood, I knew it wasn't smart to let Will follow me from Edinburgh to Paris. Instead of scaring him off,

I've sucked blood from him and screwed him until he can barely remember who Will Baumann is, let alone care about C.J. Hart's existential crisis. I all but carried him across the Swiss border. How much longer before I take it too far? Before I lose my fiancé, my art gallery, everything I treasure, and to prove what? That I can handle whatever challenges my father throws down?

More important, isn't it, to prove that I won't let this vampire self obliterate the human me? If I value everything I've been until now, and Aspect Ratio and Jackson—dear God, Jackson, what must you be thinking—don't I have to turn back?

Will shivers, the sweats of his fever giving way to chills. I wrap him in the blanket we swiped off a hotel bed somewhere in France, clutch him to my side to get him warmer. Rock him to comfort him, though he is almost surely unconscious and unable to be comforted. I'm the one being soothed, through a searing ache that rips through my gut and pounds in my head and threatens to tear the soul from my body. If death doesn't feel like this, I'll be surprised. Who expires first this morning, Will or me, might well be a toss-up. Have I dragged us so far that retreat is no longer an option? I'll never know until I try.

Time to make a run for it. I won't let Will die, even if it kills me.

I stand unsteadily, loop my courier bag around my neck, pull Will upright, wedge my body under his armpit, and boost him and the blood-dampened blanket off the seat. I half-push, half-pull him to the passage between train cars, to the steps that would lead to a platform if there were one. I pull the corner of the blanket up and over my head, down across my forehead. I close my eyes against the sun and jump.

*Chapter Two*

## ZURICH, NOVEMBER 2011

By air, it was, what, two hours from Zurich to Prague? He couldn't think, Jackson Fahey just knew it was two hours more than he had to spare. Chloe had already been missing for days. Too long, and too much ground to make up.

Uneasy through two days covering a eurozone bankers' conference. Dismayed when so many calls and text messages went unacknowledged. Scared witless when Benjamin Kwesi, her associate at Aspect Ratio, had at last reached Fahey with news that he'd asked Chloe's landlord to open her flat for him. No sign of her at all, no sign that she'd been there since leaving Ben a message Monday at her London art gallery that she was going to Edinburgh.

Why Edinburgh? Recent developments suggested she should have been bound for her parents' house outside Prague. The bodies of four murdered women, each with a dead unborn child, had been found on Sebastian and Emilie de la Coeur's estate near the Czech capital.

Almost midnight now, almost Friday. Fahey was due on a flight back to Brussels in the morning. They wouldn't be expecting him at the BBC news bureau, though; he could fly to Prague, he might find her there. But something told him no, that wasn't right.

*Trust your gut, Jackson. What else have you got right now?*

Every bone in his body clamored for rest. Every cell in his brain vibrated, anticipating a signal that the blood bond Chloe was forever talking about had activated, transmitting her coordinates like a GPS. He'd open any one of his Irish veins to make it happen. "*Just a bit of a signal, I'll take it from there,*" he demanded with some inner voice he hoped was connected to her, but it gave nothing back.

Up the lift from the hotel bar, two beers and a bratwurst barely staying down. He swiped the key card for his room and turned on the overhead light.

Someone had tossed the place: dumped his suitcase onto the floor; threw his things about; dragged the sheets off to one side. Fahey made his way slowly, listening for something, he wasn't sure what. Looking for whoever had gotten into his locked room, ransacked it, then locked up again without taking the bank envelope containing 500 euro he'd stashed in his luggage. Cash was scattered across the carpet with his socks and briefs.

A moan, mournful like a wounded animal's, drew him to the far side of the bed. A man was clinging to the mattress, but mostly on the floor, his chest scarcely rising and falling. Fahey crouched next to him, felt for a pulse. Faint, but there.

Circling back to the phone on the nightstand, Fahey called the front desk, described what he'd discovered, retraced his steps until he was once again looking down at his unexpected guest. Something about the body, its position, something about the bend in its back, the hand dangling, brushing blood on the floor, just a small amount, still dripping from the man's wrist. Too familiar, as were the bloodstains he now noticed on the man's collar and sweater, about a third of the way down his chest.

Level with the man's left hip but tucked almost under the bed was a folded napkin. Fahey could see words bleeding through from the underside. He stretched as far over the body as he could without touching it, tipped the napkin with a knuckle.

"*HELP HIM.*" Her handwriting.

Fahey scooped up the napkin, thrust it into his pocket. The man's eyes opened. "Wasn't too much," he rasped. "Tell her."

"Tell who?"

"Pretty. Afraid."

"Where is she now?"

The man shook his head, agitated. "Forget."

Fahey loomed over him. "What's her name?"

"Forget. Made me forget."

"Forget what? Who she is, or what she did?"

"Unforgettable." The man smiled.

Fahey knew that smile, had seen it in the mirror reflecting back at him after he and Chloe made love. Even at the airport in Ireland, after their first quick time together, he'd seen it.

"What did she do to you?" Fahey demanded, but the man lost consciousness as police officers arrived, announcing themselves, first in French, then in German, followed by two paramedics, who checked the man's vitals before loading him onto a stretcher.

"Unforgettable," the man murmured again. An officer looked at Fahey, eyebrow raised. Fahey shrugged. Truly, what could he have said?

Through the next few hours—through the half-dozen recitations of what he had found and questions about how it was possible that this man, with an Oregon driver's license showing him to be William Baumann, age twenty-nine, might have come to be in his hotel room—the bloody napkin burned a hole against Fahey's leg, incinerating the fabric of his pocket and the skin below it. He felt dizzy and slightly nauseated, as if the blood on the napkin had been his own.

Alibi checked and statement given, he was more than halfway to Belgium when the sleeping pill he'd chased down with beer at the hotel bar finally kicked in. As Fahey dozed, a memory stitched: a man bent back over a woman's lap, her face concealed by a fall of red hair; his arm dangling from his body, his finger trailing in his own blood. A too-familiar image. In his dream, Fahey traced the outline of the man's wounds, his finger red, wet. In his airplane seat, he squeezed the napkin in his pocket, the paper still damp against his thumb.

Wheels bounced hard on the runway, brakes whined loudly. Fahey opened his eyes, and Sebastian and Emilie de la Coeur's sitting room in upstate New York vanished, as did the inscrutable tapestries on which he had first seen those wounds, that blood.

*Chloe, what have you done?*

Through the terminal, through the taxi ride home, the ruby pendant that once scorched him with her passion thudded cold against his chest.

* * * *

His Brussels flat was in a retrofitted candy factory. Fahey swore he could smell the nougat and chocolate that once boiled in kettles there. His fourth-floor space was tiny and all-purpose: eat, sleep, and everything else in one room. No privacy, except for the toilet.

No privacy at all, and no security, when the street door was propped open. His brain screamed a *déjà vu* when he discovered the door to his flat had been forced. A random intruder would be disappointed with its contents. After Zurich, after what he had found there, Fahey hoped for random.

Vomit, or something like it, greeted him: saliva, blood, green bits of lettuce maybe. What might once have been a black cashmere sweater curled on itself like a dead cat. Black tights, a short skirt; tall black boots collapsed next to the bed. In the doorway to the bath, a red wig.

She was lodged behind the door, half in the tub, the tap running, water perilously close to overflowing. He stepped over her legs, straining to reach the faucets to stop a flood, standing in the same whitish-reddish-greenish slime he'd found in the other room.

Her body convulsed against his legs. He peeled her hair back from her face, startled by its pallor. The water was scalding, the steam rising as he lifted her, washed blood from her mouth, dunked her head beneath the surface, whether to cleanse her or kill her he wasn't sure. Maybe both. Probably both.

He yanked her hair and pulled her face out of the water, moved his other hand down her outside leg, felt it stick to what he guessed might be semen. He picked her up and placed her fully into the tub. Her eyelids fluttered.

"Jackson!" Unconscious yet somehow aware.

His pendant, supposedly powered by the chemistry between them, seared his chest. "Okay, I get it: She's the only girl for me." Maybe for someone else, too, judging from the slickness of her thigh.

"Jackson?" Plaintive. Contrite.

"It's all right, love, I'm here. I have you. Let's clean you up and get you all warm and down for a rest."

She tried to climb out of the tub, slipped and splashed them both with water now turned pink. Fahey pulled the plug, let the water drain, ran the taps as hot as he could; she could take the heat, it seemed.

"What?" she moaned, after some minutes of soaking and scrubbing, when he helped her to her feet, wrapped his lone clean towel around her, and carried her to his bed. He rubbed her briskly, to get her dry before setting her down. He fished a soft, old shirt from his closet, folded her into it; slipped socks onto her feet, laid her on her side. Pulled the covers up to her shoulders; pulled a trash bin close to her head.

"What?"

"Something you ate, and drank, and maybe screwed, but I'm just speculating." He pretended not to hear her persistent "Whats" and went to the kitchen, found his mobile, texted Benjamin in London: *"I have Chloe here in Brussels. She's not feeling well. Will call later."*

Over the next hour, Fahey cleaned the place. Scrubbed hydrogen peroxide into the rug; during his Afghanistan assignment with the BBC, he'd seen it take blood out of anything. Scoured the tub with cleanser then filled it with a cold water-peroxide mix and dumped her clothes into it to soak. Wiped down the tile, the mirror, the toilet, anything else she'd spewed into or on.

When there were no more bodily fluids to wash away, he retrieved from the very back of a kitchen cabinet the bottle of scotch he'd pinched from Castle de la Coeur and smuggled over the Atlantic from New York, Sebastian's very old, very good whisky. He could use a buzz right now. About a third of the way through the bottle, Fahey more or less passed out on a too-small, too-short chair. After a while, he heard his ringtone but couldn't raise his head far enough off the vinyl cushion to care.

"Daddy, answer the phone! Daddy, please, it's so loud!" Her cries pierced Fahey's stupor. She was sitting up on the bed, her eyes a flat black instead of their usual brilliant green. She was looking directly at him, but it was clear she couldn't see him. The phone rang again, and he stumbled out of the chair to get it. Aspect Ratio was calling.

"Ben . . ."

"C.J. never gets sick, not once in all the time I've known her, and I've known her longer than almost anyone in the world. What's wrong with her?"

Shit, Meredith Grainger-Todd *would* be in London now, romancing Ben, handling some publicity thing for the gallery. She had to stay there; Fahey couldn't let Meredith see what he'd just seen.

"She has the flu, I think," he lied. "She's been vomiting and feverish and a bit delirious." Okay, semi-lied, that last bit was true.

"Aspirin and liquids, now, to bring the fever down, and you have to get her to a doctor!" Panic infused Meredith's every syllable.

Aspirin might help, though, might thin Chloe's blood or whatever consumed blood she hadn't yet thrown up.

"Call if you need me to fly there to look after her. Ben can postpone the opening of the new exhibit. If Chloe's sick, he should postpone."

"The opening is a week away. This will pass, I'm sure." He wasn't.

"I need to talk to her, Jackson." Not bloody likely, not anytime soon.

He hung up before Meredith started in again and ran to his medicine cabinet. A couple packets of the fizzy bicarbonate stuff with aspirin would have to do, at least it would be liquid, and hopefully Chloe would keep it down. He opened the packets and dissolved two tablets, got about half of it into her before she started to scream in a language he didn't recognize. Like German, but not exactly.

"Stefan, Stefan! *Vati!*"

*Daddy*, he understood that much, and Stefan was the name Sebastian's birth parents had given him.

Perspiration poured off her and she trembled with fever, retching, threatening to bring up what she'd just drunk. He wrapped her in the blanket, sat up against the headboard behind her, pulled her to his chest, held her as close as he could until there was no space between them, kissed her head to comfort her.

"*Nein, Vati!*" she shrieked.

The pendant rocked him with a jolt of heat. The skin beneath it crackled, he felt the blisters rise. She fussed in his arms, as if she'd felt the burn too.

She'd made him wear the fucking pendant, where was hers? He eased out from behind her. Against the wall near the door sat her courier bag, right where she'd dropped it. He felt her pendant's burn through the velvet pouch it was in, watched as the pendant practically combusted when he removed it. Gently, he lifted her head, gently slipped the pendant over and positioned it between her breasts. The ruby brightened the minute it made contact. She clutched at it, twisted it, tried to break the chain, but the metal, forged an age ago, held strong, defying her attempts to snap it. After several minutes, she gave up the fight, gave in to whatever it was she was trying to resist.

"Jackson, help me."

He returned to his place behind her on the bed, his own pendant calmer now against his flesh. "I'm here, love. I'll take care of you."

"I'm sorry," she whispered, then slumped in his arms, asleep, unconscious, he wasn't sure which. Wasn't sure he cared. Wasn't sure he wanted to know just what she was apologizing for.

He caught a few hours' sleep, cradling her between his legs, but the position was awkward, and even his exhaustion could not quiet his mind, or distract him from the thought of Chloe with her teeth in William Baumann, with her lips and other parts in contact with him. Fahey extracted his body from hers, stood and stretched, started a pot of coffee in the kitchen, switched on his laptop at the low table that served for meals and work at home.

He began searching databases for Baumann. By the time he'd downed two cups of coffee, he'd discovered that Chloe's new friend was a University of Oregon graduate in chemistry; date of birth, 6 April 1982, Sacramento, Calif.; living in the UK under a twenty-four-month work visa, employed by a Scottish microbrewery; current address, Edinburgh. As far as Fahey could tell, Baumann hadn't gone to even one of the many universities Chloe attended, hadn't lived any of the same cities.

"Wasn't a business trip, Jackson, or I'd have known about it," Benjamin had told him Tuesday night, when he'd first reached Fahey in Zurich. "And why would she go to Edinburgh for a non-gallery trip and not tell you about it?" Ben had done security work, had been Chloe's bodyguard for a while; his antennae had immediately gone up, envisioning worst-case scenarios.

With her screams still ringing in his ears, Fahey thought to beyond the worst. "Pretty. Afraid," Baumann had said. Chloe was peaceful enough now, but how long might that last? He needed to understand what had happened since she left London at the start of the week. He googled major Edinburgh hotels, scratched out a list of five, and started making calls.

The third hotel, a posh place on the Royal Mile, proved the winner. A desk clerk there was willing to tell the BBC reporter a tasty little tidbit about a certain Miss C.J. Hart, whose name said clerk had recognized immediately because of the reports about corpses being found on property owned by her late parents, Sebastian and Emilie de la Coeur of Court of Cruelty fame.

"Attractive redhead, checked in at seven o'clock Monday evening, checked out about half-past eight on the arm of a handsome blond man with a Swedish name. I don't dare divulge whom—hotel policy. He said she'd be staying in his room, and he paid her bill. Elderly chap and his wife came down from the man's floor a few minutes later, complained that Miss Hart and the Swede practically ran them down as the pair got off the elevator. Musician, we think he was, one of the concierges here is sure he looked familiar."

A handsome, blond Swedish man. Not Baumann then. More like Teppan Nilsson.

"You say Miss Hart was a redhead?"

"Yes."

"Which day was their last at the hotel?"

The clerk tapped a few keystrokes. "The room was paid for in advance. Housekeeping found it empty, with the key cards left behind, about ten the next morning. Tuesday, that is."

So Monday night into Tuesday morning, Chloe was almost certainly with her father; the red wig she'd been wearing was in his own bathroom right now. He hung up, flipped through some old text messages until he found the one alerting him to the Matins and Vespers show he'd gone to in Brussels a few weeks ago.

"*Urgent*," he texted.

At the Zurich hospital where the ambulance had taken William Baumann, a woman checked the patient logs at Fahey's request; there was no one by that name currently. Damn.

Maybe Baumann had headed back to Edinburgh. Fahey searched for microbreweries, then brew pubs, and cross-referenced. Six breweries also had pubs; he'd bet anything Baumann worked at one of them.

"Jackson? Where are we?"

Her voice was weak, but Chloe's color was closer to normal. Relief pounded through him, muted immediately by what he knew and what he suspected. "We're in Brussels, love, at my flat. You've been ill."

"Can I have something to drink please?"

An unopened bottle of sparkling water was chilling in his refrigerator. He poured her some. "Slowly, love, don't want you vomiting again."

"I don't remember traveling with you."

"We came separately. I was in Zurich covering a banking conference. You were here when I got back earlier today."

She nodded, but he could see she didn't remember. What did she recollect, he'd love to know? Instead, he asked whether she was hungry. She wasn't, though her stomach was surely empty. Fahey wasn't sure he needed food, but he did need to avoid the deep subjects for a bit longer, until he knew more.

"I need to go out for a little while, to pick up a few things for us."

"Peanut butter."

"If that's what you'd like."

"Hmm, yes." She sank under the covers. Fahey waited until she was asleep again, threw some water on his face, then went out to hunt for supper.

When he returned, Chloe was still sleeping. He took a quick shower and got into bed with her. It was either that or the chair again. At some point during the night, she nestled into his arms, as if nothing had happened, as if they were the same as they always had been. He woke hard and hating himself for it.

Before departing very early Sunday to do an on-camera summary of the week's euro-crisis developments, he made her a pot of coffee and two peanut butter sandwiches and left a note saying he'd be back about eight o'clock that night. He needed time away from her to think, but he couldn't just toss her out, not the way she'd evicted him from the Castle after that ugly business with Meredith. Christ, hadn't he deserved it? He'd slept with her best friend to gain access to a sample of Sebastian de la Coeur's semen, to confirm Chloe's parentage. Still, he and Chloe were engaged now, and this thing with Baumann was tough to accept.

As the day progressed, he called her mobile three times from work, texted too, but didn't raise her. Sleeping and, he hoped, not sick again. He wasn't sure how much more vomit he'd be able to stomach. Later, en route to the flat, he picked up some mild cheese and some saltines, some ginger ale and some yogurt, things he hoped she'd tolerate. He wasn't sure how long the effects of her blood binge might last; eventually, she'd need real food, wouldn't she?

Later than he expected, he unlocked his door, found the flat in darkness. Fahey flipped the closest switch, to the overhead fixture in the kitchen, and the light blinded him. When he could see again, he saw the full coffee carafe, the sandwiches undisturbed in their plastic bag. When he turned to the bed, a fresh bloodstain lay inside the distinct imprint of her body.

He followed drops to the closed bathroom door and shoved it open. She was standing at the sink, staring at the mirror. In blood—it was running down her wrist—she had written the word *vampire* on the glass. Slowly, he stepped in behind her, careful not to startle her.

"Love, let me wash this for you." He ran the water cold, tucked her wrist under the stream, soaped it, rinsed it, dried it with a towel, the whole time watching her face, watching her eyes, wide, black, unblinking. He eased her head aside, opened the medicine cabinet, wrapped the wound with a series of small bandages he found there, his only emergency supplies. Then he leaned her against the door and washed blood and skin from underneath her fingernails, which she'd apparently used to cut herself. When he finished, he carried her back to the bed. He poured some ginger ale into a mug and wrapped her fingers around the handle, tilted her head back a bit so he could hold it to her mouth. She lapped at the liquid with her tongue, coated her cracked lips with it, breaking his heart with each shy movement.

"Not a vampire, just my only love," he whispered, brushing her matted hair away from her face.

She looked past him to some unknown truth beyond that room, and he saw tears well in eyes that were green again, hers again. For the second night in a row, he cradled her in his arms until the torment passed and she could sleep.

* * * *

Monday: No fever; no vomiting; no cutting. *Catatonic* seemed apt. He spent his first day off watching for signs of improvement and seeing none.

Tuesday: He handed her a saltine with some peanut butter, eventually got four more down her and some ginger ale. All day, she watched him but did not speak, did not attempt to communicate at all.

Wednesday: He had to go back to work, but how could he leave her like this, quite capable of starving or drowning or slicing herself until she bled to death? He didn't dare take her to a hospital. He couldn't gauge her mental state, what she might do among strangers, and how to explain that she'd been like this, more or less, for days now? How did one recount what he'd discovered, or what she had likely done to get herself into the state she was in?

*I'm not sure, and I'm being conservative in speculating. Talking to myself, as well. Get a grip, Jackson, think this through.*

About half-past seven, he took a serrated knife from the kitchen, slashed across his wrist and raised it to Chloe's mouth. She moved her tongue through the blood, locked her lips onto him. When bright flashes sparked before his eyes, he wrested the arm away, wrapped a dish towel around the cut, wiped blood from her lips, kissed her forehead as she moaned. He dabbed some of her saliva onto the towel, patted his wound with it, and watched the laceration seal. He made her as comfortable as he could, locked the door behind him, and went to work. For once, the blood thing hadn't left him rock-hard, and he thanked whichever god had seen to that on his behalf.

About noon, as he prepped a piece about the new Italian prime minister and his fiscal agenda, Fahey's desk phone rang.

"I'm at your flat, I'm taking her home. You've done well, Jackson, but a girl needs her mother at a time like this."

Emilie, or, rather, Katarina Nilsson.

"Home to London?"

"Home to the Castle. Tell no one, especially Meredith. Wait a week before coming to New York. Chloe should improve by then. She'll have made the transition."

Always, Fahey navigated interviews by instinct. First, he asked questions to which he already knew the answers, and if he had none, he'd pretend and wait to see what was disclosed once he got someone talking.

"The transition, of course."

"She's like us now, and so help me, her father will pay."

Something more than anger underlay that vow, something Kat was not saying. The woman he loved was altered forever, what more could the de la Coeurs do to shock him?

So much more.

"Chloe is pregnant, about five weeks' along. It never occurred to her, but I vomited the same way, I knew. It's yours;

she insisted I tell you there was no one else before Edinburgh."

He dropped the receiver, heard it crash against vintage linoleum, worried for a moment it might be his head instead hitting the floor. The small office went silent around him. "Chloe and I are having a baby!" he announced, astounded. Applause rose, as did a chorus of congratulations.

By the time he got home, the flat had long since been vacated, slamming the brakes on his soaring spirits. The place smelled strongly of clean, of citrus and bleach and fresh air. Bed linens had been changed, towels replaced in his kitchen and bathroom, and with them all trace of Chloe obliterated. Fahey yearned to be with her and their child.

In his freezer was a bottle of her favorite lemon vodka; he'd bought it to share with her on a visit they'd never gotten around to planning. He reached for it, to taste her, since he could neither see nor hear nor touch her. His hand brushed against a package in the freezer: the vial containing Sebastian's semen, evidence of Fahey's latest sin. He had kept it on impulse, insurance, he supposed, against the day when he'd need some leverage against one or both of the de la Coeurs. Though now, of course, the baby their daughter carried—his baby, begotten of human father and vampire-inclined mother—had raised those stakes. More precious than the potential fruit of Sebastian's loins, surely to all of them, was this child, the fruit of Fahey's.

Now that Chloe was fully a vampire, how much more valuable might she and the baby be to Sebastian's enemies? Hard to envision a more perfect way to blackmail the King of the Cruel. Hard to know the best way to defend against that for the next eight months, but staying in Brussels for even another day was not it. Fahey shoved the vial back into the recesses of the freezer, repositioned the vodka bottle in front of it. You never knew when something would come in handy.

He booked an early morning flight to New York, called his bureau chief on the drive to the airport to ask for—and, luckily, be granted—a week's emergency leave, so he could be with Chloe when she saw a doctor back in the States. A possible complication with the pregnancy, he explained, a genetic issue, and he wanted to be there for her. All true enough.

* * * *

Fahey found a limo driver willing to take him from JFK Airport to the outskirts of Ithaca for the $362 he'd gotten in exchange for his euro. The car came with sodas and snacks. "Breakfast of vampire champions," he muttered in the back seat.

Once past the city, they hit surprisingly little traffic, and Fahey was reminded how lovely upstate New York was in the fall. Yet he hoped Chloe would be as eager as he to get back to their lives in Europe, to figure out again what normal was for them. It seemed they'd done that every few months since they'd met in April. Change had become their one constant.

When the driver deposited him at the Castle gate, Fahey saw that security was twice what it had been before June's tour-bus bombing here at Vineyard de la Coeur. Though he had lived at the Castle for several weeks before the blast, even the guards he knew were reluctant to admit him to the grounds. He showed identification, greeted at least three of them by name and asked about their families. Nothing cracked their resolve to keep him out. He hesitated to do it but had no choice: He punched in a number on his mobile, and prayed for an answer.

"Come get me," he implored. A green pickup approached the gate in minutes.

"About time you got back, Jackson Fahey. This house is too quiet by half without you blaring music night and day." Gloria Dennehy stepped out of the truck and into his hug. Fahey whispered his thanks, kissed her loudly on the cheek.

"Then maybe you could be persuading the gentlemen over there to let me in to see my lady fair?"

Gloria bit her lip. "Mrs. Nilsson will not be pleased if I do.

She was adamant that you not be admitted onto the property."

Katarina had reassumed command of the Castle, had she? "How fortunate that the property doesn't belong to her, but to Chloe. Shall we ask her thoughts about that?"

A sly smile crossed Gloria's lips. "Let's not."

She climbed into the truck and leaned over to unlock the passenger door. Fahey tossed his bags in the back and slid in.

They entered the Castle through the kitchen, an aromatic paradise of apples and cinnamon and autumn.

"Where's Chloe? I want to see her right away."

Gloria filled a mug with coffee, sliced into a pie cooling on the island, pulled out a stool, and motioned for him to sit. "Slowly. She's been very sick, what with the baby and everything else. This can't be rushed; the transition took a lot out of her."

So Gloria did know the de la Coeurs' big, bad secret. "Take me to Kat then. She'll talk to me."

Except it turned out Kat wouldn't, and Gloria wouldn't intervene. As manager of the Castle, she assigned him his old room, the one with the grand four-poster bed that had been the backdrop for tormenting dreams of sexual and vampiric awakening. His pendant sizzled like a just-struck match, and his cock saluted the power pulsing around him. Chloe was close, very close, but not close enough to touch and burn off the desire. Close by, he guessed, her pendant would be blazing, too, heralding his arrival.

Once past the sentinels at the gate, he moved freely through the Castle and surrounding compound, with access to all but the areas housing the women he wanted most to see. The doors to Sebastian and Emilie's quarters were locked. His first full afternoon back, Fahey inspected the newly reopened winery, admired the retrofits that created a new shop from what remained of the damaged one, sampled the favorites and a new white, a pinot-chardonnay blend called "Innocents." Meredith, public-relations genius that she was, had set up a charitable fund using the wine's sales to benefit the families of those slain and injured in the explosion. He spent his last ten dollars on a bottle and sat in a familiar patch of dappled sunlight outside, under a familiar tree, to drink away the chill and his anxiety.

Beyond the confines of the winery and the vineyard, with their separate entrances from the road, no one but Castle staff came or went as the week unwound. Fahey supposed blood was being supplied to Chloe somehow, wished there were a book he could read to research what might be going on around him but just out of sight.

To amuse himself, and Gloria, he played through Court of Cruelty's catalog, imbibing Sebastian's potent scotch as the music reverberated off the Castle's old walls. He studied the concert posters and the paintings and the Cruel's tour memorabilia yet again, looking for something he couldn't describe but was certain he'd recognize if he saw it. Yet what was there now was what had been there before: images of Emilie and Sebastian; the guitarists Zeke Segal and Ronnie Hamilton; Esteban Gronlund dressed as Stephano the Jester; some images of the band's lawyer, Ed Chestack, back when he was the drummer and called himself Eddie Check; the keyboard player, Theo Martin, before his fatal motorcycle crash; and a few other musicians who appeared on some albums but not others. Also photos of Chloe: as a baby; on the tour bus, bouncing on someone's knee; laughing as she conjured balloon animals with Esteban; and in her boarding-school uniform with Meredith, scowling at the camera. This was her family, the one she loved and loathed. The parents she would know forever more, unlike him and quite possibly unlike their child.

Loneliness gripped him, and Fahey mourned those many future years he would not have with his Juliette, as he first came to know her. By the afternoon of the sixth day, after too much time to think and prowl without purpose, after more liquor than any man should be allowed to consume, he was ready to blow up the Castle himself. He raged at Gloria, demanding to see Chloe, or at least talk to Katarina.

"I won't be denied any longer! Tell Kat to get her immortal arse down here and explain what's going on in this house, or I swear I'll burn it down around her. Can she survive a conflagration? Shall we give it a shot?"

Gloria made a pot of tea, Irish breakfast, a mutual favorite that reminded them of home; she pushed a cup toward him, then another, and another. Afterward, she led him to the window seat and left him there. Fahey stared outside, watching the sky streak pink, then red, then go black. He felt compelled to turn back to the room. Katarina met his eyes, turned and walked upstairs, to Sebastian's music studio. He followed.

Kat's hair was dyed now like Teppan's, an almost-white blond, cut short, very 1960s Carnaby Street. Her distinctive green eyes still hid behind contact lenses in a blue several degrees less icy than her husband's. Less forbidding, yet, Fahey must remember, no less dangerous. Arrestingly gorgeous, he had forgotten how beautiful she was. His cock twitched, his balls tightened, his pulse accelerated; he clutched at the pendant, but it was cold against his chest. She laughed at the effect she was having.

"I'm not here to toy with you, though I'm sure we'd both enjoy it. You wanted to see me. Here I am."

She snatched a bottle of something, maybe brandy, out of his reach and fixed those eyes on him. He struggled to focus, to articulate even one of the hundred questions he wanted to ask. "Chloe?"

Kat took a chair, pointed to its mate next to her. He sat.

"Getting stronger every day, she'll be ready to see you tomorrow, just as I promised. These things take time."

"What things?"

*Are you sure you want to know?*

The challenge hung between them, loud though unuttered. Fahey felt himself nod that, yes, he was.

"What you saw her go through was her transformative experience. That usually involves death, and a subsequent purging of the human casing. The amnesia, the catatonia, the fever, that's all part of it. Body and mind cast off what they no longer require, so they can re-form into what will be needed thereafter. I don't fully understand how it happens, just that it does."

"I spent days cleaning up the 'human casing', trying to keep her body and mind intact. I can't believe she survived it."

Worry danced across Katarina's features, and he sensed Chloe's survival was still not ensured.

"Yes, it was terrible. I suppose that's because she didn't actually die. She's been almost equally human and other up to now, I think, and when she made the decision to transform, her body had to figure out how to remain both but in different proportions, without destroying itself."

"Both? You mean she's not a vampire?"

"She is, but remember we're human and more. It's the more that almost killed her: Chloe was not made a vampire; she was born with that inclination and for some reason has only just matured into it. Being pregnant complicated things."

Unable to keep blood down one day, or food down the next. How would Chloe and the baby coexist? "I was afraid she'd starve or dehydrate or both, that's when I gave her my blood. She'd been vomiting for days, sweating with fever. I couldn't think what else to do." What if it hadn't worked, if he'd come home that night to find her dead?

Kat stroked his hand. "You saved her. I was desperate to find her after I saw your text and I realized what her father had done. When your blood hit her system, I could sense immediately where she was and that she was in distress. Without you, I might have spent days stumbling around Edinburgh and Zurich."

She knew about William Baumann then.

"Chloe went to Edinburgh to see Teppan. I know that much."

Kat stood, paced the way her daughter often did. Weighing how much might be better left unsaid? She grabbed the bottle she'd kept him from earlier, poured them each a drink, handed him a glass.

He breathed in the brandy's fire. It stung his throat as it went down, like the scrape of Chloe's teeth, so pleasingly painful, until he envisioned her nibbling on her virgin vampire conquest in Edinburgh. It would take all the brandy there was to wash that image away.

"It's sensual, sexual, always. Unless we have been starved and pushed to our limits, there is no reason to kill, no reason not to give pleasure for pleasure. Sex with Baumann was not personal for Chloe, you must understand that."

"She wasn't being unfaithful, is that what you're telling me?"

"Trust me: You'll know when she's being unfaithful. Sex with someone else will have very little to do with it," said the voice of experience with perfidious vampire partners.

"She brought Baumann to me in Zurich, left him in my hotel room like a cat leaves a dead mouse for its master."

"She was suffering, and she panicked. She knew you'd take care of him, knew you'd realize that in doing so, you'd be taking care of her."

"Why did she need taking care of in the first place? Where was her father, and why are you so angry at him?"

That relationship was verboten territory, though Fahey sensed that whatever offense had been committed this time was beyond the pale.

"I didn't want this for Chloe. I was perfectly content for her to have you and not explore her other side further. Our daughter could have lived a human life and had its human joys and sorrows."

"Teppan disagreed? He seems to do that a lot, seems to thrive on provoking you, actually."

"Nothing about Chloe's life has been predictable, not the day she was conceived, not today. He had no business doing what he did."

"Which was what exactly, besides encourage Chloe to decide for herself that she wanted this? It's been on her mind since you two told her about the de la Coeurs' unusual family heritage. You know she's been practicing on me for months. How has your husband done anything but help Chloe fulfill her destiny?"

Green streaks shot through Kat's blue contact lenses. Rage radiated from her in successive waves, knocking Fahey to his knees, pressing on him until he was on all fours and shielding his head and neck from the ire she had unleashed.

"He tricked her into playing with fire, and Chloe very nearly went up in flames." White heat permeated every soft-spoken syllable. "He doesn't know how precarious a thing this existence of ours can be because his transition went smoothly; others are not so lucky. We might very well have lost her."

She swallowed the remainder of the brandy, hurled the glass so close to his ear Fahey felt it skitter across his cheek as it passed.

"Her father crossed a line. I won't allow him to cross another."

Suddenly, Fahey was quite sober.

* * * *

A fragrant freshness surrounded him, the scent of grass after a light rain. Her weight pressed down on the mattress, warmth melting over him like chocolate. Whatever Chloe was now, whatever she had done and would do, she was here and he loved her.

She moved over his chest. Her hair, longer, softer, teased his nipples to attention. His cock, too, was ready, and when she sank onto it, his breath left his body.

"I love you, Jackson, only you."

He couldn't speak; his only functioning sense was tactile. She slid along the length of him, squeezed against the width of him, a slow, rocking rhythm. Her hands gripped his hips, steered confidently, gently accelerating until he could bear it no longer and he bucked off the bed, clutched the globes of her rear end, thrusting relentlessly until finally he could see again.

What he saw was that still she was his Juliette but lovelier, and he stretched to take her lips, wanting to be joined to her in every possible way.

Surprising him, elating him, she came first, shuddering around him and over him, shivering her satisfaction. He climaxed and fell back onto the bed, dragging her down with him, holding her fast. She had taken no blood, just given him everything he'd longed for.

"Love, I missed you, and our baby." He pressed his palm against her belly.

Chloe cuddled under his chin. "We all need our sleep now. It's after midnight."

He pulled the blankets over the three of them and followed her very good advice. When he woke, she was standing near the lone window, stained glass in a Tudor rose design that cast the morning's first glow as a deep magenta. She sighed, pulled the blackout shades shut.

"I'll miss the dawn. I love the sun rising to shed pure light on the world. When I was growing up, everything turned quiet around here as the day took over from the night and the Cruel and company finally settled down. The silence would wake me, and I'd listen and watch from my window."

"You won't burn up if you stand in the sun. Your parents performed outside all the time."

She turned to look at him, smiling wistfully. "I must avoid exposure to the rising sun. While it's still making its ascent in the sky, its rays are harmful. When it starts downward after noon, it's safe."

She slipped into bed next to him, rested her head on his chest. "I thought I was prepared. I thought I knew what I was getting myself into, but there's so much I didn't anticipate, and the baby . . ." She kissed his chest, ran her lips over the hair curling there. "If I had known about the baby, I never would have done this. Please believe me."

There was no hiding his apprehension. Fahey took a deep

breath and let it out slowly. "You didn't suspect you might be pregnant?"

She fastened her green gaze onto his. "I was aware of an urgency, of something building. I mistook it for a growing need to know myself, when it was actually a life growing inside me. I can't regret what I've become, but I was human when we conceived, and now I've shifted the balance. The baby might not survive."

Tears glistened in eyes greener now than ever. Everything about her was more enchanting: her hair more lush; her skin more luminous; her beauty more fragile though he knew a tensile strength underlay it. He reached to catch a tear as it fell. "We'll figure it out, love. We will."

*Because we have no choice,* his head finished, and her eyes flashed. Chloe had heard him, or sensed his thoughts, how wasn't important. She got up, pulled one of the blankets around her, settled into the chair by the now-shaded window, putting distance between them, fortifying her defenses, as she always did to protect her private self.

"My parents look different, they have new names." She watched him through the semi-darkness. "All my life, I've been Sebastian and Emilie's daughter, but now I spend time with new friends who look my own age, Teppan and Katarina, and I have to call them by those names so I don't forget, so I don't expose them and myself for the non-orphan I really am. Becoming a vampire isn't nearly as bewildering as trying to sort out who they are now and why. They've changed, and not for the better."

She tucked her legs under her, folded herself further into the tent of the blanket. "They're going to kill each other if this keeps up. That night in Edinburgh, my father was erratic. One minute, he was taking care of me, encouraging me to resolve my questions; the next, he was terrifying me, pushing me into the change. Not compelling me, I could resist that, but pressuring me, insisting that I be the vampire I was born to be instead of sticking my toe in the water then running away from the rushing tide.

"As for my mother, this last week with her was revealing for what she didn't reveal. She won't talk about him, but it's clear she's unhappy."

Fahey knelt before her. In the half-light, she looked unspeakably pale.

"I think Emilie had Esteban murdered back in June." Chloe's voice trembled with pain, or maybe guilt. "I think she wanted to know what Esteban had done on my father's behalf and what he said in the hotel bar that night and what I said to him. When Esteban wouldn't tell her, she arranged for Anton to kill him. Nothing would have hurt my father more than losing his truest friend, so she had him eliminated."

Fahey placed his hands on either side of the chair, close but not touching, for fear she might shatter. "What else, love? What do you know now that you didn't before?"

He could feel the sobs building, a dam beginning to crack inside her.

"Sebastian hired those men to abduct me in London last summer. To beat me and cut me and break my arm so I could see how quickly I'd mend—a demonstration for my eyes only, so I could experience my own invincibility and he could use it to sway me." Chloe opened the blanket, moved forward in the chair to gather Fahey inside, and wrapped the blanket around them both.

"Did your mother know this?"

"She does now."

Weeping, Chloe clutched at his shoulders, nipped at the space low on his neck that she favored, drew blood, sucked gently as her tears fell onto his skin. Lightning flashed through his veins, jolted through his cock. Her mouth still attached to him, Fahey lifted her and brought them both to the bed, lowering his body over hers. Pleasure for pleasure, he could give her that.

Afterward, he watched her sleep, wishing it could be like this every day, wishing that sometime in the next few days, they wouldn't have to part again, with him heading off to BBC Brussels and her heading back to London and Aspect Ratio. He wanted to be with her as their baby grew inside her. He wanted to be with her to nourish her. The thought of her turning to someone else was unbearable. Fahey tightened his hold, and eventually he slept too.

What roused him, he couldn't have said exactly, except that a clock seemed to be ticking in his head, telling him there were things that must be said today, questions that must be answered before the opportunity was lost.

He threw on yesterday's clothes, still smelling of yesterday's bath in scotch and brandy. Still fighting the last of his hangover, he hurried down the hall to the de la Coeurs' quarters. He tried the knob and, to his surprise, it turned and he was allowed to proceed.

Fahey entered, nervous about breaching the sanctum without permission, fearing he might disturb Chloe's mother at whatever repose she took. Not that he expected to find her in a coffin, arms crossed over her chest, but what did he know of vampires, even allowing for the fact that he now was intimately linked to three of them?

When he reached the sitting room, he found her on the floor in front of the three aged tapestries that had inspired Chloe's work with textiles, in the spot where he and Chloe had sat months earlier, when those relentless dreams first lured him to the Castle.

"Emilie?"

"Katarina. You mustn't forget. This is who I've become for now, though for how long I can't say."

"It's hard to think of the Castle as anything but Emilie and Sebastian's home." He sat beside her and immediately felt a chill, whether from the drafty old pile they inhabited or the woman herself, he wasn't sure.

"We built it in the 1890s, when we first came to America, but it never seemed more ours than it has these last four decades. We built Court of Cruelty around this house. Sebastian had the idea of our personifying the mystical rulers of this keep and telling tales of lords and ladies, masters and servants and everyone in between, a society of chivalry and fealty and superstition and religion. We had this glorious fortress; all we needed was to supply the legend. We had such a grand time giving birth to our finest creations here, our daughter and our music, my art and his photography. Perhaps that's why it's so hard for me to leave it now."

Walking away from a life clearly got no simpler with practice. "I don't want to be the one left behind when it's time for Chloe to move on. I want what you and Sebastian have. That's possible, isn't it?"

Kat stood, moved to the first needlework panel, ran her fingertips across the raised surface. "I stitched these tapestries. Our story, Stefan and Eugenie's, is here. This is our beginning."

Fahey rose and joined her at the triptych, hoping she wouldn't rebuff his questions. He wanted to see how it started, how Stefan and Eugenie Herz begat Sebastian and Emilie de la Coeur, then begat Teppan and Katarina Nilsson.

"I want to have more than just a beginning with Chloe. I want to have my middle and my end with her, too. Can that happen for us?"

She moved to the last panel of the three, still charred from the night in June when it revealed he had been unfaithful to Chloe with Meredith. The representation of his bloodied face was still distorted, as if his infidelity was being viewed through rising flames.

"This panel must be rewoven now that more of your story has unwound. Think carefully how you want this restoration to take place. Are you looking for permanence, or are you just seeking reassurance?"

"I'm a stupid mortal, Katarina. Say what you mean, please."

She pointed to the pendant visible under his half-buttoned shirt. He looked down at it too. No luster, no fire.

"You're afraid of losing her, of losing them, Chloe and the baby. That's natural, under the circumstances—if you weren't fearful, you *would* be the stupid mortal you claim to be. It won't happen, though, you're the only man Chloe has ever loved, and she'll love you until your end, if you let her. The blood bond can be severed, you see, and you can walk away—you can ask her to compel you to forget, or you can keep her in your heart, with fond memories of what you shared. The alternative is to stay with her, her lover in public for a time, then, as you age, in private. When you die, she will continue to love you. In her heart, you will live forever."

That, he understood, was what Kat meant by reassurance. "I get to stay who I am until my body fails us, and I pass away. Or, if that's more than I can face, I can move on now, with or without the memory of what we've meant to each other. Correct?"

She nodded.

"Then it's permanence I want. I want to live with Chloe and our child forever. When this life has to change, I want a new one with her. Tell me I can have that."

She rubbed her temples, as if at a headache that refused to fade. "It's easy to lose yourself in this, and later hate the person you gave yourself up for." Sadness shimmered around her. "It's a decision that, once made, cannot be unmade."

Who, Fahey wondered, regretted the decision more, she or her husband? He wanted to ask, but he knew Kat wouldn't tell him. "If I want to be a vampire, can Chloe make me one? Must I see some elder, pass some test of worthiness? If I have to, I will."

A half-smile crossed her lips. "Nothing like that. Any vampire can sire another, but in creating is responsible for that offspring for eternity. In return, the offspring must be loyal. There is no stronger blood bond. There's also no rush, is there?"

Understood: Forever was a very long time. No denying he

thought more clearly when he had some distance from Chloe, when his desire for her didn't cloud his reason, but in the meantime . . .

"How can I protect her? Shield her from wooden stakes, silver bullets? She's vulnerable, a perfect target if someone wanted vengeance."

Kat laid a hand on his shoulder. "The stake thing is just a myth; so are silver bullets. No one slays us. We kill ourselves. Despair can be lethal, and losing one's life over and over without the finality of death can be overwhelming. Eventually, most of us step into the rising sun and let it take us, until we are no more."

He felt her inside his head, listening to his questions.

"Thus far I have never regretted my choices," she said. "Without Sebastian, I might never have had my daughter. He would like to think he possesses some magical potency that made her possible. I prefer to think it required both of us to work a miracle."

Katarina walked toward the door, the time for confidences at an end. "Chloe is my true immortality, and her father's as well. Not our music, not our art, but our flesh and blood, just like normal people. How ironic is that?"

How ironic, indeed, that Sebastian and Emilie's lives were as defined by Chloe as hers was by them. Theirs was a uniquely dysfunctional family, but a family nonetheless, and damned if Fahey didn't want one for his child too, if there was a child in the end. He crossed himself three times quickly, to ward off whatever evil eye had caused Sebastian's babies to die in their soon-to-be-murdered mothers' wombs.

* * * *

The afternoon air smelled like snow, though it probably wasn't cold enough. Fahey imagined the Castle standing majestically amid drifting icy whiteness, its natural aloofness softened by endless layers of small, intricate flakes. As he jogged the last curve and the mansion came into view, a sports car, convertible top down, gunned past him. "ECHECK," the license plate read. The car blew by the parking area at the front of the mansion and rocketed toward the back.

*The lawyer makes a house call.* Odd. Fahey detoured to the entrance off the kitchen, the closest exterior access to Sebastian and Emilie's private apartment. He was rounding the corner when he saw Katarina get into the front seat and pull Ed Chestack into an embrace. He thought he saw a flash of fang as Kat's head dipped low along Chestack's neck.

He ducked behind the partial wall that separated patio and pool from kitchen and pantry, peering around the wall every few minutes once it became obvious the engine would not be starting again. To hell with it, he finally decided. It was likely Kat knew he was there anyway, and he stepped out behind the car and into the weak afternoon sunlight.

Kat was facing him, astride Chestack's lap, clearly astride Chestack's cock as well, judging from the up-and-down motion of her body. She winked at Fahey, showed two long, sharp incisors, and bit into Ed's shoulder. Fahey winced as he heard Ed moan toward orgasm. Too much information and much too easily revealed, as if he'd been meant to witness it.

A lesson, of sorts, in Court of Cruelty as self-sustaining organism: Ed and Emilie, and before that, Zeke and Emilie. Maybe Ronnie and Emilie, too, and Esteban and Emilie, or maybe Esteban and Sebastian? Certainly, Eric and Kat back in Brussels that night, the promiscuity model transferred to Matins and Vespers. Were he asked to choose up sides within the Cruel, Fahey would have put Chestack firmly in Sebastian's camp, along with the late Esteban Gronlund and the weapons-dealing Ronnie Hamilton, even though Ronnie's daughter, Chloe's mentor Genevieve Hamilton, and his daughter's mother, the glorious Gloria, had both been Sebastian's lovers.

Fahey waved at the copulating couple and turned toward the kitchen. He arrived at the door just as Chloe jogged up the path. They went in together, and she flopped onto the window seat.

Fahey pulled two bottles of water from the refrigerator, opened one and handed it to her. "What do you know about Stefan and Eugenie?"

She swallowed hard, coughed. "Why do you ask?"

"I had a conversation with Katarina this morning, while you were asleep. She mentioned the tapestry that told their story. I was wondering, you know, how they hooked up. Your parents behave as if it's a big secret."

Chloe took a slower pull on the water. "Can't be that big, Daddy says it's all in the Herz family Bible."

"Too bad the book is at the gallery in London, or did you manage to stop by there with your mother before you came here? You seem to get around more than most: Edinburgh, Zurich, Brussels."

Fahey immediately regretted the crack and lowered himself into the small space next to her. "Sorry, I didn't mean to be hurtful."

Chloe kissed his cheek. "I'll forgive you, for now. I may have to whip you later, after a light snack." She flashed him a wicked smile.

Which brought him around to his original question, more or less. "Yes, well, Stefan and Eugenie, what do you know?"

"Not a lot. I know Eugenie was French, and I know Stefan was a musician in the Habsburg court; his parents were German Bohemians from the borderlands that are the Czech Republic now. My research on the tapestries suggests that my maternal grandmother was, indeed, French Canadian, but how Juliette Roget came to be in Canada I don't know. I also don't know how my mother came to be in the Habsburg court, but I'm fairly certain that's where she met my father."

Chloe went quiet, and he could tell she was connecting some heretofore-invisible dots. Suddenly, she grabbed his hand, squeezing so tightly he feared he'd lose feeling. "I've figured out what the tapestries have been telling me all these years!"

"Aside from the 'You are going to meet a tall, dark stranger and possibly kill him' part?"

"Not the panel that changed mysteriously as we changed, but the panels that changed before you even arrived here." She rushed for the main staircase. Fahey chased after her. "Those photos I took of the tapestries in April," she said. "They're still on the computer upstairs. They'll confirm it."

Oh, Lord. She'd gone all thread geek on him. He might lose her for hours, on what was likely their next-to-last day together for two weeks. "Tell me what we're looking for. I'll help."

She powered up the desktop she'd left behind when she moved to England. She rummaged through the files until she found what she wanted, then enlarged the image on the screen and pointed. "See that?" Chloe drew a circle with her finger around a shadowy figure in the rear of one panel. "A third person, faded into the background, someone watching Stefan and Eugenie embrace, as if supervising it all."

Fahey stopped her circling hand. "Love, just tell me."

She took a deep breath, and he saw the now-familiar signs of Chloe about to hyperventilate. Maybe vampires didn't, though. She rallied.

"I assumed, from what little they said before faking their deaths and the way my father behaved toward her, that Sebastian—Stefan, I mean—had been the one to turn my mother into a vampire. It was the other way around: She turned him, and she did it because she had lost the person who turned her. That's him, the man in the background, the one who seems almost faded into a memory."

Because that man had walked with the rising sun? Did he live forever in Emilie's heart, a rival Sebastian couldn't eliminate if he tried?

*Chapter Three*

# LONDON, DECEMBER 2011

Aspect Ratio, the art gallery I inherited from Sebastian (and, indirectly, from Esteban Gronlund), is the place where I feel most in equilibrium: creative; productive; but also aggressive, predatory when necessary. The art world, I have discovered, can be quite the stalk-and-take-down experience.

Yet, as the one-hundredth person accepted our invitation to tonight's opening of *Sass & Brass*, all I felt was exposed, my stomach in knots that even saltines and ginger ale couldn't untangle. Benjamin, my non-pregnant sidekick, looked queasier with each passing minute toward zero hour.

When the head count hit 250, which meant every invitation we'd sent out came back a "yes," panic set in. Between Jackson's BBC pals and Meredith's tweets, was there anyone who hadn't heard that he and I were expecting, and oh, by the way, that Aspect Ratio's new exhibit was the hottest ticket in town? How could we accommodate that kind of crush in a gallery that, packed to the corners, held about 125? We set up staggered admissions, emailed the schedule to our guest list, and said a rosary or two that some of the invitees would actually honor the changes.

Now, an hour into the exhibition's first-night festivities, we can breathe again, all seems to be going smoothly. The crowd is navigating a winding path through our Tansu-inspired presentation, taking in the elevated small fiber works, circling the larger, more solid sculptures. Hardly a single square foot of gallery floor is unoccupied, which may be why people are weaving through efficiently, then flowing into the bar-and-hors d'oeuvres area for meeting and greeting the artists we've set up in the temporarily leased vacant storefront adjacent to the gallery. A few outsized pieces that didn't fit in our space have migrated there, and the whole milieu is spontaneously, organically blended. God, I really have turned into a gallery owner, which is more unexpected than the vampire thing, to be honest. No one seems to mind having to exit one building and enter another. The champagne and sparkling cider are bubbly, the puff pastry is nicely browned, and the four of us—Benjamin and our intern, Daphne, Meredith and I—are exhausted already.

The first sale came quickly, a small bronze piece perfect for holiday gift giving at £2,600, fifty percent of which goes to the gallery. Pairing three-dimensional fiber art with sculpted works via the Tansu motif was my idea, so that sale is a real rush. I feel like my secret and public identities are in sync at last, as if events are following the script I've written for my life.

Benjamin is circulating through the exhibit, answering questions, applying stickers to prospective purchases, sales to be finalized later. Meredith and Daphne are playing hostess next door, where a string quartet is playing J.S. Bach and L. von Beethoven, as well as the occasional instrumental work by S. de la Coeur. At my station by the front door, I am welcoming our guests, finally relaxed enough to believe that this, our second show since reopening the gallery, will prove that Aspect Ratio can be independent of its celebrity founders, my publicly mourned musician parents. I am confident C.J. Hart can succeed in her own right before an audience. So poised.

So naive.

Nausea washes over me as Ronnie Hamilton walks in, flashing the invitation I sent his daughter, my friend and former teacher Genevieve, and leering at me as he's done since I hit puberty. I sway behind the table arrayed with exhibit catalogs and gallery brochures. I grip the wooden edge to steady myself.

"Had to come see you, girlie. You're all grown up now, a chip off the old de la Coeur block, I hear. Let's have a look at you." He runs his eyes up and down my so-far unswollen body and smiles. "Hmm, your mum's curves and your dad's intensity. Lovely."

He leans in and kisses my cheek. It's a wonder I keep my crackers down.

"Where'd you get that?" I point to the invitation.

"You sent it to my Genevieve, and I suggested we come together. Good for her and me to spend some family time, and you two being such fast friends, it'll almost be like the old days. She's been delayed with musty museum work at the Victoria and Albert, so I'll just wait here with you, catch up a bit."

I'm at a loss what we might catch up on. Through high school, in those last years I lived among the Cruel, we never had an encounter that didn't end with Ronnie licking his lips, no doubt remembering Sebastian had already rogered his daughter.

My father, of course. Why else would this snake slink here? "If you're expecting some kind of reunion tonight, you'll be disappointed."

Ronnie checks his expensive Swiss watch. "You don't know much, as it happens. A new one like you, you should watch tonight and learn how it's done."

An invited guest inches around him to get closer to the catalog table. I smile and hand over a booklet, answer a question about the exhibit, point out Benjamin for future reference. Ronnie maneuvers around the table and parks himself against the wall behind me, his head resting against a painting by Emilie, *Iscariot*, whose main feature is a visage remarkably reptilian, just like his. Wise woman, my mother, to know what she was dealing with.

When my parents, as Katarina and Teppan Nilsson, walk in arm-in-arm, I know they have called a truce. Maybe it's just to show the flag, to support my latest venture. Maybe it's to unite against a common enemy—say, Ronnie, international weapons dealer and all-around son of a bitch. At my opening, however? I think not. The three of them need to go, and now.

"Kat, Teppan, you weren't on the guest list."

She leans in for an air kiss. "Teppan and I were in London, and we read about the opening. I insisted we gate-crash, didn't I, love?" She smiles sweetly up at her husband, who smiles sweetly—and insincerely—in return. "I just had to see it, Chloe, and you, of course."

Teppan inclines his head to me, polite but keeping his distance in mixed company, much as he did on his last visit to the gallery. He tugs my mother back to his side. "Now that we've crashed, Kat, let's take a look around and let Chloe tend to business. Perhaps she'll have the chance to chat a bit later. Perhaps Mr. Hamilton will agree to join us for a drink afterward. Such an honor to be with one of the true Cruel."

Teppan's eyes burn behind their ice-blue façade. Ronnie ignores him and smirks lasciviously at my mother, obviously well aware who they are. No one picks up on my hint that they take it elsewhere.

A newly arrived Genevieve holds out her arms to embrace me, starts to congratulate me on the exhibit and the baby, sees her father and stops short. She notices Katarina and Teppan, but doesn't appear to recognize the Nilssons as anyone except the musicians she's seen here before. How is that possible? She presses a kiss to my cheek, slips behind the table to stand with Ronnie, and suddenly I feel like a United Nations peacekeeper in a cease-fire zone. Kat makes a move toward the artwork; Teppan steps into the line behind her. Ronnie follows then looks back at his daughter.

"Start without me, I won't be a minute," she assures him.

A handful of people enter, stop for the catalog, offer thanks, and head for the queue. I wish them safe passage, given the bellicose trio ahead of them.

Genevieve puts her arm around my shoulders. "I'm sorry about this, about him. He showed up at the museum two hours ago, intent on coming tonight. I'm sure I don't understand what's so urgent; you'd think he was here to see the Nilssons. That is them, right, from that cover band?"

I pat her hand in shared bewilderment. "Yes, that's them. They weren't invited either. Such a popular place, this gallery, who'd have guessed?"

Genevieve cranes her neck to locate her father. "I don't see him, but I see them. That's odd. Well, actually, odd is normal for Ronnie, isn't it? Where's Jackson? Isn't he here?"

"Covering a banking thing in Frankfurt. I won't see him until Tuesday or so." I hand out two more catalogs, to a conservatively dressed gentleman, a member of Parliament recently in the newspapers for reasons I can't recall, and a woman young enough to be his daughter yet wearing clothing and jewelry that suggest a different relationship. Without commenting further on my Fahey-less state, Genevieve slips into the queue behind them. Sugar daddy, skunk daddy, vamp daddy, it's a full house tonight, except for my baby daddy. The thought makes my stomach roil, and I doubt my pregnancy is the cause.

The next two hours pass quickly by, with no apparent bloodshed. I have seen neither my parents nor the Hamiltons since they arrived. Meredith assures me via text that food and drink are being happily consumed over at the party, which I will join when the doors officially close at ten o'clock and the last of the guests proceed to the bar. Benjamin emerges from the hallway to the office and gives me a thumbs-up. He's made another sale, a dozen in all for the evening, one-third of the pieces on display. Quite the satisfactory launch.

I beckon him to come spell me at the door, so I can grab a few more crackers and some sips of water on behalf of my unborn passenger.

"You should probably sit a bit, too, Chloe. You'll be here hours more even after we've moved the action to the other side."

"If you promise to send buyers in, I'll sit for the next twenty minutes. Deal?"

I wander back past the office, first to the restroom, then to our small kitchen. I've collected a bottle of water and am restoring the twist tie to a wax-papered stack of saltines when I hear pounding on the back door. My phone rings simultaneously, revealing the caller ID: "Metropolitan Police."

Warily, I open the door to two men with badges. Detective Chief Inspector Neil Blackwood of the local constabulary introduces himself then a detective named Julian Gippel from Interpol. They know who I am without inquiring. That can't be good.

"Sorry, I'm in the middle of an exhibit opening. There are 250 people here at my invitation. Can this wait until tomorrow?"

"That's why we came to the back door, Miss Hart, so as not to disrupt your soiree," Blackwood replies. "This is a matter of urgency regarding the bodies discovered some weeks ago near your parents' property in the Czech Republic."

Love to say I've never heard of those bodies, but alas, I show the men into my office, offer seats and refreshments. They take the former, decline the latter. I stand, seeking a position of strength.

"I will be direct, Miss Hart: Interpol believes your father has some connection to the murdered women, possibly to the murders themselves." Gippel's perfect English is tinged with a German accent. He locks his gaze onto mine.

I don't blink. "My father passed away in April, almost eight months ago. I was under the impression that the women died in October."

"All four were sex workers. Cameras were concealed in two of the four women's flats in Pristina, their footage now collected by the authorities in Kosovo. Videos, time-stamped on more than a dozen occasions beginning in January and ending in October, show the same man engaging in sex with the two women in question. He is seen only from the back: long dark hair, over six feet tall, dressed at the start of each rendezvous in the stylized black clothing Sebastian de la Coeur was known to favor."

Yes, the style he wore until he became the blond Swede currently drinking champagne next door.

"It's also the type of clothing favored by thousands of my father's fans worldwide, maybe tens of thousands. As for hair color and height, the description matches thousands of men in the UK alone, even my fiancé."

Blackwood clears his throat. "Jackson Fahey's voice does not match the voice on the audio. Based on your parents' albums and a 2009 television appearance in Italy, however, it is your father's voice. Recognition software confirms it, which leads us to the possibility that Sebastian de la Coeur was alive after April, despite the reports of his suicide."

I collapse onto the nearest chair, dropping my weight heavily for effect. I feign unconsciousness, hear Gippel come around to my side of the desk, feel a cool tissue pressed against my forehead. I silently count to one hundred, then let my eyelids flutter and slowly raise my head from the back of the chair, which is now wedged up against the filing cabinets that line one side of the office.

"I'm pregnant. I haven't eaten as well today as I should have." I point to the crackers on the desk.

Gippel hands me the crackers and my water. I sip slowly, my breathing ragged whenever I come up for air. A few awkward, silent minutes pass. Benjamin sticks his head in, alarmed to see me with two strangers. He moves aggressively closer. Gippel moves his hand to his coat, reveals a revolver.

I nod to Ben then to the police officers, hoping they will stand down. "This is my associate, Benjamin Kwesi. Ben, Inspector Blackwood of the Metropolitan Police and Detective Gippel from Interpol. I'll fill you in later. If our guests have finished in the gallery, go ahead and lock up out front. I'll meet you at the party shortly."

Benjamin eyes the men suspiciously, takes my word, for now at least, that everything is as it should be. I smile my gratitude and he leaves, pulling the door almost shut but not completely.

"Forgive the interruption, it's been a hectic day here," I say, in apology.

Gippel retakes his seat.

"How can any of this be possible? My parents killed themselves. The bodies were found by their housekeeper. I have the death certificates, signed by the Tompkins County, New York, medical examiner."

"But you did not see their bodies." Gippel does not ask. He knows I didn't.

"I was in Barcelona, where I lived at the time."

"They were cremated. Where are those remains?"

"Scattered on a lake at their estate just outside Ithaca, as they stipulated in their suicide note."

"Samples from the lake will be required, and statements from the housekeeper and any others who can help establish the circumstances of your parents' deaths." Gippel fishes a business card out of his pocket. "My number here in London."

"I really must return to my guests and the artists. I'll call my attorney in the morning."

Gippel rises, signals for Blackwood to follow. "Mr. Chestack, a most unpleasant man."

"Apologies for upsetting you," Blackwood adds, as he exits behind Gippel.

*Upset* doesn't begin to describe what I'm feeling. Stupidly, I'd believed that when my father said the four women had been inseminated artificially, it was the only technique used. That night in Edinburgh, he didn't say they'd never had sex, now did he? I call Benjamin on my phone; ask him to come get me. I need a calming influence right now, so I don't do something I'll regret when I lay eyes on Teppan.

After setting the gallery's alarms, Ben escorts me next door, past the party crowd gathered by the entrance of our rented storefront. He steers me along through well-wishers who stop to congratulate us on the exhibit, up to the thicket of artists who have been waiting for me for more than four hours. I am hugged, kissed, cooed over repeatedly. Ben watches me closely, alert to the fact that something is amiss but knowing this is neither the time nor place to ask what that is. When the creators of two now-purchased artworks inquire about the deals made on their behalf, I defer to Ben's superior knowledge and excuse myself to get a drink and catch my breath.

The sugar in the sparkling pomegranate juice a bartender hands me cuts my baby-induced fatigue. What I can really use right now is some A positive. If only Jackson were here for a quick nibble.

I make small talk with the covey of artists and exhibit-goers that has attached itself to me, many of the latter regulars from when Esteban ran the gallery, patrons I inherited with his mailing lists. Must keep the clientele happy, so I eagerly listen to their musings on whether fiber art ought necessarily to be functional. I offer opinions and my business card, inviting them to come again when the gallery is less crowded for a closer look at any pieces they might be considering, pocketing their business cards for follow-up calls in the next few days to remind them of their interest.

One woman asks if I might look at a needlework piece she purchased on the Portobello Road, to ascertain its age. I suggest she consult my friend from the V&A and maneuver her over to where Genevieve and Meredith stand, acting surprisingly friendly considering they've never liked each other. I wonder if they've finally deduced that Teppan Nilsson is their former lover, the man they once knew as my father. I introduce Gen to Needlework Woman and ease away, saying that I need a word with Meredith.

We sequester ourselves in a corner with good sight lines of the room. "Did I miss anything?"

Meredith arches a perfectly tweezed eyebrow. "Oh, you mean

besides your whole party? You should have let me mind the door, so you could greet the people. They came here as much to see you as to see the art, celebrity gallery gal C.J. Hart."

Whose fault is that, old PR pal? "Nope, you're the party girl, Mer; I'm the artsy, aloof one. Those are the roles we were born to play, remember?"

She nudges my shoulder. "Ben said something about police."

"More about the bodies found at Sebastian and Emilie's Czech estate. Nothing worth going into now, trust me." I scan the crowd for the Court of Cruelty contingent. Kitty-corner from us, Katarina leans seductively on a bronze coffin that's part of the exhibition overflow, chatting up Ronnie and Zeke Segal. When did he get here?

"I didn't see Zeke over in the gallery."

Meredith thinks a minute. "I don't remember seeing him come in, but Ronnie walked over and pointed Kat Nilsson out to him. They joined her and have been all cozy over there for at least a half-hour. They haven't ventured over to the artists, I'm sure of that."

Teppan, where is he? With Daphne, looking for candy where he shouldn't. I steer Meredith toward them. "Get in the middle of that. Tell her you need help with the cleanup. It's about time we cleared folks out anyway."

"The caterer will break down the bar in about fifteen minutes."

I give her the patented de la Coeur glare. Works like a charm.

"All right, but what's the big deal? She's twenty-one, let her have some fun, it's a big night for her."

I try not to dwell on Teppan's idea of a big night. "He's fun to look at, but best to not touch."

Meredith swallows a comeback, like maybe, "How would you know about that?" She hands me her wineglass and heads over to disrupt the *tête-à-tête*. As she leads Daphne away, Teppan waves to me. I stop at the bar, exchange Meredith's glass for another sparkling pomegranate, and join him by the store window.

"Killjoy," he whispers, too close for just polite conversation, no doubt hoping someone will notice us.

"She's my intern. I'm responsible for her on-the-job safety. You are not safe."

He pulls a flask from his pocket, raises it to his mouth and drinks. "Ah, but I know an awful lot about art. I once owned this gallery, in another life, of course." He offers the flask to me. "Type A negative, I was feeling sort of minor key tonight, being here without Esteban."

I can feel my father inside my head, looking for something about Esteban; I don't know what he knows about how his friend died. I focus on a Duran Duran song I liked as a child, and he scowls at me. "I think you could use a drink, Miss Hart. Your bad musical taste is showing."

"No, thank you, Mr. Nilsson. Mustn't drink. I'm pregnant."

He nods, takes another swig. "I heard felicitations were in order. How are you feeling?"

Seriously, Daddy, you know more about vampire pregnancies than I do at this point. Other types of pregnancies, too, but I can't think about that now, better to think of Duran Duran, multi-task vampire-style, block and engage simultaneously.

"It's like there are two of me right now: one woman who wants to eat and sleep a lot, another who couldn't care less about either. I never know which one I'll be at any given minute. Who knows which one I'll be by the time the baby comes in June."

"Perhaps indecisiveness runs in the family, Miss Hart."

Laughter from the coffin corner attracts my attention. Teppan's eyes follow.

"What's that about?"

He shrugs. "Couple of old men who want to get laid?"

Always a possibility, though I'm guessing that's not the only reason they showed up here tonight. "Awfully long way to travel for sex at their age."

Teppan gives me the wicked grin I've come to know so well. "Some sex is well worth the trip, Miss Hart, do I really have to explain that to you?"

I want to slap him. "Explain this: How is it those two old men know exactly whom they're sniffing around, but your two old flames don't recognize you at all?"

"They'd recognize me if I wanted them to. I don't." He heads over to investigate what the Cruel clique finds so amusing.

I circulate among the remaining guests, shake hands with the last of the artists, receive cheek-kisses of gratitude. Benjamin joins us and announces that, in all, we've sold twenty of the thirty-six pieces on display. Deposits are in hand for some, full prices paid for many. He promises an accounting by Tuesday.

Meredith calls us over, Daphne secure by her side. "We've tidied everything next door, switched off the lights and drawn the shades, reset the alarms. Ben, sweetheart, we should see Daphne home."

He looks uncertainly at me.

"I'll be fine. I'll get a cab back to my flat after I've scooted the musical crowd along." I reel the three of them in for a group hug. "Now off you go. You've done all the hard work here, time for me to mop up."

Meredith shakes her key to the storefront, hands it to me. "I hope for your sake the Court of Cruelty love fest doesn't last much longer."

They're making no move to leave, and Ronnie's presence adds just enough unpredictability to give me *agita*.

The caterers finally close the bar, pack up leftover hors d'oeuvres in takeaway containers, box up bottles, glasses, pitchers, napkins, limes, olives, etc. They break down the tables, fold the chairs, dump tubs of half-melted ice, and clear out the trash. Thirty minutes later, as the Cruel continue to reminisce, the workers load the last of the party equipment into a van parked out back. I write their check and see them out.

Before I can lock up this space, I need to move the spillover art back to Aspect Ratio. Should have thought of that before I let Ben leave: I may be vampire-strong, but I still have only two hands. I push a giant copper tuning fork toward the door, open it, struggle to keep it open with my back while tilting the fork through and out, but the angle is wrong and it won't clear the lintel. Damn.

"Need some help? I'm not just a pretty face, you know."

Daddy to the rescue.

I go outside. He tilts the fork down until it clears and pushes it through the opening. "Easier to take this through the alley and into the storeroom. You be the guide, I'll be the muscle."

Teppan maneuvers the piece efficiently up the block, through the alley, in through Aspect Ratio's rear door, and into the space in the storeroom where it sat until this morning. "Coffin should go in through the front, to replace that hideous table," he decides. "You can put catalogs on it. The artist won't mind. It'll be impossible to miss."

He knows the gallery game, I never realized. Once all the big works are safely back, we lock up and reenter the leased storefront. It's empty now. My mother, Ronnie, and Zeke are gone.

"Little Goth Club in Soho, they'll be there. Come with me, Chloe."

"I have a few more things to attend to here. Text me the address. Maybe in about an hour?"

He nods, knowing I'll do what I'll do. He watches as I give the storefront one last check and lock up. "Take care, baby. Love you."

Suddenly, all I want is to keep him safe, too, if that's still possible.

By the time I walk down the steps to the Little Goth Club, it's two o'clock in the morning at least. Cigarette smoke and the smell of cheap beer assault me, as does the music, amps fully cranked. A facsimile of the Cruel is killing it onstage: Teppan on his feet behind a Hammond B-3 organ, sharing vocals with Katarina; Zeke and Ronnie on lead and rhythm guitars; Eric the Terrible, Sebastian's understudy from Matins and Vespers, on bass; and a drummer who looks young enough to still be in high school pounding through the beat of "Inquisition."

True believers crowd close, swaying, keening along with my father as the song soars then dips relentlessly, daring the heretics to test their mettle against his might.

*Face a flogging, lowly infidels. If you're lucky, I'll be brief.*
*Should I find that you are miscreants, then I'll bring you all to grief.*
*First the questions, then the moment comes, when you say the words I seek.*
*Be persuasive, parse your answers well, this is no time to be meek.*

*I must believe your base entreaties.*
*I'm the one to convince, just me.*
*God may know the ugly depth of your lies.*
*But I alone will judge the worth of your cries.*

*Meet your inquisitor. Your future is in my hands.*
*Greet your inquisitor. Beware the blows I land.*

His fingers dance through an intricate organ riff. He bares his teeth, pumps his fist, and the crowd erupts. He has established dominion here. Teppan smiles from the stage, waves at me. Kat tracks his gaze, spots me, and waves, too.

I slip back into the shadows. Hiding from them, from their fame, is my default instinct. After a few minutes, the old terror passes, and I force myself to breathe and step forward. Apostasy, after all, is no longer an option: There can be no renouncing who and what I am, and what this troupe means to me. These people are my family, my history. My child and I are their legacy.

"There on the far wall, ladies and gentlemen of this earthly kingdom, is a proud daughter of the Cruel," Teppan proclaims as the song's last notes fade. It's as if he's read my mind. "You may know her as C.J. Hart, owner of the art gallery Aspect Ratio, where we were guests at a reception earlier tonight. But vassals worldwide watched her grow up as young Clothilde de la Coeur, Sebastian and Emilie's little girl. A bow of honor to you, *mademoiselle*, to the fine, accomplished woman you have become." He steps out from behind the organ and sketches that bow, like the royal musician he once was.

A spotlight finds me, bathes me in brightness. The crowd cheers, I curtsy deeply. Zeke launches the opening notes of "Sanctifying Grace," the song Sebastian wrote the day I was born. The light goes out, the show resumes.

It takes hours to extricate myself from vassals who grieve for my parents, who hear in their music inspiration I do not. Still, their determination to keep Sebastian and Emilie's spirit alive and pure gives me the strength I need to run back to the gallery through the fog-shrouded streets of predawn London, to step into the middle of what I'm sure will be a shit storm. If there is even the chance I can minimize the damage, I have to try. Winded, woozy, I fumble with the alarm and the lock, stumble back to the office. Maybe I should have taken Teppan up on his offer of the flask. I've ignored my needs in deference to the baby's. I need blood and sleep, and soon. First, though, I must set my course.

In a desk drawer, I locate the police report from that terrible night last summer when Meredith and I were abducted on a London street just to test my vampire tendencies. At the top of the form is the Metropolitan Police non-emergency number. I call it and punch in the extension it gives for Detective Chief Inspector Blackwood, who on first meeting seemed the less hard-assed of the two cops who darkened my gallery's door last night.

"This is Chloe Hart. I'd like to see the videotapes we discussed. You have my number."

If only that weren't true.

* * * *

A kissing sound rouses me, and I open my eyes to see Jackson's face on the computer screen next to my head. I squint at the beam of sunlight that's snaked its way through from the gallery's display windows.

"Sleeping at your desk? I'm not sure that's good for the baby."

"What time is it?"

"About eight o'clock in the morning here in Frankfurt, sunshine. Been breaking into the blood bank? You seem a little hung over."

Very funny, and so not true. God, he's cheerful this morning.

"I got in very late, after a very long day, and then did some research. Not hung over, just exhausted."

"What kind of research? One of my specialties, you know."

I unplug the laptop from its battery, carry it to the gallery's kitchen, set it down, and pour what's left of yesterday's—or was it Friday's?—coffee into a mug and pop it into the microwave. Jackson whistles for the required two minutes of heat time, applauds when my face reappears before him.

"In case you've forgotten my question, what kind of research? Not more on that bloody Bible your parents bequeathed you, which you said you could translate with your new skills but apparently can't?"

I glance at the safe. I do have to get back to the Bible locked inside it and whatever it is Sebastian intended me to find there. "No. Voice-recognition technology, as used by police agencies."

"That doesn't sound good."

"Sounds complicated." I drink the coffee down black and much too quickly, curse as my tongue burns but heals immediately. There's no way I can discuss this on Skype, someone might be listening in, which Jackson somehow intuits, smart boy that he is.

"Here's what I know, love: Voice recognition is pretty accurate, but it can be gamed. Put a clever mimic on a crisp recording, and it's hard to know who might have been speaking in real time. There have been legal cases disputing the authenticity of voices heard and supposedly recognized."

I feel my eyes droop, and I smile a sleepy, grateful smile.

He blows another loud kiss to keep me awake. "Give me a few more minutes, love, and tell me about the opening. Ben texted that it was a great success."

"Hmm, yes, we did well. It was a full house, and we sold a ton of pieces. This week, we'll update the exhibit with some works we held out and integrate the larger sculptures, now that we have the luxury of a little more space."

He looks positively delicious, his hair perfectly mussed, probably in preparation for an on-camera appearance.

"Wish you could have been there. Wish you were here now."

Jackson reaches away from his computer, grabs his new smartphone and fingers the keyboard. "Just two more days, love. Meanwhile, I get to watch this—I just forwarded you a link one of the guys here sent me. Seems you had quite the trip down memory lane last night."

I look at the link; it's for a video titled *Cruel, Recombinant.* "No escaping my past, and no avoiding it when the vassals come camera-ready, God love 'em." I try to stifle a yawn, then simply give up and give him a view of my tonsils.

"Okay, get some sleep, even if it is at your desk. I'm off to babble something to the world about the Spanish real estate market's collapse, heady stuff. Love you."

The screen goes dark.

My lights go out too, but I don't nap long. My body wants rest, but I am restless. I should head home, shower, change my clothes, but I can barely motivate myself to leave my chair, much less dodge the morning sun to find my way back to the flat. I dump the dregs of dead coffee, start a new pot, nibble on a few leftover cheese puffs. Fair-trade caffeine and phyllo dough, my baby could do worse, right?

Mug refilled, paper plate crowded with bite-sized nutrition,

I resume my place at the desk. It's almost nine-thirty; I call Gippel's number this time, but it takes me to a generic police voicemail box. I try the non-emergency number again and let it take me to a human being, ask for Blackwood, and identify myself. I am patched directly through.

"Miss Hart, I thought we'd be hearing from your solicitor instead."

"About that: I'll feel a lot better about my conversation with him if I've seen the videos, if I understand why you and Detective Gippel think dredging the lake on my parents' property is necessary. Ed Chestack will fight your petition. If I agree with you, he'll fight us both, I assure you. I must see what you've seen and what you've heard."

Detective Chief Inspector Blackwood is silent, as if weighing what I've said. Surely, it's not such an outrageous request.

"Events last summer—the murder of my gallery's former owner, the bombing at my parents' winery in upstate New York—have cast sinister shadows on their memory. If the man in the video, on the audio, is my father, I have to know, and if it's an impostor, I have to know that too."

My voice catches; I choke a bit and sniffle. He has to believe I'm crying, that I am distraught at the prospect of more scandal.

"Miss Hart, this evidence is not mine to disclose. Detective Gippel involved Scotland Yard as a professional courtesy, but I'll contact him, and if he agrees, I'll be in touch."

He rings off. I'm in, I can feel it. It's early, I've got all day.

I open the safe, drag out the Bible. I've been meaning to devote more time to translating Stefan Herz's writing, but I keep finding excuses not to. I'm afraid there will be still more surprises.

*Buck up, C.J., you're waiting for the cops to call so you can eliminate an element of Daddy-surprise.*

Nothing like impenetrable nineteenth-century calligraphy to distract me from the anxiety and blood hunger, right? What has it been now, six days without? I can taste Jackson and Will.

I imagine them bending to my will, opening themselves to me, allowing me to enter their heads, to draw their fluids into my mouth. My brand-new fangs descend; the space between my thighs throbs and moistens. I am hungrier, thirstier, hornier than I ever remember being.

"Focus, focus, focus!" I scream, and the words echo off the walls around me. I unlock the clasp and tear open the Bible's leather cover, dump a sheaf of ornate Fraktur pieces onto the desk, and work my way through the documents I've seen before to the small leather portfolio containing papers written in German Bohemian, in my father's unmistakable handwriting. I should probably learn more about the Herz family, my forebears, through the more official entries in this Bible, but these writings are what Sebastian wanted me to see, I think.

Folded and resting at the top of the portfolio is another illuminated document, a marriage license: "April 1865, Stefan Herz takes to wife Eugenie Roget Verlaine, widow of Auguste Verlaine."

Eugenie was a widow. Auguste must be the figure in the shadows of the tapestry panel—the man in the background has a name at last. He had to be someone of consequence, to have brought Eugenie to the court of the Habsburgs. I do an online search for his name and the year 1860, allowing for a few years of mourning between his death and her remarriage. I'm amazed to find a reference to a French diplomat who negotiated a trade agreement considered an early modern example of "most favored nation" treaties, but there is no personal information about him. "Eugenie Verlaine" and search variations including her maiden name yield nothing. Crap.

Back to the documents. The quill-and-ink script is a bit medieval, even for the nineteenth century; then again, my father has always been about the trappings. It makes the going slow, but after about an hour staring at the words I come up with a plausible translation of what reveal themselves to be journal entries.

*"Thirty-one October, in the year of Our Lord eighteen hundred sixty-four. She is absolutely celestial, the most enthralling woman I have ever met. Beautiful, intelligent, there is art and music in her. My body throbs with need of her, I who have lain with so many and felt so little. Tonight, she allowed me to sheath myself inside her for the first time, after she presented me with a gift, a ruby pendant that burned my chest and seared my cock. When we came to climax, I felt humbled by my love for her. In her ecstasy, she took small nips of my neck, as though to find another way to join with me. No, to consume me. I would give her my soul if she but asked . . ."*

My father was overcome by his passion for this young widow, this young vampire who would become his wife, my mother. How sweet that it began that way, with him in awe of her.

How things have changed.

My phone rings; the caller ID reads, "Metropolitan Police."

"Miss Hart," says an officer whose name I don't catch, "DCI Blackwood will see you at two o'clock this afternoon. I will text you the address. He will meet you at the front door."

It's not quite noon. That gives me time to clean up and have some real breakfast to satisfy the precious little parasite that lives inside me now.

"I'll be there." I promise, and dismiss as pregnancy-related the wave of nausea that sweeps over me.

* * * *

Gippel is the one who meets me. Blackwood is nowhere in sight. That's disconcerting: I get the bad cop, but not the good one. He escorts me into a screening room. A large panel is suspended at the far end, a TV monitor with a computer hookup positioned next to it. He gestures to a chair, bids me sit.

"Are you certain you want to see these, Miss Hart? The videos are explicit."

"I was surrounded by musicians and their groupies for much

of my childhood. I don't shock easily."

He studies me, which is more unnerving than the prospect of watching my father have sex on these tapes.

"You are acquainted with a Swedish musician named Teppan Nilsson, yes?" Gippel walks to the computer, punches a few keys, launches a video of last night's show at the Little Goth Club, probably the one Jackson sent me earlier. We listen to Teppan's rendition of "Inquisition," watch the guys and Kat on stage, and scan back to the wall where I stand after Teppan's little speech about me. See me squirm under the spotlight, more than a little uncomfortable—like now.

"Yes, obviously I am acquainted with Teppan Nilsson, and his wife, Katarina. They belong to a tribute band called Matins and Vespers that performs my parents' music."

"You met the Nilssons when?" He strides before the screen like a prosecutor.

"In September, though I first learned about their band in April. Matins and Vespers played a memorial concert in Barcelona after my parents' deaths were disclosed. Why do you ask?"

He looks at me as if I am mentally deficient. "Mr. Nilsson's voice is very much like that of the man on the tapes found in Kosovo. Very much like Sebastian de la Coeur's."

*Breathe, C.J.* I close my eyes, inhale, exhale.

"Miss Hart, are you unwell?"

"Just pregnant. May I have some water?" I point to a carafe on the table behind him. He pours a glassful, delivers it to me. I sip, and try to figure out where he intends to go with this.

"It is curious, is it not, that of several Matins and Vespers videos online, Mr. Nilsson appears in only two: this one, in which he dominates the performance, and one from September, from an appearance at your art gallery?"

"I wouldn't know how often Teppan Nilsson appears or doesn't with his band. I barely know the man."

The second I utter the words, my lie slaps me: The unsmiling Detective Gippel winks. He knows Teppan and I were in Edinburgh together. The hotel records there suggest something utterly misleading, and I've left myself with little leeway to reinterpret that story.

"Okay, Teppan and I were together last month, as you are aware. It was one night, and I regretted it immediately. I hadn't seen or spoken to him since. When he and his wife showed up at my gallery last night, I was caught off guard."

I hold out my glass for more water. Gippel pours.

"He is the father of your child?"

"Absolutely not, I was already pregnant when we were together. If I had known, I wouldn't have . . ." If that truth could set me free right now, I'd be so grateful.

"But for his coloring, Teppan Nilsson resembles your father."

"People also tell me all the time how much my fiancé looks like my father." I swallow some water, to give that thought a moment to sink in and distract Gippel with whatever daddy issues he might imagine I have. "But Teppan and Sebastian, no: They're like fire and ice, black and white."

"Just so," he replies, whatever that means.

Gippel taps the keyboard, and one of Daddy's performances gives way to another, time-stamped January 2011. He is fully clothed in his usual black, his back to the camera. A blond woman he addresses as Anya is lying on her back on a bed, partially obscured by his body but clearly naked.

"Anya, you are so ready." He runs his tongue over the length of her, into her, savoring her at his leisure. I am thankful he doesn't smack his lips or show his fangs, though he might be biting her, drinking from her in places the camera cannot see.

He lifts himself from her body, pushes his long dark hair from his shoulders, pulls his shirt from his waistband and takes it off. He kicks off his boots, unzips his slacks and removes them. Stretches to his full height, with his bare backside facing the camera at an angle. The same view Emilie posthumously presented at Aspect Ratio's grand reopening in her painting *Annunciation*—the Angel Gabriel, only less holy, what with the object of his erection so close by. He climbs onto the bed, opens Anya's legs, presses forward and enters. He reaches back, grips her by her ankles, penetrates deeply, rocks into her, pounds her.

Anya makes appreciative noises, moans with increasing intensity as the video progresses. Daddy wisely keeps his mouth shut and his posterior to the camera. When she cries out in an apparent orgasm, he hammers her more forcefully until his body shudders and he presumably ejaculates. He hovers over her, breathes deeply, allows her to roll out from underneath him.

The camera shuts off. I release a breath I didn't know I was holding.

"There are six additional videos with Anya Morina, and seven with the second woman, Viktoria Tolaj. I would like to show you two more."

Gippel waits for me to object.

I turn the de la Coeur glare on him. "That's why I'm here, Detective. As I have said, I am no frail flower."

"Your father . . ."

"I've seen nothing yet to convince me that man is my deceased sixty-year-old father. Show me more."

Gippel queues up a second video. The same bedroom appears on the screen; the time stamp reads June 2011. Anya, obviously pregnant, backs into the room, sheds a green silk wrapper in a Japanese print; she sits on the bed, glides upward, toward the headboard, eases her legs open, licks a finger and runs it along her inner thigh. A man follows her into the room, his back again to the camera; he stops to look at her.

His hair is shorter, curls against his collar. Jackson, only not, though close enough to raise some doubt. "Anya, you are beautiful," he whispers. "You are lovely and round and full with sweet new life. Luscious."

He disrobes slowly, standing in front of the bed, allowing

the camera to take in every inch of his long body as he bends to remove his boots, stretches to relieve his torso of his shirt. Muscles ripple along his smooth wide back, which tapers to a trim waist so much like Jackson's that I squirm, wet, in my chair. He lowers his trousers over naked buttocks and kicks the trousers away, flexes his firm ass, bends forward and pulls her by the ankles to the bottom of the bed, takes her as he stands, his back to the camera all the while.

This time, the sex is fiercer, more vocal, though no real words are uttered and Anya's pleasure in the act sounds thoroughly authentic. She comes repeatedly; he covers her screams with his mouth, or so it appears from the restricted angle. He is relentless, his hips in constant motion, an untiring pile driver bringing her to the edge, pushing her over, dragging her back. At one point, he seizes each leg, bites each calf, appears to suck her flesh, but I can see no blood, so it's hard to know whether he's feeding and driving them both to climax that way, his sculpted back obscures much of what the camera is there to see.

Finally, he finishes, lowers her legs, and twists away, revealing a just-spent penis bigger than many are fully erect. I close my eyes; order myself to block the reverberation at my core. That is not Jackson up there, that is not Jackson up there, and, Jesus, how is it I'm aroused to the point of almost wanting to jump Gippel by a perverse combination of blood lust and the sight of my father in all his fine physical glory fucking a now-dead woman?

What is the matter with me?

The video player switches off. Gippel breathes harshly, as if the pheromones in the room are suffocating him. He stares at me accusingly, if only for a second; he coughs, unwraps something covered in cellophane, sucks on it.

Sweat is running down my chest, pooling underneath my breasts. I feel flushed and dizzy. I bend over and put my head between my legs. Footsteps pass me; the door opens, swings shut. The baby flutters, or at least I think it's the baby. I have no idea what the hell is going on inside me. This is more disturbing than I imagined, and I have no doubt that's just what Gippel was hoping for. Can I compel him to just drop things here? Right, how do I pull that off, when I don't feel capable of compelling myself to stand?

He returns with a can of cola, pops the top. "Perhaps this will help."

I take a few short sips. He hands me a pack of crackers, scrutinizes me as I rip it open and shove one, then another, into my mouth greedily, examines me as I chew them. After the third, his fascination diminishes and he returns to his station at the computer.

"This video is from the camera in Viktoria Tolaj's rooms, from early October. It was the last one made, taped after Anya Morina's final video in late September."

Gippel hits play, his unease unmistakable, and the video opens on a nude, very-pregnant brunette approaching the bed, crawling onto it and getting on all fours, her posterior angled toward the right of the frame. The man in black steps in behind Viktoria, caresses her derriere, kisses the cheeks, appears to run his tongue along her anus, though it's hard to see exactly. He reaches below her and fingers her, runs a hand under her abdomen, strokes her there for several minutes, nibbles. He does not disrobe this time. He enters her from behind, thrusts wordlessly, repeatedly, enthusiastically, his head flung back though not enough to render his face visible to the camera. His black hair is significantly shorter, teasing the bottom of his ears, curling up around his jaw. As he pumps into Viktoria, he begins to hum, adjusts his rhythm to the music, whistles then begins to sing hoarsely as he builds toward his climax: "Meet your inquisitor, your future is in my hands. Greet your inquisitor ..."

Ultimately, he comes and collapses face-first onto the bed next to Viktoria, who says not a word. Gippel cuts the tape.

I slide down in my chair, lean my spinning head back onto the plastic-covered metal, grip the rest of the crackers so hard they crumble between my fingers and spill onto the floor.

"What is it you'd like me to say, Detective?" I ask, eyes shut tight. "What you've shown me is nothing but a voyeuristic look at a man and his sexual partners over the span of almost a year."

"We believe this man to be Sebastian de la Coeur. But as you have said yourself, Miss Hart, he could just as well be Jackson Fahey."

I open my eyes, snap erect on the chair. "That's ridiculous. As *you* said yourself, it isn't Jackson's voice."

Gippel fusses with the computer again, and again the video from the Little Goth Club flashes onto the screen: Teppan singing "Inquisition;" Teppan speaking into the microphone; Teppan seeming more like Sebastian with every syllable, seeming more like his true self, for everyone to see.

"It *could* be Teppan Nilsson's voice," he says frostily. "We will need whatever contact information you can provide for him. Also, I must insist that you call Mr. Chestack, as we discussed last night. If you do not, Interpol will take steps with the authorities in New York to procure a search warrant for your parents' lake without your cooperation. I have too many victims and too many questions, and little time to waste."

I could snap his neck in seconds, or drain him so dry Scotland Yard would need only a vacuum cleaner to tidy the mess. I hear his blood flowing, more calmly now that he's finished our session with the amateur porn tapes. His pulse throbs serenely in his throat; a man supremely satisfied that he has rattled his witness, supremely satisfied that he has successfully sprung his trap.

I want him dead. Every fiber of my new vampire being tells me it's the only way to protect my father, but I know better, truly I do. So I fish around in my courier bag for my phone, find on it the number Kat gave me back in the summer, the number with the always-full voicemail box, scratch the number on the back of an Aspect Ratio flyer, get up and hand it to Gippel. I've already given him so much to implicate the man Sebastian has become. This red herring is the last of what I'm willing to give.

Or not. Pain tears through me, and I throw up on Gippel's shoes. My baby's revenge leaves him the sparse contents of my stomach in exchange for the pieces he requires for his investigation. I fall against him, too weak to stand. He grips my upper arms, seemingly with his fingertips, as if he is afraid my digestive issues are contagious. He is so close; I smell the O positive within him, and my mouth waters. I could rip out his throat and solve both my problems at once, but that would be counterproductive, and I've created enough trouble.

Gippel settles me back into my chair, pulls a white handkerchief from his inner jacket pocket, wipes down his shoes, walks to the door and shouts out for a cab to be summoned. I flutter my eyelids, breathe heavily and loudly. He brings me more water, sticks the glass under my nose, as coldly solicitous as an undertaker.

"I'm so sorry," I whisper, and it's not wholly a lie. If he only knew how I regret being here. When a uniformed officer knocks and announces that the cab has arrived, Gippel beckons the officer to come assist me.

"Please tell the driver to take you straight to your home, Miss Hart. Clearly, you need much rest and a good meal."

Neither of which I will find there today.

* * * *

Quite the box Detective Gippel has suckered me into. I can warn Jackson about the tapes, but I mustn't do anything that smacks of warning my parents. The usual difficulties getting in touch with them aside, any call, text, comment on a Cruel message board, or shout-out on Twitter will be dissected. I have no doubt that Interpol has hacked into my phone and email accounts by now, and the Aspect Ratio accounts, too; no doubt that it will extend its reach to Jackson; Meredith and Benjamin; Genevieve and Ronnie Hamilton; even Zeke Segal, all here in the European Union and thus fair game.

I am expected to contact Ed Chestack. If I fail to make that call from my own phone, more eyebrows will rise, and I neither know nor trust my lawyer well enough to be confident he'll understand whatever coded message I try to deliver. But what choice do I have? He surely knows my parents' secrets. Someone mopped up Sebastian's messes with those women after Esteban died. If Chestack didn't, he knows who did.

It's after seven o'clock in the evening, London time, about mid-afternoon in Ithaca. The son of a bitch should be well into the back nine at his country club by now. This should screw up his swing but good. His phone rings several times. I can almost see him weighing whether to let the call go to voicemail, but Chestack eventually answers.

"If it isn't the princess," he snarls. "How nice of you to call in the middle of my golf game."

"The rest of your foursome must be well aware by now who signs your checks," I growl back. "It's the price of celebrity, even reflected celebrity such as yours. Boils down to this right now: I speak, you listen."

He is quiet for several beats, stewing no doubt, but also deducing, I hope, that I haven't made a trans-Atlantic call just to insult him. He tells his buddies to play through; he'll catch up.

"How can I help you, C.J.?" he asks, his voice free of a return barb this time, a telling nuance.

"It's about the Czech estate and the women's bodies found there. Interpol believes my father may still be alive, and it intends to seek a court order to dredge the lake at the Castle to retrieve Sebastian and Emilie's ashes, to confirm their deaths."

Another pause, this one longer. "That's preposterous, can't be done forensically. Plus, I was there when the medical examiner claimed their bodies, and I have a copy of the documentation given to Zeke Segal when he picked up the cremated remains. Gloria Dennehy and I and about a dozen others, friends and Castle staff, watched Zeke scatter their ashes on the lake. What evidence does Interpol think it has to justify this? I'll fight it, assert there's no probable cause."

That's my attack dog, good boy.

"There are, it turns out, about a dozen sex tapes made by two of those women at their apartments in Kosovo, all starring a dark-haired man of Sebastian's height and build. The man's face is never on camera, but he speaks on the tapes, and voice recognition suggests to Interpol that it might be Sebastian."

I let him process that a minute that before I drop the next bomb. "I pointed out to Detective Gippel, the investigator from Interpol, that the man on the tapes could not possibly be my sixtysomething father. Gippel countered that, based on the visuals, the man could well be Jackson, and based on the audio tracks, it might also be Teppan Nilsson."

"Fahey, hmm, that's interesting, isn't it. Teppan Nilsson? I don't know the name, who is that?" Chestack catches on quickly, thank God.

"He and his wife have that Court of Cruelty tribute band, Matins and Vespers. I just sent you a link to a video of a performance they did last night, after a reception at my gallery. Ronnie and Zeke were in London, so they came to my exhibition and one thing led to another, a Cruel love jam. Teppan does a great impersonation of Sebastian's lead vocal on 'Inquisition,' and the drummer was perfection."

Can't resist that last jab at Ed's former role with the Cruel, as if I can afford to be petty right now.

"Give me a minute to watch it," he says, then hangs up.

I can almost hear the music playing, almost see Chestack perspiring, feel his brain swelling. I almost wish we had a blood bond so I could get inside his head, soothe his blood pressure down to something near normal. Because at the risk of his stroking out there on the fairway, I have to tell him the rest of it. The worst of it.

Ten minutes pass before he calls back. "You were saying?"

"Gippel showed me three of the sex tapes. Obviously, the man in them can't be Sebastian, and even Gippel admits the voice isn't Jackson's. But maybe it is Teppan Nilsson; on one tape, the guy is actually singing 'Inquisition.' Teppan's blond, but dye his hair darker and, from behind, it could be him. Maybe he was in Pristina on a pretty much monthly basis earlier this year and visited those women? You could see they were pregnant. Those babies, it's so sad . . ."

There, done. All of it communicated as best I can under the circumstances. Now, I can hear Chestack's heart pounding, sense the blood beating in his ears, drowning out everything around him.

"Ed? Hello?" Pretending the connection is weakening buys him some time to recover, time to react and get back on script for our listening audience.

"C.J., are you still there? Can you hear me?"

"I was afraid I had lost you. I'll text you Detective Gippel's number here in London, also the number of a Detective Chief Inspector Blackwood, the Scotland Yard liaison. They expect to hear from you soonest."

Chestack's end goes quiet, which makes me uncomfortable. I begin to sniffle, sob, gradually increasing volume and intensity. He recognizes it as a signal to wrap up.

"I'll take care of this," he says. "Don't worry. No way will those ashes be disturbed."

Now, two of us are stuck in Gippel's quicksand; I wish company truly were the cure for this misery. As if on cue, my phone rings. It's Jackson. I make a run for the bathroom, phone still in my hand, to throw up again. On lifting my head from the toilet, all I can think of is raw steak, road kill, anything bloody, any kind of blood. I have to hang on, just until day after tomorrow, until he arrives.

The buzz of a text cuts through my fog: *"Change of plans. Developing story, working Tuesday, arriving on later flight but can stay two days longer. Love you. Call me."*

Will the waiting never end? I can't let him hear how weak I am, he'll kill himself trying to get here tonight, so I text back: "*Torture here without you. Love you.*" I slump back down to the bathroom floor, the tile chilling my bottom even through my leggings. I'm not sure I can last another hour, let alone another forty-eight.

I stretch out and close my eyes, oblivious to the hard floor, oblivious to the near darkness, even to the dry heaves that have begun. Maybe I'll just die here, but vampires don't die, do they, they just live to screw up another day. I wish the night away, wish the time separating me from Jackson's return would dissipate like so much dust.

*You love me, Jackson Fahey. I invoke the blood bond. Come for me, please. Come for our baby.* As if incantation or even prayer will actually work.

At some point, I open my eyes again. I'm still on the bathroom floor. My wrist is stinging mercilessly, a pain worse than the one in the vacant pit of my stomach. A ray of morning sunlight has peeked around the blind and landed directly on my forearm. I roll out of the way, toward the doorway to the hall, and crawl to the living room. I pull myself onto the sofa, bury myself under the afghan Jackson's mother crocheted and sent when she learned we were expecting. A woman I've never met loves my baby, loves me because I love her son. Please, God, make Tuesday come.

I doze off or pass out, maybe both, for who knows how long. When I pull my phone out from under a cushion, it's after noon. I sit up slowly, and the room doesn't spin. Holding onto the furniture, then the walls, I make it back to the bathroom, strip off the smell of vomit, brush its debris off my teeth, and stand under a lukewarm shower so I don't weaken myself further. I wash the stench from my hair and body, caress the slight rounding that is my child. Baby seems to flutter under the water's massage.

I emerge and wrap my torso and head in towels, shivering from an inner cold that can't be conquered without blood. I make my way back to the sofa, to Maureen Fahey's afghan, and curl up again within its folds, lose myself in my weakness.

An urgent beeping brings me back to consciousness. A disembodied voice follows. "I'm downstairs in your lobby. Buzz me up."

I stare at my door and the intercom next to it. I don't get visitors.

"I'm here to help." The American accent is vaguely familiar, friendly, and truthfully I don't care who it is, as long as he's a breathing, blood-filled human. I press the button that unlocks the elevator entrance, and minutes later someone is banging on the door to my flat. I unlatch the deadbolt, open the door.

Will Baumann crushes me in his arms, kisses my cheek, whips off his coat, rolls up the sleeve of his sweater and the shirt beneath it. "Drink," he commands, shoving his wrist up to my mouth and slamming the door shut behind us.

I bite down hard, gorge on the cinnamon of his blood, a sugar high and a sexual rush gripping me in one sweet burst from this darling, trusting man. Must be careful not to kill him. Soon, his lean, six-foot frame slumps against me, and it's hard to tell who's holding up whom.

I need to stop, and he needs to recover. I half-lead, half-carry him back to the bedroom, help him up onto the mattress, take off his jeans and boots, tuck him in under the duvet, then lick the wound on his wrist so it will heal. My body is flushed with his heat, with the warmth of his blood as it courses through me, with the warmth of desire for more of him. I get into the bed beside him, snuggle up against his back, rest my hand against his groin, feel his cock lengthen and nudge my fingers. Will lifts his head, tugs off the sweater and shirt.

"Too hot. Too wonderful." He turns and nuzzles my neck, running kisses along my throat, down to my naked breast. "You taste like flowers. Like more." He shifts me into his arms, covers my mouth with his, wraps a long leg around me. I suck on his tongue, feel his erection burn the inside of my thigh, rubbing until I am wet and aching for him. He slides deliciously through me. I nip at his nipples, draw beads of blood, lick and suck, feeling stronger and wilder with every swallow. I raise my head and bite the untapped wrist, lapping at the blood that coats Will's skin, dipping my tongue inside the puncture, drinking more deeply each time he thrusts.

He pummels me, matches my lust for his blood with his own for my body. He tears my mouth from his wrist, leans on his elbows and takes my face into his hands, kisses me as if his very life depended on it, as if I were his salvation rather than his likely damnation. He comes into me, and I bite his lower lip to taste his orgasm, dissolving into a bliss I had despaired of never knowing again.

We separate, and Will rolls me over onto his chest, keeps me nestled in his embrace. I let him sleep; keep my teeth to myself. I lift my body from his, stretch beside him, my head against his left arm. By the time my eyes open again, streetlight is slipping past the window shades. Will is sitting up against the headboard, watching me.

"Didn't think I'd ever see you again. Couldn't stop thinking about you."

"You were supposed to forget, Will. I told you to forget."

"I remembered feeling fabulous, but I couldn't think why. In my dreams, I saw your face and made love to you, but I couldn't remember who you were or how I knew you. "

"Yet here you are. How?"

He swings his legs over the side of the bed, locates his jeans, fishes in the pockets, pulls out a phone. "Your Edinburgh friend says to tell you that sometimes the strongest bonds fail and the weakest hold. This is for you."

I sit up, study the phone, search for whatever will bring up received calls and voicemail. "Password?"

Will smiles. "Clothilde."

In Will's voice is a message dictated by my father: *"Für immer werde ich dich lieben. Stefan."*

Oh my God, Daddy, I'll love you forever too. I call the number that originated the message. In the living room, a phone rings, Will's of course, I should have guessed. He looks at me as if he doesn't understand, and maybe he doesn't, maybe he's been compelled to forget by someone far more skilled at compulsion than I.

"Juliette," he says, his aquamarine eyes darkening. He strokes my thigh, pets me like a kitten he hopes to start purring again. He pulls me toward him, into a kiss fierce with yearning and hunger. I wish I could feel more for him than just the latter. He hovers over me, my pendant, its ruby dull and lifeless, abrading his chest, his soft light-brown hair brushing my skin. He licks the column of my neck, past my collarbone and along the curve of my left breast, then covers my nipple with his tongue, teases it until it puckers, sucks and rolls it in his mouth. He drops light kisses along my ribs, onto the gentle curve of my stomach, down past my hipbone, detouring to the dark curls between my legs. He blows warm puffs onto my labia, swirls his tongue over the sensitive folds.

Distracting man, he pulls my brain away from Jackson, draws me into the game he's been sent to vie in, following the rules taught him by Teppan. Will lifts my arms over my head, dips his tongue inside me, sparking shock waves everywhere. I latch onto whatever I can reach with my teeth, bite lightly, draw just enough blood to tantalize him further and power his tongue into a higher gear. When he lifts himself over me, he leans in to give me access to his neck then penetrates me to my core, his cock engorged with blood I cannot taste but savor all the same.

He is skilled, my handsome play-date, and sweet tasting, I wish I could keep him. Will rocks against me, works me until I am stretched to my fullest, my arms still high above me, my ankles gripping his shoulders, my muscles strained around his thickness. I sink teeth into the flesh under his left pectoral, tiny bites that release a nutmeg flavor. He comes with a fury that fills me with his essence and his complete delight at our reunion. He cries out, subsides with exhaustion, releases my arms; breathes me in as if I were oxygen itself.

I flip him onto his back then likewise begin to lick him, pleasure for pleasure, teasing his cock back to attention. I complete the anointing, then climb atop him, ride us both to completion, sipping from the wrist he offered to save me as he caresses my face and kisses my chest, breasts, whatever part of me he can to prolong the contact. My body blushes with the warmth of him, but that's all, it's nothing more than skin deep. He deserves better.

"You're the sort of man I always walk away from: beautiful, smart, but not smart enough to know I'll hurt you."

Will laces his fingers with mine, deftly rotating the ring on my left hand. "Smart has nothing to do with it. I want to be with you. I won't forget you, don't think you can make me this time."

He wrests his upper body from the mattress, folds me into him for another searing kiss. I reward him with a long fingernail slash above his right nipple and suck us to another mutual, albeit non-coital, climax. One last time, no matter what he'd like to believe.

"*Okay,*" I say wordlessly, astride him and burrowed into his thoughts, asserting my dominance. *"You won't forget me, you won't forget this. But you will forget where to find me and who told you where I was."*

He battles the compulsion, holding me close while pushing the voice in his head aside. "Stop that. You needed my help, and I came, doesn't that count for anything?"

"It does, yes," I say aloud, resting my forehead on his chest, "but you have to understand, I love someone else. You should have so much more than I will ever give you."

"We're good together."

"I'm good with everyone, it's who I am. You have to leave here and go back to your life."

He gets up, walks out of the bedroom, comes back carrying the leather jacket he dropped just inside my doorway. Out of a pocket he fetches the phone I called not too long ago.

"Listen." He pulls up the voicemail, hands me the phone. "*Go to Juliette*," Teppan's voice orders. "*Make her well, and tell her this for me: You are her backup plan.*"

I grip the phone so tightly the plastic case begins to crack. I stop myself before I crush it completely. I call the number the message came through on; it is, of course, no longer in service.

"Neither of us has a choice, do we?" Will kneels on the bed next to me, scoops his hands under my ass and draws me to him.

I turn my head, lick along the outcropping of his Adam's apple. "No," I whisper. "We never did."

* * * *

About eleven o'clock at night, after a quickly arranged delivery of food from the Italian place down the street, the ravenous baby beast within me is taken care of, and Will falls asleep, now satisfied in every way.

I, on the other hand, am restless. My mind does somersaults, and the pendant burns a hole between my breasts, beats a rhythmic reminder that my heart lies elsewhere, that this man in my bed is a stand-in, despite my father's efforts.

*Are you trying to help, Daddy, or interfering in my life again? When will I stop expecting you to just let it be?*

I throw on some running clothes and shoes, leave Will a terse note—"Pull the door shut; it will lock behind you when you leave"—and hope he takes the hint. I stretch on the wet sidewalk outside, then head for the gallery, where I can at least busy my brain with something more productive than trying to divine my father's motives.

In minutes, I am in the alley behind Aspect Ratio, a place

that holds memories of the night when I was the kidnapped thing that went bump. A shadow at the far end, by the gallery's back door, gives me pause, but if I can't defend myself now I should turn in my vampire-club membership. So I jog toward my business, keys clutched between my fingers, an old-school precaution. I set off the motion-sensor light Benjamin has installed. It throws a glow onto a familiar, most unwelcome face.

"Knew you'd show up, always were one to keep strange hours. Your parents would put you down for the night, but up you'd pop, wanting to party with us. Course, one of them always walked you back and stayed until you finally conked out, but come sunrise, you were up to watch us drag our sorry arses off to bed, now, weren't you? You thought you were hiding and no one could see, but I did, I knew you were there, eyes wide, takin' it all in."

I unlock the door; whatever it is he wants is best discussed indoors. Better to be out of sight, in case I need to kill him.

"Been waiting here long?"

Ronnie smiles, his teeth a faint tobacco yellow I've tried for years to forget. He takes off his jacket, shakes off the rain. "A bit, maybe. Could use a little tot of something to take the chill off, if you've got it."

From the fridge, I pull out a sparkling water for me and a split of champagne left over from the opening-night bash for him. He takes it from my hand, stroking my palm as he does; works the cork out, takes a long drink.

"Cheers! Quite the hostess you've become. Emilie taught you well, that was clear from your soiree."

"Nice of you to come thank me and all, but I have work to do here. Take the bottle with you."

He drains it, smacks his lips annoyingly.

"Time for you to go, Mr. Hamilton. You're done stalking me for one night."

Ronnie walks out of my office toward the gallery floor, knowing I'll follow. He's counting on my curiosity, just as he counted on my showing up here. The bronze coffin, now positioned by the front door, draws his eye. He finds his way to it, guided by the dim glow of a security light, and hoists himself atop it, pleased with his choice of seat and his view of me silhouetted at the other end of the exhibit space.

"Obsessed with this gallery, aren't you, just like Sebastian? Whenever we were here in London, we always knew where to find him, even before he bought the place. Said something drew him here, some *creative force*. Then he became a silent partner and installed Esteban here and they did their little thing together, it was like their baby. Sebastian became Sir Fine Art Photography, made all those photos just so Esteban would have something to show off. Unnatural, the way he loved this gallery.

"But you, Miss Clothilde, you love it for a different reason: It gives you a stage of your own to perform on, doesn't it? You're not just some woman with a loupe around her neck anymore, poking at threads like my Genevieve. You're the one bringing art and space together in time. Driven into the spotlight, it's in the de la Coeur genes, just showed itself a little later with you. No use denying it, girlie. I'm part of the family, remember? Uncle Ronnie knows what he's talking about."

I lower myself into a lotus position on the floor, prop my back against a wall straight across from him. "Fascinating insights into my personality, Uncle Ronnie, but maybe there's a point you'd like to get to?'

"You're the type that studies something, wrestles with it until you make it your own, but in a good way, to make it work. Unlike your father, who just decides he wants something for himself and pulls at it until it becomes his, no matter who it belongs to, no matter who he hurts in the taking."

It's chilling, the resentment I hear. Maybe it's because I recognize in it the sound of someone, once loved, trying to comprehend why that love has been withdrawn. I spent my teens wondering why I'd been rejected by my parents, until I could no longer bear it and simply had to leave.

So I ask: "Why stay then?"

His eyes brighten, as if my question has led him into the light. He looks less like the sixty-nine-year-old man he is; more, I imagine, like the man who first wielded his guitar with abandon at my father's side.

"Why stay? Because in the beginning, it's like Christmas every day, with some shiny toy waiting for you. A little blood, that's all, a little secret, no one is the wiser, and you're young and there's women and booze and drugs and such amazing, amazing music for you to play, and you're so high on it all, all the time. Who'd even think of giving that up? You'd have to be crazy. But then one day you wake up, and your wife is in his bed, she leaves you, and someone else is raising your baby. Your music is all you have, and that's tied to him, to the goddamn band, and you have to cleave to him, and whatever destiny might lie beyond the goddamn band is beyond your reach. So you stay, because it's who you are and you don't know who the hell you are without it, without him."

He looks as if he could use another drink, but I don't offer. He smiles knowingly.

"Eventually, like you, I tried to master my own life. I stepped out of the music and did something else. I'm real good at it, real good at taking things people want to sell and finding people who want to buy. I know how to twist the screws and tighten them to get the deal I want, I learned from the master, right? Except he wanted in on that, too, so I let him in because getting around with the band was a fantastic cover and making the deal was so much sexier with the great Court of Cruelty behind me. Just like that, it was all of a piece, until he owned my side business as well, just like the fucking soul I sold him when I first believed his lies that we'd all live forever, that we'd never age, never diminish, that we'd always burn white hot."

A life too good to walk away from. I watched it my whole childhood, how thrilling it all was, how inviting. Like he said, I wanted to play with them, too.

Ronnie eases himself off the very expensive coffin, joins me on the floor in the gallery's moonlit shadows. He eyes me up and down, assesses me for something, shakes his head.

"The lives we led, Christ have mercy, then he took those away, too, what with him and Emilie all of sudden being dead. Doesn't know how to do things halfway, doesn't care that the rest of us become collateral damage. You, too, even though you're his flesh and blood and you've inherited his almighty Sebastian-ness. More's the pity for you, with all that implies."

I smell the champagne on Ronnie's breath, mixed with an older musk of scotch. My stomach clenches, and I shift away from him, but he grabs my wrist, clamps it to the floor between our thighs. I glare at him. He laughs.

"Think you're gonna stare at me with the de la Coeur evil eye and I'll just snap to attention? Think again, girlie. You don't scare me. Fact is, you're the one who should be afraid."

I believe him. What is it they say about a man who has nothing left to lose being the most dangerous of all?

I break free from his grip, careful not to break his fingers. He might need them to play his guitar, if not to continue supplying certain fearsome goods to certain fearsome states and non-state perpetrators of terror. My hand trembles with restrained fury. He realizes the degree to which I am holding back, takes it as his cue to leave. He stands, offers me his help getting up. I refuse.

"Word of advice, little one," he whispers: "Best be prepared."

He hurls the empty champagne bottle at the bronze coffin, watches it shatter against the polished metal, glass skittering along the floor toward us. He kicks a shard aside, turns to the hall and makes his way to the gallery's back door.

Sort of like John the Baptist leaving the building, having heralded something that portends nothing but grief.

*Chapter Four*

# FRANKFURT, DECEMBER 2011

Murderous rage gripped him, a seething jealousy that manifested every time the pendant kicked against his chest, every time it glowed until the stone burned hot against his skin, every time he felt the evidence that Chloe had fed, that she had pleasured whoever was supplying the blood he'd neglected to bring to her. He'd been away too long, it was his fault for not rushing back to nourish her, but that didn't stop Fahey from wanting to lay hands on whatever lowlife prick had laid himself bare in front of his woman, after offering his veins to her.

All Monday evening, the ruby seared a path from his pecs to his cock, until Fahey had given in and masturbated repeatedly in hopes of getting some relief, enough to bring him just a little sleep. But it didn't work, he couldn't rest, his brain assaulted him long after the pendant settled down. He stood under a cold shower this morning, in hopes his fists would unclench, his jaw would loosen, his teeth would stop grinding in sheer fury at himself and the person who dared step into the arms and the spell of the woman he loved.

He swiped his credit card viciously through the reader at the hotel desk, pushed his luggage at the attendant after he checked out. He left his bags because he had to return to the banking conference for one more round of idiocy on bond yields and bailouts. Needed to find a new job, any job, he didn't care what, anything with anyone who'd assign him to London and deliver him from the eurozone forevermore.

Thus was Fahey in a foul mood already as he entered the makeshift pressroom at Deutsche Bank headquarters, the whispering preceding him, then surrounding him. That it was him they whispered about was clear, his name and the words *sex tape* and *Sebastian* repeated too often for him to pretend nothing was amiss. He scanned the pressroom for an ally, some way to figure out what the hell was going on. A friend from Agence France Presse waved him over to the table where she sat, opened a CNN video post from about twenty minutes earlier, stood back and offered him her chair. She shook her head as if to say, "It's bad."

In the video, a naked man with longish dark hair, his back to the camera, his buttocks blurred for public consumption, stood before a strategically blurred naked woman on a bed. An English-language voiceover identified the woman as a sex worker from Kosovo; described her pregnancy and death, the discovery of her body outside the Prague home of the late Sebastian and Emilie de la Coeur of the rock band Court of Cruelty; the uncanny resemblance of the man, in body or voice or both, to the late Sebastian de la Coeur, a Swedish singer named Teppan Nilsson, and BBC journalist Jackson Fahey, fiancé of the de la Coeurs' daughter, C.J. Hart.

Plus this, the CNN correspondent reported: Interpol was investigating the connection between the man on this tape, already dubbed "The Lethal Lover" by the British tabloid press (a cut to a shot of the headlines), and a dozen more tapes discovered in Pristina, Kosovo. Also being investigated: The murder of this woman, Anya Morina (cut to her photo) and three other women, whose bodies had been found recently outside Prague, all of whom had been pregnant, all of whose babies had been dead in the womb. The effort by Interpol, led by Detective Julian Gippel (cut to footage of his 6 a.m. GMT press conference), who was seeking to gain permission from authorities in New York State to dredge a lake on the grounds of the de la Coeurs' famous Castle (cut to footage from after the winery blast) to verify that the remains of the singers had been scattered there after their reported April double suicide. Protests by Edward Chestack, attorney for the de la Coeurs' estate and onetime Court of Cruelty drummer, that assertions made by Interpol that Sebastian de la Coeur might himself be the naked man on the tapes were absurd (cut to footage from a midnight EST press conference in Ithaca).

And then: footage of the arrest of Teppan Nilsson, leader of a Court of Cruelty tribute band called Matins and Vespers, on suspicion of murder by authorities in Stockholm (a short perp walk from a black sedan into the police station). Nilsson had surrendered to police after a warrant was issued early that morning. Footage of Nilsson's wife, Katarina, trying to avoid reporters outside the precinct where her husband turned himself in for questioning; footage of C.J. Hart, Jackson Fahey's pregnant fiancée, as she entered her London art gallery, Aspect Ratio, that morning, refusing to talk to the press assembled outside. Live cut to Miss Hart's representative, Meredith Grainger-Todd, telling reporters in London that the de la Coeurs' daughter was cooperating with law-enforcement authorities to see that whoever was responsible for the women's deaths was brought to justice. Miss Grainger-Todd declining to comment on a report, attributed to sources at Interpol, that Miss Hart had acknowledged a romantic rendezvous with Teppan Nilsson last month in Edinburgh.

Promised by CNN: further details as they became available.

Fahey bent over to keep his head from spinning off his neck. The AFP reporter pressed a cup of water into his hand, crouched beside him, asked whether he needed her to call anyone. He drank, breathed, reached for his bag, pointed to the pocket where his smartphone rested; saw a half-dozen urgent texts broadcast on the screen, gave her his pass code. She searched through his contacts, found BBC Brussels, returned the phone to him.

"You'll want my resignation," Fahey said when the call to his bureau chief at last went through.

Nonsense, the bureau chief replied. No charges had been lodged against Fahey, and the BBC could verify his whereabouts on the dates time-stamped on the videos in Interpol's possession. He had been working out of Madrid much of that time, and the bureau chief there, Amanda Witt, had verified Fahey's assignments and found his video and audio feeds corroborating the log sheets.

"You'll want a statement then."

Not necessary, the BBC had already issued one, decrying the attempts by Interpol to sensationalize an already salacious case by unnecessarily involving a respected journalist. The BBC stood by Fahey and was dismayed that his personal relationship with C.J. Hart had been made part of Interpol's blatant attempts to gain publicity for its investigation.

"You said all that before you were able to reach me?"

No reason not to, Witt had vouched for him, had the evidence to back her up, and there was no time to waste. Damage control.

"You want me to proceed here, as if I haven't become a bit player in a drama of international intrigue and murder?"

Not appropriate, under the circumstances. The banking conference's conclusion today would be covered via pool material from the news services.

"You'll want me to come back to Brussels then?"

No question he should instead make haste to London to be with his fiancée, and plan on returning for his regular assignment Tuesday a week.

"You know that's not me on that tape."

Never a doubt. The voice was wrong, that was perfectly clear from the outset, and of course Fahey had never breached the standards of behavior BBC staff must abide by in both their professional and private lives.

True enough, he thought, unless you counted as a breach his considerable undisclosed knowledge of other people's bad behavior.

As he ended the call, journalists filed out of the room; the conference's morning session was about to convene. The AFP reporter gave him a hug and departed. Fahey soaked up the silence, sat immobilized in the uncomfortable banquet-room chair his friend had given up for him.

His jealous anger was doused; Chloe needed all the strength she could muster right now, its source very much beside the point. His career appeared intact, though who knew how long it would take for this to die down, or how many more times those nude "Lethal Lover" images would be associated with his name. As for how everything else had transpired as it had, the man with some of those answers could be found, at least at the moment, behind bars in Stockholm, surely surmising that it was better to cooperate and find a good lawyer to arrange for bail than flee and sort out the consequences later.

Fahey opened his laptop, found the CNN feed his French friend had shown him, watched it a half-dozen times more before sensation returned to his legs and he could stand again. Teppan Nilsson in a jail cell. Sebastian de la Coeur in custody, unbeknownst to the very police who'd love to prove him still alive and charge his naked ass with murder. Katarina acting the dutiful wife, standing by her man.

"Holy Mary and the saints, save us," Fahey whispered. This was what Americans meant by a come-to-Jesus moment. He understood now.

He had to talk to Chloe, had to be there for her in spirit if not in fact. He called the gallery, wanted to scream when Benjamin picked up, though he hardly should have been surprised.

"She's on a conference call with Meredith and Ed Chestack. Interpol got the warrant to dredge her parents' lake; Chestack got a court order to block it, and there's a hearing tomorrow in Ithaca. Meredith wants them to do a preemptive statement:

'We'll cooperate with reasonable requests, but this isn't reasonable.' "

"Everybody knows Sebastian de la Coeur is dead, and I'm sure as hell not the guy in those tapes, so they've got their man and the rest is just for show. That business about her being with Teppan Nilsson in Edinburgh, I know it's nothing but a bunch of lies."

Benjamin cleared his throat, and an awkward silence fell. He might well believe Fahey wasn't the man on the tapes, but the rest? Ben didn't know who Teppan Nilsson was and what had actually happened, and Fahey couldn't tell him.

Now that he thought of it, Fahey saw why Chloe had lied about meeting Nilsson for a tryst in Edinburgh. The police would have run Teppan's financials, checked reservation records, and put them together at the hotel. A fib made a lot of sense when there was such an enormous lie to preserve.

"Tell her I love her, Ben, and I'll be there as soon as I can. It will be late though, tell her I'll go straight to the flat."

"Not the flat, at least not if I have a say." Ben's voice sunk into the West African tough-guy timbre he'd used when they first met. "I'd prefer to book a room for her somewhere and smuggle in her through a kitchen if we have to. Meredith has some contacts. If I can convince Chloe, I'll let you know where."

Fahey gathered his things to head back to the hotel. A platoon of paparazzi fell in behind him, snapping photos, shouting questions. He no-commented in German, French and English, hopped into the first available taxi, and left the working press sucking up exhaust as the driver tore off into Frankfurt's mid-morning traffic.

* * * *

Police cars and a crime-scene van blocked the street in front of his Brussels apartment building. A television crew had skirted a barricade and parked on the sidewalk.

"There he is now! Jackson Fahey, is it you on that video?"

Bloody hell.

He shoved through to the door, the voice of his landlord pitched high above the din, yelling in Dutch about not wanting to give permission. Fahey grabbed him by the arm and dragged him upstairs, taking the steps two at a time, not particularly caring how the shorter man kept up.

The door to his flat was open. A German shepherd stood at the entrance.

"Hello? This is my home, where is your warrant?" Fahey hollered, first in his nearly perfect French, then in his flawed Dutch. An officer peered around the door, tugged on the dog's leash, allowed him to pass.

A man in street clothes appeared, flashed credentials identifying him as Detective Julian Gippel, Interpol. Fahey recognized him as the star of this morning's briefing; must have taken a helicopter here immediately afterward.

"Your landlord granted us access, Mr. Fahey. Your superiors at the BBC were uncertain what time you might return from Frankfurt, given the change in your assignment today."

"You have someone in custody, and my superiors have provided proof of my whereabouts when the sex tapes were made. The so-called Lethal Lover cannot possibly be me. What is your purpose here?"

A tall, thin man, Gippel looked the type inclined to insinuate rather than charm, all staid black trench coat and dour demeanor. This was a hunting expedition. Fahey guessed that Gippel was in no way sure the man he'd arrested was the man he wanted, and he would take no chances.

"You are aware, Mr. Fahey, that there are too many connections between you, your fiancée, and four murders to be ignored."

"Deliberate on the killer's part, no doubt. What better way to attract attention than to hitch one's star to celebrities. I certainly don't qualify, but it can't have escaped Interpol's notice that Sebastian and Emilie de la Coeur's fame has already been appropriated by unstable individuals bent on mayhem."

"*Natürlich*, I have heard this litany recited by Miss Hart, Miss Grainger-Todd, and Mr. Chestack, as well as Mr. Nilsson's attorney." Gippel backed Fahey out into the hallway, casting a withering look at the landlord. "Yet it is intriguing, is it not, that in more than thirty years only the occasional incident of vandalism was attributed to a follower of Court of Cruelty, while in the months following the de la Coeurs' deaths seven people have been horrifically slain? I go where the investigation leads."

Fahey leaned against the railing opposite his flat, watched through the door as gloved officers bagged a diverse assortment of his belongings. Gippel pulled a cigarette from his coat pocket, lit it, drew on it deeply. Part of the act, Fahey surmised: feign a moment of relaxation, ease up so the subject drops his guard. Gippel would lob some sort of verbal grenade soon. He had to be ready for it.

"Miss Hart, you have known her long?"

"You surely know that Chloe and I met in April, after her parents' deaths. That we met, in fact, the day after I covered a concert in memory of Sebastian and Emilie de la Coeur in Barcelona that featured Teppan Nilsson's band, Matins and Vespers."

"A performance at which Teppan Nilsson did not appear onstage with his band." Another drag on the cigarette. "You traveled to the US in May and stayed with Miss Hart at her parents' home for several weeks."

"I presume you're more curious about my fiancée's relationship with Teppan Nilsson than her relationship with me, which I'd wager almost any fifteen-year-old in Europe or America could brief you on. We've been a fairly public couple lately. "

Gippel took two last pulls on the cigarette, crushed it under his shoe on the hallway's wooden floor. "Miss Hart acknowledged a sexual rendezvous with Mr. Nilsson in Edinburgh late in November. You were aware of this?"

"Aware, yes, if unhappy about it. I believe we have come to an understanding about our future course, since we expect a child in June."

Gippel moved back into the flat, gestured to an officer. "A child, yes. Perhaps you can explain why we have just found in your freezer a container of what appears to be semen? We will, *natürlich*, perform tests to determine whose it might be."

The grenade, ready to blow.

Fahey focused on his breathing, the techniques they'd taught him after the ambush in Afghanistan—anything to cope with the memory of so many soldiers slaughtered in front of him, killed with the BBC correspondent also embedded in their unit, the reason Fahey set down his video camera and picked up a microphone for the first time. He inhaled, held the oxygen in his lungs, slowly let it out, counting brief puffs, readying his body for the blast. Worst case, Gippel tested the semen, matched the DNA to Nilsson, then to Sebastian and the dead babies. Best case, well, he didn't exactly know what that might be. His options here were limited to another half-truth in service to the big lie.

"Semen, but not mine. Sebastian de la Coeur's actually, given to a lover of his, who gave it to me because she wanted to be rid of it so she could move on after his death. It's been in and out of kitchen freezers for many months now. Not sure why I kept it."

The information seemed to surprise and delight Gippel, whom Fahey would not have guessed capable of either.

"This woman, her name?"

In for a penny, in for a pound, Fahey supposed. "Meredith Grainger-Todd, who, I may as well tell you because you'll learn it anyway, gave it to me after we had sex together in June. Fidelity has been a bit of an issue for me and Chloe: I slept with her best friend; she slept with a man who apparently looks like me, at least from the rear and when his hair is dyed dark. I like to think we're even now, she and I."

A smile turned up the edges of Gippel's mean, thin lips. He shouted in Dutch and French for the search team to wrap things up. "My regards to Miss Hart, Mr. Fahey. I do hope she's feeling better. She was unwell when I last saw her. Perhaps she is not eating as she should during her pregnancy? Or perhaps I should not ask?"

A reminder Fahey didn't need about the weekend and what Chloe had done to satisfy her hunger. "The baby's mine, not Nilsson's or anyone else's."

Gippel nodded and turned for the stairs.

* * * *

Lights still blazed in the main exhibit space at Aspect Ratio, though it was well past eleven o'clock. Fahey asked the taxi driver to stop at the far end of the block; fumbled through his wallet for some pound notes while scouting for press types who, like him, would wait out a story as long as it took; spotted a guy with a camera standing outside the café across from the gallery. Hoisting his bags onto his shoulder, he took the back way down the alley.

Fahey buzzed at the delivery entrance and wasn't altogether surprised when Meredith opened the door after he identified himself, though he thought perhaps he'd find Chloe here alone, as she so often was after-hours on a weeknight. Maybe it was just as well.

Meredith pulled him into a hug, a desperate embrace if ever he'd felt one, as if she required his strength to stand. She began to cry, and her arms tightened around his waist.

"Are you here by yourself? Where's Ben?"

She gulped back tears, brushed the moisture away from his sleeve, pressed her forehead against him. "He needed some space, away from me, frankly, though he was too polite to say so. I should have told him about Sebastian. I should have told him about us."

Fahey pulled back, wiped a mascara smudge from her face.

"My fault, I should have known those details would get out once the police left my flat in Brussels. Gone viral by now?"

Meredith flashed him one of her professional smiles. "I should hire Julian Gippel, he's a media master."

Fahey led her to the office, sat her in Chloe's chair, and dropped into the one opposite. "No more secrets from Ben, it must be a relief."

"When I heard Interpol had searched your apartment, all I wanted to do was smack you, Jackson. Why did you keep the semen? Why didn't you just dump it?"

"I did, or rather Chloe did, or so she thought—I sent it to her from Madrid in September, in care of the gallery, with a note telling her what it was. Someone sent an identical package to her flat. From her description, it was an exact duplicate, my handwriting, my return address in Spain, everything."

She groaned and opened a desk drawer, brought out a bottle of ibuprofen and popped two without water. Fahey crooked his finger, and Meredith passed him the bottle; he downed three, acutely feeling the day's exhaustion.

"So Gippel found which?"

"The one sent here. I've kept it all these months since, don't ask me why."

*Don't ask me why*, he silently repeated, *because I won't tell you if Sebastian hasn't. Too many people already know.*

She leaned back in the chair, kicked off her heels, and stretched her very nice legs. "Thus the world, and of course Benjamin, now knows that you and I did the nasty, and that I was Sebastian's lover for years, and that he left me a piece of himself, which I gave you and which you've kept in your freezer. Are we demented? It feels like each day reveals again how insane we are. As if the sex tape that's all over the news weren't bad enough, you know there's an uncensored full version of that video online, right? Gippel wanted a big bang, excuse the expression. He obviously wanted every possible Sebastian-like john that Anya Morina might have serviced to see it."

How funny, then, that Fahey himself hadn't. He unpacked his laptop from his bag, set it up in front of Meredith. "Find it."

She tapped a few keys; he moved his chair around the desk next to hers. The video opened, and Fahey was struck again how, if he didn't know better, even he might think the man was him. The resemblance was strong if not exact, but the hair was too long, the clothes too well-made.

At the point several minutes on at which the man began to disrobe, Meredith grabbed Fahey's hand and squeezed. At the point at which the man climbed onto the bed and into Anya, the pendant grew warm on Fahey's chest, beat a tattoo down to his crotch. Meredith squirmed by his side.

At the point, twenty minutes in, that he felt the fires of Hades intensify against his skin, felt the sweat against his shirt, Fahey wished he could take off his jacket but was afraid to move for fear he'd take off everything, his cock was twitching to get out and jump into Meredith, just as it had the last time he contemplated the copulatory gymnastics of one Sebastian de la Coeur in her presence. She couldn't take her eyes off the man on the video; who knew how many times she'd watched it already and relived how it felt to be under those hands, wrapped around all that muscle.

At the point the video cut off, Meredith was panting, curled so tightly into a ball, legs tucked under her, that it was clear her thoughts echoed Fahey's own. He jumped to his feet and pounded the laptop's keys until it shut down.

She closed her eyes, as if summoning the images again. "It's not you, the differences are subtle, but they're there. All I know about Teppan Nilsson after meeting him twice is that he's handsome, blond and has blue eyes so hard they could cut through steel, but I know that's not him on that video either."

"Sebastian then?"

"Oh, yes, every inch. He had better moves than men half his age." Meredith opened her eyes, looked at Fahey, shrugged.

The air crackled around them. Fahey steadied the pendant

on his chest, guessing Chloe had just felt its every vibration, just as he had felt her sexual arousal the other night.

"I need to get out of here, Meredith."

The look she sent him said otherwise, but she agreed. "Yes, you need to go."

He grabbed his bags, ordered his legs to move toward the exit. The minute he passed through the door, he felt it, felt Chloe inside his head. He'd have to walk to the flat if he had any hope of arriving with something less than the bulge now groaning in his pants. Meredith would always be somewhere near Chloe, near him if he was with Chloe. This couldn't keep happening. Fahey pulled the pendant over his head, shoved it into the pocket of his jacket. It burned his hand.

After twenty-five frigid December minutes outdoors trying to get his privates and his brain in sync, he found Chloe standing at the dining table, her back to him, studying papers spread out before her.

"Are we done ruining lives or will there be more, Jackson? That's what we've done: broken hearts; shattered souls."

He let the door slam behind him. She was pissed off, jealous, who knew what else. That made two of them.

"You think I don't know that?" Fahey dropped his bags to the floor. Would he be staying long?

The flat smelled like an Army surgery, like bleach and hydrogen peroxide and rubbing alcohol, like the tent where they took his mates in Afghanistan, filled with the smells of whatever could eliminate the blood, kill the germs, sterilize the living hell out of what was left of their bodies. Chloe had been cleaning.

He walked into the bedroom—the covers were smooth and tucked, no stained sheets barely clinging to the mattress—then into the bathroom. If not for the waste bin and the telltale bits of a torn ticket stub for the Edinburgh-to-London train, he might not have guessed the name of the visitor she'd been so busily tidying up after. Fahey flushed the toilet, wishing he could flush away the memory of his barely conscious guest in Zurich not so long ago.

She was jealous? Screw her.

"Stinks in here." He threw his jacket onto the sofa, walked past her into the kitchen, opened the refrigerator and pulled out a beer. She'd been shopping too. How very domestic.

She didn't look up from the papers but knew when he was close, he could see her shoulders tense. "Couldn't have you picking up any diseases. Blood carries all sorts of things."

Like resentment and regret, for starters. "Blood relations are especially messy all the way around, don't you think? Full of opportunities for infection, contagion, especially yours."

At that, she laughed, lifted her head. "Hadn't noticed. Too busy branding myself an unfaithful little whore on multimedia news platforms. You?"

Fahey swallowed half the beer, wished fervently for something stronger. "Much the same, though I'd characterize myself more along the lines of semen-saving unfaithful little whore. Sounds so much more perverted, don't you think?"

He leaned over her, rested a hand on her arm, and peered down at what he could now see were papers written in old-time script. "Sebastian's?"

She shook him off. "When he was Stefan, yes. I'm channeling my anger at him productively, or trying to. You'll have to find your own way. Meredith is probably still at the gallery, not too late for you to fondle Daddy right out of her memory. I'm sure you'd both like that. Wouldn't be surprised if she didn't sleep there tonight. She's too scared to go to Benjamin's place, afraid she'll find him gone, but even more afraid she'll finally have to talk to him alone."

Crouching next to her, Fahey took her face into his hands, stared into those green eyes. "I don't want Meredith," he said, certain Chloe knew that wasn't precisely true. "Lust after her? Yes, I do, from time to time. There's this thing that comes over me when she's talking about Sebastian, some obsession with how I look like him, and I have to compete and be better than him, and I have to prove it, and Meredith's the only one I can prove it with. She gets wrapped up in it, too, and she wants me, wants me to prove that I'm better than Sebastian because then he doesn't drive her crazy from the grave, it's like she gets to screw him and tell him to screw off simultaneously. You know that's the truth, you know how she is about him."

Fahey rested his cheek against Chloe's forehead, hoped she'd let him, if only for a minute. "This thing with Meredith and me is an aberration. I love you, and she needs to forget Sebastian. Ben is what she needs, he's nuts about her. Idiot that I am, even I see that."

Chloe wrenched away. "I was at the gallery today when your revelations to Gippel hit the news and hit Benjamin like a truck. He spent the rest of the day trying to recover from that double sucker punch you delivered: that Meredith had not only been Sebastian's girl toy for years, but that she had given you his precious fluids after you two had shared a few of your own."

Fangs on display, she hissed, to force Fahey out of her personal space. "Meredith lied to Ben, we all lied to him—he took one look at my face and could tell none of it came as a shock to me. So now, maybe he loses her and the gallery. How does he continue to work at Aspect Ratio and not be caught between you and Meredith, me and Meredith, you and me? If he's smart, he runs while he can. I spent thirteen years hiding from that unblinking public eye. I know just how he feels."

Fahey grabbed a chair, spun it, sat on it backwards, and got as close and into Chloe's face as possible, daring her to strike out at him. "Like I can't relate to being bare-arsed, however metaphorically, in front of millions right now?"

She moved her head away. He grabbed her by the chin and turned her body to look at him, held her immobile, his strength greater than hers only because she allowed it to be. "Meredith knows that's Sebastian on that January Anya Morina video.

It's the only one she's seen, but she says there's no doubt in her mind. We watched it together tonight; I could see her analyzing every move, every sound. Gippel shows her the rest of the videos, the ones made after April, and that's it, game over, she'll know Sebastian is still alive, and Gippel will know, too. It's just a matter of time before Interpol calls her in for questioning."

Chloe reared back, then bulleted forward, butting her head into Fahey's nose. Pain radiated across his face, vibrated through his eyes, felt like it would shatter his cheekbones. He heard no crack, she hadn't broken anything, but he'd have one hell of a bruise.

She darted away as he grabbed for her again, putting the width of the table between them, out of his longer reach. "Then we'd better hope Gippel decides he has his Lethal Lover. Chestack says that as long as Gippel has somebody in custody, the chances are nil he gets permission to dredge the Castle's lake. Oh, except for the fact that Gippel can still do DNA comparison on the semen and the bodies of the dead babies and prove that my father is their father, even if he didn't kill their mothers. It won't matter who killed them, Sebastian's resurrection will be assured."

She didn't add, "Thanks to you." She already had, and his head throbbed from the force of it. Fahey launched himself over the table, locked his hands onto her shoulders defiantly. If she wanted to show off her vampire strength, he'd counter with a few moves of his own. He dug his thumbs into her flesh, flexed his fingers around her upper arms, wrapped one of his longer legs around her waist and tumbled them both to the floor, shifted his weight and threw her under him, flat on her back, his forearm pressed against her cheek, her mouth aimed away from his throat.

"*I* gave Gippel the semen; *you* helped deliver Teppan on a platter because the old gang got together at the gallery, which begat the Little Goth Club performance video and the voice track Gippel needed. If you want to blame me, find yourself a mirror while you're at it. This has been quite the team effort."

He felt rage swell within her as her body strained to get leverage against his, to push him off and away. She kicked every part of him she could reach; he pulled his groin out of range. Then abruptly, like a switch had been thrown, she stopped and he could feel her will to fight him draining away. She pushed against the forearm holding her face down; Fahey lifted it.

She stifled a yawn. Fahey rarely saw Chloe fatigued. Must be the baby.

"Jesus, the baby. Did I hurt you? Are you all right?" He scrambled to his feet, helped Chloe to hers. What was he thinking? It was late, too many tense hours into a very long, tense day, he felt like his brain was unraveling, felt dizzy from the blow she'd administered. He dropped into the only dining chair still upright, sat down quickly, before he fell and took her with him. She bent until her eyes were level with his, kissed his face where she had struck, licked across the bridge of his nose. The pain receded from the concussed parts of his skull, and all he felt was hungry.

He couldn't remember the last time he had eaten. Fahey got up, made his way around her, walked into the tight galley that passed for a kitchen. There were eggs in the fridge, he'd seen earlier, and some cheddar and butter. He searched in the mostly empty cupboards for the frying pan he knew had come with her furnished flat.

"Omelet?"

Chloe looked at him uncertainly. "You're going to cook?"

"If I want to eat, apparently I am. To reiterate: omelet?"

"That would be wonderful."

"Let's not get carried away, it's just scrambled eggs with cheese." He took six of the eggs out of the bowl they'd been stored in, found another bowl in which to break them, added a bit of water.

"Whisk?"

"Somewhere in that drawer to your left, I think. If not, there are forks there—or there were. I haven't been paying a lot of attention the last few weeks. When Guinevere gets fussy, I order in."

Indeed, there was a whisk. He added salt and pepper and stirred, then sliced some of the cheese and put the pan on to warm before he added the butter.

"Guinevere?"

"Or Lancelot. I might learn tomorrow, if you want to join me. I'm scheduled for an ultrasound."

How would that go, Fahey wondered, as he gave yokes and egg whites a final whipping. She heard, or intuited, his question.

"I found a doctor from the National Health Service who's willing to restrain her curiosity about my inner workings in exchange for cash, amounts more than she'd ordinarily get for an obstetrical case. No blood work, I insisted; she agreed, but was firm about imaging, said she needed to see what was going on—to limit her legal liability, no doubt, but what the heck. I made the appointment purposely for a day you'd be here, but if you don't want to come . . ."

Eggs sizzled as they hit the hot pan; his dry, weary eyes burned as he turned down the heat. Chloe stepped into the narrow space behind him, reached around to remove a loaf of bread from the metal box on the counter, put two slices into the toaster.

"Of course, I want to go with you. How can you think I wouldn't?"

She stood on tiptoe next to him, pressed a kiss to the back of his neck. "It's a girl, I'm sure of it." Her breath brushed warm against his skin.

"How can you possibly know that?"

"Blood bond?" Chloe, who never giggled, did. She replaced the toasted bread with two untoasted slices.

"Guinevere it is, then," he said, pulling dishes down from an upper cabinet.

They ate in silence. Too much had been said already, and more still they feared revealing. Much simpler to be naked than candid, to share orgasms rather than honest exchanges; always, they struggled for full disclosure. He was, Fahey recognized, too quick to think he had surmised the answers, in contrast to her instinct to preserve her privacy, to never give up everything at once. Chloe was ever a book one had to read, then re-read, to determine whether one had correctly interpreted what had gone before. He loved her, but he recognized he might never know her completely because she no longer knew herself. Not since that night in Edinburgh with her father. Their wrestling match earlier demonstrated an aggressive side Fahey had never before seen in her. That he'd been focused only on fighting back was disturbing.

He finished his eggs, drank the tea Chloe had brewed while he plated the food. "Come away with me tonight, to Spain, where we were happy."

"I was living in Barcelona, you were living in Madrid. Could be that's why we were happy, or at least why you were, far from the cursed de la Coeurs."

"You, me, and Guinevere, we could go off and love each other and live our lives, everyone else be damned. We'll get married, find some way to make our livelihood and just be normal people."

For a minute, Fahey thought she might agree. She wanted to, he was certain, but she looked so sad.

"I'll never be normal again. Though really, I never have been, have I? We can try to run away from the trouble my father has bound us up in, but we'll never be free of it. If there's any hope for us, we have to see this through, see what happens, and when it's over—please, God, it has to be over eventually—I'll close the gallery or sell it and we'll take the baby and head for Madrid or Barcelona or wherever you want."

"You love the gallery."

"I love you more."

She began clearing plates and cutlery, defaulting to perpetual-motion mode: loading the dishwasher; rinsing the kettle; returning the butter to the refrigerator; wiping the counter. She reached over him to collect the condiments. Fahey pulled her on to his lap, wrapped his hands across her midsection, and hugged his girls tightly to him.

"Tell me about Guinevere. She's just starting to make her presence known here." He sketched finger circles on Chloe's stomach.

She leaned her head against his shoulder. "I feel her moving when I'm in the shower. She doesn't like the water pounding over her; she flits away from the spray."

Fahey swept her hair from her neck, kissed along the length of it. "Tell me more. Is the morning sickness gone?"

"We've achieved a truce, baby and I, as long as I keep the food and blood in balance. Too much of one, or too little, and there's hell to pay."

*Like the weekend just past*, he thought.

"Like the weekend just past," she echoed. "Not enough blood, and nothing I ate stayed down properly either. I shouldn't have gone so long without."

*You wanted to wait for me, to stay faithful to me because that's what I wanted.*

"I wanted to wait for you, yes, but I wanted to be faithful also," she countered. "I want you to be sure of me, to be sure that I love you."

"But I am sure."

"You're not, and I don't blame you. The next time Will Baumann shows up here to feed me because you can't, you'll see what I mean."

*Next time?*

"Inevitably, yes. Teppan overrode my compulsion. If Will senses a need, he'll find me and slake my blood thirst."

This flat would smell like bleach and peroxide again. He couldn't take that, or even if he could, he couldn't like it. Fahey vowed again to look for another job, this business of being away from her had to end.

"Did you mean it: If I wanted, you'd leave your life and your career in London for me?"

"No, Jackson, I'd do it for me."

Emilie, or rather Katarina, had been right: It was easy to lose yourself in a relationship like this. Everything you thought was solid was ephemeral; everything you cherished, tenuous. Chloe seemed so fragile now, and he wanted to safeguard her, his delicate, precious jewel, when in fact her body was preternaturally strong, her will stronger.

She slid off his lap, offered her hand. "Let's go to bed. Neither of us is thinking straight." He scooped her into his arms and carried her. He doubted she'd gained an ounce of baby weight so far. He deposited her gently on the mattress, undressed swiftly and eased under the sheets next to her, draping his body around hers like a second skin, her breathing even against him in mere minutes, his breathing slow, steady for the first time all day.

When his eyes jolted open, he was alone. Fahey padded into, then out of, the bathroom; found her in near-darkness at the dining table, a candle lit, her father's papers before her—slightly rearranged from last night, he judged, since the leather portfolio had spilled its contents. She was staring at her computer, at a webpage for French-to-German translation.

Over her shoulder, he read: "*One life only to complete the change. One life only to survive.*"

It was just after four, the clock on the microwave glowed; Fahey figured he'd slept about three-and-a-half hours. He was dying for some coffee, to be able to stay awake as she did whatever she was doing, but he was too exhausted to think about making some, so he dropped onto the sofa and spread over his midsection the afghan his mother had crocheted.

"What is that 'one life' bit?"

She was fixed on the words, didn't turn at the sound of his

voice. "Stefan writes that Eugenie said this to him in French on their wedding night. Then he mentions it again in describing the night he transformed, which was about six months later."

The room was freezing; Fahey folded himself into fetal position under the blanket. Couldn't Chloe feel how cold it was? The chattering of his teeth would soon make conversation impossible. "How romantic," he managed.

Chloe redirected her attention to him, got up and punched buttons on the thermostat. Heat whooshed through the vents, and she shoved him over on the sofa so she could snuggle against him. "Doesn't sound like my mother at all. Sounds like some dusty old motto."

Fahey settled between Chloe and the back of the couch, soaking up her body heat. "You're sure you've translated it accurately? Move one *only* and you might change the meaning."

"I've done it French to German, and German to Czech, it comes out the same. So unless Stefan misheard her, that's what Eugenie must have said. Unfortunately, I can't ask my father in person since he's in a Swedish jail right now. I have the disposable phone he gave Will, though. I can try to reach Katarina on it."

Fahey looked at the room around them. Blank grayish walls, like the ones found in bad hotels across Europe. This flat looked about as much like home as his place in Brussels did, if you considered generic rented furnishings welcoming. Not what he wanted for Chloe or their baby or himself. He wanted more, and peace of mind besides. He, like her, wanted this nonsense behind them.

"Text the words to Kat. She must know where they came from, and why Sebastian left you that Bible."

Chloe sprang from the couch, found the phone and texted the message, in French, to the number Kat had given her over the summer. "Brilliant."

"Or not. We'll see."

She pulled the afghan off him, and Fahey felt as if he'd been dropped onto a glacier, it was still that cold despite the laboring furnace. "Come on, back to bed. I promise to stay put so you can rest." She put her right hand over her heart, then over his.

"No more vampire insomnia?"

"Nope, you sleep, I sleep, but I'll set the alarm clock. We have a princess to visit with later."

Fences to mend, too, and riddles to solve, just the sort of thing likely to keep sleep from overtaking him, even with Chloe snug by his side. Fahey rested his hand on her belly and willed himself to dream of their daughter.

* * * *

The ultrasound exam proved a good distraction, in and out of the doctor's office. Chloe had seen the obstetrician once before and had walked away with prenatal vitamins, having made up a story about not wanting her blood drawn for religious reasons. But she worried how a human baby in a vampire uterus might appear on a sonogram. Fahey worried about, oh, any number of things related to fatherhood, like where they would live and on what if they decided to chuck the careers they now had, and whether in twenty or thirty years he'd be wondering whether his daughter would one day transition the way her mother had, and whether he'd be gray and stooped over while Chloe looked as young as she did today.

His bigger worry was not what the monitor showed—as it turned out, that was quite extraordinary and totally normal—but whether it would continue to show it to full term: a beating heart, a female fetus growing apparently according to plan. Looking yet again at the three photos the doctor had printed, Fahey wondered how he would sleep the next six months, especially when he had to be in a different city much of the time; wondered how best to schedule his stays in London with an eye to avoiding further visits from the willing Will Baumann.

They had no sooner set foot into Aspect Ratio when Meredith and Benjamin, clearly tiptoeing around each other, rushed over for a view of the very similar, not very sharp, images of the unborn child now officially known in the database of the United Kingdom's National Health System as Baby Hart-Fahey.

"Everything's okay?" Meredith clung to Chloe's arm, determined that the answer would be yes.

"We seem to be doing fine. Blood pressure is good, weight good, fetal heartbeat is strong. She's on the small side, but I was a small baby, too, only five pounds when I was born. The doctor is happy."

Ben offered Fahey his hand. "In Ghana sometimes, a girl child is named for the month in which she is born. That would make her June."

"Chloe calls her Guinevere," Fahey pumped the hand heartily, relieved not to have lost a friend. "I'm hoping there's room for compromise, though. Maybe Gwen?"

The women looked aghast. "How," Meredith asked, "could a granddaughter of the Court of Cruelty have anything but a name that conveys majesty? How about Boudica, after the Celtic queen?"

"Don't think that didn't occur to me," Chloe said, "but I worried we'd all end up calling her *Boo*. No way. I am, however, willing to explore other possibilities with Mr. Fahey."

"C.J., where is that photo Jackson brought from his parents' house, the one from back in the seventies with all the members of the Cruel minus Sebastian and Emilie? Some of the so-called ladies-in-waiting gave themselves medieval names, didn't they, like Aislinn and Freya? Not majestic exactly, but period-appropriate." Meredith searched a file drawer and found the picture. "How cool is this, they look so young, all knights brave and maidens fair."

She held the photo out as far as she could, assessing something. "I never noticed this before from the old album covers: Every one of the guys in the band has got to be over six feet tall,

all a uniform size, like soldiers. See, they loom over the women and some of the vassals and other people near the stage."

Fahey, looming over these two women, moved in for a closer look. There was, indeed, an almost military precision to the lineup of Zeke Segal and Ronnie Hamilton, Ed Chestack, Theo Martin, and Esteban Gronlund. None had Sebastian's stature, but none fell too short of the mark either. Even with Esteban in his jester's bells, they looked quite formidable.

Sebastian's personal army. Maybe Emilie's too?

A memory flashed, of Anthony Kirkpatrick's description of the man he encountered after a tryst with Chloe the night he killed Esteban. Anton had met Chloe, and Esteban, while tending bar at a hotel, serving them as they chatted. The man told Anton to kill Esteban unless he gave up information the man wanted. A tall man, with cold hands, Anton had said, a face in the shadows, maybe Fahey's height. Not Teppan, though, if Chloe was right about her mother being behind Esteban's death.

Fahey left them looking at the photograph, moved behind the desk and sat. An accounting spreadsheet for the gallery displayed on the computer screen. "Ben, may I, for just a minute?"

Benjamin circled around the desk and cleared out of the program. Fahey logged into the BBC video archive, did a quick search and located the footage he'd shot of Matins and Vespers at the memorial concert for Sebastian and Emilie in Barcelona. On stage surrounding Katarina Nilsson were four tall men. Tallest of all was Eric, the bassist, a stand-in for Teppan in any number of ways. A Sebastian clone with his own bent for violence?

Exiting the archive, Fahey stood and clapped the group to attention. "You have important Aspect Ratio business to attend to, whereas I have none. Wouldn't want to impede the progress of art sales so close to Christmas, so I'm off to run an errand."

Chloe eyed him curiously. "What are you up to?"

"I'll be back in a few hours, love, before closing time." He kissed her cheek. "We'll have dinner out, my treat, yes?"

"How about a baby celebration, the four of us?" Meredith suggested, ever the event planner. "Back by nine o'clock, Jackson, no excuses."

Possible, though it might be slicing things a bit fine. Figure two hours to travel and navigate security at HM Prison Belmarsh—assuming the strings he'd pulled on his last visit remained taut—then an hour with Anton Kirkpatrick, then the trip back, all to play a hunch that might not prove worth the playing.

On the train, Fahey made calls to the prison and Kirkpatrick's attorney, requesting and receiving permission for a short meeting and to bring his laptop into a private interview room. He would show Anton three videos: his own of the April concert, the YouTube video of Matins and Vespers & Co. from last Saturday night, and the Anya Morina sex tape released by Interpol. Maybe Anton would see someone he recognized. Not that any knowledge gleaned would help his cause: the butchering of Esteban was deemed too professionally done not to have been premeditated. Claim that a man had gotten around his dick and inside his mind? Too little, too odd to be believed, and much too late to make a difference.

*That might be me in that cell, doing life for murder, if not for some dumb luck of physical appearance and Esteban's efforts at matchmaking.* Kirkpatrick deserved to be more than a forgotten piece of this intricate puzzle. He was a victim of sorts, too. He deserved to know who'd done this to him, and Fahey did not intend to walk away today without an answer.

A guard guided him to the interview room in which he'd seen Kirkpatrick last month and, grumbling, left them alone there, a concession typically reserved for attorneys that Fahey had requested and was surprised to have been granted once again. It was a spare, cold room, painted a greenish-gray: the color of misery. The prisoner wore a jumpsuit in the same shade. Anton had picked up a few more pounds of muscle, all chest and biceps, looking more now like a man hardened by his fate than the frightened soul he had been last visit. Fahey's presence seemed to faze him not at all.

"Knew you'd be back," Kirkpatrick said, hands cuffed to a bar at the center of the table. "You don't give up, do you? Told you, I don't know who the guy was or why I felt like I had to follow his orders."

Fahey powered up his laptop, queued the video files; pulled his chair around to Anton's side of the table, so they could watch together. "Think you'd recognize him if you saw him again?"

"Might. What's in it for me?"

Honesty was certain to piss Kirkpatrick off. Fahey wanted him angry, motivated to find the bastard who'd jerked him off, screwed with his brain then screwed him for life.

"Probably nothing: You know you did it, Anton, the police know you did it, end of story, except we both know it isn't. I want you to watch three videos with me. Tell me what you see, anyone who looks familiar. On the first, you'll hear me doing a voice-over; it's from an assignment I covered when Sebastian and Emilie de la Coeur died."

"Court of Cruelty, they committed suicide, yeah? I saw this bit before, when it happened. Didn't know that was you talking."

"The de la Coeurs were my fiancée's parents. You remember Chloe." Fahey remembered all too well the security camera footage of Chloe and Kirkpatrick in the alley, bodies twisting, tongues tangling.

"Absolutely, wish I could forget her. Forgot they were her mum and dad, that's sad."

Hardly worth shedding a tear for, actually, but Fahey couldn't tell Kirkpatrick that. The clip opened on Katarina Nilsson swanning across the stage, microphone in hand, wailing "Faithless Servant" as Eric and the other members of the faux Cruel tried to keep up, Eric seeming especially clueless on bass.

"Singer's brilliant, but I remember you said the rest were shit, especially the tall blond guy, yeah? He wasn't having a good night." When the clip ended, Kirkpatrick looked confused. "Didn't see anything I didn't see before."

"On to the next, then. This is a performance by the same band last weekend, but they're playing with a couple of the original members of Court of Cruelty."

Kirkpatrick peered at the computer, watched Kat cavort, but seemed more focused on the music. "Little Goth Club, yeah? Much better. The band is really killing it. Who's on organ?"

"Teppan Nilsson, he's married to Katarina Nilsson, the singer." Fahey tapped at the screen when Eric came back into the frame. "Teppan usually plays bass with the band, but this guy, Eric, fills in when Teppan can't make it. On the first video I showed you, that was Eric."

About six minutes in, Teppan launched into "Inquisition." Kirkpatrick closed his eyes, mimicked the rhythm, banged his handcuffs up against the bar on the table, hummed along. When Teppan stopped singing and started speaking, opening his arms to the crowd to acknowledge Chloe at the back of the club, Anton reared up, practically capsizing the metal table to which he was shackled, hurtling the computer toward the edge.

"That's him, the accent."

"Matins and Vespers are from Sweden. Kat, Teppan, Eric, they all have a bit of an accent."

Anton shook his head, stamped his shackled feet. "I don't give a bloody fuck about Eric, whoever he is. The guy on the organ, Nilsson, he's the one who came after me in the hotel. I could see his hands, beautiful long fingers that tore open my fly, milked me until I couldn't breathe, I was coming so hard."

Gasping, Anton looked down. A wet spot had formed near his crotch, where the tip of an erection was straining his prison jumpsuit. He gripped the bar he was cuffed to, held tightly, shuffled closer to the table, maybe to conceal his standing cock. After a dive to rescue his falling laptop, Fahey wasn't sure of much beyond the fact that Anton seemed to be reliving the moment in the hotel physically as well as mentally. Sweat beaded on Anton's forehead; he bit his lower lip till he drew blood, grimaced in pain; struggled against the handcuffs, closed his eyes.

"Make him go away! I don't want to feel him again, not there, not there!" Anton was screaming now. The guard pounded the door, demanding to know what was going on. Fahey opened the door wide; Kirkpatrick quieted immediately.

"He's fine," Fahey said.

"I'm fine," Anton insisted.

"I'll be shoving you both out if I have to come in here again." The door clanged shut behind the guard.

Anton slumped, heading for the floor. Fahey stepped behind him, braced him by the arms. "Don't touch me," Anton hissed. "Not like that."

Fahey pulled a chair under him, and one under himself. Anton gulped in air and bent over at the waist, looking ready to vomit, his face a sickly yellow-green.

"He was tall, taller than you, I think, and he had to lean back to keep his face in the shadows. The whole time he was talking, I didn't hear the words. I felt them, in my head. He grabbed my wrist and stared down at the dried blood on it, then locked his free hand around it, I thought he was going to break it off my arm. He moved around me, slipped his hands down my jeans, jerked them over my hips, stuck a finger up my ass, then two, pushed, ground into me, told me I wanted him, and I looked down and I was hard again. I could hear him tell me it was him I wanted, not her, never her, she could never be mine, and he rammed his dick inside me."

Raped him, Fahey corrected. Had Anton told his attorney?

"Who was the man talking about?" he asked, but he knew.

"Your girl. He knew I'd just been with her, he'd been watching her with that Esteban Gronlund, then watching us, watched her suck my wrist, then go down on me. After she left, he followed me. He was angry, shouted inside my head, 'Find out what she told him. The man at the bar, find out what he knows. Make Gronlund talk, and if he doesn't talk, rip his throat out.' Said I'd have to send a signal that she couldn't be kept from him forever. I had no idea what he was talking about, but I didn't have a voice, I couldn't concentrate on anything but the dick pumping inside me, his body banging against mine and the words roaring through my head. I couldn't move except to clutch my own dick as I came again. I'm not sure how I was still standing."

Vampire sexual torture. "How long did this go on?" Fahey asked.

"I wanted him to keep going until I was blind, but I also wanted him to stop raging in my head. When I felt him come, the voice disappeared. One second he was there, the next I was stalking Gronlund and killing him."

The guard stuck his head into the room. "Five minutes. BBC special privileges, my arse, wrap it up."

Fahey checked the laptop for damage, opened the video Anya Morina had made at her flat in Kosovo, the more explicit version Meredith had showed him, unsure what more he was after. "Tell me if anything about this video seems familiar to you. This is from January. The woman was found murdered last month."

"There's a connection between my case and hers?"

"Not necessarily, but I thought you should watch it just the same."

Kirkpatrick nodded. Fahey played a few minutes from the beginning: Sebastian whispering sweet nothings to Anya, his voice devoid of Swedish inflection, soft but clear. Anton's posture stiffened, he leaned forward, closer to the laptop. Fahey reached in to advance the play bar, to the point where Sebastian, his naked rear facing the camera, penetrated Anya.

Anton took in the long dark hair, the muscled nude body; turned to Fahey, arched an eyebrow. Fahey hit pause. "It's not me, don't even think it. I was on an assignment in Portugal at the time."

"Not your voice, yeah, but still."

Yeah, but still. Sebastian was a born exhibitionist, always eager to perform. What did that say about him and his fascination with Sebastian's on-camera sex romps, Fahey wondered. He shifted in his chair uncomfortably.

There was little audio, not much of Sebastian's voice for Anton to listen to and maybe recognize, but the action was quite enough to rivet his attention until the guard banged on the door. "Time's up." Fahey quickly shut down the computer.

"It's him, isn't it?" Kirkpatrick said. "Same voice, same hands, even if the hair is different and the accent is gone. That woman is dead now? The bastard."

"Can't say I disagree." Fahey crossed to the other side of the table to face Kirkpatrick, shook his manacled right hand.

On the train ride back to London, Fahey sorted through new questions: Why bother to have Anton kill Esteban? Why the sexual humiliation on top of it? Why didn't Chloe's father just kill Esteban himself, and, if there was a point to be made, why lie to her about it months later? His head felt like someone had taken a mallet to it, and Fahey didn't want to think anymore about the de la Coeurs. That's all he'd done for as long as he could remember, though he'd known them for only a few months. He settled back into his seat, tried to doze, but the opening line to "Inquisition" ran on a loop through his head:

*Face a flogging, lowly infidels. If you're lucky, I'll be brief.*

Fortune was a spiteful bitch, though. Liked to prolong the agony.

* * * *

It was a quarter to nine when he returned to Aspect Ratio, with time to spare, amazingly. Fahey was hungry enough, just not looking forward to dinner with Meredith after watching even a short part of Sebastian's sex video. Under those circumstances and in a public place, he had no clue whether he could keep himself together, whether Meredith would sense his unease and choose that moment to be provocative, as he knew she could be. It was important they be on their best behavior. He couldn't imagine what Chloe would do without Benjamin at the gallery. He couldn't say whether Ben was better off with Meredith, but she certainly seemed steadier when he was by her side. Best to not jeopardize that.

Through the storefront windows, Fahey could see the exhibit space brightly lit, but saw neither customers nor staff. No one was sitting at the coffin-turned-reception desk. He tested the door, no alarm sounded when he entered. He set the lock and walked toward the office.

Chloe stood in near-darkness, a pizza box on the desk in front of her. "Just delivered, still hot. I'll get some paper plates." She turned to find them, switched on the overhead light.

"I'm taking you out to dinner, remember? Where are Meredith and Ben?"

"With the police, I suppose. She was summoned by Gippel and Blackwood about three hours ago. Meredith would have called or texted by now if she could." Chloe handed him a plate and a napkin. "There's water in the fridge, maybe some juice. Nothing harder, per Guinevere's orders."

She smiled, a thing both sweet and bittersweet, and folded her hands over the barely visible bump that was their baby.

"You need to eat, too." He lifted a slice from the box and placed it onto the plate for her. "I'll get the water, you sit."

He had wolfed down three slices before Chloe nibbled her way through a single piece. Preoccupation—with Meredith, with her father, with the police investigation, hell, maybe even with him—was deflecting focus from taking care of herself. Fahey was sure she hadn't consumed a thing since he'd made her eggs the night before.

"Another slice, and no arguments." He put the widest wedge in the box on her plate. "Then later, if you're good, I'll feed the rest of your appetites." Fahey waggled his eyebrows suggestively, hoping to make her laugh.

She smiled again, ever so briefly. It would have to do.

He was snagging more pizza for himself when a text pinged through on Chloe's phone: "*Done with me, am heading to Ben's to pack. Gippel got court order to dredge Castle lake; booked on 9 a.m. flight to JFK. Turn on TV; got to get busy. M G-T.*"

"I'll check the World News 9 p.m. feed." Fahey fetched his laptop, connected to the gallery's Wi-Fi, but he could hear another phone receiving a text. He checked his; nothing there. He rechecked Chloe's, then noticed her purse on the floor. "Do you have that phone from Teppan here with you?"

She spun the desk chair around, stared at the red leather satchel. "I hate that purse. Meredith picked it out for me the night we were abducted by my father's goons." She turned back to her pizza, took a tiny bite, grimaced and pushed it aside. Fahey walked behind her, set the purse on the desk. "Check the phone."

"Leave it," she hissed. "Gippel couldn't have gotten permission to dredge the lake unless they'd released Teppan. I have no desire to deal with my father right now."

"Mightn't it be your mother?"

"Because my mother is so communicative? She speaks only when she chooses, appears only when she chooses. Not a day goes by that I don't regret reentering their lives. Maybe always running from my parents wasn't such a bad strategy after all."

He wrapped his arms around her, kissed her neck, licked along the pulse throbbing there. "Let's run away now."

She seized his wrist, bit softly into the vein there, sucked gently; ran her tongue along the small hole, watched it close. "Let's go dancing. The old C.J. Hart went dancing four, five nights a week."

He swayed slightly, lightheaded from the blood loss. "I look like shit. I've been on trains all day."

She pulled his head down to hers, pulled his lips into a kiss, pulled his tongue into her mouth, pulled away much too quickly. "You look gorgeous, and you know it, Jackson. Give me a minute."

With another spin of the chair, Chloe escaped into the washroom. When she emerged less than ten minutes later, she was the girl on the plane again, the witch who cast her spell on his heart and his head, the siren who lured him to her side and straddled him in an airport janitor's closet. Red sweater dress cut low on her breasts, high on her thighs, Empire waistline camouflaging the infinitesimal baby bulge. Textured black hose, tall black boots, hair the color of chestnuts, just off the fire, feathering her jaw line.

"Out the back, I know a place."

"Which place?" he whispered, having lost his voice somewhere.

"This is London. There's always a place."

A cab slowed down, waited for them at the end of the alley behind Aspect Ratio. Near Leicester Square, the taxi stopped. Chloe led him down a narrow stairwell to a space doused in colored light and sound and perfume. Electronica ricocheted around them. She found a table shrouded in shadow, mere steps from the dance floor. She let her leather jacket slip onto a stool, laced her fingers through his, and guided him through the crowd.

She pulled him close, flung her arms around his neck, gyrated against him, slow-dancing in the middle of an up-tempo rave. His cock stiffened to granite hardness. By contrast, she was all softness and tender pressure under his hands, against his chest and thighs, undulating to a rhythm only she could hear.

"In Barcelona," her voice caressed his ear, "I'd work ten hours a day at the museum, examining worn tapestries and rugs and upholstery, making decaying things impressively antique again. Then I'd seek out my friends, the bartenders at the clubs I was most comfortable in. I attracted men, which meant more tips for my barkeep friends. They, in turn, knew when to intervene and what to ignore, and that if I was alone at the end of the night, and if I was in the mood, I'd go home with them. They were handsome and very good in bed, and there was absolutely no obligation for me to ever return, not the next night, not the next week. I did, because I felt free and wonderful, and sleeping regularly with five hot Spanish men was all the companionship I required."

He clutched her tighter, ran his hands over her hips and cupped the cheeks of her backside possessively. "Are you trying to make me jealous? It's working."

She rubbed up against him. "You had more than your share of women in Spain, my love. I know you worked the crowd at Casa Cruella the night of the tribute concert, cast your line at some lovely senorita and reeled her in. When I first met you, her scent clung ever so lightly to you. I could imagine you with her. It was very arousing."

"Do you like to watch?"

She reached up on tiptoe to nip at his jaw. "I'm not a spectator."

He raised his hands to her face, turned her lips to his, kissed her deep and long, buried his fingers into her hair, wanting to bury himself inside her until neither one of them remembered who they were.

The music changed, pounding fiercely. Around them, the crowd bumped, swayed, bounced, swirled, exactly what Chloe wanted. Fahey knew what he wanted, and it couldn't be easily achieved on the dance floor. He swept her up, carried her to their table, her eyes holding his captive. He set her down, massaged the soft skin between her shoulder blades, let her feel the ridge of his erection against the small of her back. Felt the rumble of his phone against his rear end.

"*Matins and Vespers play 'Christmas at the Castle.'* " He

reached around to show Chloe the text.

Astonishment lit the face she turned toward him. "It's the annual fund-raiser for research into bone marrow and blood cancers, Sebastian and Emilie's charity. Back when I was a teenager, they'd sell about 500 tickets at $200 a pop for a nighttime concert, and charge $20 for tours of the Castle earlier in the day."

"Clearly someone decided the show must go on. Chestack?"

Chloe massaged her temples, shutting out the Donna Summer dance mix reverberating from the speakers. "He must have told Meredith to handle it, and she booked Matins and Vespers to stand in for Sebastian and Emilie." Her fists clenched; Fahey watched her struggle to tamp down her anger. "How can Meredith not recognize who Teppan is? Everybody else in the inner circle sees him and Kat as they really are."

"You said Genevieve didn't recognize them either time she, Teppan, and Kat were at the gallery together. So maybe it's true people only see what they want to see, or, in this case, what Teppan wants them to see."

Except when he doesn't expect them to make the connection, as Anton Kirkpatrick had, and as Gippel might eventually.

A cocktail waitress hovered. This was not a conversation he wanted overheard. Fahey waved her closer and dropped cash onto her tray. "Be a love and leave us alone." The woman aimed her fishnet-clad legs in the opposite direction.

He leaned in, licked a trail of heat from Chloe's lips to her ear. "How did Teppan game the DNA test, the only thing that could have persuaded Interpol to release him?"

"His lawyer's DNA, had to be." Chloe wrapped her arms around his neck. "Compelled his lawyer, fed on his blood before surrendering to the police, and probably again before the DNA swab was administered. They wouldn't swab his attorney, he knew that."

So the investigation would shift back to Sebastian, whose

ashes would never be found at the bottom of the Castle's lake because they were never there in the first place. At the benefit concert, in plain view of the authorities trying to disprove reports of his death, the man who had become Teppan Nilsson would no doubt give the performance of a very long lifetime.

"Back home for the holidays then?" Fahey stretched, bowed over his lady's hand. She shivered, and he felt her fear.

"If only to remind me I was born human there. God, I don't want to be like them."

"You won't be. You couldn't be." Fahey settled Chloe's jacket onto her shoulders, shepherded her up the stairs and into a taxi.

Company awaited them at the flat: half a dozen photographers, plus a news video crew, staked out on the sidewalk, clamoring for Chloe's comment on the dredging. "Let me handle them," he said. "If they get something from me, though I have nothing of value to give, maybe they'll pack it in."

He got out on the passenger side, walked around to pay the driver; opened the rear door to help Chloe out.

"C.J. Hart, will you let them take your parents' remains from the Castle's lake?" the TV reporter shouted. "Is Sebastian de la Coeur alive after all?"

Fahey put his body between Chloe and the lenses. "She has no comment."

"We want to hear it from her, Jackson. We can listen to you any day."

"And watch your naked backside as well," said a voice from behind a camera.

Chloe pushed through to the front door of her building. "No comment. Happy?" She jammed her key into the lock and stepped inside.

"Talk to Edward Chestack in New York if you want to know about the Castle lake," Fahey fired back.

"What about Teppan Nilsson, Jackson? Is it true Chloe's leaving you for him now that he's out of jail?"

Fahey glared at the reporter then envisioned that belligerent expression broadcast to the masses. He smiled sweetly. "You don't expect me to comment on that rubbish, now do you? If you'll excuse me, my fiancée is waiting for me." He winked at the camera and went inside.

He sprinted the four flights up to the flat.

"Don't let them get to you, love." He encircled Chloe, and the electric kettle she had just filled with water, in a warm, steamy hug.

"It's nothing a nice cup of tea can't help me forget. I must be getting used to this. See, no hyperventilating. My new indestructible, candy-coated shell is working."

She ducked to escape his embrace. Fahey moved toward the cabinets to gather mugs and spoons, and toed the hated red satchel out of his way. Chloe kicked it over, tipping its contents onto the ugly beige carpeting in the dining area. Two phones spilled out under the table, hers and the one Teppan had sent via Will Baumann.

"You never did look at that text." Fahey rescued the purse, took the mug Chloe had prepared for him.

"I know what it says."

"You're a vampire, not a soothsayer. Read the bloody text."

She carried her cup to the sofa, sipped, ignoring him; took off her boots, flinging one in his direction, clipping him in the hip. "Jesus, you're a nag."

"You'd try the patience of six Irish saints. I'll name them for you, if you like." He handed her Teppan's phone.

She typed in the pass code, turned the screen with the text toward Fahey: "*You are the one life. You are the survival.*"

"That's it? Who sent it?"

"Not a number I recognize, and really, I don't care, Jackson, not tonight. I'm going to bed."

Starved for his one life, his own survival, he wasn't about to argue.

*Chapter Five*

# NEW YORK, DECEMBER 2011

Call me crazy, but I regard it as an omen that *Iscariot*–the last of my mother's, shall we say, postmortem artworks–sold the day after my father was released from jail. As a Hanukkah present, of all things, for a Houston oil executive whose wife flew to London to pick it up and bought a return seat for it in first class. I see wife and painting boarding at Heathrow. I am wearing a short, peroxide-streaked, very-Goth black wig; she does not recognize me as I move up the aisle past her, back to my seat in coach, which is how I intend it, of course. Not to be noticed.

The last of Sebastian's seemingly inexhaustible output of cityscapes also have sold, leaving the cupboard at Aspect Ratio quite bare of this year's must-have gifts. Dead-but-maybe-not artists are in vogue right now. I must remember to scour the Castle for examples of their respective *oeuvres*; no doubt Emilie left some sketches behind. The tapestries at the Castle might fetch a few bucks, as well. What I wouldn't give to foist them onto someone, and throw Mom and Dad in free of charge.

I have abandoned Benjamin at the gallery this week before Christmas. Poor man can use some peace and good will right now. Our usually quiet workplace has been overrun by patrons and paparazzi since Teppan went free and the legal wrangling over dredging the Castle's lake for Sebastian's ashes became fresh news again.

In eight hours, all the parties, me included, will gather at the Tompkins County, New York, courthouse to argue about an injunction delaying the inevitable. My money—literally, but also figuratively—is on Ed Chestack. His face has peered at me on daily Skype calls, and I've been treated to panoramic views of the "Christmas at the Castle" preparations: the decorations; the vendors' booths within the bailey; the dining areas throughout the winery; the stage set up in the Great Hall. Chestack will argue financial hardship to the beneficiaries of my parents' charities, as well as the local economy, if the show is disrupted by the police investigation. Dead is dead, he will say, the remains are not going anywhere and will prove nothing in any case, thus Interpol and Gippel and their liaison with the local prosecutor should have to cool their heels until after the concert.

Well, that's the hope. The musicians, caterers, light and sound teams, and rented tents, tables and chairs have all arrived, per Meredith's precise planning, so the show will go on either way. There's no such thing as bad publicity, as she constantly reminds me, and the court hearing will provide it. The whole business is making me queasy, over and above the morning sunshine streaming through the windows of the airplane, plus jet lag, plus pregnancy. I feel like total crap and the prospect of having to pick up a rental car and drive to the environs of Ithaca from Queens makes me want to cry. Why didn't I book a connecting flight closer?

I emerge from Passport Control and Customs, luggage and other accessories hanging from my limbs like Christmas ornaments. "Hey, give me something to carry," says the blonde in a black business suit and ridiculously high heels whom I have known since pre-adolescence.

"I'm a lousy tipper, I warn you."

"Fortunately, you have me on retainer." Meredith takes my suitcase and wheels us toward an escalator.

"Didn't know I was paying you for chauffeur services."

She shrugs, looks tired. "I had to get away from the circus, so I left last night and stayed at a motel here. I can't decide who I hate more at this minute, Eddie C. or Teppan Nilsson. Okay, I can decide: It's Teppan; he's a whole new category of jerk. I'm used to Ed's particular brand of insufferable."

I yawn, hoist my backpack and the despised red leather satchel higher on my shoulder. "So head south on I-95. We can be in Florida in twelve hours or so, away from the crazies."

"If only." She glides over to her white Mercedes convertible, which is being watched by a nice airport security guy who clearly so enjoys Meredith's girly storm that he looks the other way as she violates the no-stopping-or-standing rules. She loads my gear into the tiny trunk and even tinier backseat, and we're on our way upstate.

I sit back, shield my face from the sun with the hood of my coat, close my eyes to the maze of highway ramps and merge lanes that Meredith maneuvers. Some sights are too painful to be witnessed. Feeling the twists and turns isn't pleasant either, and I pray for a straightaway.

Motion sickness? I'm a vampire, for God's sake, this isn't happening. "Mer, I'm going to do something unspeakable on your dashboard."

From the enormous purse on her lap, jammed between her chest and the steering wheel, she yanks a bottle of ginger ale and hands it to me. "Sip. In another minute or so, we'll be out of this and so stuck in traffic you'll think we're sitting still." She navigates; I drink, the sun pricking my skin, a sharp pain tearing through my stomach. I grit my teeth and, after the road turns into a cloudy stretch, the discomfort finally passes. Hallelujah.

We inch bumper-to-bumper for about forty-five minutes, Meredith intent on the highway. There's no way I can sleep, so I turn on the radio, scan until I reach a station playing Bach. So soothing not to listen to the clamor of progressive rock, likely the only time that will be true in the days to come. Still, I feel my body tense as we begin to ascend from the downstate flatlands into the Hudson Highlands, along the New York Thruway toward the Catskills. Meredith rolls her neck, to loosen her own tightening muscles.

"I'm not nauseated anymore. Do you want me to drive for awhile?"

"No, it's a good distraction. A few more hours and I'll be in the thick of things, and there won't be any relief until the concert is over and the crowd has left."

Evergreens tower as we rush past, standing proudly in contrast with their leafless deciduous companions. The sky is a gray-blue, the sun now a thin yellow streak visible through thickening clouds. "I want to say it looks like snow, but it's been so long since I've been here at Christmastime."

"Snow would be a great touch, but a pain in the neck; we'd have to move all the vendors indoors. A blizzard a few years back postponed the show for a week, and people were stuck at the Castle because it didn't make sense to cart everything out then back in again. It drove Sebastian screaming nutso."

"Short drive."

She laughs, and sighs. "God, I miss him, C.J., even though he messed me up something fierce. I have Tweedle-Dee and Tweedle-Dum to thank him for, don't I?"

"They tried to be good husbands. They loved you. You loved them too, however imperfectly. Hell, you're still carrying their names around, and I know it's not just for professional reasons. You're Meredith Grainger-Todd, formidable businesswoman, because of them, not in spite of them. Because of Sebastian, too, probably."

"Fierce, feisty, and freshly medicated, that's me."

I stroke the hand resting on the stick shift. "Friend, fiercely loyal, fiery competitor, that's what I see, and why I love you. That's what Ben sees too, why he loves you."

We pull off to a rest area. She parks, rests her cheek against the steering wheel. "I don't want Ben to love me, not when I'm like this, my brain all twisted up in memories, I'll just end up hurting him. I watched that dead sex worker's video with Jackson, and it was like the night in my apartment last summer all over again: I wanted to rip his clothes off, but I wasn't seeing him, I was seeing Sebastian. Yesterday, with Teppan Nilsson, it was the same way. He was walking around the Great Hall, giving me orders like he owned the place one minute, cooing into my ear about something the next, and it was as if I was looking at Sebastian. I swear I got so distracted, so turned on, I had to walk around the grounds twice to settle myself down."

Teppan is like that, he can blindside a girl, as I know too well. "All the publicity must be going to his head. Don't beat yourself up, he's trying to bait you, trying to play sex-symbol rock star. Just ignore him."

She swipes at her tears, smearing her mascara. "Did you ignore him, C.J., in Edinburgh? You scratched your itch, isn't that what I should do, too?"

I scratched an itch, just not that one. Dear Lord, I can't think of anything that would screw Meredith up more than having sex with yet another version of my father.

"No, keep a safe distance; a few more days, and he'll be gone. Despite what I told the police, I never slept with Teppan. Denying it wouldn't have helped, too many people had seen us in the hotel bar and the lobby, and he performs for whoever will watch. So I just let everybody believe what they already thought was true."

I fish through her purse for a tissue and hand it to her. Meredith pulls down the visor, tries to repair her makeup in the mirror. "Toilet? Starbucks?" I ask. She shakes her head, so I get out of the car alone. This conversation isn't finished, and we have hours of driving and soul-searching ahead. I hit the bathroom, bring back two full-caff lattes and a bag of salt-and-vinegar potato chips to settle my stomach. I hand her a cup and fold myself back into the Mercedes, drink and chew as she pulls back onto the roadway, shifts and takes it up to ninety mph. Speed and Meredith in a manic phase, not the perfect combination.

I let her run it out for a good half-hour, until she blows by an on-ramp and just barely gets us out of the path of an eighteen-wheeler. "Slow down! What the fuck!"

"Think if I drive fast enough, I'll be able to race everything Gippel showed me out of my head? Think I'll stop knowing what I have to pretend not to know?"

"Which is what?"

"That it's Sebastian in those videos, in all of them."

"Meredith, come on . . ."

"The way he looks from the back and front and side is branded into my memory. Damn it, I may be crazy, but not about this. Those women, did he kill them? Did he kill Emilie? Did she even have cancer?"

So many lies fill the space between us that I have to grope for something true to tell her. I give her the only thing I can: "I know my father didn't kill my mother."

"Are you saying he's not still alive?"

"Gippel showed me the same videos he showed you, but I didn't see what you saw. What do you want me to say?"

The car decelerates, slows to something approaching the speed limit, then less. Meredith hits the emergency flashers, coasts to the shoulder, stops and cuts the engine.

"What do I want you to say? Tell me you're being straight with me, C.J., that you're not protecting him if he's done something terrible, and if he has, tell me that too. We're all up to our necks in this now. When they dredge that lake, then what?"

That's something I don't have to lie about. "I don't know what they'll find. I wasn't here, remember? I was in Spain."

She produces from her purse a *cloisonné* pillbox, tosses two tablets down, sips at her now-cold latte. "I'll drop you at the Castle, let you unpack and rest a bit. Then we'll go to the courthouse together, okay? I'll draft two statements beforehand, one for if we get the injunction, one for if we don't. You'll be on camera at some point; I hope you brought one of your nice suits and some heels."

Her eyes are far brighter than they should be. I can feel her blood pumping double time, her pulse skittering faster than it should, yet she also seems calmer, distracted by the things she can manage. She can manage my schedule, my wardrobe. "I have the black suit with the black-and-tan pumps and the tan cowl-neck sweater."

"Everything still fits?"

"Still fits. Not much baby bump yet."

She looks down to confirm, restarts the engine, and pulls back onto the highway. Settles into the traffic flowing by at about seventy-five mph, breathing air no longer quite as thick with deceit but still reeking of half-truth. As long as she can control the message, she'll keep it together, I think.

Realistically, we have no choice but to stay on point: *"Your honor, there's no need to dredge until after the benefit concert, no deadly creatures are hiding in our shallow little lake."* That's because they'll be on the stage, sucking wallets dry for a change instead of circulatory systems, and after we've raised gobs of cash, we'll all go happily to jail for perjury, accessories after the fact. Well, all except Zeke Segal, who'll take the rap for dumping whatever it is he dumped in the water and get nailed with a conspiracy charge.

By the time Meredith pulls into the driveway behind the Castle's kitchen, the day has gone from cloudy to just miserable, a cold drizzle tapping against the old stone walls and the pavers underfoot. We unload my suitcases, slide them under the covered space where groceries are delivered, and Meredith drives off to check on a few details with the vendors in the front courtyard. I ring the doorbell, hoping for a few extra hands to tote my stuff inside.

Expecting Gloria, I get her daughter instead, holding the door open, holding her arms out to me. I don't think Genevieve has ever visited the Castle, certainly not since her mother became a permanent resident here, which is to say longer than I've been alive. "Hope you don't mind an extra guest. I'm here for the party Ronnie insisted I couldn't miss." She wraps me in a hug then picks up the heaviest of my bags, leaving the wheeled suitcase to me.

I can use all the allies I can get if Ronnie has big plans for the concert that no one has thought to mention. "Elaborate, please. This is my house now, a fact people seem to forget."

Genevieve hesitates, which is disturbing to say the least. "Truth to tell, I'm not entirely sure what he means. He goes on about it being like the old days, musicians who played with Court of Cruelty will be here tomorrow, even guys who just did a couple shows after Theo was killed. Could it just be a stunt to get press, 'Show the flag for Sebastian, our great leader?' "

Somehow, I doubt that. "Meredith didn't mention it. She's focused on pulling the show off, period, what with the court hearing today."

"Not that Ronnie would think beyond what he considers important. He's walking around shouting, 'It's a freaking family reunion.' "

"We've always been a family of freaks, now with Swedes added to the bloodline." I punch the button for the freight elevator behind the Great Hall and lead Genevieve to the Dream Chamber, the room I've come to consider Jackson's. I wheel my bag into a corner, sit on the side of the bed; Genevieve takes the desk chair.

"Gloria has put the Nilssons in Sebastian and Emilie's wing of the Castle. Did you know about that?"

"Of course," I lie. More like they just moved themselves into their old rooms.

Genevieve studies me. I know she senses something off about this gathering of the Cruel, actual and aspiring.

"I was hoping to study the tapestries while I'm here," she says, "but Katarina Nilsson turned me out. Such nerve! I told her I was sure you'd want me to have access. Tactile experience of them would be most revealing, especially given the changes over time that we've discussed."

Revealing, oh yes. "The last week hasn't been a lot of fun for Kat. I'll have a word with her; we've always gotten along fairly well."

"Since Edinburgh? You slept with her husband, Chloe."

Again with that. "Didn't happen, despite reports to the contrary. The cops wouldn't have believed me, and the gossip rags don't deserve the truth from me. If Teppan hasn't reassured Kat, I will. I'm guessing it wasn't a priority while he was being arrested on suspicion of murder."

Genevieve seems to accept my version, and the mere fact we're talking about it certainly suggests that she, like Meredith, has no idea Teppan is Sebastian. A variation on compulsion, a skill I must explore.

Below us, in the Great Hall, the clock chimes the hour, only three left until I see a judge about an injunction. I unpack the suit I'll be wearing, liberate it from its plastic cocoon. The sweater emerges next, then the shoes. Gen watches; I multi-task.

"You've watched the famous sex video by now, right? Is it Sebastian?" I ask. My back is to her as I line the hangers with my clothing in formation on the closet rod, but I can feel tension building in her neck and shoulders. Her long-ago relationship with my father is not something she's comfortable acknowledging.

"Yes," Gen sighs, "every blessed inch."

"Meredith has seen them all now, through to the last video made. My father, not Teppan or anyone else, she says."

Genevieve lifts my smaller suitcase to the bed, unpacks lingerie, hosiery, toiletries, arraying the latter on top of the room's double dresser. "He's alive then?"

"He was in October, if Meredith's right. I'm not familiar with him from that particular perspective." Close enough, though, I can't shake that night with him in Edinburgh out of my memory, my vampire coming of age.

"We're quite the pair, aren't we? You don't know whether your father is dead, and my mother hasn't acknowledged that I'm alive in the twenty-four hours we've been under the same roof here. Really, Chloe, how did our lives get so mucked up? Accident of birth doesn't quite cover it, does it?"

Genevieve zips the empty suitcase, stashes it on the floor of the closet. "You should get some rest." She gives me a quick hug; a minute later, I hear her heels on the stairs, heading downward.

On the chance that one or both of my parents are in their private apartment, I make my way in that direction. As I enter, Kat stands at the door to the sitting room. "Good to have you home. I thought you'd never get here."

"I stayed away as long as I could."

My mother frowns, and I am fifteen years old again. "Be serious, please. There's a lot to do before the concert."

"Not for me. You and Daddy and your merry men are in the spotlight now, all I have to do is keep the dredging equipment from blocking the view."

She pulls me into the space where the tapestries hang. "You aren't doing yourself any favors keeping Genevieve Hamilton away from these things, not when I spent weeks consulting her about them. We really don't need anyone suspicious of *you*. It's bad enough we have to deal with your husband's mess."

Kat lowers herself into a lotus position in front of the tapestries; I sit next to her, the way I used to as a little girl. "Those women were always going to die, whether their babies lived or not."

"He told me he'd arranged for them to be cared for."

"More lies, about the women, about Esteban, he always lies and gets others to do his dirty work. So many layers of fixers stand between him and the corpses that he conveniently forgets how their deaths came to be in the first place. 'See no evil and no evil exists.' "

It's a line from one of his songs, "Plague of Fools." The plague has descended on this house again, on those of us snookered by the man behind the band.

"So what's the plan, Mom? After we've distracted the world with 'Christmas at the Castle' and raised some money and done some good works, then what? Ed Chestack stonewalls the FBI and Interpol some more, and I do my 'I wasn't here when they took their lives, I didn't see the ashes scattered' song and dance indefinitely?"

She grabs for my hands, squeezes them. I see in her eyes the green behind the pale-blue irises Katarina shows the world, but also despair and fatigue. "I will love your father forever, he is my one life, but I have had enough."

I start to perspire, a cold sweat. I am nauseated and dizzy and my stomach cramps, a dull pain that shoots from right to left across my midsection and around my back. I lie down on the floor, close my eyes; wait for it to pass, pray for it to pass.

"What do you mean, he is your one life?"

She strokes my forehead, her hand warm, dry. "Have you met other vampires, Chloe, in London or Barcelona, anywhere?"

I raise my head, instantly sorry that I did; lower it back to the floor, the rug soft beneath my hair, dust stinging my eyes. "Would I know one if I saw one?"

"Yes."

"Then no, I haven't met other vampires. Should I have?"

"Not necessarily. There aren't that many of us, though pop culture would have you believe otherwise. We'd never survive if there were. We're very territorial."

"So I've been told, unless Daddy lied about that too."

She strokes my stomach, and the cramping doesn't seem as bad. "What maintains the balance among us is this: Each vampire gets to create only one other."

" 'One life only to complete the change.' What does the rest mean?"

" 'Only one survives'? That a second likely will not. You don't take that life on the mere hope this time will be different."

My father is her one life, and I am his, that's what the message meant. "Those babies died because of me, and then their mothers did, too."

Pain stabs through me, and my daughter writhes inside. I roll over, pull my knees up, fold myself as small as I can to escape the ache, but it doesn't go away. My mother wraps herself around me, rocks me to comfort me. I feel tears against my cheek, her tears. I don't ever remember her crying.

"No, my girl, those babies died because of him, and so did their mothers, and so did Esteban, all because Sebastian couldn't accept that he didn't get to choose."

"He loves me, don't say that!" His face comes into view, my memory conjures the image of my Daddy Bastian, singing me to sleep, carrying me back to my bed through the halls of this drafty old house all those years ago. I hear the sounds of my sobs, feel my eyes fill and empty, a flood of remorse and sorrow.

The blond woman who once looked like my mother coos into my ear, her breath calming. "I didn't say he doesn't love you, I believe you're the only person he's ever truly loved, but he never wanted to believe that having you meant there could be no more. As long as we didn't know whether you'd be like us, he persisted in the hope that there could be more, and when those women became pregnant, it looked as if he might be right. Then the babies died, and you transitioned. I think he's convinced at last, but at such a terrible, terrible cost."

*Such a terrible, terrible cost.* The words echo around me then slowly ebb to nothingness.

I hear no sadness, yet sadness exists.

* * * *

Chestack paces the corridors of the courthouse. The judge has decided to hear in chambers the arguments for and against a delay of the dredging, presumably to keep the press out. Ed knows his theatrics work best with an audience; bluster is his forte, subtlety is not. He was a drummer, after all.

Meredith stands with Zeke Segal; they wear sober expressions and somber attire like mine. This should go quickly, Chestack assures me, the judge has heard the arguments twice before. I am the newcomer to the group, though, and he may decide to grill me about the events of last April and the April before that. I must be prepared to recite again what I know: that Zeke picked up my parents' remains, scattered them in the lake, and delivered to me two stained-glass boxes with only some fine residue where their ashes had been. DNA analysis of cremated remains is fruitless for identification purposes, my lawyer has explained, though the investigators already have insisted on testing that residue. For law enforcement, he says, the aim now is to debunk the story altogether, to establish that no human remains exist in the lake.

They have no idea the lengths to which my parents might have gone. For that matter, neither do I. I lean on the wall behind me, afraid to stand without support for fear I will fall. My head is pounding, and I know I look like crap after almost five days without Jackson's blood. He may be able to get to the Castle late tonight, if his latest Brussels-to-Frankfurt-to-JFK plans go off seamlessly. I check my phone for messages, but there are none from him.

At four o'clock, Gippel and the FBI's supervising agent in charge of this region of New York arrive. Together, the six of us enter a courtroom, and a bailiff ushers us into the judge's chambers, where a court reporter sits ready to record the proceedings and the Tompkins County district attorney waits to defend the state's interests. The judge positions himself behind his desk; we arrange ourselves around an oval conference table, the home team to one side, the away team from Interpol to the other.

"Mr. Chestack, we have been here before," says the judge. "Tell me again why I shouldn't let these good people sift through the dirt at the bottom of the lake at Castle de la Coeur."

"Your Honor," Chestack stands and begins, "the circumstances have not changed since the last hearing."

"Your Honor," the district attorney interrupts, "Interpol has released the suspect it had in custody. Teppan Nilsson's DNA matched neither that of the dead fetuses nor other evidence found in the two Kosovo apartments where the sex videos were made. On the other hand, Sebastian de la Coeur, whose DNA is a match, remains at large."

Chestack shakes his head vigorously, protesting the logic. "Detective Gippel may, indeed, feel a greater urgency to delve into Sebastian de la Coeur's suicide, Your Honor, but a delay of another seventy-two hours will make no difference. If Sebastian de la Coeur is alive, as Interpol contends, then he has been at large since October and has thus far eluded detection. Disrupting the 'Christmas at the Castle' fund-raiser planned for the day after tomorrow will not cause undue hardship for law enforcement, only for the charitable foundation Sebastian and Emilie de la Coeur founded twenty-five years ago to underwrite research and treatment of blood-related cancers. Miss Grainger-Todd can supply the court with updated numbers on ticket sales and vendor fees; we project the foundation stands to see at least a $250,000 improvement. We are counting on the recent passing of the de la Coeurs to push ticket sales even higher in the next two days."

"You're asking me to decide in your favor so this charity can capitalize on the de la Coeurs' being dead, with law enforcement's priorities taking a back seat?"

"Interpol made an arrest, Your Honor, and at that time the court was right to delay action on the order allowing dredging of the lake at Castle de la Coeur until the question of Teppan Nilsson's apparent involvement had been resolved," Chestack argues. "To do differently now would not serve the court's purpose. Justice will be neither delayed nor denied if the court grants our request for sufficient time to facilitate the benefit concert without the disruption the dredging would create. We promise to abide by our commitment to allow the dredging as soon as practicable after the benefit concert."

Gippel clears his throat. The judge, annoyed, glares in his direction. "Go on, Mr. Chestack."

Larger than he should be, lumpier than a man in a $1,000 designer suit should look, Ed gestures to me and Zeke. "Already included in the record are affidavits from Miss Hart and Mr. Segal regarding the dispersal of Sebastian de la Coeur's ashes, as well as copies of the medical examiner's report and the receipt from the crematory. Miss Hart and Mr. Segal are here today should you require additional testimony from them."

The judge, a man of nondescript coloring and medium height, is younger than I expected him to be, about forty-five. "Miss Hart, do you have anything to add today?" he asks.

I glance at Ed, who nods almost imperceptibly. "Nothing, Your Honor," I stammer, getting to my feet, "except my hope that you will delay the dredging. The foundation's work was very important to my parents, and keeping that work moving forward and in the public's eye will be difficult enough now that they are gone. 'Christmas at the Castle' is the blood and marrow of our fund-raising, providing vital infusions of research dollars each year."

The judge winks at me. "Mr. Nilsson's presence at this event so shortly after his release can't hurt, I'm guessing. Makes for a better show?"

I wink back, what the hell. "We're hoping a few people will see it that way, yes."

"I've heard enough." The judge stands, signaling no one should dare attempt to dissuade him. "You get another seventy-two hours, Mr. Chestack, and not one minute more. So ordered." He pounds his gavel, and we are dismissed, our collective execution stayed three more days.

Chestack rushes us out through the courtroom, into the hall. "Well done, Chloe. From here on, I'm counting on you and

Meredith to keep everything under control. One whiff of additional scandal and this order will be rescinded, worthy cause be damned. Keep Teppan Nilsson on a short leash, do you understand?"

"Short leash, got it," Meredith says, intent on her tablet and tweeting the judge's decision.

Gippel, his FBI counterpart leading the way, passes our triumphant little group and heads for the exit, unsmiling and without acknowledging us. He has no suspect in custody and no indisputable evidence that his prime person of interest is still alive. Sucks to be him today.

"Ed, final rehearsal tomorrow, sound checks start at two o'clock sharp," Zeke sternly reminds Chestack, whose face and neck right now are the color of a cooked Maine lobster.

"I told you I'd be there, I'll be there." Chestack shoves some papers into the outer pocket of his briefcase and makes his way to the door. "Give us ten minutes to make a statement to the media. You two head out the side exit to the parking lot. Let's go, Meredith."

Zeke ambles over, embraces me. "You did good," he drawls, a worn smile stretching across his face. "We're gonna put on the baddest do-gooder show we can. Might be the last time the old gang gets together."

He walks me out to the limousine that awaits us. Sayid, my parents' driver, emerges the instant he sees the courthouse door open, bids us inside; starts the engine, waits for a signal to pull around to the front to collect Meredith and Ed. We deposit the latter outside his office five minutes later, and take the former directly to her condo, too dead on her feet to pick up her car at the Castle and drive home.

Zeke has declined to use his usual accommodations at the Castle and is staying at a hotel downtown. When the limo pulls over to the curb, he grabs my hand, squeezes tight. "I know we just won some breathing room, but I got a bad feeling. This is Sebastian's perfect revenge: No matter what happens, the odds are real good I'm looking at jail time. If you were a cop, would you believe I didn't know that the ashes in those stained-glass boxes weren't Sebastian's and Emilie's? And you know, sugar, I haven't been questioned directly. Ed's kept the investigators away from me. He knows I'll never pass a polygraph."

"Talk to Katarina, she can make it happen."

He shakes his head sadly, proudly, and I know he won't ask for her help. "Your mother and I, we've moved on."

"I can make it happen." I grip his arm in an unintended show of my superior force. "I won't let you go to jail for what Sebastian did."

Zeke stares at my hand, looks into my eyes. "I kept thinking the change I was seeing in you was because of the baby, but that's not it, is it? You're more beautiful, just like your mother, and stronger like her, too. Maybe you're Emilie's perfect revenge against Sebastian."

I want to protest that I'm not like either of them, that I'm no one's revenge, but the words die on my lips. Zeke senses my self-doubt; his muscles strain against my hold, asserting his strength against mine.

"Here's my two cents: Enjoy the good things this new life gives you, but be sure to fight back against the temptations. From what I've seen, they can make you forget you used to be human." He doesn't have to offer specifics. Zeke pries my fingers from his coat, kisses my cheek, gets out, and taps on the limo's roof in farewell.

Sayid carefully navigates the roads between Ithaca and Vampire Ground Zero, which have gone slick under a coating of sleet. I drift into a restless sleep until a voice comes through the divider and pierces my exhausted haze. "Miss Chloe, your phone is ringing. There, on the seat next to you."

Jackson's number blinks at me. "Hi," I mumble, my mouth dry. "Are you here?"

"Don't I wish, love. It's snowing in Frankfurt, flights are delayed, and it looks like they'll cancel some if this storm continues. I have no idea when I'll take off." He sounds tired, but happy. Just talking to him makes me forget how long I've been running around.

"I saw Meredith's tweet," he says, the connection fraying. "You got the dredging postponed."

"A small victory, at least we'll get through the concert before the heavy equipment moves in."

"How's my other best girl? Did Guinevere behave herself on the plane?"

"Fine on the plane, not as good afterward, between jet lag and stress. I'm definitely calling it an early night, barring on-site disasters. The Castle is crawling with people already, there must be forty of them at work on the set-up, not to mention Matins and Vespers and their crew. Everybody but Zeke is staying on the grounds. Oh, and Genevieve is here with Ronnie, which is weird. She says her mother is ignoring her, but more likely Gloria's just busy with the horde of light and sound guys and roadies and Swedish musicians."

Jackson's laughter tickles my ear, and I'm so hungry I could eat the phone.

"Major production, I'm exhausted just hearing about it. Must go now, they're making some announcement about my flight, which may not be a good sign. I'll text you as soon as I know something. I love you."

I blow a kiss, and the connection breaks. Almost immediately, the phone pings, and I figure he has more news about his flight, but the text begins, "*Super 8 Motel. Room 116.*"

The message shreds whatever resolve I might have had about rest: "*Dinner. I know you're ravenous for me.*" I bang on the divider, tell Sayid to turn around and head back to the highway.

Room 116 is toward the far end of the two-story white building. About three doors remain between me and my destination when he steps out into my path, wraps me in his arms and kisses me greedily, leaving the question of who is the hungrier jammed into the non-existent space between us. He smells like lime and honey, tastes like cinnamon and nutmeg, and that's just his lips. He picks me up and carries me into the room.

"Will, how?"

"I'm here, what more is there to know?" He rips back the sleeve of a gray Henley shirt that hugs his pecs nicely, raises his wrist to my mouth. I'm a goner, and an idiot, and I don't even try to fight it. I bite down and suck his spicy blood into my mouth, swirl it, savor it before I swallow and drink in more. I feel him harden as I press closer, and my body hums with a need other than the obvious one.

"Will, now," I command, and he leads me to the bed, lies on his back, unzips his fly and frees himself. I kick off my heels, peel off my skirt and pantyhose, climb on top and sink my teeth into a nipple. He surges up off the mattress, driving deeper into me, and I bite harder, action and reaction. Delicious.

I lift off my sweater, taking pendant and bra with it, and toss them across the room. I seize his unpunctured wrist and bite into a vein, consuming the blood as I grip his cock with some small, very effective muscles. As his breathing grows more ragged, I pick up the pace, agitating around him, against him, moving like a piston atop him until sensation rips through me, past my labia, along my ribcage, and up out of my throat. I grab his face between my hands, nip along his jaw, bite into his neck, and quake until my body glows with a sheen of his blood, my juice, our sweat.

He pulls away from my clamping fangs, pushes deeper into me, swivels and flips us, so I am below and he is on top. Rougher this time, like he can't get there fast enough, he bucks like a rodeo rider, bounces and bangs, abrading my body with bruising impact until he comes ferociously. Then, like a switch has been thrown, his face turns beatific, his smile otherworldly as he kisses me, my lips, my eyelids, my nose, my forehead, dives down and dips his tongue inside me and swirls and sucks me to climax again, such sweetness after such violence.

"I know you don't love me," he says when our senses return, his head cradled against my midsection, his hands kneading my bottom tenderly, teasing my slit from behind. "I know you won't love me, but I love you, Juliette."

"Don't call me that." This is too much, I should go.

"What does he call you?"

"That's what he calls me. That's what I called myself my first time with him, too, when I was using him the same way I used you that night in Edinburgh. I'm not the person you think I am. I'm not even the person he thought I was."

As if that matters. I can smell the blood as Will's throat pulses against my stomach, I can smell his semen slick within me, on my skin, and I can smell my own liquefying arousal. We want what we shouldn't have. We want what's bad for us.

Will pushes up on his forearms, climbs aboard, eases into and out of me, rides lazily at first, spurred faster by the fingernails I dig into his hips. He drives, I steer; we race until we break the speed limit and are both gasping for oxygen, gasping for release.

"I don't care who you think you are, Juliette," he growls above me. "Try to tell me right this minute you aren't mine. I know better."

I spear him with a fingernail, drag it upward from his waist, along his ribs, leaving a rivulet of blood. I lean in, lap it up, lick the wound closed, arch my pelvis to accept as much of him as he can give. I *am* his this minute. I cannot be otherwise. I quiver beneath him, melt again under his heat. He comes and collapses onto his right elbow, sparing me the weight of his upper body, pinning me to the bed with his lower self. He whispers my name as he falls into a sated sleep. All my names. He knows them, he wants me to know.

Drained, we lie there for some time, conscious only of our connectedness. When finally I try to lever him off me, so I can slip away, the shaft that joins us hardens again, and there's no way I'm escaping.

"Will," I whisper, blowing a light-brown wave from his ear.

"I have to get back to the Castle. I have things to do to prepare for the concert."

"It's being taken care of, Teppan said you shouldn't worry yourself."

Teppan lies, in addition to acting the fatherly pimp when my blood levels are low and Will's services must be arranged via this odd blood bond once removed.

"I have other things to attend to. My fiancé will be arriving early tomorrow. I need to get a room ready for him."

"He'll stay in the same room as always. Your things are already unpacked. There's nothing for you to do." Will grinds against me, licks the valley between my breasts, circles one nipple then the other with his tongue; moves lower to sprinkle my stomach with kisses, blows into my navel, sets my flesh on fire. Makes it hard to think of anyplace beyond this bed, beyond this man affixed to me.

"How do you know that?" I ask dreamily, his every move igniting a different tactile spark.

"Teppan told me you'd fuss. He told me not to let you, says you need me now. He loves you like a . . ." Will stops, unclear how to describe what Teppan feels for me. "Like a brother, I guess. I know you two didn't have sex in Edinburgh, despite what they're saying about you on the news. I know it's different between you and him."

"Different, yes. Complicated."

I don't want to talk about Teppan. I spend my entire life talking about my father, defending my father, anticipating my father's next rash move, when I should be focusing on my own stupidity, stretching now into hours of lust I should accept cannot be sated and just stop trying. This man cannot resist me, so I should be the strong one and leave.

"You don't love me, you're here because Teppan has compelled you to be. Do you know what that means?"

Will leans in, nibbles my lower lip, takes possession of my mouth, nodding as he does. "I really don't care; I'm where I want to be. Get up and walk away, but that won't stop me from wanting you, Clothilde Juliette de la Coeur or Chloe Hart or whatever other name you call yourself. *You* don't have that power over me."

His aquamarine eyes are clear, his voice is steady, his words firm. He is not drugged or bewitched. He means what he's saying.

"I love Jackson. The baby inside me is his, a little girl. Come June, our daughter will be here, and Guinevere and Jackson and I will be a family. You can only get hurt if you keep this up."

He eases out of me, then impales me, every inch of his desire impelling me to pay attention to the present, the future be damned. He lifts his hair and presents his neck to me.

"Let me know when you get tired of this, and then we'll say good night. Cross my heart and hope to die."

I scrape my teeth across the vein he offers and bite down. There's surely time for one more taste.

* * * *

The light is on in Sebastian's music studio. A melody trills just below the level of human hearing: "Bride Price," from Court of Cruelty's first album. A song I learned only recently, during my convalescence here, about a boy with nothing but his honor to offer in exchange for the girl he loves.

Teppan lies on his back on the leather couch, his feet extending over the far arm. "Isn't it past curfew, little one?"

"Doesn't count when Daddy knows exactly where I've been."

He grunts in agreement, stretches until he can practically reach me in the doorway, tilts his head so he can see me upside-down. "Inspirational performance by your Will Baumann: four times in how many hours? I'm surprised you can walk right now."

And off he goes. Will wasn't far from wrong: Teppan does act like an annoying, crude older brother, which might be charming if he weren't also selfish and very deadly. I let him read the disgust on my face and turn to leave.

"What, after three decades of lies from me you can't appreciate a bit of candor? A man can't win around you, but then poor Will knows that. Had to give him a piece of your mind while you were wrapped around his dick. Better to give a little carrot while he's giving you the stick."

I throw my purse at his head, not the most mature response but the one that seems the most honest, since we're being honest. He sits up, dodging the red satchel.

"You're a real son of a bitch, Daddy. You all but brought him to my door. Did you want me to ignore him? Because it's a funny thing: Based on the only vampire lesson you and my mother have managed to impart so far, I thought fucking Will in appreciation for his blood was what I was supposed to be doing. 'Pleasure for pleasure,' isn't that the new family motto?"

"Not what I planned to engrave on the de la Coeur crest." He grins like the 140something-year-old vampire man-child he has devolved into.

I don't remember him being like this before. Certainly not last year, after he and my mother announced their grand suicide plan. Was what I saw then less what he actually was, and more what I wanted him to be?

"Do you know how to be serious?"

"Okay, sweetheart, tell Daddy your problems and he'll make them all better."

"Since my problems start and end with you, I doubt that's possible."

"Go ahead, then, blame me for everything: You're in love with a handsome guy who thinks the sun rises with you; you're having his baby; you have a successful career; and a promising business, which I happened to have founded. Have I left something out, is there something wrong with your life? Because if there is, stop whining and fix it. You opened a door in Edinburgh, either pass through or back up. Get out of the way so the rest of us can keep moving."

I wish I had more leather goods to throw at him. I could

clear out a Prada boutique and not have enough.

"Is seeing your reflection in me more than you can bear, Daddy? I'm your 'one life' after all, created in your image. Does it make you feel better to make me feel dirty?"

"Of course not. I love you more than anything, more than myself."

I walk around to the side of the couch, sink to my knees next to him, grab one of his big hands, thread my fingers through his stronger ones, fingers that can pluck strings and wrest magic from them. "Behave like my father then, instead of like a four-year-old. If you'd deferred gratification just once in the last year, we wouldn't be in the shit storm we're in right now. Once the world figures out you're still alive, Emilie's found out, too, this Castle will topple like the house of cards it is, and I'll be the one holding the bad hand. I'll be forced to give up all those good things you just mentioned. Hell, I'll be lucky not to be in jail, and Jackson and Meredith and what's left of the Cruel with me."

He says nothing, looks past me, lets his hand go limp in mine. Shuts me out and shuts me down. If the Sebastian de la Coeur I once knew ever inhabited Teppan Nilsson's body, he is gone now. Reaching behind me, I grab the strap of my satchel and drag it back, abandon my subservient position next to him. He clearly desires my whining presence no longer, and I no longer care what he desires.

Purposely blocking the passage leading to the rest of his third-floor play space, I stop. "I didn't open a door in Edinburgh, I opened one the minute I left Barcelona last year at your request and walked back into this house. I never should have listened to your lies. You were supposed to go away and start a new life and give me a chance to lead mine. I should have known better."

Out of the music studio and down two flights of stairs to the kitchen, I run, rip the lid off a quart of milk, and drink it down, washing away the taste of Will's blood. Up one flight, I rush, to the chamber of the slumberous sex fantasy I shared with Jackson. I fling my coat onto a chair, my pendant glowing red as it hangs from the pocket. Does Jackson know I've been with Will again, sampled his blood again, sampled every inch of his body again and liked it far more than I should? A vein throbs over my left eye, a guilt headache.

I kick off my heels, strip, and pad into the bathroom, run the shower until the water is fit to scald and the steam seeps into my soiled soul. I stand under the stream, Guinevere fluttering occasionally, until the temperature fades to cold. I wrap myself in a bath sheet and fall onto the carved four-poster. I curl into a fetal position and close my eyes, my back chilled by a December draft seeping in behind the blackout curtains on the old windows.

Finally, fitfully, I sleep, exhausted by my long day, my strenuous evening, my troubled thoughts. I dream, and instead of huddling cold in the dark, I am warm. I am being lifted, carried to my own bed, safe again in my father's arms. He hums to me, sings me a German lullaby, sets me gently down onto the mattress, pulls up the blanket and hands me my teddy bear, tucks Galahad under my arm to keep him from falling.

"Good night, sweet Chloe."

"Good night, Daddy Bastian."

"Sleep, little one, my darling girl."

When I wake, I am lying widthwise atop the comforter, my shoulders and toes stiff when I try to move, though there's no discomfort from the cold, no feeling at all, a state of numbness, truly. A pre-LED digital clock, circa 1970s, stares at me from across the room. It's half past four, time enough for a run before the sun rises and bites into my strength. I throw on a few layers up top plus leggings and heavy socks appropriate for weather I will not notice, and, last, my sneakers. Stretch, bend, flex out of habit; head out the front door, past no one and nothing, under stars bright despite clouds that portend snow.

I take my time, run at human pace through a familiar two-mile circuit of the grounds, then hop a low gate near the winery and take the dark country road until it links with the four-lane highway into Ithaca. Double-back down the country road, past the infamous lake, toward a perimeter route behind the staff cottages, many of which are now occupied by members of the Cruel and Matins and Vespers and the sound team and the light techs. Farthest from the main house, at the woods along the edge of the property, light is visible from Gloria's cottage. I approach quietly. If she is awake, I don't want to startle her.

Through draperies so sheer as to be nonexistent, I see her, dressed in an emerald-green negligee. She is lovely in the way so many older British actresses are—her hair cropped short and feathered silver-gray across her forehead, her bearing straight and strong—and she is laughing as she pours tea and hands a cup across the table to my father. He is dressed as he was in the music studio, white shirt and blue jeans, feet bare. He looks relaxed as he sips whiskey, a bottle of Jameson's next to him, then nibbles on a cookie—oatmeal raisin, I imagine, one of his favorites, baked for him by another of his favorites.

I stand very still; slow my breathing to almost nothing, wary of intruding yet unable to avert my eyes. Gloria drinks from a fragile porcelain cup, part of her mother's tea set, brought from Ireland when she first followed my parents to America. I have drunk from those cups here, and eaten her cookies. Teppan reaches across and caresses the back of her hand, strokes skin as translucent as the cup she holds. He kisses the hand, the fingers.

Something inside me shivers. He looks up and out the window, sees me. He shakes his head as he faces Gloria again, as if to say there's nothing outside, nothing to be afraid of, then rises and kisses her lightly on the lips, presses his mouth gently to her throat.

I move away, stepping lightly until I am well past the cottage, picking up the pace as I approach the Castle itself. Purple and pink streak the horizon; I should get inside, get more rest. Jackson's plane may land in just a few hours, and the next two days are sure to be full and exhausting.

Yet I know I will not sleep anytime soon. I ascend the grand staircase, return to the third floor seeking something, a book, maybe some music to divert me or perhaps bore me enough to knock me out. I start at the west end of the space, over near the darkroom, where my father's photos are arrayed and his library of art books is neatly shelved. But art will feel too much like work—I must remember to call Benjamin to see how the gallery is faring without me; quite well, I suspect. Moving along the wall of books, I pass coffee-table tomes about cars, architecture, history, science; acres of novels and plays and short stories; and, as I reach the portal to the music studio, bound copies of librettos of the great operas. None appeals to me.

I enter the music studio, move to the bookcase on the opposite wall, next to French doors that lead to a Juliet balcony. I locate the book about late Baroque composers I started during my sickbed visit last month, pull it down and thumb through it, to see if I can find where I left off.

"Are you just getting up or just getting in?"

My mother stands half-in, half-out of the studio, dressed, oddly, the same as her husband is: white button-down shirt, jeans, feet bare, riding boots in her hand.

"I might ask you the same thing."

"I heard someone up here. I expected to find Teppan locked in with his music and his scotch, waiting until the very last minute to put his hand into the fire then snatch it away."

No idea what she's talking about, which my face must reveal. She points to the French doors, gestures over to the floor-to-ceiling windows on the adjacent wall. "Almost total eastern exposure. At this time of year, the sun's first rays should come through that glass in about three minutes and bounce all around. For the baby's sake, time to get out of this room. "

I tuck the book under my arm.

"Baroque composers, really? I think of you as more Patti Smith, less Henry Purcell, Chloe."

Whatever, she can think what she likes.

The sky's purple glow shimmers across the French doors, and I back out of the studio, joining her in the main space. "Teppan is at Gloria's if you need him."

"With a cup of tea and a plate of cookies and a bottle of Jameson's. It's their thing, not for me to interrupt."

Again, she must see bewilderment on my face. My mother loops her arm through mine and guides me down the stairs toward the bedroom I have claimed for Jackson.

"The night we met Gloria, at a basement club in Belfast in 1970, she was stunning—beautiful long dark hair, those great big blue eyes and pale skin. Hard to know who fell in love first, Gloria with us or us with her. Immediately, she was my best friend, it was so lovely to have a woman around to talk to. So lovely to be able to get her away from Ronnie permanently. Great guitarist, waste of a human being always, he would have gotten himself and her killed, running with the brigades the way he was. Always loved guns and bombs, no matter who they killed. Sebastian sent him to music school in Dublin, and we brought Gloria here."

I'm still trying to wrap my head around the "she loved them, they loved her" thing, but my mother is actually sharing with me, which she almost never does. Not exactly news I need, but it is progress, so I let her tell her story, walking into the bedroom, toeing off my running shoes, burrowing under the covers.

"Gloria filed for divorce in this country as soon as she could. Genevieve had been in the orphanage for years by that time. Giving the child up to the nuns was her revenge on both of them, Ronnie and her own father, Gloria said, for being such a heartless bastard and making her marry the man who'd raped her at fifteen."

"Sounds like you and Sebastian saved her life." They probably saved Genevieve's, too, who knows what growing up in a house with Ronnie Hamilton and the Irish Republican Army would have been like.

Emilie recedes into Kat's persona, smiles at me wistfully, sits on the bed to put on socks she's pulled from her back pocket and the boots she's carried in. "Sebastian saved Gloria's life, by saving Ronnie from himself. Gave him a sense of self-worth and an education in music; distracted him from his anger at Gloria and delivered an ultimatum. Sebastian swore to God he'd kill Ronnie if he ever touched Gloria again, and has checked in on her every night Ronnie's been at the Castle since then, to make sure he doesn't."

She leaves without a goodbye. I lean back against the pillows, trying to picture the three people who raised me in a time before I was born, trying to sort out their odd partnership, but I simply cannot keep my eyes open.

At some point, rays of sunlight slip past the edge of the curtains, stinging my face and startling me awake. The Baroque-composers' book digs into my hip, wedging my phone into my flesh through the fabric of my clothing. When the phone buzzes, I want to ignore it, but Jackson is surely on his way here by now, so I pull it from my pocket and answer without checking to see that it's him.

"*Guten morgen, Fraulein Hart.*" Julian Gippel's iceberg-cold voice blasts through my sleep fog. "I find myself in a noisy restaurant off the roadway."

"The diner? Good choice, what a shame I can't join you. Too much preparation to do here for the concert, and I'm expecting my fiancé shortly."

"Pity, as we have so much to discuss."

"Such as?" I run a quick inventory of what has been said already, and what more I can say without making things worse.

He sips at something. I imagine him to be a black coffee kind of guy, no sugar or sweetness ever passing his lips. "It occurs to me, Miss Hart, that you are the center of the de la Coeur universe. Every flashing star, every spinning planet, every fleeting comet is drawn by a magnetism you possess. Most unnerving, to discover this."

I think so, too. "I can be there in thirty minutes."

Teeth brushed, hair tucked under a Mets cap, sunglasses affixed, I take the shadiest route to the garage and grab the keys to the Bugatti. Doing eighty all the way, I pull into the diner lot with three minutes to spare. Naturally, Gippel is sitting in full daylight; I sit across from him, nudge the gingham curtain on the window enough to allow me to open my eyes again.

"A bit upset this morning," I lie and pat my slightly protruding abdomen. "I thought it would pass by now." A waitress appears at my side with a coffee pot; I turn the cup in front of me up. "Buttered rye toast please, that's all for me."

The waitress looks to Gippel, fills his cup, takes his plate. "Lovely omelet," he offers curtly, encouraging her to leave.

"You have limited jurisdiction here, Detective. Let's stop being coy and get down to business."

He twists the wedding band on his left hand, once, twice. "*Coy*, a good word, yes. You appear to cooperate, Miss Hart, yet I am unconvinced I have had the full story from you. I continue to be interested, for example, in what actually transpired between you and Teppan Nilsson in Edinburgh last month."

I add sweetener and cream to my coffee, stir it slowly as the waitress returns with my toast. I take a bite, chew thoroughly, just to annoy him. "I'm sure I don't understand why," I finally reply. "Teppan has been cleared, and surely my sex life can't be that fascinating."

He smirks his inscrutable, irritating smirk. "What further fascinates me is your relationship with William Baumann, a man whose coworkers say you apparently met that same night in Edinburgh. A man whom you brought back to a hotel room Teppan Nilsson had booked for himself. Security footage from the streets near the hotel shows you returning rather late with Baumann, with no sign of Mr. Nilsson, though you had left the room with him earlier."

"Embarrassing evidence of my promiscuity, no doubt. Haven't you ever had second thoughts about a major life decision and acted inappropriately, Detective?" I take another bite of toast, which really is nauseating me right now. I swallow it with difficulty, push the plate away.

“Never, Miss Hart.”

Of course not, the man is a robot. “How is any of this significant?”

“I have reserved a room nearby. I was standing outside having a cigarette last night when an impressive car stopped and you stepped out. I followed and watched as a man greeted you quite enthusiastically. Imagine my surprise when, after I obtained his name at the front desk, my further research revealed that this man had been found injured and disoriented in Jackson Fahey’s Zurich hotel room mere days after meeting you in Edinburgh. To learn, as well, that Mr. Fahey had told the Swiss authorities he had never seen Baumann before in his life and had no idea how the man had gotten into his room with no sign of forced entry. Curious, no?”

Obviously, saying anything will be a mistake. Gippel nods, acknowledging my non-response.

“It is curious, too, Miss Hart, that the day after you and I met in London to discuss the sex videos, William Baumann traveled from Edinburgh to see you. Video-surveillance footage shows him arriving at your flat and leaving about twenty-six hours later. One might conclude his presence both here and in London to be welcome, casting your relationship with Teppan Nilsson in Edinburgh in a different light. Perhaps your relationship with Jackson Fahey, as well.”

I slide out of the booth. “Conclude what you like. As I said, I have things to do today.”

“As do I, such as calling on Genevieve Hamilton at your parents’ home, a matter well within my jurisdiction given that she, too, is among your father’s former lovers. It will be most interesting to observe her reactions to the sex videos. Miss Grainger-Todd seemed quite, how to put it, unnerved.”

Even if Gen manages to bluff Gippel, letting him anywhere near Meredith at the same time can only mean trouble. “Let’s see what Mr. Chestack has to say about your planned visit." I storm out of the diner, phone in hand, Gippel's eyes boring into my back. Ed Chestack's secretary answers before I reach the car.

Before I get to the Castle, Chestack calls to say he's doubled the security at the front gate and his already ample yearly contribution to the local Republican Party. A certain district attorney hopes to run for Congress.

"If Gippel wants in, he'd better bring the FBI, the county sheriff, and a search warrant for the house and grounds as well as the lake, though I'd like to see him try to get one. Meredith's working up a statement about police harassment, just in case."

Chestack's breathing fire, raging like the official dragon of Castle de la Coeur. I'm starting to believe he's worth what we pay him after all.

* * * *

It drifts in, something faint and shrill I can't distinguish from the sound of my moans, of Jackson's heart beating harder, faster, of his blood washing through his body and mine. A persistent whine.

Every nerve pinging, every cell alive, I block out the high-pitched whatever-it-is and focus, soaring to a place where I exist alone with this man I love, his lips welded to mine, his body pinning me to the bed beneath him, joining me to him. But after I finish and regain my separateness, after Jackson collapses half on me, half off, I can't shake it, that faint wailing, something barely audible even to my vampire senses through the amp feedback shrieking beyond the ceiling and up the staircase from the Great Hall, past the shimmer of cymbals as the drum kits are set up for Ed and the boy wonder from Matins and Vespers.

I try to sit up, but Jackson's left leg is curled around me, and I am his captive. I push up against it, try to lift it, knowing I could easily do so if I were willing to use the strength I now possess. But he is stronger, too, from all those hours in the gym when we are apart and he is alone in another European city, covering another financial crisis. Keeps him out of trouble, he says. The opposite is true for me.

I shove at his muscled thigh, enough to ease partially out, and the sound is suddenly recognizable: sirens, in the distance still but closing in.

"Uh-uh, you're not going anywhere." He pulls me back toward him, dips down to bite my ear. "Hmm, tasty." He runs his teeth slowly along my throat, in a languid imitation of my feeding ritual. "I'm very hungry. No way I'm setting you free."

Sensation ripples through me. I want him again, and the last thing I want to do is leave him with less than I gave Will the night before. I reach up through black curls, pull his face closer, nibble the beard stubble on his jaw, lick the tip of his slightly crooked nose.

"Do you hear that?"

"I hear musicians bashing about below us, ruining the moment." He tucks his hands beneath me, cups the cheeks of my behind, squeezes. "If I make you scream loud enough, that will disappear. And I'll work very hard, I promise you."

"Police sirens. There's nothing out here but the Castle. No doubt where they're headed."

He steals one more kiss, reluctantly releasing me. I spring from the bed, lift the window shade. Through a steady snowfall, I see miniature lights, blue, red, white, getting bigger, approaching the main gate. I throw on my clothes, pull on my sneakers and my leather jacket, and set off at a run, knowing he'll follow as soon as he can.

Vehicles surround the guardhouse: black sedans that I've learned spell FBI; blue New York State Police cruisers; and a Tompkins County sheriff's van. Lumbering up the road behind them: trucks and other machinery that can only mean the dredging is somehow back on. I sprint to the gate, where the sentry has his phone plastered to his ear as he eyes the official-looking document they've provided him. Beyond the construction flotilla is Gippel. I put out my hand, and the guard relinquishes the court order. "Get Ed Chestack out here now," I bark.

"On his way. Keep those guys outside, his secretary says."

The court order is terse, stating simply that the judge has rescinded his previous ruling and decreed that dredging may begin immediately. Gippel points to me. Behind me, the Bugatti's door slams shut, followed quickly by warmth at my back.

"What is the meaning of this?" I shout at the assembled officers, fists clenched at my side. Jackson places a restraining hand on my right arm.

A state trooper approaches, his hat's wide brim blocking my view of Interpol's finest. "Miss Hart, there's been a shooting. Zeke Segal is dead."

Jackson's arms move around me to hold me up. Gippel shifts, closer to the front of the group now, watching, listening.

"What happened?" Jackson asks, rubbing my shoulders slowly to calm me.

"Bullet wound to the head," the trooper says, "possibly self-inflicted."

"When?" I ask, but I know the answer: before I met Gippel at the diner. He didn't tell me, didn't show his hand until he had played his own with the judge.

"Time of death was between 7:45 and 8 a.m."

"Was there a note?" Jackson's breath is hot against my ear, his ungloved hands cold as they settle protectively at my waist. The trooper shakes his head.

A horn blares, and Chestack guns his SUV up to the gate, scattering a few sheriff's deputies. Waving a copy of the court order, he stomps over, dragging Meredith in his angry wake.

"This is bullshit, back those trucks away! Give me some time to fill my client in, then you'll get to dig, drag, or whatever the hell it is you think you can do in the middle of a goddamn snowstorm."

A cable-news van pulls up; Meredith picks her way across the icy road, prepared to go on air with a statement. "Fahey, let's get Chloe up to the house, it's freezing out here," Ed declaims for the benefit of the crowd. "No place for a pregnant woman who's just had a shock."

They lead me past Gippel, who's moved even closer, assessing. I spit in his direction. "You're a cold bastard, Detective. I've known Zeke Segal all my life, yet you purposely chose not to mention his death this morning. I hope you rot in hell."

"Chloe, that's enough." Jackson pushes me into the SUV. Chestack reverses until he's clear of the clot of trucks, spins us and floors the accelerator until we reach the back of the property, swipes us through the automated security gate there. As the news van speeds up the access road, Jackson rushes me into the Castle, points me toward the grand staircase, away from any first-floor windows that a long-range lens might peer through. I climb a dozen steps, and drop to sit with my back against the railing. Chestack takes the bottom steps, opens his briefcase, finds the police report he's brought with him.

"I no sooner get off the phone with you this morning when the judge's clerk calls to say the order for the dredging is being reinstated. At the courthouse, they make me cool my heels for two hours until they get this paperwork together and the judge can reconvene the hearing. We're screwed. Zeke just screwed us good."

"His perfect revenge." Jackson sits next to me, curious. "If Zeke shot himself, no more worries about having to lie about the ashes. If somebody else shot him, it keeps the heat on Daddy Dearest. All good, all around, I'm sure that's how Zeke saw it. No other way to see it."

"Keep her away from cops and cameras, Fahey, she's obviously in shock." Chestack yanks off his necktie, opens the button on his straining shirt collar. "Let's get everyone here assembled; everyone needs to be on board. I can't have random roadies and Swedish musicians talking to anybody without my knowledge. Gloria!"

Chestack stalks into the Great Hall, bellowing about a pre-rehearsal meeting. Jackson picks up the police report, whips through several pages. "Looks like there's reason to question whether the gunshot was willfully self-inflicted." He turns the papers sideways for a better look at a computer printout showing Zeke's body on the floor of his hotel room.

"No note found. Residue from the gun on his hand, and the angle of the bullet's entry is right for suicide, but it seems Zeke wasn't alone this morning. He was nude, recently showered apparently, towels and bath rug were still damp, as was the carpet under him, and the medical examiner notes there were traces of what appear to be recently deposited semen and vaginal fluid on the body. Bed sheets were still sticky with the same. Prostitute?"

"The Cruel are legendary around here. Maybe a local woman he was friendly with," I lie.

The more likely possibility: After my mother left me, she went to Zeke's hotel and they spent a few intimate hours together. Did he shoot himself afterward? Did she compel him to? Or was it some combination of the two, he wanted to die and she helped him?

Where is my mother anyway?

Before Jackson can react and follow, I race up the stairs to the second floor, back to Sebastian and Emilie's apartment. The door is bolted from the inside. I put my shoulder into the wood and split the jamb. A keening lofts from her bedroom. I walk in without announcing myself, close the damaged door behind me, follow the sound of her mourning.

Kat rocks in Teppan's arms; her eyes spill blood tears, spotting her white shirt, his white shirt, and the white bedding they sit on, the stain spreading slowly around them.

His hand supports her head; he leans down, murmuring into her ear, so softly I can barely hear. "Hush, sweetheart. You gave him your love, and now you've given him his peace."

"We took so much. I could have released him long ago." Kat raises eyes wild with self-recrimination.

"Release was not what he wanted. You did nothing wrong."

My mother's petite body shudders against my father's large

chest, wracked with a sorrow too big to carry alone. His arms tighten around her, as if to take the brunt of her pain. Perhaps after all their time together, he is the only one who can comprehend the depth of her grief. Perhaps he is all the comfort there is for her.

Feeling like a voyeur, I rush away to the main part of the house. At the end of the hall, on the top step, waits Jackson, the professional voyeur, filled with questions, I'm certain, about my rage at Gippel and about why I called Chestack this morning. Wondering, I'm certain, how much more insane my family can prove to be, but not bolting the way any sane man should. He pats the space next to him, opens his arms and collects me close to him. He strokes my cheek with his hand, wipes away a newly shed tear; holds me until I catch my breath.

"She's heartbroken. I can't imagine how many times she's endured something like this." I rest my head against him; listen to his heartbeat, such a steady, normal sound, reassuringly constant. Intruding suddenly from outside, from down by the lake: the groaning of winches; the staccato beeping of trucks backing up; the whirring of motors. Mechanical wailing that seems apt in this particular moment.

"We're doomed," I shout above the din.

My darling man presses a kiss to my hair. "How long will this dredging take?"

I try to remember what Chestack has told me. "Two days, maybe three, to cover the whole lake bottom; a few weeks after to analyze all the samples. I'm guessing they'll find someone's cremated remains."

Jackson wraps me even more tightly against him, as if he is all that stands between me and the ugliness ahead. "So, two days, maybe three, before the gods of water and molecular biology decree our fate. The gods can be fickle, you know. A twist here, a twist there, and the unimaginable is realized. It happens every day."

Such a lovely delusion. If only this were Delphi, the lake a sacred spring and divine favor something the de la Coeurs deserved. I wish something augured redemption. "I don't have your faith. I wish I did."

Too loud, as if it's been wakened harshly by the noise without, the Hammond B-3 roars to life on the floor below us, followed by a thin melody, noisily but sweetly played. "It Came Upon a Midnight Clear" taps out, one finger on the organ's keyboard playing the simple right-hand notes Gloria taught me as a little girl to surprise my parents. It might be her playing now, I can see her trying to prod our collective memory of good times when we were all together, when their pretty artifice was the truth my parents and their troupe happily lived by, and I was happily ignorant.

A hymn of hope to lift our sagging spirits. Unless those angels bending near the earth back away in horror.

* * * *

Only three bars into a new attempt at the now-prescient-seeming "Slaughter of the Innocents" and the shouting starts again, disrupting the rehearsal.

"The bloody organ is drowning out my guitar, to say nothing of Eric's bass." Ronnie's face darkens to the same purple as Katarina's thigh-high boots. "Technically, the cue comes when she sings, 'Wolves in the pens, lambs in their jaws.' "

Behind the keyboard, Teppan rolls his eyes. The kids from Matins and Vespers look bored. Kat storms over, an angry gale capable of knocking over a man twice her size.

"Technically, really? Who wrote the song, Ronnie?"

"You know who wrote the song, Kat, we all know who wrote the song."

"Should we ask Sebastian, then? Oh, wait, he's dead, and so is the Cruel's better guitarist. Adjustments must be made. Make them."

Teppan beats a count of four on top of the organ, and the notes rise the way Sebastian composed them, through bars one, two, and three, on through the wolves and the lambs and the blistering left-hand riff Zeke would never have let overwhelm him.

Jackson dozes at the rear of the Great Hall, his legs sprawled into the row of folding chairs in front of him, his chin dropped onto his chest. He snores lightly through sinuses still congested from the flight over. His comfort level here is not much better than it would be in coach, though the food clearly is—the crusts of his third roast beef sandwich sit on a paper plate on the chair next to him. I can't look at them, my stomach feels as if I swallowed a jagged rock, nor can I take much more of the musical discord onstage.

I need something to wear tomorrow, for my mistress-of-ceremonies role. Meredith and I were going to shop, but PR crises have superseded wardrobe emergencies. My parents are rehearsing, and Emilie has hundreds of costumes she can't wear now that she's become Katarina, so I make my way to their rooms again, past the door I've damaged, to the mother lode of Cruel female fashion.

Emilie's closet is the size of some of my European apartments, bigger than my first flat in Spain, now that I think of it. Clear garment bags are organized by concert tour; dresses—no slacks for the medieval miss—hang from the rod, coordinating shoes in clear bags below them, each outfit numbered so the corresponding under-things and stockings and jewelry and hats and scarves can be located in the dressers that edge the space. I've decided on a red-and-green ensemble, naturally. I'll wear my ruby pendant, so I need a green gown. I have something specific in mind, and get lucky when it's the second gown I pull out: rich, mossy velvet in an Empire style, cut low and gathered under the bust so I'll look more voluptuous. The dress is number 89; I grab the shoes from their bag and fetch the matching accessories to try on downstairs.

A rustle to the right catches my ear, someone in the sitting room.

“These are breathtaking. Horrific, but breathtaking,” a voice says from the shadows: Genevieve, standing rapt before the tapestries. “There’s a gruesome beauty that can’t be conveyed in two dimensions, nuances that must be seen up close.”

I see her moving back and forth among the panels, taking in the three of them. When she stops again, she is blocking the light from the hallway, and I can’t tell which tapestry has drawn her renewed attention.

“This one is particularly disturbing,” she says after an awkward silence, as I stand riveted to my spot just outside. She is looking, I surmise, at the no-longer-charred depiction of me feeding on Jackson. “I could never quite make out the faces on the images you emailed me, but it’s clear in person who they’re meant to be. It’s happened, hasn’t it, Chloe? The change has come over you.”

She makes it sound like a passive thing, like a fever that descends rather than the violent, convulsive transformation it is, but how could she possibly know what it’s like to cast off one form for another within the same body? I don’t respond, which, if she were not a scientist, Genevieve would take as confirmation that what she suspects is true. She is an investigator, no less thorough than Gippel, as she has taught me to be, and I know half-answers are, to her, no answers at all.

“He’s done this to you, hasn’t he, that bastard Sebastian?”

“If you mean am I like my parents now, yes, I am, but no one else could make it happen. Only I could.”

“I don’t believe you. I’ve known you since you were eighteen years old. You couldn’t just turn into them. You *wouldn’t* just turn into them.”

How to explain this, when I don’t fully understand? “It didn’t just happen, it was happening all along. I didn’t recognize it for what it was, because I didn’t know what Sebastian and Emilie were. But I’m still me, Gen, still that girl you met fresh out of boarding school.”

She looks at me, and even in the dim light I see what cannot be mistaken: pity. "Sebastian has taken from you the thing he wanted most, the freedom to choose."

"He didn't do this."

"He didn't stop it either. Nothing happened for thirty-two years, why now unless something or someone pushed you into it?"

"You don't know what you're talking about." I move out of my parents' apartment, toward the stairs, my mother's dress and shoes and the rest weighing on my arms, weighing down my heart. Genevieve follows me, hurries to keep up, as I rush through the house, not sure myself where I'm going, but heading toward the music, toward Jackson. She grabs hold of the arm carrying the dress. The bag falls to the floor, and I crouch to scoop it up, but she won't let go, won't let me escape without hearing her out.

"I've been around these people longer than you have, and I wouldn't have wished this on you for the world. You think I don't know about the 'one life' command, or how Sebastian wouldn't accept you as his one life as long as you hadn't changed? You think I don't know how my father exploited Sebastian's vanity, bought him those women to impregnate then arranged to have them killed when their babies died? Sebastian knew what the likely outcome would be, but he did it anyway."

So it does, indeed, come down to this: The babies, the women, Esteban, all of them died because of me. Gippel is right: I am the center of this dreadful universe.

Genevieve gathers up the dress, takes my hand; leads me around to the back staircase. I climb, then walk, not to the room I share with Jackson but to the frilly monstrosity that was my childhood bedroom. She hangs the garment bag from a hook on the back of the door, unzips it, removes the dress and shakes out the creases; unzips the bag with the undergarments, shakes them out and lays them across the bench at my vanity table. I sit on the bed and watch, not knowing why she feels the need to play lady's maid, knowing only that I feel too exhausted to ask.

"Gen, I want to sleep."

She sits at the edge of the bed. "I can't bear the thought that Sebastian has cursed you now with the same uncertainty that tormented him."

I can't bear another riddle. "What does that mean?"

She puts her hand on my stomach. "This baby, is she your one life? How will you know till you know?"

That's wrong, the baby doesn't count. "I was human when Jackson and I conceived Guinevere."

She smiles indulgently at me, at the flaw in my logic. "You said the change didn't just happen, that it was happening all along. If that's true, when were you ever merely human, Chloe? It took all those years to make the transition, but can you say for sure: Was it the beginning of a process, or the end of one?"

I don't know, all I know is that I will not be like my father. I'll wait for my daughter to grow up, wait to see what happens. And like my mother, I'll watch as my love grows old and dies, and weep for him when he's gone.

*Chapter Six*

# UPSTATE NEW YORK, DECEMBER 2011

Mud was the great equalizer, Fahey quickly discovered, the great leveler of the battlefield Castle de la Coeur had become.

Mud that had heavy equipment sinking along the shores of the now-infamous lake, to the point where all but the machines needed for the actual dredge work had to be moved back, then back once more when their tires dipped deeper into the viscous brown stuff. Mud that had two men in hard hats walking a path from the edge of the water to the road, calculating how best to transfer the silt, plant sediment, animal remains, and whatever else would be brought up to the surface so it could be transported to a forensics lab.

Mud that had security guards and parking attendants continually recalibrating where to put the tidal wave of vehicles filled with vassals and assorted other concertgoers that began to crash over the grounds at eight o'clock in the morning, an hour before the gate was to have officially opened.

Mud that had TV news vans splashing their presenters with every shuttle they were forced to make between the lake and Vineyard de la Couer, where the much more appealing stories were, for now, unfolding: the tale of the rebuilt home of Blood of the Bards, a vintage now tainted by the blood of the summertime bombing victims; the tale of the food and crafts vendors, who were more busy with each succeeding wave of ticket holders. Chloe, astute judge of the media that she was becoming, had dictated that only one set of credentials be granted to each network or press outlet, compelling the same team to cover investigation and concert, with no relief crews permitted. "One and done," Fahey had heard Meredith repeatedly declare at the main gate. "We have ample food and toilet facilities and rest areas. You leave the grounds, you leave the story."

The source of all that lovely mud: an unanticipated warming trend that had raised the temperature seventeen degrees overnight. Couple that with a brilliant sun now liberated from the cover of clouds, and more than a day's worth of snow had liquefied to inundate the Kingdom of the Cruel.

Fahey had known things outside would be bad when, so caked was she in mud after her predawn run, Chloe had refused to rejoin him in bed until she'd showered. Not that Fahey would have minded, but she was touchy enough, so he hadn't pressed the issue. Nerves, he knew, kept her running, despite her obvious exhaustion. He'd found her asleep in her old bedroom last night, crawled in next to her after two o'clock, only to have her rouse when she sensed his presence. About seven, when he got up, he went downstairs and persuaded Gloria to bring Chloe some tea and a grilled-cheese sandwich for breakfast, which Chloe ate and finished under his scrutiny. She'd eaten a container of yogurt last night but nothing else, as far as he could tell. Almost into her third month now and the baby nausea hadn't subsided. Gloria reassured him that Emilie had been the same way, always moving, seldom eating.

He had left Chloe in her office a half-hour later, memorizing the short welcome speech she would give to open the show. Stopping in the kitchen for some coffee, he found Ronnie Hamilton and Teppan Nilsson arguing over the playlist, music charts scattered across the island, Ronnie ticking off the songs he was perfectly capable of taking lead guitar on, Nilsson agreeing about half the time. Gloria handed Fahey a travel mug and pointed to a pair of work boots near the window seat. "Escape while you can. This will go on until they step on stage. Ronnie will win, but he'll have had to work so hard to earn it, he'll play the show of his life. You'll see."

Fahey walked the grounds, with no clear role in the concert preparations—largely to avoid any more notoriety deriving from his ties to the de la Coeurs, which the BBC had thus far seen fit to overlook. He was impressed anew by the Castle, the hidden nooks and open spaces where Guinevere would play, as little Chloe had done. He couldn't stop smiling at the prospect, couldn't wait for June.

Couldn't stop smiling until he saw Detective Gippel up ahead, on the path leading to the dredge site. He followed, and eventually Gippel turned around.

"Perhaps you would like a tour, Mr. Fahey? We are not fully operational yet. Conditions are not as we had hoped."

"Snow would have been preferable?"

"Traction would have been better, yes, for the many trucks. However, it is not critical what we accomplish today, just that we are here to accomplish it."

"Anything to disrupt the show, in other words?"

Gippel grinned, stopped to light a cigarette. "The show is of no importance. It is the players in whom I am interested."

Interesting, that interest. "Well, of course, the Cruel now has just two surviving original members here."

"I've had quite an education in Court of Cruelty these weeks, Mr. Fahey. I have learned much. Mr. Chestack, who called himself Eddie Check when he was the de la Coeurs' drummer, yes? He left the band early on, for law school, and was replaced by another man for quite some time, a James Fritz." Gippel drew on his cigarette, lifted each shoe gingerly, disdainfully, from the mud. "Fritz left in the nineties, after the band ceased recording and touring each year. He has been living in Arkansas, where he is a professor of percussion at a university."

"Tim Sutter, what happened to him?" Gippel no doubt had a

dossier on everyone who'd ever played within ten miles of the Cruel.

"Dead, heroin overdose, May 2005, Bangkok. Lost his girlfriend in the tsunami in Phuket five months earlier, stayed on in Thailand, but acquaintances said he never recovered from her death."

Along the near perimeter of the lake, posts supporting crime-scene tape sagged toward one another, struggling to resist the suction of the mud. A tank-like vehicle resembling an elephant, trunk-like tubing waving back and forth, seemed to be sweeping the lake water at the surface.

"What's that for?" Fahey pointed toward the metallic mastodon.

"Control samples, to gain baseline knowledge of the water's chemistry and what exists in it. I do not pretend to understand all the science, just those parts that make my investigation go smoothly."

"So they might not dig today?"

Gippel opened his hands innocently. "The machines are quite noisy. We have no desire to ruin the charitable event. Just because I believe Sebastian de la Coeur to be a murderer does not mean I want to impoverish his cancer-research foundation. Emilie de la Coeur had cancer, did she not?"

Emilie's name seldom came up in connection with the murder investigation. *Tread lightly, Jackson. Act dumb, say nothing you'll regret.* So he said nothing at all.

They walked in silence around the lake, stopping briefly on the far banks to survey the vast property—the house, the vineyard, the outbuildings. Encroaching closer to the Castle was the public parking area, both shoulders of the road from the main gate now dense with vehicles, with more coming in.

"I must check in with my colleagues. Perhaps later, we'll converse more," Gippel said, irony dripping from his voice.

"I think I'll stop by the press village, I've worked with several of the reporters before. Anything you'd like me to pass along?" Fahey felt Gippel's stare centered on his back as he walked away, past the equipment, both active and temporarily marooned, toward the sidelines where the news vans were parked. It was clear the crews had abandoned their mud-challenged rides and hoofed up to where the action was, at the winery.

He arrived there to see Meredith in full frenzy, scurrying amid media types and event staff, laying down the law to the former, offering guidance to the latter. Yes, she assured, credentials meant coverage of the full concert was permitted. "We can't very well insist that you stay without allowing you to work, can we?" she repeated at least twice a minute. "That said, the photo pit will be open only for Miss Hart's introduction and the first three songs; after that, you're at the back of the Great Hall. Ticket holders come first."

She spotted Fahey and stuck her tongue out.

"Very mature," he mocked and strode off, Meredith's laughter letting him know she was relaxed enough to joke with him. That must mean things were going well so far.

Several yards away, Genevieve distributed maps of the vendors' area and the home of Blood of the Bards, busy but not nearly as frenetic.

"Pressed into service?"

She smiled at him warily, handed him a stack. "There's a lot to be done, in case you hadn't noticed."

"Hint taken. I'll stay till these are safely in visitors' hands, but then I want to check in on Chloe. She was pretty stressed earlier."

A group of five approached. Genevieve pointed the way to a short line for the winery visits. "Guided tours run every thirty minutes until 12:30 p.m. The show starts at 2 p.m.," she told them pleasantly, then turned to glare at Fahey.

"There's a bit to be stressed about, don't you think? This might be the worst day of our very private Chloe's life, and that's saying something, considering the year's events."

A vassal couple in full 1970s Peasants' Faire regalia—Fahey recognized it from his parents' closet—asked him for directions to the restrooms. He consulted a map, pointed out the nearest loo, and accepted a handshake from the male of the devoted-fan species, all under the disapproving gaze of Professor Hamilton.

"Why do I feel as if I've somehow failed a test? If you're finding fault with me, just spell it out and tell me how I've erred."

She laughed. "Not just a pretty face, he's perceptive too. Perceive this: You have come to a crossroads with Chloe, and you have to decide whether you want to be present and support her, or let her be. Gippel knows the truth, and what he doesn't know he suspects."

"Not *that* truth."

"No, the big lie is intact, but the rest is just a matter of time. This dredging business is mere theater."

"I've loved Chloe since the first moment I saw her, and now that we're having a baby, I couldn't love her more. None of the rest pertains to me."

Genevieve nodded, clearly skeptical. "When she falls, she'll need you—and she will fall. All the de la Coeurs are about to fall."

"You sound almost eager for it." Was Genevieve's animosity toward Sebastian heightened by being here at the Castle, where he had brought her mother and where Gloria had happily stayed, far away from her daughter?

"Much as I don't want to see Chloe hurt," she said, "if Sebastian were here now, I'd happily introduce him to Detective Gippel myself."

Genevieve still had no idea Sebastian was, indeed, here—no idea, like Meredith, that Teppan Nilsson was Sebastian. How, Fahey wondered, had Sebastian managed that?

Twenty minutes passed before his hands were empty, the maps all distributed. He turned to leave, but Genevieve halted him with a firm grip on his sleeve.

"Chloe is very vulnerable right now, for all her newfound

strength. She may be like her parents, but I don't think she truly has the stomach for what they are. Love her as she is, Jackson, and if you can't, take care not to destroy her."

Eyes shimmering with unshed tears, Genevieve released the fabric, and Fahey could see she knew that narrative in its entirety.

"She told you?"

"The tapestries did. They're a family chronicle; that must be why they fascinated Chloe as a child. I can see they were always meant to be her story, as well."

"Mine, too, or am I to interpret being eaten alive as a metaphor for something else?"

"I have learned the hard way that nothing is ever as it seems with the de la Coeurs. You can trust Chloe. What you can't trust is what you think you know about her."

More inscrutable nonsense, and this time from the most coldly rational person in the lot of them. Fahey shook his head and walked away, before Genevieve could confuse and frustrate him further. He wasn't sure which of the de la Coeurs he hated more at this point: Sebastian for pushing Chloe into the change or Emilie for stitching the evolving reminder that there was no turning back from it.

Just ahead, stopped as concertgoers flowed around him, the ubiquitous Julian Gippel faced the winery's entrance, standing with a man whose back was to Fahey but whom he recognized nonetheless. Talking freely to Interpol's chief investigator of the four murders attributed to Sebastian de la Coeur was Will Baumann, Edinburgh brewmaster and emergency vampire blood supply. To Fahey's knowledge, they knew few people in common, one being Teppan Nilsson, which was to say Sebastian, the other being Chloe, who had spit at Gippel in a rage the previous afternoon and had yet to explain why. Fahey began to think he knew the reason.

The path forked a few yards away from them. Fahey considered veering off toward the staff cottages, knowing he could reach the back of the main house that way undetected. Before he could choose, Gippel and Baumann were upon him. Gippel merely nodded, as if expecting them to hail each other as friends. Fahey said nothing; Baumann waited for an introduction. Fahey knew the minute Gippel comprehended that they had not met, at least not officially—at least not in any way Baumann recalled. Finally, Baumann extended his hand.

"You're Jackson Fahey, I've seen you on the BBC, and of course you're C.J. Hart's fiancé."

"So sorry, Mr. Fahey, I thought you were acquainted." Gippel failed to hide his delight at the moment's awkwardness.

"We've met before, briefly," Fahey acknowledged.

Baumann frowned. "I don't think so, I would have remembered."

"In Zurich."

"Indeed." Gippel stepped around them toward the winery. Fahey did not see Genevieve Hamilton, and had the momentary thought that was a good thing, that the detective really needed to stay away from this particular former girlfriend of Sebastian's, when he noticed Baumann once again offering his hand. He ignored it.

"It was your hotel room? I had no idea how I got to Switzerland, or who had found me there. I spent two days in the hospital, with no memory. Thank you for your help."

"I didn't do it for you. She didn't give me much choice."

"Juliette brought me to you?"

Fahey struggled to keep his hands off Baumann's neck. "You don't get to call her that."

"It's what she told me to call her."

"Forget you heard it. Why are you here?"

Baumann smiled. "I'm American. I came home for Christmas, of course."

"You're here because of her."

"Teppan Nilsson invited me; got me tickets, reserved a room."

"Too bad, you need to leave." Fahey figured he had a couple inches on Baumann and about twenty pounds. He'd toss the bastard himself, if necessary. He took a step forward; Baumann took a step back and put up his hands in mock surrender.

"I'm doing what I've been asked to do: take care of her and keep her satisfied."

Fahey moved closer. "I'm here to handle that."

"Today, sure, but you'll be gone again. I'll be here if she needs me, or there in London, wherever she needs me. I have no intention of neglecting her."

Fahey swung, and Baumann's backside made contact with the brick walkway. He shook his sore fist, droplets of Baumann's blood flying from his hand. "If you're smart, you'll leave."

"No more convincing than when she says it." Baumann scrambled to his feet, blood dripping from his swelling lip. "She can't make me go either, but she knows I can make her come, and come, and come. Just ask her."

Fahey kneed him in the testicles and stalked away, glad he'd put a little extra Irish in to make the point. People rushed to help. "Nothing an ice pack won't cure," he yelled to the crowd gathering.

The closer he got to the Castle, the more disembodied melody filled the air around him, the more Fahey thought Genevieve was right, that maybe he was capable of destroying Chloe and everything between them with a few ill-considered words and a few thrown punches. Chloe warned him they hadn't heard the last of Will Baumann, she told him he'd have trouble dealing with Baumann's compulsion to be with her and her inability to resist what he offered.

Baumann was right, too: Fahey would be gone again, day after tomorrow in fact, and unless Chloe returned to Brussels with him, it was inevitable that too many days would go by and Will would show up, unasked, to give her what she needed. Unasked didn't mean unwelcome, and every part of Fahey vibrated with anger at the thought of his woman with that man.

He ran through the patio entrance, through the crowded kitchen, past yet another argument between Teppan and Ronnie, up the back staircase to Chloe's office. Empty, so he backtracked to the bedroom they'd been sharing, now empty, too. Notes from the piano above sent him up the stairs two at a time to the music studio. He opened the door but didn't make it over the threshold, arrested by the sight he saw.

She was at the keyboard, playing a tune he knew well, one of her parents' but different somehow. Where Court of Cruelty's version was arrogant, this one was plaintive yet just as demanding. She hummed a few bars, then began to sing in a light, lovely alto he'd never dreamed she possessed.

*If you're seeking Joan of Arc, I am not her*
*If you want a heroine to rise up for your cause*
*I will not give you aid, I must demur*
*Cri de coeur*

*If you want a gentle soul, I am not her*
*If it's a sacrificial virgin you desire,*
*I am no lamb for you to maim and martyr*
*Cri de coeur*

The green of her dress matched the green of her eyes, and Fahey was mesmerized. God, she was gorgeous, everything more vibrant since her transition, despite the stress of the investigation and the concert and the pregnancy. Yet she looked more fragile, as well, like someone he must love and protect rather than the otherworldly being she had become.

Fahey joined her on the piano bench and folded her into his arms, kissed her hungrily, melted around her as she fitted her body to his. When he remembered that one of them still needed to breathe, he lifted his head, inhaled the scent of her hair, battled not to lose himself in her gaze.

"The song is 'Croix de Guerre,' isn't it? You've rewritten it, rearranged it. I didn't know you could sing like that, or play like that."

Chloe pressed a kiss to his chest, to his heart. "I'm their daughter; I was born with the music. I simply chose not to be defined by it." She stretched and bit into his neck just above his collar, sipped at the bubble of blood that rose, licked the wound closed. Fahey felt his body harden, inhaled deeply, fought to think of something else.

"The song, is there more of it?"

"I hope so."

Fahey couldn't tell whether she really didn't know. She ran her fingers over his battered right hand, bent to taste the dried blood there, then quickly pulled away from him.

"Will's blood. You hit him."

"Bastard deserved it."

She walked to the door, pressed her forehead against it. "No, he didn't. If you want someone to punish, punish me."

"When did he get here?"

"Day before you did. He just comes."

*And comes, and comes, and comes.* Fahey mimicked Baumann but did not say the words aloud. He didn't have to; he knew she had heard. Chloe walked out, leaving him to stew in his jealousy, but he pursued her downstairs to her office, slipped in before she could shut him out.

"Must you indulge him? Is Baumann so irresistible?"

She crossed to the window. Well past one o'clock, the sun's rays streamed in, surrounding her in a halo of gold and orange, and Fahey knew her answer, though he hated that he knew.

"You can't expect me to not feed, any more than I can ask you to fast when we're apart. Please don't make more of this than it is, not today."

Fahey couldn't stop himself, couldn't stop thinking about Chloe and Baumann together, doing things she should be doing only with him.

"Did you rush to Will when he got here? Suck from him and

fuck him and drain him while he impaled you? How many times?"

He was acting like a brute, but it felt like someone was gnawing at his skin, and Fahey couldn't help picking at the wounds. Chloe stared out at the brilliant winter day. The hum of voices grew louder below them as the Great Hall filled. Forty minutes till show time.

He stepped behind her, put his hands over the rounding that was their child, saw Baumann putting his hands there too, and his lips on her, and his cock inside her. Fahey twisted Chloe to face him, took her mouth possessively, thrust his tongue inside, and grasped her tightly to him, kissed her until his lungs screamed for him to stop.

"Come to Brussels with me on Monday, close the gallery until the New Year and be with me. I can't live with the possibility that the next time you're kissed it won't be by me. Marry me in Belgium, and we'll figure out what comes next."

She pressed her forehead to his chest, her breathing as ragged as his. "This is not something a marriage vow can solve. Neither one of us is thinking clearly now, there's too much going on."

He dropped his arms, stepped away. She swayed and reached back to brace herself on the window ledge.

"What is there to think about? If the only way to keep Will Baumann away from you is for us to be together, change me and we'll be together for eternity."

Eyes sad, she walked past him, out of yet another room. Again, Fahey followed, to her parents' chambers. She opened the portal, wordlessly defying him to enter her parents' sanctum without her permission.

"I'm sorry, love, stop. Don't push me away in favor of him."

"Can't you see past your ego? Where Will is, or whether you and I are living in the same city, it doesn't matter if you can't accept me as I am now. I can't change you, Jackson. You can't be my one life because I've already created one."

That couldn't be true. This woman loved him and only him, he knew that as he knew his own name.

"What one life have you created?" He inched closer, because he had to know, and he knew she had to tell him.

She caressed the bulge that was their daughter. "This one," she said, slamming the door.

* * * *

A herald's trumpet sounded. Obediently, the vassals took their seats.

"Welcome to the twenty-eighth annual 'Christmas at the Castle' celebration. A joyous holiday to one and all!" Meredith's voice rang out from backstage. "Please make your bows to a true daughter of the Court of Cruelty, your mistress of ceremonies, C.J. Hart."

The curtain opened to reveal the princess of the Cruel. Applause and cheers bounced off the walls of the Great Hall in greeting. From stage left, Chloe moved to a piano to perform in public for the first time, as naturally as if she had done it all her life, this woman he loved who had so shied away from the spotlight but now accepted this role, however reluctantly. Fahey watched from the wings at stage right, a plastic cup of Sebastian's fine scotch half-empty in his perspiring hand.

She sang effortlessly, with no apparent fear of flubbed notes or bad rhymes. What, after all, did she have to lose?

*If you seek the master's daughter, this is her*
*If you befoul the name he gave to me,*
*I will not sit*
*and countenance your slander*

*If you want a gentle soul, I am not her*
*If it's a sacrificial virgin you desire*
*I am no lamb for you to maim and martyr*
*Cri de couer*

*If you defame the glory of this house,*
*I vow you'll feel the fire of my anger*
*I vow you'll feel the fire of my anger!*
*Cri de coeur*

She played an instrumental repeat of the chorus and gazed into the crowd. Fahey followed her stare to the back of the hall, where Gippel leaned against a pillar and offered her a bow few others witnessed, the cry of her heart loud and clear. The vassals roared, appreciative of the newly blossomed chanteuse de la Coeur they perceived Chloe to be. She rose from the piano bench and strode to the standing microphone at the center of the stage, looking quickly over at Fahey, then quickly away.

"Thank you all for coming, to offer your support and your dollars to the charity my parents founded. If they were here today, this Great Hall could not contain their gratitude. It is important to remember them and that they loved us and that we can continue their work through our generosity to the Sebastian and Emilie de la Coeur Foundation for Blood and Bone Marrow Cancer Research. Cancer took their lives, after all. Let us devote ours to discovering a cure."

The curtains closed, the house lights dimmed still lower, and Fahey watched Chloe exit via the opposite wing. He hoped she'd circle around to him, but he could see only musicians taking their marks, and the person stepping next to him instead was Ed Chestack, in his Cruel regalia, sticks in his hand.

"Why aren't you up there?"

"Only one drummer for the opening number, Teppan says. That kid Lars is at the far kit."

The herald's trumpet sounded three times then played the first eight notes, appropriately, of "Hark, the Herald Angels Sing." Invisible to the audience, Meredith took the microphone once more.

"Hear, ye vassals, and obey the call. Raise your voices in praise and your hands in applause for today's musical guests, Matins and Vespers."

Chords reverberated an ecclesiastical keyboard riff, the organ looming sonically from the rear of the stage, followed by the pealing of cymbals and the lilt of a flute that rose then faded to a shimmer. Two figures took their marks in the shadows at the front of the stage, one tall with long hair down his back, one much shorter and holding the flute. Teppan and Katarina, of course, but not, and Fahey felt his chest tighten and the breath desert his body.

Teppan leaned forward, pulled the microphone stand closer, like a lover initiating an embrace. He intoned into its metaphorical ear, spinning a web meant to ensnare:

*Call me pretender to the throne?*
*Regard the man who sits on it*
*I'll seize the land the people own*
*From those who lie and ravage it*

*I have no love for anarchy*
*I have no lust for wealth or power*
*I am by right no less divine*
*Than he to rule this day, this hour*

*For I was born to slay the king*
*To slay our bloody bastard king*
*To make him rue the very day*
*He thought our worth to be nothing*
*Yes, I was*
*Born*
*To*
*Slay*
*The*
*King*

Guitars squealed, drums pounded, the stage flashed bright in an incandescence of white and red spotlights, and before all they stood front and center, clad in black, the king and queen of the Cruel, Sebastian and Emilie de la Coeur themselves.

The music quickly muffled whatever collective gasp rose from the audience, but it did not quell the collective shriek of adoration that replaced it.

"Alive! Alive! Alive!" the vassals chanted as Ronnie shredded the notes of a fiercely electrified version of the song that made Court of Cruelty famous. Eric drove through the bass line like a man possessed, and maybe he was. Beside him, Fahey felt rage blasting off Chestack's body, saw him splinter the drumsticks he held and reduce them to toothpicks.

"Goddamn it! They planned this, deliberately wanted me nowhere near the opening number. They knew I'd never let them do it."

Following Ronnie's manic lead guitar, Matins and Vespers rocked through verses two and three. On verse four, Eric took up the vocal. Two roadies emerged from the wings, pushing fabric-covered folding screens onto the stage, positioning them as close to the edge as possible.

The screens encircled Sebastian and Emilie, concealing them as they methodically tossed medieval clothing, then modern wigs over the top and, in Sebastian's case, into the seats. When the monarchs lifted their voices for the final, fifth verse, emerging from behind the screens, clad in white, their hair blond and eyes blue again, they were Teppan and Katarina Nilsson.

Impersonation over. Hoax intact. Coup complete.

Chestack slumped against Fahey, in relief or from cardiac arrest he wasn't sure. The older man wheezed and shut his eyes, trying to compose himself, trying for deep, even breaths. Fahey turned from the stage, let his vision adjust and peered into the audience, hoping for a break in the sway of the bodies that might afford him a view of the one person this performance was intended to impress. Past the enraptured vassals, standing at the back of the hall, he at last saw Gippel, a small smile etched across his tight face, as visceral a reaction as the detective likely would allow.

"Megalomaniacal, daughter-fucking son of a bitch, I swear I'll kill him," Chestack seethed as he stepped away to walk onstage.

Fahey grabbed Chestack's arm, wrenched it, painfully he hoped. "Whose daughter?"

Chestack pulled free. "You mean beside Ronnie's? Mine, for one, and who knows who else's." His eyes drifted to the opposite side of the stage, where Meredith stood watching the show.

"Wait. She's *your* daughter? Does she know?"

"Only if she equates my throwing work her way with paternal love. Her mother meant nothing to me, and I meant nothing to her. It was one night, a married woman I would never have given another thought to, but Sebastian was there, and he never let me forget."

The music stopped, and Chestack had to go. "This is between us, don't you dare tell Meredith. I should have protected her from Sebastian, but I couldn't. Was his own daughter even safe from him?"

"He didn't," Fahey protested. "Edinburgh was just a lie they told the police."

Chestack pushed past him. Through the blood pounding in his head, Fahey heard Kat's introduction: "Ladies and gentlemen, pay tribute, if you please, to the Court of Cruelty's own Eddie Check, resuming his place at the drums for the first time in decades."

Through chants of "Ed-die! Ed-die!" Fahey circled behind the stage and down the right side of the hall, to where Gippel stood. He didn't know what Chestack was trying to say, whether he didn't know or whether it was true: that Sebastian had taken his own daughter that way, or just the fact that you couldn't put anything past him. Fahey wanted to tighten Gippel's noose around the bastard's neck regardless.

Chloe's relationship with her father had always been complicated, and Fahey couldn't believe she would have hidden something like that from him. Still, she'd never revealed what had happened in Edinburgh, or why she'd chosen to let Gippel believe she and Teppan had been lovers—or why, when she lay fevered and delirious in his flat in Brussels, she'd cried out in German, "No, Daddy, no!"

He had to know, or at least know what Gippel had discovered. He had information to trade, if Gippel were game.

If Fahey's appearance at his side surprised him, Gippel didn't let it show. "Quite the performance they are giving, the Nilssons and their band. The musicians are much improved since your recording in Barcelona earlier this year."

It was true, they were, but Gippel wasn't making small talk, he was making a point: Even with Kat fronting them, Matins and Vespers were only a passable cover band. With Teppan, they sounded like the real deal. Because they were.

"Shall we get some air, Detective? You want a cigarette, and I want to hear myself think."

Bodies flowed through the vestibule in front of the Great Hall, traversing the space between it and the bathrooms and the temporary concession stands. Fahey led the way to the inner courtyard and outside to what had been cordoned off as a smoking area. The sun had all but set, leaving only reddish streaks low in the late December sky over upstate New York. Fahey pressed close to the wall, bracing against the wind because he had no coat. Gippel lit a cigarette, offered Fahey the pack.

"It's one of the few vices I've managed to quit. Well, mostly. Ask me again in an hour."

Gippel smiled, sort of. "I have succeeded at no longer trying. A man must accept his shortcomings and work at what he does well, yes?"

"Like you, what I do well is ask questions and weave a narrative. Care to do a little weaving with me?"

"If I choose not to answer, you will, of course, understand."

"I will, of course, answer a question of yours in return."

After several silent minutes, Gippel took one last deep drag on his cigarette and crushed it under his heel. Fahey chose not to see symbolism in the gesture.

"Let us go back inside, Mr. Fahey. I might find your questions more agreeable were your teeth not chattering with the cold."

In the vestibule, the music was near deafening. Through the main door, Fahey could see Ronnie sawing across his strings and whirling like a dervish, dancing across the stage toward Katarina, grinding his instrument as she matched his movements on air guitar. Teppan's baritone fomented Dark Ages discord from behind the organ's keyboard.

Sounded damn good to Fahey, the vibration of the dual drummers and Eric's bass pounding through the air, across the floor, assaulting whoever dared stand in its path. He caught Gippel's eye, nodded to a far corner. The investigator followed.

"I want to know about Edinburgh, about Teppan Nilsson and my fiancée. Will Baumann isn't important to her, but Nilsson—let's say I'm no longer sure."

Gippel pressed his thumb and forefinger to the top of his nose, as if warding off a headache. He sniffled; sinus headache, Fahey mentally amended, and the music's volume couldn't be helping.

"There are surveillance cameras in the public spaces at the hotel they chose. Miss Hart checked in first, went up to a room she had booked online only an hour or so before her arrival; she is seen shortly afterward in the bar, sitting alone for a time. The barmaid described her as nervous, saying that Miss Hart quickly drank down two glasses of wine but that she seemed no more at ease. When Nilsson joined her, the barmaid and the bartender said, she seemed transfixed. That was the word they used, as though they had consulted on it. I pressed them: They said she seemed in awe of the man, though annoyed to be so, especially when he took certain liberties in public."

"Liberties?"

"He stroked her cheek and kissed it, and put his hand on her buttocks and squeezed. The bar was not crowded, they said, but Nilsson and Miss Hart were not its only patrons, and her body language suggested she was not pleased with his behavior. They argued, though the barmaid couldn't say about what. About thirty minutes later, the barmaid said, Nilsson stood behind Miss Hart's chair, leaned down and left a trail of kisses along her neck. The barmaid assumed they had settled their argument.

"The front-desk camera records Nilsson ordering that Miss Hart's bill be given to him to pay and her luggage moved to his room. They enter an elevator. A hall camera upstairs shows an older couple watching Nilsson and Miss Hart embrace as the elevator door opens. They run down the hall to Nilsson's room."

"And?" Fahey didn't like what he was hearing, feared what more there might be.

"That is all. Lobby cameras show them leaving several hours later, quite late, in fact, but Nilsson is never observed returning, and Miss Hart is seen subsequently only with William Baumann. Everything else I have gleaned—credit-card expenditures, travel arrangements—you already know."

Not enough, but clearly all Fahey would get. His turn.

"I visited Anthony Kirkpatrick at Belmarsh Prison a few hours before you released Teppan Nilsson from custody."

"The authorities have no further interest in Kirkpatrick. He confessed to Esteban Gronlund's murder."

"Hear me out, Detective. I remained curious why Kirkpatrick was unwilling to talk about killing Gronlund, except to admit freely that he had done so. Odd, don't you think, given that he claims never to have seen the man before that evening at the bar?"

Gippel unwrapped a stick of gum. "Odd, so you say, yet not unheard of."

"No, of course, random acts of violence occur every day. Still, something seemed off when I spoke to Kirkpatrick a few months back. It was clear there was something he wasn't saying. When I pushed, he eventually said he had been compelled to kill Gronlund by a tall man who approached him out of the shadows, sexually assaulted him, and took over his will. He said he had been advised by legal counsel that such a claim would not exonerate him, and might, indeed, land him in a mental institution. Anton saw prison as the more tolerable alternative."

"This tall man? Kirkpatrick could identify him?"

"He said he didn't see the man's face, but I was intrigued. When I was last in London, I visited Belmarsh again. I brought my laptop and showed Kirkpatrick several videos, including my Barcelona shoot of Matins and Vespers' concert and the YouTube video of the impromptu show the Nilssons put on with Ronnie Hamilton and Zeke Segal earlier this month, after my fiancée's gallery reception. Teppan Nilsson speaks in that video. Kirkpatrick recognized his voice."

Gippel's eyebrows arched, ever so slightly, a telling twitch he quickly caught and tamed. "The tall man assaulted Kirkpatrick? Esteban Gronlund was known to be bisexual, but we have thus far found no connection between Gronlund and Teppan Nilsson, sexual or otherwise. To be frank, we know of few connections between Teppan Nilsson and anyone. What news clippings exist maintain that he and his wife were childhood friends in a town outside Goteborg, Sweden, but personal and financial records offer little to substantiate that."

"What do they tell you?"

Again, an eyebrow lifted, as if to suggest Fahey knew exactly what the records told. "That Teppan Nilsson, and Katarina Nilsson for that matter, did not exist until the early part of this year. Nilsson is a very common name in the Swedish databases, and in other parts of Scandinavia, so it is possible we are looking at the wrong Nilssons. It is further possible those are not their real names. We continue to search the records, to whatever end that may lead."

Gippel dug out his cigarettes, pointed to the door, and stepped outside. Fahey was struck by how quiet the Castle had become. He slipped inside the Great Hall, taking the spot Gippel had occupied during the early numbers. Onstage, seated at the piano, was Chloe, accompanying her mother on "Piety," a soulful refrain about unconditional love.

A concept, Fahey knew, he must embrace or lose everything dear to him.

* * * *

Auditorium seats rolled out, banquet tables wheeled in, and tantalizing aromas wafted through the Great Hall. A full bar flanked a buffet of hot roast beef, baked ziti, and grilled salmon; bowls of Caesar salad and trays of cheeses; baskets of bread; and stands of cupcakes. Fahey estimated one hundred people remained of the winery, security and parking staff, in addition to the musical-event crew. All had worked hard for hours, before and after the concert, most without breaking for lunch, while he had stood around with nothing to do but observe.

He was used to observing, it was what a journalist did. Observing with no purpose was unsettling, though, and had stretched his last nerve taut. He needed to get out of this place. Tomorrow, he'd go for a run, with Chloe if she'd allow it, without her if she wouldn't. Off the premises, off to where the world revolved nicely on an axis tilted away from the de la Coeurs.

Fahey hadn't seen Chloe since she left the stage, never returning for the encore the crowd demanded of Teppan, Katarina, and the others; not emerging to acknowledge the congratulations Meredith heaped on them when the final tally was made and the checks written amounted to a windfall for the foundation.

Nor had Fahey sought Chloe out. For a while, he'd mingled with the BBC crew covering the show—what with the sex videos, and Teppan Nilsson's arrest and subsequent release, and now Zeke's suicide, Court of Cruelty was a hot topic again all over Europe. Outside the Castle, packing up for the night, journos were agog about the resurrection bit at the start of the concert; one repeatedly played the chant of "Long live Sebastian and Emilie!" that a sound tech had captured.

Being among the broadcast teams had merely reminded Fahey he'd rather be working just now; made him almost long for Brussels and the daily report of euro-versus-sterling-versus-dollar spreads.

Over at the bar, he noted Ronnie and Ed arguing whether to give the roadies more money because they'd had to haul the piano down from the music studio for Chloe's number then back up again. Genevieve sat nearby with a dish before her and a glass of red wine, pushing food around with a fork, as if she'd prefer to be anywhere but here. Like him. He took a plate from the stack at the far end of the buffet and made his way along, surprised to discover his appetite had returned.

"Jackson Fahey, your girl is fabulous, a fearless performer! I am totally in love with her!" Lars, the drummer wunderkind, yelled. "Watch me steal her heart from you. I'll do it."

"What would she want with a puppy like you?" Eric asked, reaching over the table to pat Lars on the head. "She clearly favors dark, brooding Irishmen over handsome blond Swedes, or else I'd steal her for myself."

Lars groaned, joined by Katarina, who wore a mock pout while contentedly bookended by Eric and Teppan, her lovers for all seasons. Fahey swore he felt Nilsson's eyes burn through his back and a challenge hang in the air.

"Yes, Chloe clearly prefers the dark Irishman who looks like her daddy," Teppan said. "Still, I got her to test-drive a Swede in Edinburgh. Ask her about it."

Fahey dropped his plate on the buffet, nearly upending a

chafing dish, and charged their table. "*Håll käften, Teppan!*" Katarina shouted, and dragged her husband away before Fahey could reach them.

"She told him to just shut his trap. He gets like that, always has to be the star. Best to ignore him." Eric handed Nilsson's untouched whisky glass to Fahey. "Drink, sit with us. They won't be back. Kat will tame the lion, and we'll be lucky to see them before noon."

Fahey tossed back the scotch, shook his head. "Thanks, but no thanks." Retrieved his plate, navigated to the chair Genevieve pulled out for him, and threw himself onto it.

"Eat and soak up some of that alcohol. Hunger makes men so stupid." Genevieve handed him a fork, pushed a bottle of water toward him on the blood-red tablecloth.

"Good of you to suggest I wasn't stupid enough already."

"That was good of me." She looked past Fahey to where Ronnie and Ed Chestack stood. "Must be on my best behavior, so Father Christmas will bring presents. Maybe this year I'll ask for a sports car, though where I'd park one in London would be a puzzle. Oh, I know, I'll ask for a sports car and a year's term in a garage. Ronnie can afford it, and he owes me for coming here with him. It's as if the man needs moral support suddenly."

Fahey swallowed a forkful of ziti, sipped some of the water. "Maybe he does. The terrain has shifted a lot this year."

She raised her wineglass to her lips, drained it. "I suppose, being here without Sebastian and Emilie and now without Zeke, with all the publicity. What Ronnie can't afford is to have the spotlight trained on his little side business. Wouldn't want someone to follow the evidentiary thread from those four dead women in the Czech Republic to his cronies in every ugly corner of Eastern Europe."

"You sound as if you care."

"Not in the slightest. I only came to see my mother. I've seen her, time to go. I'll be on a jet to Sydney tomorrow for a conference. I'm hoping for some beach time; I've packed my swimsuit. If the concierge can order up a handsome Aussie as well, I might stay through Christmas and into the New Year. Either way, it will be good to get away from Swedish men and their inflated egos, don't you agree?"

Oh, he certainly did. He needed to get far away from Teppan Nilsson, but first . . . "May I ask a personal question, Professor Hamilton?"

She twisted her wineglass, rolling the stem between her palms. "As if you ask any other kind, Jackson Fahey. Fill this and I'll ponder your request." She laughed as she watched him stroll to the bar, walk behind it to retrieve a bottle of Blood of the Bards' finest pinot noir, then return to her with it and a second glass.

Fahey refreshed hers, poured some wine for himself, settled into his chair, stretched his legs. "Now then, how did it start with Sebastian? You seem . . ."

"Smarter than that?"

"You seem to despise him, even now that he's gone. I wondered whether he'd forced you."

She ran a hand through her hair, the Great Hall's candlelight catching the random silver streak. "Not at all, Sebastian was a gentleman. I wanted him. I loved him the way only a fifteen-year-old can: unconditionally, unobjectively."

"You were awfully young."

"I was alone and in the middle of this weird bunch, brought along for a summer Peasants' Faire by a father I barely knew, a non-child amid the so-called adults. Sebastian spoke to me as if I were older, treated me as if I were a beautiful woman, told me stories about the mother I had never met and how like her I was, looked at my sketches and made me feel like an artist. He made me feel as if I belonged to his little family. I'd never felt loved by my aunt and uncle; the Hamiltons had adopted me, but I felt like baggage they carried around with them. Sebastian made me feel loved."

Fahey saw tears glisten. "Then he made you feel unloved?"

She reflected a moment. "So wonderful, that first flush of romance; so special. It's when you discover that it's no longer special, that you are no longer special—you can imagine how wounded I was. I knew I would never supplant Emilie, I even knew Sebastian had other women, but when I realized I was a pawn in his game with my father, his chess piece to manipulate Ronnie into a misstep, I knew I couldn't stay. I found my way back to Ireland, back to the Hamiltons' house, and told Ronnie I was done with the Cruel."

Genevieve drank her wine, held the glass out for more. "When I applied to art school in Dublin the following year, they asked me to name a party responsible for my tuition. I put down Sebastian's name and this address, and he paid the bill sent in the post. The next summer, I asked Ronnie to take me on tour with him again. I wanted to dare Sebastian to berate me about the money, but he never did. Even after I took up with Theo, even after Theo was killed and I publicly accused Sebastian of tampering with the motorcycle, he kept writing checks. When I finished university and got my first textiles position, he sent a check equaling the amount of my rent. I tore it up, and the next month's, and the next, until he eventually stopped sending them. But he never forgets, so I knew it wasn't over between us. It wasn't until Chloe showed up at Cambridge during my first year as a teacher that I knew exactly how he'd demand repayment."

She was slurring her words, and Fahey debated giving Genevieve more wine, kept his hand around the neck of the bottle but made no move to pour. She encircled his hand with hers and lifted the bottle over her glass.

"He demanded that I watch over Chloe; that I look for anything that might suggest she was becoming like him and Emilie, that I inform him where she was and what she was doing. I quite resented it, told him he couldn't compel me to care about his daughter, but I discovered I did care, as I came to know her. You see, we both understood how it felt to have family cast you off, and she was so brave, armed against the world with her new name and not much more. She looked so much like Sebastian, and she was smart and witty, as if she embodied all that was good in him. She became like a younger sister, and I wanted to be her friend."

"You didn't tell her you knew who she was."

She slowly shook her head. "Being Chloe's friend meant accepting her as she presented herself to the world." Genevieve got to her feet shakily; put her hand on Fahey's shoulder to steady herself. "Go find her, Jackson, and be her friend. Things are not so different for her now."

He looked up, the chandelier overhead blinding him long enough to obliterate the scene but not the sense of what Genevieve had said. He moved over to the buffet, made a platter of cheeses and bread and fruit, covered it with a napkin and carried it out of the Great Hall, around to the back staircase and up.

The door to their bedroom was ajar. Chloe stood at the window; beyond her, Fahey could see the stars. At the sound of his footsteps, she lowered her head, her smile reflected in the glass. "Cheddar and provolone and Italian bread, perfect. I'm hungry for a change, or I guess I should say Guinevere is. Thank you."

Fahey set the plate on the vanity table. The green velvet of her dress swirled around her as she stepped closer, then sat on the bench. She chose a chunk of white cheddar and breathed in its scent. "One of the few good reasons for being home: The winery's staff creates some of the finest artisanal cheeses in these parts."

"Sebastian and Emilie recognize the best, that's a rare skill. Today, it was clear how well Matins and Vespers flourishes under their tutelage. Lars is amazing; Eric switches instruments effortlessly now, stands in on whatever Teppan needs him to play. The band wasn't doing much more than showing up when I saw them in Barcelona in April. If that hadn't been a memorial concert, the crowd might have risen up with torches and pitchforks."

"Don't forget garlic, to ward off vampires."

He sat at her feet. "I'd like at least one vampire to stay. I want to spend my life with her, however long that turns out to be, or however short. I don't want to miss a minute of being with you, Juliette, but if I have to, I know you'll take care of yourself and Guinevere the best way possible. I love you as you are, and I hope I'm right, and you still love me too."

She stroked his hand, threaded her fingers through his. "You're an idiot if you think loving you is the issue. I'm different in a lot of ways, but none of them have to do with that."

"Then tell me about Edinburgh."

"You know what happened."

"I know the result of what happened."

"I allowed my body to finish a process that had been underway since the day I was born. The human me had to die physically in a body that was still alive, that's what caused the fever and the vomiting and the delirium you saw later in Brussels."

He wrapped his arms around her waist, kissed her stomach. "How did it happen, after all those years? What triggers something like that?"

"I had to want it, Jackson. I had to fight for it."

Chloe untangled herself from his embrace, enough to reach for another chunk of the cheddar and a slice of bread. She nibbled at both, distracted, but when she picked up a branch of white grapes, her eyes grew bright with tears. She plucked one and bit into it; its juice dripped over her lower lip, her tongue slipped out in time to catch it. Another grape, then another, she concentrated on the feel of them in her mouth.

"Grapes remind you of that night."

"I hadn't been alone with my father for more than a year, hadn't spent more than a few minutes at all with Teppan. We had more than three decades of history, yet it was like being with a stranger, someone with Sebastian's brain who wasn't

Sebastian, or at least not the Sebastian I knew. It was unnerving."

She bit into another grape, sucked on it, closing her eyes. "We quarreled from the time he arrived at the hotel, him in his new Teppan skin, me in my Barcelona disguise, the red wig and the thigh-high platform boots and the leather skirt. When we weren't arguing he was doing shtick, trying to convince the people in the bar and at the reception desk and everyone else we encountered that we were lovers, mostly because he knew I couldn't do anything about it, I couldn't very well turn around and say, 'Hey, I'm C.J. Hart, and this is my supposedly dead father.' "

Fahey had to move, anything to relieve the pressure inside his skull. He needed to give her a chance to breathe, as well. She was pale, as if she were reliving those moments the bar staff had described: Nilsson's hand on her behind, lips and tongue along her throat. Fahey stretched out face down before her and levered his torso up and away from the floor, down again, up again, lost in the push-up motions, counting, focusing on the numbers. After twenty-five repetitions, he sprang to his feet, pulled Chloe off the bench, pulled her close to his chest; nuzzled her neck, his breath hot against her skin, his body pressed against hers. *Remember this instead*, he wanted to shout, but didn't.

"He was aroused by me," she whispered, "or rather by me in the red wig because it reminded him of Emilie, that's what he said. He didn't hide it; he was just annoyed. I was embarrassed, mortified and fascinated at the same time. He ordered room service and sat there nibbling at grapes while I ate dinner, then announced he was going out to hunt. I wanted to go with him, and he basically said, 'Vampires, only, little girl.' He was goading me into making a choice, into deciding how much I wanted it."

Enough to do whatever brought her, half-dead, to Fahey's flat in Brussels. "You said you had to fight for it."

She looked away. “I had to prove myself to him, exert my power against his and come up the winner. My will to embrace my destiny had to be stronger than Teppan’s will.”

Teppan’s will for what?

Fahey led her to the bed, sat her down beside him, beat back the bile rising in his throat so he could reassure her . . . about what? That she could share as much or as little as she liked, and he’d never wonder whether she had shared it all?

“How?” was what he managed.

Chloe stared at her right hand, still clutching a grape. “I wrestled my father to his knees and made him beg, how else?” She crushed the fruit, its feeble juice spraying Fahey’s cheek. She licked away the sweetness, and her issues with her father, then sank her teeth into his skin.

“Show me how you love me, Jackson.” She stripped him, and he happily, desperately, demonstrated how.

He woke chilled, a cold that rousted him from a pleasant dream of her in his arms. He felt for her body and, finding her gone, patted her side of the bed, seeking the blanket.

The sheets were wet beneath his hand. Chloe’s blood, he somehow knew, not his.

*Chapter Seven*

# UPSTATE NEW YORK, DECEMBER 2011

Panic propels me away from Jackson and the fear I will see in his eyes, away from the bloodied sheets and the proof I am no fit vessel for his child. I race for the door through hidden passageways of the Castle, unseen by musicians and roadies and sound techs and their girlfriends who, accustomed to hours much later than this, are still partying in celebration of one hell of a show, man, or whatever the Swedish translation is. A half-dozen of them are glued to Eric's tablet. I slow down, stand in the shadows, hear myself singing. Lars pounds the table, waves his phone over his head, swaying to the sound of the soldier's anthem I turned into a daughter's dirge.

"We are all over YouTube, BBC, CNN, all showing Matins and Vespers, all showing our beautiful Chloe's song and Teppan and Katarina's magic act. We are famous, yes? Superstars, yes?"

"Poor musicians today, poor musicians tomorrow," Eric yells over his shoulder. "We are a kick-ass tribute band, yes, but still just playing in the shadow of Court of Cruelty, so get over yourself. Drink!" He tosses a bottle of vodka for Lars to catch. It slips through his waiting hands and smashes. Heads bob up, following the noise.

Someone hands Lars another bottle, and he clambers up onto the table. "To the lovely Chloe, whose lips I long to kiss, whose throat I want to stick my tongue down! I'd gladly face certain death by Fahey to do it! To Chloe!"

Only Eric hesitates. Matins and Vespers, he must realize by now, has no future unless Teppan and Kat decree it. This is a limited engagement, and, if they're lucky, he and the rest of the Goteborg boys will get what they need and move on. After a minute though, he, too, raises a plastic red cup, and they all drink to the fulfillment of Lars's amorous expectations—or at least I think so, it's just more Swedish to me.

I have no desire to be anyone's crush. Time to put on some speed while escape is still possible, before I am seen and again plastered all over social media. I can taste the intoxication here: who is amped-up on booze, who has shot heroin. I smell it on their breath, hear it in their blood as it rushes through their veins. I spent my childhood eavesdropping on these special brands of happy, spent a bit of my pre-adolescence following musicians and their friends through their after-gig highs. As I got older and more curious, I watched them couple off and get it on in these same corridors, sometimes doing a little coupling myself if a guy was especially cute and I was feeling especially vengeful. Even Emilie could keep me at boarding school only so many months of the year. During term breaks and summer vacations, my education took some very interesting turns.

Funny to be thinking of summers past now as I flee the house naked, trying to elude my woeful present, sprinting through freezing rain under a waning half-moon that would brighten the sky well enough for anyone to see me if they took the time to look. But the bailey and the grounds beyond are deserted, the night too frosty for outdoor frolic; all the fun is inside. Sex, drugs and rock-and-roll: best distractions ever.

I move through the grove of walnut trees farthest from the lakeside, past Gippel's metal hulks, toward the westernmost cluster of cottages, tree limbs as nude as I am blocking some of the moonlight. I reach Zeke's cottage, lift the Texas Longhorns welcome mat, retrieve the key, and let myself in. The simple floor plan was easy for five-year-old Clothilde to memorize; I find the bed without turning on a lamp. I pull back the covers and ease my body—dripping from the rain, my toes gritty from the mud, my inner thighs sticky from the blood—down next to the dog. Axel presses his black basset hound nose against my shoulder. I pull him close. There's no way to avoid getting his plush aqua fur wet, so why not cuddle my once-beloved toy?

"Axel lives here, he'll protect my house when I'm gone," Zeke promised the first time the Cruel left for a tour without me. "Somebody has to take care of him. Think you can do that, Clo?" I nodded, and he reminded me where to find the key, and I was comforted for a little while, knowing I had a job to do while Daddy Bastian and Mommy and Zeke and Stephano and Ronnie and the rest of my family loaded onto a tour bus and I stayed home with Gloria so I could go to full-day kindergarten. It was only for two weeks, until school was over for the summer. Then they would be back for me, and I would get to ride the tour bus again, too. The day they returned, Axel and Gloria and I met the bus at the gate and hugged everybody, and Sebastian got off and gave me a piggyback ride up the driveway to the Castle.

My stomach cramps. I feel for fresh blood, am relieved to find none. Maybe I'll manage to not lose this baby. Two prenatal visits, one here, one in London, have been my only brush with gynecology since boarding school, but even I know bleeding doesn't bode well during pregnancy. I reach for the blanket lying across the foot of the bed and pull it up over me. I'm cold, or rather Guinevere is. Eventually someone, probably Gloria, will figure out where I am. I want to be alone with my child in the meantime, here where I was good at being the protector and was all Axel needed.

Growing up, I always felt safe, so I took foolish chances. It was what my privileged classmates and I did. I lost my virginity at fourteen to an adorable grunge-band drummer named Adam, who bleached his hair to Kurt Cobain perfection. There was a brisk trade in fake IDs, so we could get into the bar where Adam played, and he slept with so many of us it's a wonder my pre-vampire self managed to avoid a sexually transmitted disease. I hoped I would get knocked up, just to piss off Emilie.

The summer I was fifteen, I slept with a college guy working at the vineyard. Juan Pablo was a rich kid from Caracas; his parents were old Venezuelan aristos, not nouveau-riche oil types, he boasted. He was studying electrical engineering at Cornell, but that season he toiled alongside the grape-picking migrants and acted as translator, shirtless more often than not, which my hanging around certainly encouraged. He liked the physical activity, he said, after having his head in the books. I let him get as physical as he wanted, let him put his head and anything else anywhere he wanted, hoping we'd get caught. We didn't, so disappointing. Back then, I wasn't happy unless I could stir up trouble. So mature.

The cottage's heat pump kicks on, and I immediately feel warmer. I peel Axel's ear away from my still-damp face, tuck him under my arm, and slip farther under the blankets. Screw maturity, here I am, hiding. All I want to do is sleep and be somebody's mother as long as I can. I will Guinevere to stay strong, to stay put where she is, I promise to take better care of her if only she'll give me more time. I drift off, praying she won't drift away.

After a while, I'm aware of a door opening, of a whoosh of cool air past my cheek. I ignore it, turn over, pull the bedding around my head. A gentle folk melody gradually nudges me awake, someone murmuring something vaguely Catalan, like the music that plays in Barcelona during the festivals. A ghost with Zeke's guitar.

"I used to play you lullabies, remember?"

Tears burn beneath my eyelids, threatening to spill over.

"Such a sweet child. Such a happy little one, grown more quickly than I could have imagined. It's hard to believe you're having a baby of your own."

Trying to. Trying very hard right this very minute to hold

onto the few ounces that comprise my daughter.

"I knew you'd be here when I heard Fahey tearing around the Castle, asking everyone if they'd seen you, and no one had. The key was still under the mat?"

I give up the pretense of sleeping. "Still under the mat."

"Zeke's things are still here. Guess he thought he'd be back for them eventually."

Maybe. Who can say what was in Zeke's head when he left in April, after writing to say he'd scattered my still-living parents' ashes? "He said he couldn't be here if you weren't. That meant one thing when I thought he believed you were dead. Quite another once I learned he didn't."

"Just like your mother, Clothilde, all worry and fuss. No wonder it's so easy for Gippel to rattle you and your boyfriend. You two just play into his hands."

Right, it's not a certain person's abominable behavior that has brought trouble here, not at all. "I've lied for you, don't forget. So has Jackson."

He moves closer through the darkness, choosing not to step out of the shadows. "He had no business holding onto that semen, no business having it in the first place."

"You were the one who decided to play sperm donor and hand it off to Meredith as a keepsake."

"Meredith liked what I gave her just fine. Liked what Fahey gave her, too, in exchange for it. Don't throw stones, Clothilde, unless you're also prepared to dodge a few."

No sense arguing. In a few hours, the investigators will pick up where they left off. Their machinery will roar back to life, digging and carrying off, ripping up the slopes along the lake and the roads. If he doesn't care about his precious feudal estate, why should I?

He examines perfectly shaped yet asymmetrical fingernails, shorter on his left hand than his right, differentiated for fingering a fret board or working the strings.

"It will make no difference, that machinery you're so preoccupied with. The police will find human remains in the lake, won't that be a surprise? Still, they won't get anything they can use—even a nineteenth-century relic like me knows there's no DNA to be found in crematory ashes. Well, none to speak of, they could find teeth, but without dental records—no cavities, no need—there's nothing in that water for them. This is all theater, sweetheart. Nothing more."

He pulls on a string, sends it twanging, then bangs on the back of the guitar. "Zeke shouldn't have pulled the trigger so quickly. This would have been done before he knew it, and we would have gone our merry way, as always. Such a waste."

Footsteps again, the sound of the guitar replaced in its stand. I open my eyes. A sliver of moonglow slips into the dark room, but I can't see my visitor, so my visitor can't see me, or so little Chloe would have believed here in her Uncle Zeke's cottage, safe and warm with her stuffed doggie. My game of keep-away ends abruptly with the incandescence of a bulb near the front door. I lift my head, squint at the shimmering figure standing between me and the light. He is magnetic, my father, attractive or repellent, depending on which pole of his personality is manifest.

"Leave me alone."

"Your fiancé is frantic to find you."

"If you found me, he will, too, soon enough. Until then, can't you just let me be?"

"I let you be for thirteen years."

"Not now, please. I may be having a miscarriage."

Moving closer, he scrutinizes me, focuses his heightened senses on me. "I can hear her heart beating. She's still in there." A sniff at the air. "You were bleeding, but not anymore."

"Yes, some blood, but not now. No clots, that's good, right?"

"I think so."

"Nothing to worry about then, just go and let me get some rest."

He laughs. "You think I'm leaving you with no one but a

stuffed dog to help if you start to bleed again? If you're staying here, I'm staying with you."

"Suit yourself." I pull Axel out from under the covers and growl at him.

My father smiles his Sebastian smile, the one I love, the one that's been buried under layers of jackass Teppan, and the tears prick at my eyes again. This time, I can't stop them.

"Don't make me cry, please. I've been on an emotional roller coaster for days now, don't stress me out more. I don't want to lose this baby."

He pulls up a chair, grabs the guitar again, tunes it, softly plays "Silent Night." I've left Benjamin to handle holiday business at Aspect Ratio—I trust we're doing some. Christmas is one week from today. My halls are not decked; my gifts, not purchased. I have to get back to London, with Guinevere, I hope, but if not, well . . . anywhere but here at the Castle, where I was so happy once, but am not anymore. So much will never be the same here, my happiness the least of it.

The carol completed, he stands, shirtless and shoeless, and switches on the nightstand's small lamp. Notices my now-illuminated shape under the blanket; looks around the cottage.

"Bold move, dear daughter, walking naked through a houseful of people then out into a rainy December night." He goes to the wall of closets that runs across from the kitchen and back to the bathroom. He fishes out something, tosses lumps of gray fabric onto the bed: a hooded Longhorns sweatshirt and a pair of sweatpants.

"Put these on. You don't want to get sick."

"*We* don't get sick."

"*We* don't get pregnant with human men's babies who might get sick. Put them on."

I lean over to pull the clothes toward me, but I misjudge. The blanket slides down, off my chest, and suddenly I'm topless in front of my father. He looks, then looks away, but I can hear his pounding heart, his ragged breathing.

"Damn it, Chloe, cover yourself."

I scuttle down and try to reach the sweats, but I can't, not without risking a repeat peep show. I tuck blanket and sheet under my armpits for now.

He turns back toward me, fangs visible for the merest second, and retrieves Zeke's guitar, plucks the opening notes of my song, "Cri de Coeur," our song really, my reinterpretation of his "Croix de Guerre."

"I like what you did with this. It's defiant, unyielding—a lot like you, my darling girl. Way to tell Julian Gippel where to shove it!" He slaps the bed triumphantly; the sweatshirt falls to the floor, totally out of reach. I pull the blanket closer, pretty sure there's no cause for celebration here, damn sure Gippel will go on with the dredging just because he can and has nothing to lose.

The good detective's prey mulls something, his handsome brow wrinkled in thought for several moments. " 'Cri de Coeur' was an odd choice for an opening number, but the benefit concert wasn't your typical show either. Next time, we'll put it later in the set, the penultimate song before we break, maybe rolling right into 'Croix de Guerre.' "

He's making plans for me to join the band, seeing visions of Matins and Vespers as the second coming of the Cruel. A delusion.

"Put the song anywhere you like, Daddy. I'll make sure Mom gets the lyrics in time for Matins and Vespers' next gig now that you're all famous, especially after that 'We're back, it's Sebastian and Emilie!' stunt. So amazingly believable. Just ask Lars, he'll be happy to find the video on YouTube for you."

He shakes his head, blond hair glowing in the low light. "The song only works because of you, the daughter of the realm."

"Then, sorry, the song will never work again."

"Oh, but it will, sweet child: your voice, your story."

He likes defiant and unyielding?

"Story's over, book's closed. I'm going back to London, to my life and my job and, I hope, to raise *my* daughter."

"Ooh, and marry the handsome newsman and live happily ever after! That will set more than a few girlish hearts aflutter across Europe. Can't wait for the hashtag." He stands at the foot of the bed and fixes the Sebastian stare on me.

"I came here for 'Christmas at the Castle' to help the foundation. How would it have looked if I missed the first benefit since Daddy's sad, sad death? Oh, and let's not forget the court hearing and that business with the lake—something to do with four dead women and their babies buried near your Czech manor house. Come Monday, though, I'll be on a plane, and unless someone shoves a subpoena at me, *hasta la vista.* I've spent years trying to keep my life private; I won't expose myself anymore just to satisfy your need for the spotlight. Go back to wherever the hell it is you call home these days. I'm done here and done with you."

Anger radiates off him and slaps my face. He leaps, fangs fully bared, eyes simmering red, and pounds on the bed, shakes it, somehow lifts it from the floor, lifting me off the mattress. The blanket slips away, exposing me in a vastly more uncomfortable way. His hands clench into fists, knuckles purpling from the tension, blood dripping as nails slice into flesh.

"You were always meant to be like us. You changed just at the right time. We look like contemporaries in age, the three of us. It's perfect."

No. No. No. "You and Mommy Dearest have lived, what, three or four lifetimes, and I don't even get to finish this one? Forget it. See you in forty years."

"Didn't you learn anything in Edinburgh?" He hisses. The cords in his neck tighten, animal fury surges through his chest and arms, and the beast unleashes itself from human bonds, its visage horrific. The primal vampire bursts like lava from inside him.

Every instinct tells me I should be terrified of this being with more than a century of accumulated vampire strength, yet I am oddly calm. I am the offspring of two vampires, not the creation of one. What if that hybrid yields a tougher me than he expects? What happens if I tap this raw emotion whipping through him?

I shift my center of gravity, rear back then hurtle forward, tilting the balance. The bed crashes to the floor. I raise myself onto my knees, my body now completely displayed. This time, he does not shift his gaze away. I suspect he cannot.

I have never felt more powerful.

"Did I learn anything in Edinburgh? So much, most especially that it's pathological, this need you have to control everything. I know of no other way to explain what you did to me that night. You wanted to see how far you could torture me, to see whether I'd break. 'Meet your inquisitor,' aren't those the words you sing?"

He looms over the bed, frozen there, eyes riveted on me, red as the blood he consumes. "Your future," he sneers, "was, indeed, in my hands. Don't you forget."

I move closer, thrust my breasts forward, all but into his face. "You might have compelled me to rob a bank of millions, or burn a building down. Instead, you attempted to compel me to have sex with you, my own father. What were you thinking?"

"I told you, I knew it would be the thing most repugnant to you."

"Considering the variety of vile acts you've perpetrated? Why not order me to kill someone, kill hundreds?"

"You had to resist, not just refuse."

I put my hands on his chest, as I did in that Edinburgh hotel room. His fevered skin burns beneath them. "My will against yours, wasn't that the point?"

He pries my fingers from his body, crushes them in his grip. His eyes shift from red to black to almost white, so hot is the rage flaming through them. "Triumphing over your ambivalence was the point. You had to choose your destiny. Where there is no choice, there is no test!"

"Where there is no doubt, there is no test! Unless you weren't sure of anything that night. Oh God, you weren't . . ."

He roars and pins my arms to my sides.

This is ugly, this game we're playing, this game Jackson now knows my father and I have played before. What he doesn't know, what I don't even know: Had it not been for Jackson, would I have been able to deliberately sacrifice the human me that night to become the vampire me? Would I have unwittingly sacrificed something else entirely to my father's will?

I rip my arms free of him. Catch him off guard and barrel against him, forcing him to stumble back several steps. He shrinks back to human form. His human face re-emerges.

"You had no idea what the outcome of your test would be, did you, you son of a bitch?"

"Damn it, Chloe, you resisted me."

"What if I hadn't? What if I'd gone over that edge, what would you have done? Tell me, I have to know."

He inhales deeply, turns away, unzips his jeans, lowers them over his bare behind, kicks them viciously aside. My heart hammers. I smell my own fear, where was it before?

I smell fear in him too. I watch his body tremble, watch his spine unfurl as his lungs suck in air, as he struggles to regain command of himself.

What have I done?

He turns back toward me, points to his penis, unerect, unaroused.

"Nothing!" he bellows. "I would have done absolutely nothing! Do you see? Are you satisfied?"

He pivots and stalks to the window, stares out into the almost-faded night; extends his arms to their full length and yanks at the drapes, the panels trapped in his fists snapping into position over the glass. "Wouldn't want all your lovely skin to burn, would we?"

I scramble off the bed, over the cold hardwood, tuck my head through the sweatshirt and pull it over me. I scoop up the sweatpants and pull them over my feet, up my legs and over my hips, tighten the drawstring as much as I can. I climb back into the bed, lie on my side in a fetal position facing the door, tug Axel close to me and wait for my father to calm down.

He shakes the curtains viciously, makes sure there are no gaps sunlight might penetrate. Picks up his jeans, picks up the guitar he dropped so disrespectfully. I want to pull the covers over my head, though there is no hiding anymore, not after every nerve has been stretched, every emotion flayed. What has happened has happened, what's been said has been said, there's no taking it back, not for either of us. I have my answer, but it feels like no answer at all.

The door opens, and cold air blasts inside. He stops at the threshold, silhouetted by the last of the moon's brightness, a cheetah about to spring, the muscles of his naked back and legs taut. When my father darts away from the cottage, for a fraction of a second I see Jackson, but he quickly vanishes, too, and I don't know whether I've seen him or imagined him.

If Jackson saw me, what must he imagine?

I run to the door, see my love running from me. I shout his name, I know he's heard me, but I feel him shut his mind to me, and he doesn't look back. The doorjamb is all that keeps me upright, and that only for the minute it takes Ronnie to catch me as I slump to the ground, my limbs no longer capable of supporting me.

"Let's get inside, girlie, it's freezing out here. Now try to stay with me, you'll be okay. Tell me what you need."

Blood seeps through the cotton at the crotch of Zeke's sweatpants; I am sticky, wet, woozy. Ronnie picks me up and carries me in to the bed, pulls his phone out of his pocket, hits a stored number.

"Call me, Kat. I'm taking Chloe to the hospital. She's bleeding, could be losing the baby."

Not a good idea, a hospital. "Take me to Sarah, the midwife who delivered me. My mother took me there when we learned I was pregnant. She'll figure it out."

His phone rings immediately, so no figuring will be required.

"She wants to go to someone named Sarah. I'll send Genevieve for her purse and some shoes then I'll drive her. You need to take care of things here. Himself, naturally, and find Fahey."

Ronnie ends his cryptic conversation, feels my head for fever, and gently bundles me up in a blanket. "Yeah, I know, I'm a proper bastard, but I'm all you got, Chloe, my girl. I'll get you to Sarah's in time, I promise."

In one of the vineyard's panel trucks, the better to move off the grounds without alerting either newshounds or cops, Ronnie pulls up to the cottage. He plunders the closets for whatever extra bedding he can find, and then we wait for Genevieve for what seems like forever, just me and the weapons dealer-slash-presumptive murderer of my father's paramours who now has become my rescuer. Phone in hand, he paces the room, checks his watch, a designer piece that must have set him back quite a lot of his blood money.

"We should go," he says at last. "I'll carry you into Sarah's when we get there. She'll know you, right?"

"We de la Coeurs are hard to forget."

A tight smile breaks on his lips. "Don't I know it? Let's get you wrapped up in the blankets, then, and pull up that hood. The sun is starting to rise, and I need you in the front seat to navigate. These bloody back-country roads don't all show on GPS."

Sleet grays the new morning's sky. The pre-noon sun doesn't know it's supposed to be shining, let alone slowly toasting my cells, but I do as he says. Ronnie carries me to the truck, texts Genevieve to come instead with my mother, pulls out onto the main road. We pass a van labeled New York State Police Forensics. No Sundays off for our pals, the dredgers and lake-water analysts.

"Sarah's place is off the highway northwest of Ithaca, about twenty-five minutes away." Just a house, nothing more sophisticated than stirrups and an ultrasound machine about as old as I am. Sarah is no prenatal wizard, just a woman about to treat the second vampire mom in these parts. Maybe anywhere.

He floors it, and we reach the interstate in six. "You gonna talk about what happened back there? I know what I saw. Lucky thing Fahey didn't."

Changing lanes, Ronnie glances quickly across me to check the mirror on the passenger side. "I'm walking from the Castle to my cottage and I hear Teppan roar in full-on vampire fury, not a sound you ever forget. I see a light on at Zeke's place at the far end of the row, which is odd since Zeke's dead, so I keep walking. Sure enough, facing the window, arms spread wide like a pair of bloody wings, prick raised like a spear, stands your dad without a stitch on. Behind him, kneeling on the bed in pretty much the same state, there you are. The drapes whip shut; a few minutes later, I hear the door open. Coming up on the other side of Zeke's cottage, standing directly in front of the door as Teppan walks out naked is Fahey. He sees you through the doorway."

A cramp spikes through me, followed by screaming—mine. Ronnie pulls over onto the shoulder, gives me his hand, tells me to squeeze until the spasm passes.

I try to breathe through the pain and my other misery. "Emilie was right to ship me away to boarding school, wasn't she? She had to get me away from Sebastian."

Ronnie leans back against the headrest. "Your mother's always right, except for her first mistake, choosing him. In the end, sending you off didn't change anything, did it? What your father wanted, he took, that's what he does."

"It's not what you think."

"Doesn't matter what I think, now does it? All that matters is what Fahey thinks, that's his baby you're hanging onto for dear life. The pregnancy thing generally ends badly for your dad, and now he's managed to screw it up for you, too. "

"Fuck you, Ronnie, for equating this baby Jackson and I created with Sebastian's videotaped rutting. It's not the same, not at all." I double over with another cramp and the stinging of the feeble sun's rays. "We have to go!"

He starts the engine, and an awkward silence settles between us. It follows us as we leave the highway for the route that leads to Sarah's door; persists as we pass her startled expression when she sees Ronnie carrying me. Stays with us in the back room Sarah uses for exams, where he leaves me to her care. I don't know what he believes; it's enough he knows what was all too possible.

Sarah strips the foul sweatpants off me, tosses them into a bucket of cold water, splashing my abdomen and legs. She washes the blood from my skin, pats me dry, switches on the ultrasound monitor, squeezes the cold gel over my skin, and moves the wand slowly across my stomach. Once, then again, then a third time.

The screen shows no movement, no sign of life. She turns off the monitor, presses down on my belly to feel for masses, reaches with gloved hands up between my legs for whatever has not already passed through. An agonizing cramp seizes me, crushing my insides as it's already crushed my hopes. Sarah clutches my hands, murmurs syllables meant to comfort the inconsolable, but I can't focus on her, I can't focus on the pain, my senses reel with the anticipation of the void, of the emptiness within that was filled for such a short while by a small spark of Jackson and me.

Finally, a reddish-black clot slides out and settles between my thighs. Baby Girl Hart-Fahey is no more. Sarah covers us with a sheet and leaves me to say goodbye to my daughter, whom I will love as long as I live, eternally.

A shaft of sunlight sneaks through the window blinds and lands on my midsection, but instead of burning, I feel warmth there. I feel her there still.

*Chapter Eight*

# UPSTATE NEW YORK, DECEMBER 2011

He wandered the grounds after leaving Zeke's cottage, walked through every part of the significant acreage that surrounded Castle de la Coeur. Depressed perhaps, he prowled from the mighty metal monsters stationed at the lake, to the dormant vines of red and white grapes at the farthest west point of the property, past the winery and its outbuildings and the main road, past the empty security guard's shed at the front gate. The terrain was shrouded by thick clouds that stalled the sunrise.

The east cottages, occupied mostly by members of Matins and Vespers' odd tribe, had quieted at last. He skirted the first house, where Eric was staying, with or without Katarina, depending evidently on her mood and her need to be alone with her memories of Zeke. Something drew him to the cottage at the far end of the row, the one closest to the garage and the Castle's fleet of Range Rovers and Italian sports cars. Meredith's white convertible sat mud-spattered in the driveway a few yards from the shiny red Bugatti, snug in its automotive shelter, though someone had left that door open. Had Meredith stayed at this cottage rather than drive back to Ithaca? He sniffed the air. A scent lingered, hers.

He knocked tentatively, then more assertively. She opened

the inner door, hair rather adorably matted on one side, glasses sitting crooked on her nose. She rubbed her right eye under the lens, maybe still groggy from whatever she'd taken to push the overwhelming exhaustion aside, too tired to sleep without a little chemical assistance.

"What time is it?" She sniffled as cold air stung her sinuses; shoved her hands into the front pockets of a hooded Cornell sweatshirt that fell to mid-thigh; shivered, shifting from one bare foot to the other.

"Seven maybe. A bit past dawn."

She yawned. "Chilly out here."

"I could use someone to talk to, if you don't mind. Sorry if I woke you."

"It's okay. I need to get up anyway." Meredith made no move to invite him inside, just stared through the glass outer door. "I need to plan a memorial or something for Zeke, and the police will be back and the news people and . . ." She dozed off mid-sentence. He rattled the door.

"May I come in, please?"

She jerked awake, unlatched the outer door and pushed it partly open, looked in the direction of the garage. He leaned in, whispered something in her ear. She squinted toward her car.

Standing next to it, leather jacket black against the white Mercedes, stood Fahey, watching, listening.

"Meredith?" Her eyes widened, and she turned toward the sound of her name. "May I come in?"

With one foot over the threshold, Teppan Nilsson, six feet, three inches of unclothed male, waited for a welcome. She blinked, as if finally realizing who he was, and nodded, clearing the doorway so he could enter. He stroked her cheek, pressed her hand against his heart, his mouth against her neck, where he lingered for several moments. A drop of her blood fell from his lower lip as he raised his head to glare at Fahey.

Who saw it for the dare it was: Nilsson had thrown down

the glove, challenging him to interfere, presuming he wouldn't. Fahey had no claim on Meredith, no right to argue with her decision, even if he wanted to smash his fist through Nilsson's jaw.

*"I can have her, just as I've always had her. They're mine: Meredith and Chloe."* Fahey heard the taunts in his head.

"Meredith . . ." Fahey stopped himself. What could he say? *It's him. It's Sebastian. He wants to prove a point and will use you to do it.*

Eyes bliss-hazed, she glanced at Fahey. Nilsson kissed her, blocking her view; reached under her sweatshirt, lifted her, wrapped her legs around his waist and kicked the inner door shut.

Fahey knew Nilsson wouldn't harm Meredith; rationalized this was one way to keep him away from Chloe. He was certain he had been spotted the minute Nilsson emerged from Zeke's cottage with a raw, angry erection. Followed him anyway. Should have anticipated Nilsson's twisted calculation that Meredith was the shortest distance both to sexual gratification and antagonizing him.

Advantage, Nilsson, for now.

Fahey wanted him dead, now.

Since that wasn't likely without supernatural intervention, Fahey would chart an alternate course: putting Nilsson in prison again, in protective custody, of course, for as long as it would take to blood-starve the bastard. He eyeballed the lock on the key box on the garage wall, easily picked it, and easily picked out the key he wanted. He started the Bugatti's engine, revved it and let it warm, pulled out his mobile and Julian Gippel's business card.

"Breakfast in thirty minutes, at the diner on the highway. Make it so, Detective. *Macht schnell.*"

"Go to the devil," a drowsy Gippel replied. Backing out of the garage, Fahey was reasonably sure he'd just left the devil's own spawn with Meredith. If there wasn't a separate circle of hell just for Teppan Nilsson, also despised as Sebastian de la

Coeur, Satan wasn't all his advance billing made him out to be.

Icy roads between the Castle's main gate and the highway were treacherous, negotiating them in a vintage sports car difficult, and when Fahey finally entered the diner's lot and switched off the motor, he let out breath he didn't know he'd been holding. He'd arrived ahead of Gippel, which gave him time to check the BBC news feed for signs their talk last night had yielded results. Fahey had just found the report about "Christmas at the Castle" when a text flashed: "*Call now. Amanda.*"

Much as he missed working for her, much as he liked and admired her, these days Amanda's texts meant bad news. He called Madrid anyway.

"I see yesterday was quite the day for you, Jackson."

He checked the time, scanned the parking lot. "I'm waiting for someone, Mandy. I may have to ring off soon."

"Looked at Twitter today? YouTube?"

Who'd had time to connect to the inevitable video of Chloe's debut performance, of Katarina and Teppan Nilsson as their Emilie and Sebastian selves, of the band's rousing reception? "Been a bit busy, lots happening here. Anyway, I have a good idea what I'd see."

"Do you really? So you meant to punch someone in full view of scores of concertgoers yesterday, not to mention the news crews swarming Castle de la Coeur? You've gone viral, you and your fisticuffs with Will Baumann, Edinburgh brewmaster. CNN interviewed him, found out he's got something going with your girl Chloe, and now that interview is linked to every video from the concert and to the fight video, and the bugger's been tweeted and retweeted all over the globe. Word is, you'll be getting a call within the hour summoning you to BBC headquarters. You'll be lucky to have a job when they're done with you, this is a flagrant violation."

His superiors will have had enough, finally, of his involvement with the de la Coeurs. Only surprise was that he'd been allowed to stay on this long. "I may not be able to get back tomorrow. Chloe may be miscarrying the baby."

"Don't give them one more reason to dismiss you, Jackson. Best case is they'll suspend you while they assess your future value to the corporation. I'm sorry about Chloe and the baby, but you'd best get yourself to London."

Amanda was right. He'd put off talking to Chloe long enough today, now he had to see how she was, how they were, and tie up loose ends before he had to leave.

"Sorry to be such a disappointment."

She sighed loudly, her frustration clear. "I've been keeping your job open. Yes, they wanted a post to stay dark in southern Europe so they could make budget, but they also knew I wanted to give you the option of returning."

A taxi deposited Gippel at the diner's entrance. Fahey ended the call, climbed out of the Bugatti, and walked toward the restaurant. Too late to turn back, in so many ways.

He rushed to the door as it closed behind Gippel, followed as a hostess led them to a booth alongside the window, asked whether they wanted coffee. He certainly needed it. Gippel looked only slightly less sleep-deprived.

"It's difficult to talk at the Castle. Too many ears. Too many unknown loyalties."

"To Teppan Nilsson? Why would that be?"

A waitress appeared, poured coffee from a steaming carafe. Fahey said they needed some time before ordering; she flounced away, no doubt already figuring them for a wasted effort and a minuscule tip. "I think you can well imagine why, Detective. You wouldn't be here if you couldn't."

Gippel sipped at his black coffee, fingers twitching on the table, no doubt in need of another morning cigarette or three. "I received a call from the Metropolitan Police in London, who'd had a call from Anthony Kirkpatrick's attorney. Kirkpatrick saw video of the benefit concert, said he recognized Teppan Nilsson's voice as that of the man who coerced him into killing

Esteban Gronlund. They were dubious, of course, but Kirkpatrick's attorney was most persistent. The authorities here will soon have a warrant to compel Nilsson's participation in a conference call with British law enforcement."

Fahey applauded; heads turned their way. "If it lands Nilsson behind bars for a more extended stay, I'll be happy. Man needs to be put away."

"A more formidable adversary, perhaps, than William Baumann proved to be?"

Did Gippel miss nothing? "I will very likely be dismissed by the BBC because of that unfortunate meeting."

"Baumann is but a minor irritant, no? Teppan Nilsson would seem to have the greater sway over Miss Hart."

"I'd watch what you say about my fiancée, Detective."

"Nilsson unnerves her, as an extortionist might."

What did he mean by that? Fahey drained his coffee cup, glared over the rim. "She's told you everything, I'm certain."

Gippel met that glare. "She has answered my questions, yes, yet there is something Miss Hart does not discuss. Something you also do not discuss, though it hangs over this conversation. Perhaps, Mr. Fahey, unburdening yourself would help advance the cause we both support."

He could tell Gippel, but not tell him. Reveal, but not reveal all.

"Since Edinburgh, there has been a bond between them," Fahey began. "Last I saw Chloe, she had just been with Nilsson. Last I saw Nilsson, he was wandering the Castle grounds like a nude madman, in a considerable upset and with a considerable erection. I can only speculate on their causes."

The waitress reappeared, refilled their cups, tossed some creamers onto the table. Gippel sneezed and drew a handkerchief from his pocket, apologized for his misbehaving sinuses; cocked his head as if to refocus his thoughts.

"Emotion—passion, greed, fear—provokes humans to act. Nilsson evokes in Miss Hart something else, an odd loyalty.

She freely ascribes to herself unflattering behavior to avoid discussing his."

Fahey nodded, and might have done more had his phone not vibrated on the table. A text: *"Guinevere's gone."*

He jumped from the booth, threw down a ten-dollar bill. "Chloe has just lost our baby."

* * * *

Slush clung to the Bugatti's tires. Fahey fought for traction on unfamiliar roads while calling Chloe's phone. Genevieve answered: Chloe was resting, she said, the bleeding had stopped.

She waited for some response. Got none. "You heartless bastard, you're relieved. Go to hell, Jackson Fahey!"

It was true, he was appalled to admit, he was relieved. No more doubts about who his daughter might become. No fears about the kind of fatherly challenges that might present.

No worries at all if one considered as an option skidding off the road and smashing into a hillside to avoid the call now coming in on a London number he recognized as the BBC's office for European news operations. He cut off a motorist in the right lane and slowed the car, wary of how his career, like the rest of his life, might be about to crash and burn.

"We expect you at nine o'clock GMT Tuesday morning; you're booked on a noon flight tomorrow into Heathrow, we'll text details." The executive director's executive assistant put enough steel into her words to assure Fahey it was show up, or else. "This will be a formal disciplinary hearing, with the panel consisting of your superiors here in London and your bureau chief in Brussels conferenced in. You should familiarize yourself with the ethical or moral standards at issue and be aware of the range of consequences."

"Has the union been notified, or must I try to reach my representative from here?" he asked, congratulating himself for a—for him, for now—rare moment of pragmatic clarity.

"Notified already, all you need do is arrive at the appointed hour." How nice to have one aspect of his life so neatly tied up and beribboned.

Almost missing his turn, Fahey snapped the car quickly to the right, lurched off the road onto the side street Genevieve had texted, hoped he hadn't wrecked the suspension as he climbed a mound of ice plowed near the mouth of the driveway at the address she'd given. Cut the engine, slumped against the steering wheel, gulped in oxygen, tried to steady his breathing. Saw blinking lights when he closed his eyes, prayed for unconsciousness.

Heard the passenger door open. Felt Kat's arrival more than witnessed it. He lifted his head, hoped he looked better than he felt, less like shit scraped from someone's muddy boot. "How is she?"

"Asleep, or pretending to be, to prevent our fussing over her. She needs you, not me or Genevieve, but I'm sensing a certain unavailability here. Do explain that to me, Jackson."

*Careful. This woman could snap your spine in a heartbeat if she chose to.*

But as Kat waited in the seat next to him, swathed from the morning sun in scarf and sunglasses like Greta Garbo, he felt unthreatened, reckless fool that he was, and willing to risk the very little bit of himself he had left.

"You know, Genevieve described Emilie to me as amoral, as being—how did she put it?—willing to let Sebastian's evil wash over her and do nothing. Everyone else, or rather all the men—Zeke, Ronnie, Ed, even your husband—portray you as the strong one, the wise one, but I think Gen had it right. You allow that man to lay your family to waste, lay your daughter to waste and now mine, and you just stand by and watch."

Through the sunglasses, he saw her eyes burn green behind pale-blue contact lenses, then flare red. He felt the rage that filled the diminutive shell that was Katarina Nilsson, yet still calculated his odds against her.

"Do not mistake the size of this body for a measure of my

force, or you will rue the day you did. I have made my husband weep blood with a clench of my hand around his throat, taken him down, and made him beg."

Fahey unfolded himself from the sports car, walked around it, looked toward the midwife's house; saw Genevieve standing at a window, witness or guardian, he couldn't say. He exposed the Bugatti's passenger seat to the brisk air and pale sunlight with a quick, smooth pull. He invited Kat's exit with a courtly sweep of his arm, to all appearances having a civil chat. Civil war was more like it.

He bent toward her, whispered: "You created him. You're responsible for the monster he's become. End him, or watch him desiccate in a prison cell. I've set it in motion, with help from the good Detective Gippel. I'm surprised you haven't already heard from Teppan's attorney."

She remained within the car's meager shelter, seeming to assess how best to crush him without been seen from the house. "What exactly do you think you've achieved?"

He crouched, eye to vicious eye with her. "The London police intend to reopen their investigation of Esteban Gronlund's murder. Seems Anthony Kirkpatrick, who previously couldn't say why he might have ripped Gronlund's voice box out, now has recognized Teppan from the online videos. Heard in Teppan's voice that of the man who ordered him to slash Gronlund's throat. Saw in Teppan's body the man who sexually assaulted him and compelled him to carry out that bloody crime."

Fahey gave her a minute to digest what that could mean. Kat lowered her sunglasses, giving him full access to the restrained black fury gleaming from her eyes.

"If you succeed in this," she hissed, "if Teppan dies behind bars because of you, Chloe will never forgive you. Whatever she thinks of her father's recent behavior, she loves him. Destroy him, and she will hate you."

Quite likely true, and Fahey was prepared to accept it. Chloe would be one more thing lost to him.

His phone vibrated in his back pocket. A text: *"Teppan's left."*

*"Do not shower,"* he texted back. *"On my way."*

He pulled Kat from the seat and onto the driveway, catching her off guard. He was out of reach and back behind the wheel in four long strides.

"I've been summoned back to London tomorrow to face possible loss of my job. I have matters to attend to before I go. See Chloe back to the Castle, will you?"

"Shall I tell her you love her while I relay your lies?"

"Tell her anything you like," he yelled through the still-open passenger door. "Chloe trusts me. Does she trust you?"

He revved the Bugatti's motor, made a three-point turn, stretched to pull the passenger door shut, and tore out of the driveway, hoping that before this day was done he'd manage to destroy Sebastian de la Coeur's little toy car in addition to the man himself.

Meredith was waiting at the cottage door, tapping the watch on her wrist as he parked in the garage, hung the key on the hook in the metal box outside. He swept past her, preceded her inside.

"Tell me you haven't washed."

"I'm due up at the Castle. Ed's already ragging me for not being at the dredge site to monitor things. I have to bathe, you know."

He steered her toward the bed, sat her down on it. "Did you have sex with Teppan Nilsson?"

"Excuse me?"

"He was primed and ready for action before he got here."

"Oh, and I happened to be the most conveniently situated woman? Thanks a bunch, buster, you can leave now."

Meredith stormed toward the bathroom. Fahey caught up quickly, spun her around. "That's not what I meant. He was wandering the grounds until he found you. You were the one he was looking for."

She sniffed back hurt feelings. “He’s been hanging around me since they arrived, chatting me up, touching me. All of part of his Sebastian-wannabe act, I’m sure, and then there he was this morning. I didn’t see you trying to interfere, not that it was any of your business. What were you doing here anyway?”

“I followed him,” Fahey said, truthfully enough. “He was hard to miss.” Truthfully, too, Fahey had been happy to have her distract Nilsson, though to what end he’d only recently realized. “You did enjoy yourself, didn’t you? Maybe several times? Teppan was here, what, two hours?”

She blushed, cheeks pink against her blondness, against the white and red sweatshirt she still—or again—wore. “Best sex ever with a man I don’t like. Liking is usually a requirement.”

Yeah, he knew.

“Actually,” she sighed, “maybe the best sex, period, but I don’t want to think about that now. I love Benjamin, and I feel so unworthy of him. This just makes it worse. I’m a walking self-fulfilling prophecy. ”

Fahey put his arm around her, felt wetness under his fingers, saw blood seeping into the hood at the back of her neck, and wanted to wring Nilsson’s.

“You are very worthy of Ben, don’t you dare think otherwise. Now, I need you to help me. There were no condoms today, right?”

“What?”

“I need you to clean yourself with a paper towel or something like that, get up every drop Nilsson left behind if you can, and put the towel in a plastic bag for me. It’s important.”

“Semen, again? You’re joking, right?” Meredith laughed uncomfortably. “What’s so important about Teppan’s?”

She needed to know some of the truth Nilsson had kept her from seeing.

“He gamed the DNA tests in Sweden, I’m sure of it. I think he really did kill those women, or arranged to have them killed. At any rate, the police are about to arrest him again, on suspicion he provoked Esteban Gronlund's murder. Anton Kirkpatrick says he recognized Nilsson's voice from concert videos, recognized from the Lethal Lover videos the size and shape of the man he encountered right before he cut Esteban's throat. The semen from today would be an insurance policy, something to compare against any future DNA samples Teppan provides."

She doubled back to the cottage's tiny kitchen, grabbed several napkins from the counter, searched the cabinets for a bag. Found one, raised it over her head and waved it at Fahey. "No way this will be admissible in court."

"Just insurance, Meredith. Gippel already suspects Nilsson cheated the system. We'll just help him confirm it."

"Come when I call you." She turned toward the bathroom again, but stopped at the doorway. "The whole time he and I were doing it, I barely knew it was Teppan I was with, Jackson. It was so out of the body, so bizarre."

Was she talking herself out of helping him? "Someday, when this is all over, you can tell Benjamin, and he'll understand why you did what you did."

A puzzled frown crossed her face. "I swear," she said, "if you told me right now, while I can still feel him on me, that it wasn't Teppan I'd just been with but Sebastian, I'd believe you. It's like Teppan has studied Sebastian, not just his music, but his demeanor, the way he carried his body, the inflections when he spoke, the things he found funny, the way he hummed sometimes during sex, tiny things. Teppan believes he is Sebastian, I think. Am I crazy?"

A rhetorical question. Meredith went into the bathroom and closed the door. Leaving Fahey to ponder the boundaries of crazy, how far beyond them he'd already strayed in one day, and how much farther he was willing to go.

* * * *

The weather wanted to break in favor of the dredging beasts. The sun wanted to brighten their way through the clear water of the lake to the murky bottom, where human remains that would prove of no use to anyone would eventually be found. Fahey craved the sun's warmth, felt as if the cold and damp had settled into his bones and replaced the marrow at their core. He was a mess: His boots were, if not ruined, in need of rehab, just like his career. He'd need to have his jacket dry-cleaned, to rid it of the spattered mud and road salt, and he smelled of the madness of the last twenty-four hours, of jealousy and rage and disappointment and duplicity and deep, deep regret. He wore the stench of his sorry life like a protective armor.

These were his final hours at Castle de la Coeur and, disregarding issues of grooming and emotional exhaustion, he felt oddly exhilarated, sustained by the anger and adrenaline coursing through him. He spotted Gippel standing on a small hill, amid a group of what looked like civil-engineering types, with state troopers stoically on watch along the perimeter of the lake. The media crews had not yet returned. Without their scrutiny, he could approach his unwitting partner, the enemy of his enemy, or however Sun Tzu and other masters of strategy might label him.

Gippel approached first, though. "I did not express my sympathy earlier, Mr. Fahey. I am sorry for the loss of your child."

A reminder why he must do this. "It was a difficult pregnancy, made more so by the stress of the murders, the sex videos, and Zeke Segal's death."

"Miss Hart, she recovers?"

"I've not seen her yet, she was sleeping, and some friends agreed to bring her back from the midwife's."

"She should be your priority."

"She is. All of this is for her." Fahey pulled the plastic bag from his pocket, handed it to Gippel.

"A paper *serviette*?"

"One coated with Teppan Nilsson's semen."

Was it possible for Gippel's eyebrows to arch higher? Fahey doubted it.

“Chain of custody has not been established. I cannot verify this came from Nilsson, nor, I assume, can you.”

“Meredith Grainger-Todd can, she spent the last two hours in bed with him. Her fingerprints will be on the bag; mine will not.” Fahey wagged gloved digits at Gippel. “I saw her invite Nilsson into her cottage earlier; she and Nilsson both knew I had seen them, and she contacted me immediately after he left. I doubt he’d try to deny he’d been there; he doesn’t seem to be shy about discussing his conquests.”

Fahey let that settle in for a moment. “If today goes as planned and Nilsson surrenders to the London police, they’ll get another DNA sample, but there’s no guarantee he won’t play you again. Test this privately. Compare the results against everything you have in your case file on the deaths of Anya Morina and Viktoria Tolaj and the other women. Test it against their dead babies. Test it to prove to yourself that your instincts are right, but test it, so there can be no further doubt. Once you know the answer, Detective, the correct questions will be clear. ”

He started back down the hill, toward the Castle. Gippel followed, stopping to light a cigarette before closing the gap between them. “What if I choose not to pursue your prey for you?”

“Then I’ve done all I can. As a journalist, my objectivity is compromised here. I’m too close to the de la Coeurs, and I’ve embarrassed my employer by getting into that fight with Will Baumann. I knew better, but still I threw that punch.”

Gippel extended his gloved right hand. “I apologize for my part in your disagreement with Baumann. I was, perhaps, needlessly provocative.”

Fahey shrugged, shook the hand, kicked a lump of black snow down the path. “Provoked, unprovoked, it doesn’t matter. Day after tomorrow, I pay my professional piper.”

He stepped around a puddle whose muddy grime he could see but whose depth he could not discern, like most things on this estate. The Castle rose on the ridge straight ahead, shimmering silver and gray-blue as its stone walls reflected the morning mist burning off at last. It was how he hoped to remember the place: iridescent and beautiful, despite the depravity within. Then again, who was he to decry depravity, his own moral compass being something less than always true?

He walked through the delivery entrance behind the kitchen; saw Genevieve speaking to Ronnie, surmised she and Kat had just returned with Chloe. He ducked out of sight and up the back stairs. He couldn't avoid Chloe any longer; didn't, in fact, want to. Didn't, in fact, know at all what to say, how to dance around the issues of what he'd seen and what they'd lost.

The setting of their pendant-induced dream was empty. From the doorway, he heard the shower turn on in the bathroom down the hall, next to her bedroom. He tried the door. It was unlocked.

Her back was to him, her lovely naked back visible still as the steam rose around her, the water splashing hot against the glass separating them. Moisture silhouetted her as she scrubbed the skin on her thighs, scrubbed her pubic area, harsh motions that seemed propitiatory, as if in stripping the flesh from her body she could atone for some sin.

Was there enough water for him too, to cleanse his soul?

Fahey stepped out of his rank clothes, stepped in behind her, felt the scalding spray lash his spine. She reached up to moderate the temperature, turned toward him, tears of blood traversing her face, tearing at his heart. He folded her into his arms, clung to her; shed his own tears into her hair, weeping as he'd never wept before.

He sank to his knees, anointed her body with kisses, caressed the slight rounding of the stomach that had sheltered their baby, washed her with his tongue, seeking the small, warm pathway between her legs, gripping her bottom, pinning her to his mouth, worshiping the place they had created life as she writhed against him, shattered against him, shuddered then pulled away. She slid down along the length of him and straddled him, sank onto him and into him and slipped between him and his grief.

Locked together they remained, until the water ran cold over them. He closed the taps, kept her lashed to his midsection; stretched an arm outside the shower stall, seized the bath sheet hanging on a nearby hook, swaddled them both. Swept her into his arms and carried her to their bed; set her down, clasped her dripping body to his, soaking up her warmth, absorbing her guilt, her shame, hoping to shed some of his own as he did.

Tucked into his side, head above his left pectoral, she drove her teeth into him, nourished herself on what he remembered of the good that resided in him. When she finished, he flipped her onto her back, flung a long leg over her; kissed her until he thought he'd used his last breath. She abraded her lips against his two-day growth of beard, nipped at the tender skin of his neck; ran her hands through the dark curls dancing below his ears, locked her fingers through them and lowered his mouth to her breast; invited him to bite and suckle his fill. Because he had to, because he felt empty and she felt empty, he moved inside her and filled her with all that was alive in him and replenished himself, knowing that he needed her more than oxygen, and that a slow suffocation might await.

How he would live without his Juliette, he didn't know, though he knew he must. Because he couldn't, despite his earlier bravado, bear the thought that she would hate him for entrapping her father. Better to leave her love than, ultimately, have her take it from him.

They dozed, wrapped in each other, her softness curved around his hardness. When he rose again within her, she rode him, left him drunk with pleasure, re-addicted to the feel of her affixed to him, fused by the fire and flame that built between them and never fully extinguished. When he rolled her onto her back and forged the bond between them yet again, she twined her legs around him, let him take her by her heels as she took him to the hilt, until not an atom of one existed apart from the other, until they were all melded flesh and synchronous motion and complementary desires sated but never wholly satisfied.

Hours later, Fahey opened his eyes, conscious of the world again, surprised to find her still with him, as she almost never was. Peaceful as she almost never was; part of him still, but not for long. He eased away from her back, settled her outside his embrace, covered her with a sheet, pressed a kiss to her forehead.

Chloe was good at keeping her distance, hiding her hurts, swallowing her tears, skills Fahey had never mastered. Hard heart, hard nose were attributes that, for his own preservation, maybe hers too, he needed right now. Still, he couldn't find it in him to leave so coldly, couldn't bear the possibility that she might misinterpret. Not after what she'd already been through today, not with so much unresolved between them. He wanted her somehow to understand what he had done, what he was doing.

So he brushed his lips across hers, stroked her cheek lightly, whispered that he loved her, which he did, too much. Gathered his belongings and slipped out of the room before she woke.

*Chapter Nine*

# UPSTATE NEW YORK, DECEMBER 2011

No point in stirring. No point in letting him see what I see: his detaching from me as surely as our baby came apart from my uterus.

He has left our bed, but is near; I feel his heart thrumming wildly. He is anxious, apprehensive. In place of the carefree, happy man I met on an airplane over Barcelona now stands someone too much like me: unsmiling, weighted with remorse. I have cost him his bright beauty, his reputation, quite possibly his career, if what my mother has told me is true.

"Save yourself, Jackson," I whisper, but I do not tap the blood bond between us. I'm the last thing he needs in his head.

Shaving things are strewn around our room; boxer briefs and some socks sit in an otherwise empty suitcase. His backpack is missing. Laundry and laptop require his attention; he'll be leaving for the airport very early tomorrow, so the mundane things take precedence tonight. We haven't talked about the events of this morning and their distinctly unique horrors. It's possible we won't, our communication being of a more body- than word-based variety on our good days. This has not been one of our best, imbued with a vaguely valedictory quality. Goodbye. The future starts now.

Next to the bed, my phone rings. He's attached it to his charger, sweet man.

"I'm outside the room, may I come in?" Meredith asks. "When I saw Jackson heading down to the Dungeon with his dirty underwear, I figured you might be awake."

"Awake, though not dressed." Wrapped in the bath sheet, I let her in.

She gathers me into a hug. "I'm so sorry. I know how much this baby meant to both of you."

She doesn't know the half of it.

"I hate to ask, but I need you downstairs, C.J., the district attorney and the state police will be here any minute. The Skype connection's all ready."

My blank expression betrays me. I have no idea what she's talking about.

"The authorities want Teppan Nilsson back in Britain in connection with Esteban's murder, didn't Jackson tell you? No, of course he didn't, so much has happened. Ed insists you be present for this call, since the Castle belongs to you and they may want to search the interior and other parts of the grounds."

I don't understand. "This is about Esteban?"

"The Metropolitan Police in London texted a warrant for Teppan's arrest to the state police here. They want him to surrender officially tomorrow, after arranging local legal counsel—Ed's filling in tonight. This call is sort of an extradition proceeding, conferencing in the prosecutor and someone from Scotland Yard and a judge and Teppan's lawyer in Stockholm, who really isn't happy to be doing this at something like midnight. No one, of course, is more pissed off than Ed. Teppan's acting like it's no big deal."

"Jackson knew about this?"

Meredith blinks twice quickly. She's hiding something. "He talked to Detective Gippel earlier, I think. Anyway, we have about fifteen minutes before this thing gets underway; Ed's rounding up Teppan and Kat now. Maybe splash some water on your face, wake yourself up a bit before you come downstairs? We're ready to go in the Great Hall, the banquet tables and chairs were still there."

Splashing won't substitute for information, but I follow her out to the hallway. Meredith turns right, toward the stairs; I go left, toward the bathroom, stopping to find some clothes. I wash up, throw on black yoga pants and a long black turtleneck, stick my feet into black flats, black being the color of the day, most appropriate to the wary exhaustion, and exhausted wariness, I feel.

I descend to discover the Great Hall bustling. They've allowed the media in because this is a court proceeding and, as such, a public event. I scan the room for Jackson, spot him talking to a BBC reporter I recognize from newscasts but whose name I can't remember. Shoptalk, I hope, a chance to catch up with a friend rather than speculate about the fate of his career.

Filing in along the opposite wall are various members of our strange, dysfunctional family: Gloria, pale, distraught, looking old in a way I hadn't noticed these last few days; Ronnie, standing smugly between her and Genevieve; Eric and Lars, the contingent from Sweden, or at least its core, watching, looking worried about the future of their own livelihood. Sayid and several other Castle staffers take up posts at the perimeter, as does with the woman who runs the direct-mail operation for Vineyard de la Coeur, here after hours on the Sunday before Christmas processing holiday orders, I suppose.

Some of them stop and ask how I'm feeling, offer their sympathies about the miscarriage. The hall buzzes with anticipation that Teppan will again own the stage.

The Tompkins County district attorney introduces the local magistrate, who calls the proceeding to order and asks Teppan and Ed and Teppan's Stockholm lawyer/former prison blood supply to identify themselves. Teppan's voice is cold and flat, emphatically Swedish-sounding, hissing the S's in Nilsson, staring bullets in Jackson's direction as he does. Meredith appears at my side, and we stand a few feet away from a video guy Ed and the prosecutor have engaged to stand in as court stenographer.

After tending to some administrative matters relating to this unconventional assembly, the magistrate intones the case against my father, obviously reading from a script the British authorities have prepared:

"Teppan Nilsson, you are charged today as a participant in the death of Esteban Gronlund in the early morning of Thursday, 16 June 2011, in the Borough of Kensington and Chelsea, Metropolitan Police District of London, willfully provoking one Anthony Kirkpatrick to carry out the killing on your behalf. Further, Teppan Nilsson, you are charged with raping Anthony Kirkpatrick in the early morning of 16 June 2011, and, by such sexual coercion, provoking him to carry out the killing of Esteban Gronlund on your behalf."

Rape? Sexual coercion? I focus on Teppan's face, try to force his attention onto mine, if only momentarily. He fights me off, growls, *"Leave it, little girl,"* in my head, shuts down further attempts on my part to communicate surreptitiously. I glance at my mother, standing behind him. She stares ahead, her face impassive, her thoughts impossible to read.

"Teppan Nilsson, you are hereby ordered to surrender to the custody of the Metropolitan Police no later than midnight GMT Tuesday, and to submit to a DNA swab test immediately, to be administered by New York State Police officers present here. Do you understand the charges, Mr. Nilsson?"

Meredith grips my hand so tightly I marvel that her fingers don't snap from the strain. She looks directly at Teppan, then pivots and stares at Jackson. He nods, almost imperceptibly, but I see it. What's going on?

Teppan rattles something off in Swedish. His lawyer shakes his head, disagreeing. Teppan shouts him down in threatening tones I don't need words to interpret. Ed Chestack places his hand on Teppan's forearm, apparently urging restraint. Teppan shakes free.

My father stands, stretches, waits for the cameraman to center him in the frame. Extends an arm clad in butter cream silk toward Jackson and the BBC reporter, now tapping furiously on a tablet.

"I will not submit to a DNA swab. I will not surrender to the London police. I will not dignify charges fabricated by certain members of the media who would conspire to libel and defame me in pursuit of a personal agenda. I will not name names, lest I be accused of similarly defaming someone, but he knows who he is, as does anyone who has been following press accounts of yesterday's 'Christmas at the Castle' events. I did not participate in the murder of Esteban Gronlund, a man I did not know. I did not rape or otherwise sexually coerce Anthony Kirkpatrick into murdering Esteban Gronlund. I am not even acquainted with Kirkpatrick except for having seen his picture at the time of his arrest."

Teppan swivels to draw my mother closer to him, takes one of her hands and clasps it to his heart. "What I am is the target of a certain vindictive individual who has conspired to sully my name and that of my wife. I intend to return to Stockholm tomorrow with her and our band mates, as our travel plans have dictated all along. The authorities in London may attempt to pursue their case in Sweden, if they choose. I will not cooperate in a plot against me; I will not incriminate myself in any way. DNA evidence procured by Interpol has eliminated me once as a suspect. I am in their database; they are free to use that sample to reach a similar conclusion in this matter."

He turns and strides out of the Great Hall, Kat trailing in his wake, some of the press racing after them, other reporters stampeding the district attorney and the magistrate, shouting questions at them and at Teppan's attorney, who sits dumbfounded via Skype. In the pandemonium, I lose sight of Jackson, who surely wants to disappear, but whether from the crowd or me, I'm not certain.

"Can they arrest a foreign national in the United States for refusing a DNA swab?" Meredith asks her smartphone. "In some cases, yes, they can," it replies.

Better not to leave that to speculation. I spot Gippel near the main portal of the Great Hall and spear him with a glare that will brook no avoidance.

"What do you know, and how is my fiancé helping you?"

"Miss Hart, I trust you are feeling better," Gippel deflects. "My condolences on your loss."

"You engineered this."

He half-smiles. "Anthony Kirkpatrick has recognized from the 'Christmas at the Castle' videos now circulating on the internet the voice and build of the man he says sexually assaulted him in June and compelled him to cut out Esteban Gronlund's voice box, causing him to bleed to death. The Metropolitan Police, of course, took Kirkpatrick's clothing from that night into evidence, and at the time confirmed four sets of DNA on his garments, the greatest quantity of which was, *natürlich*, Gronlund's blood."

He pauses to light a cigarette, blows smoke and dares me to stop him. Let him rot out his lungs, stink up the Castle; I don't care, as long as he shares information. After a few more puffs, he drowns the cigarette in the bottle of water he's set down near his boots. "There was saliva on the clothing, yours, Miss Hart, from your earlier interlude of fellatio with Kirkpatrick. There were, as well, two different semen specimens, one of which was Kirkpatrick's own. The other, we believe to be Teppan Nilsson's. A DNA sample taken here, now, will confirm what we believe."

"You heard him, he refuses the swab. Can he be compelled to provide a new sample?"

"He will not leave this country without providing one."

"Good luck with that, Detective. Nilsson's lawyers will bury you in motions to dismiss on the grounds of entrapment."

"Ed's already screaming at the DA about it," Meredith interrupts. Gippel offers her his hand and stands straighter. He smiles appreciatively, as if he's about to recite love poems.

I've come a little late to this game, but I'm figuring out the score: where Teppan went when he left me this morning; who texted Jackson, calling him away just as he arrived at the midwife's, as my mother angrily informed me.

"You already have a new DNA sample, don't you, even if you can't use it in court? Quite the *ménage a trois*, Detective: you and Meredith and Jackson. Go screw yourselves."

"C.J., please. Teppan showed up at my cottage this morning and sweet-talked his way inside." Meredith clutches my sweater. "It's not like I planned this with Jackson. The opportunity just presented itself."

I pull free, causing her to stagger. "This will never go away. Teppan will never let it die, he'll hang it over my head and yours and Jackson's indefinitely, until he gets what he wants."

"Which is what, Miss Hart? You and your undivided attention?" Gippel is so unerringly on the mark I am struck dumb. Meredith looks from me to him and back again, aware she's been left out of the conversation in a significant way. "Your interest in Mr. Nilsson is rather more intriguing to me than Miss Grainger-Todd's willingness to assist my investigation. I know Mr. Fahey would be most eager to hear you explain certain recent encounters, especially."

Meredith grabs at my sleeve again, forces me to look at her. "What is he talking about?"

I can't answer. The words that sum up my relationship with Teppan Nilsson, my relationship to Teppan Nilsson, cannot be uttered. Gippel notes my inability to articulate, sees through my hesitation to do anything but rage against my friend, my instinct to deny everything Meredith might even wildly guess at. He suspects what I cannot say, what I will not say. Jackson recognized it, and has allied himself with Gippel against Teppan.

"I'm going to be sick." Not a total untruth as I run away, struck suddenly by a need to find my mother and make her finally tell me the truth about my father.

The truth about vampires, period.

* * * *

She is staring at the tapestries, cradling her mother's coverlet. She's taken it from my suitcase, somehow knew I had brought it home with me this time.

"May I come in?"

"Of course," my mother says, and hands the coverlet to me. I sit next to her on the rug, open my grandmother's handiwork and spread it across our legs, against the chill that has settled in my heart and, quite likely, hers as well.

"Did my father do what they say? Rape Anton? Compel him to kill Esteban?"

"Can you doubt it?"

"Yes, he denied it when I asked him in Edinburgh. I thought you'd killed Esteban."

"It's what he wanted you to think; he lies, Chloe."

"For the first thirty years of my life, so did you; he knows I don't trust you either. It's clear to me now you thought you were protecting me, but still . . ."

She puts her arm around me, pulls me close. "There was so much more I could have done. So much I should have done, you're right not to trust my decisions, or my motives. This past year, I haven't fully trusted them myself."

My mother presses a kiss against my temple. "I was raised to be a proper nineteenth-century wife: decorous, decorative, smoothing the way. With my late husband, Auguste, being the righteous Madame Verlaine was easy. I think that's why I was drawn to your father: From the start, every minute with him was a challenge to all I'd been told my life would be. He forced me to look for the passion inside, encouraged me to take a stake in our success. He made me feel as if I could have it all.

Sounds so feminist, doesn't it, except it was the mid-1860s."

I rest my head on her shoulder. "Doesn't sound like such a bad thing, what you had with Daddy."

She wraps her other arm around me, rocks me like the baby daughter I once was. "It was so wonderful, for so long. Your father was always ruthless in his pursuit of our perfect life, but he did more good than harm. He found talent and nurtured it, sent total strangers to school, gave them jobs and homes and purpose, and everything up to then set us on the path that became Court of Cruelty. It was his family, his passion, and Sebastian loved us all, all out of proportion. He saw us as one. Individuals, but fundamentally one.

"People drifted into and out of the Cruel, and he was fine with that for a while. But it started to take a toll on Sebastian, and as you got older, he would talk about the day when you'd stand as one of us, when you would be one of us forever. I knew then I had to push you away; our unconventional lifestyle was a convenient excuse. I knew his bond to you would get stronger, an unrelenting love that would bewilder you and smother you, but maybe I only made things worse. Maybe I should have let it be."

She squeezes me more tightly, as if trying to press me back into her body. "Maybe you were one loss too many, Sebastian had seen so many people pass through our lives and pass away. He started to demand loyalty, manipulated those who didn't give it willingly, and then, with Esteban, manipulation became the least of it."

Like me, she blames herself for Esteban's death. I also have Anton's suffering on my conscience. I'd do anything to take back that night.

"Now," my mother muses, "it's as if, in becoming Teppan, your father has lost himself, too. It's not good, and it can't go on."

What choice do we have?

*"There is always a choice,"* her voice rings in my head.

His voice is there, too: *"Where there is no choice, there is no test."*

This feels like another one, so I must know: "Why did Auguste kill himself?"

A tear falls onto my wrist, a red drop staining my skin. "They repudiated him," she says, so quietly. "He was an honorable man, but the vampires of the realm—some of them only metaphorically vampires—cast him out, accusing him of disloyalty."

"That word again. What is it about vampires and loyalty?"

"I don't speak for the species, I've done no research; my own experience is all I have to pass on to you." Her words are laden with disdain. She doesn't respect the species, doesn't want to. She relaxes her grip on me slightly then steels it again, as if gathering from me the strength to sift through the memories.

"Auguste was a diplomat. He came to immortality later in his life, with notions of justice and honor from which he could not be swayed. He had just negotiated a treaty whose terms for commerce throughout the Habsburg empire were favorable not only to the royals and their strategists, but to as many others as possible—merchants, tradesmen. It was radically modern capitalism for the era, radically egalitarian. Those were times still of political revolution: of life, liberty and the pursuit of happiness here in America; of liberty, fraternity and equality in France. Marx and Engel had written their manifesto about communism, but no revolutionary fervor heated the blood of Auguste's creator or the masters he served. And so, after a century together, Auguste's creator shunned him, his one life, as though he meant nothing."

"Did you mean nothing to Auguste?" She was young then, younger than I am now by several years, I can't imagine what it must have been like for her.

"He adored me, but I was not enough reason for him to go on."

Her voice is a fragile melody, barely audible. "An eternal life without the love of the one who had made him was no life at all. Auguste felt humiliated, he wanted to die, so he kissed me, begged me not to follow him, stepped out under the sun at dawn unprotected and stood there, weakening, until it consumed him from within. His body was found days later, apparently ravaged by animals, but I knew."

Afterward, she mourned, then she met my father—not an honorable man, at least not recently.

"Stefan Herz was selfish and ambitious, but also handsome and reckless and fun, things Auguste, dear dignified Auguste, was not. Stefan glided through his mortal life on the beauty of his music and the power of his charm, wooed and won me with them, and has let them carry him throughout his immortal life, as well. Everyone has always been too willing to love him. I have always been too willing to love him."

So have I. Too willing to indulge him, too willing to forgive him. In spite of everything he has asked of me, in spite of everything he threatens to take from me and everything he's taken so far, the prospect of him in prison again, this time very likely isolated and without blood, terrifies me. I want him gone from me, gone to a place where he can't suck the air from my life, but not gone forever.

From my mother's desperate embrace, I disengage myself, uncomfortable in her arms after too many years denied their warmth. We will always be at this impasse, she and I. As she can't forget the good wife she was raised to be, can't be the forceful influence on my father's everlasting life she knows she should be, I can't forget the lonely child she made me, the willful daughter with so many of Sebastian's flaws. He is my creator. I am his one life. I will always crave his love, to my detriment.

As for my one life, loved for such a short time . . . now I am a vampire whose creation is gone. Have I truly lost that chance?

"Right after I transformed, after we found out I was pregnant, you told Jackson I could still make him a vampire. Because I was human when we conceived Guinevere, is that why?"

"In light of what happened to those four babies, I wouldn't advise it. Jackson deserves to live, as unworthy of you as he so often proves himself to be."

"Daddy was unworthy of you, isn't that what you've been telling me here?"

She collects the ends of the coverlet, strokes the stitches my grandmother sewed when her only daughter was still Eugenie, her little girl.

"Love is a brilliant gift, one we are all unworthy of at times," whispers the woman now known as Katarina. "It's part of being human, not part of being vampire."

* * * *

The Dungeon is spacious, sumptuously appointed, Gloria's subterranean domain beneath the kitchen and the pantries. Its commercial-grade laundry also serves the winery's needs, its napkins, tablecloths and so forth.

Jackson's clothing lies folded on a pristine soapstone counter. His suit, immaculate after being steam-cleaned and pressed with precision, no doubt by Gloria herself, hangs from the pediment of an armoire that might have accompanied my father from Bohemia all those years ago. Not a piece I've contemplated before, like so many of the things furnishing this Castle.

At an antique farm table, Jackson's laptop sits open before him. On the screen are faces I recognize as his parents'.

"I'll be flying into Heathrow tomorrow. I won't know until after my meeting Tuesday whether I'll be going back to Brussels to return to work or to pack up my flat, unemployed."

"Stay here with us," Maureen Fahey urges. "A hot meal, a friendly bed, you shouldn't be alone before such a big day. You said Chloe wouldn't be returning to London just yet."

I won't be?

He senses my presence behind him, out of Skype sightlines. His back stiffens; he's been caught in his fib. "I'd be terrible company for her and you, too wound up to sleep; I'd just disturb everyone. I'll get a hotel room somewhere closer to the BBC offices, best not to take a chance on the train."

"He's probably right, Mo, the boy's got a lot on his mind, what with losing the baby and these worries about Chloe and his job. Do what you think best, Jackson. Your mother will light a candle, and all will be well. Call and let us know how it went."

"I will," he promises, then closes the connection.

"My mother will have to set the whole church ablaze to save my stupid arse," he says, rising from his chair. "Teppan's news blast this evening put a few more nails in my professional coffin. My parents had already heard about it, and about the fist-fight, and about the miscarriage. They were waiting up, hoping I'd call."

I turn away, to hide my tears. His parents are so normal, so loving and understanding of who he is, just the way he is, and mine are—well, we know what mine are, no sense dwelling on what will never change.

He steps behind me, wraps his arms around my waist, pulls me close to his chest; rubs his chin along my hair, breathes in its scent. "Always lemon. I immediately think of my Juliette."

"Am I still your Juliette? You've decided not to stay at my flat, even if I'm back in London."

"C.J., there's so much I need to tell you."

"Yes, there's quite a lot you need to tell me. Do it, damn it!"

He leads me to the table, pulls a second chair around for me to sit in. "Let's talk, unless you'd prefer to scream."

"I'd prefer you just be honest. You're not coming back to the flat because you're not coming back to me."

He nods, and my heart breaks. "I love you, but I need to think. Yesterday, I had a baby on the way, a career I mostly loved, and my peers' respect. Today, so much is gone."

"I understand: This ugly vampire business I've dragged you into, you can still walk away from it. I envy you that."

He lifts my hands to his lips, kisses my palms. "When I

learned we'd lost Guinevere, my first reaction was relief that she would never have to live in your parents' world. How could I think losing her was for the best, even for an instant? I want to fix things for us, Chloe, but I don't see what else I can do?"

I bite into his right wrist, suck until his champagne flows down my throat and fills me with his warmth. I climb into his lap, feel his erection strain against my bottom. *"Interview me, Jackson,"* I order wordlessly. *"Ask me the questions you want answered."*

His head rolls back. I feel his dizziness, his desire, then I feel them slowly recede, until he has command of his brain again.

"Why," he sobs, "did our baby have to die?"

I lick his blood from my lips, kiss the tears from his face. "I couldn't nourish her, and she couldn't grow strong enough to hold on. She just flowed out of me."

He struggles to clear his throat. "You had already started to lose her when you left our bed this morning. Why did you go to that cottage? What was Teppan doing there with you?"

He deserves the truth. I'm done with dissembling.

"When I saw the blood on the sheets, I panicked. I ran out of the house just as I was, I didn't even stop to dress, and I hid in the cottage Zeke always used, where I played as a little girl. My father heard you searching for me, and knew immediately where I'd gone. He found me shivering under the blankets, though the bleeding had stopped. He fished out some old sweats of Zeke's for me, tossed them onto the bed and told me to put them on."

"Teppan found you naked in the bed?"

He's fixed on that, I just can't blurt the rest out. I press my lips to his cheek. "Tell me what you saw, and I'll tell you what you didn't see."

Jackson closes his eyes. "The door opened, and Teppan walked out, nude. I saw you on the bed, peering out from the blankets. I didn't know what to think except that I wanted to kill him."

I'll tell him the rest, I swear, but first I have to know: "You followed him to Meredith?"

"He stalked across every inch of these grounds, searching, and he knew I was right behind him. When we got close to her car and could smell her perfume, he presented himself at the nearest cottage and had Meredith wrapped around his waist in minutes. He wanted me to imagine what he was doing to her, wanted it to torture me."

"Did it?" I hate myself for asking.

"It's never been about me and Meredith, love, it's always been about us: I was selected to play his role in your bed, isn't it obvious? He can't let you be, he will never leave you alone, so with Meredith's help I handed Gippel enough rope to hang Teppan with. Anton's attorney had already contacted Scotland Yard; the wheels were already in motion. I helped set them in motion."

"And Meredith knew what you were up to?"

He sighs, weariness weighing him down. "No, but her body recognized him. She's this close to realizing . . ."

"He might have killed her, Jackson. He might still kill her if he figures out what she's done, what you've done with her help."

"Another reason why I have to leave, and why your father needs to be stopped."

I wrap my arms around his neck, pull his face even with mine. "Nothing happened this morning, but I've never seen him like that. That wasn't my father, it was a beast feeding off some fury raging inside him. I refused to give ground, and he backed down, turned and walked out the door, that's what you saw."

"If that was him backing down . . ."

So Teppan lied, showed his physical need to Ronnie and Jackson and Meredith, but hid it from me. "He did the right thing. The father who loves me beat back the vampire sire who expects me to bend to his will."

Jackson stares, as if at a stranger. "You defend him? Your murdering, molesting, gunrunning, and, Lord knows what else, father? The pervert who steered me into your life because I look like him and now hates me because you love me? Who compels a stranger to service you in my absence because he must somehow wrap you around his prodigious vampire ego? If you can still defend him, Chloe, nothing I've done matters."

"I am his one life. I can resist him, but I can never deny the blood that binds me to him."

There it is, what Jackson needs to say goodbye. He gently moves my arms, lifts me from his lap; pulls his computer and some papers toward him and into his backpack, gathers his clothes. "I'll find somewhere else to sleep tonight. I'll be gone before first light."

I listen to his boots fall hard on the Dungeon stairs. Listen as he ascends to the upper levels of the Castle, probably for the last time.

* * * *

These walls make my skin crawl. I want to flee, run all the way back to London, as far from these people as I can get. Who knows, maybe I could actually do it; there's no telling what this body is capable of. I've only determined what I won't do with it, not what I can't.

I am halfway to Binghamton, my clothing and running shoes soaked through by the nasty, icy rain that wants never to stop, when I turn back, redirected by some inner compass. Almost every person I care about is in that house, every person who has formed my life to this point. Someone wants me to return. *Who* doesn't seem as urgent an issue as *right now*.

It's at least one o'clock in the morning when I approach from the main drive, yet the house is ablaze in light, from the bailey, to the vestibule, to the Great Hall. I race inside, dripping on the fieldstones. Gloria waylays me before I can go farther, carrying in her arms a towel and some clothes of mine.

"Duck into the bathroom here, quickly." She hands me black leggings, socks, and a warm Aran sweater. "Shoo, you're needed in the Hall."

I strip off my wet running togs, pat down my hair and body, step into the dry things. She's brought no shoes; I pad across the vestibule in white tube socks with Cornell red stripes.

Within the Great Hall are the extant, if somewhat unofficial, members of Clan de la Coeur, minus the two men who have gone to war over me. Ed Chestack and Ronnie Hamilton stand at the table used just hours earlier by the Tompkins County magistrate and prosecutor. Gloria stands off to one side with Katarina, seeming to comfort her. In front of a rack of folding chairs waiting to be sent back to the rental company, Meredith and Genevieve stand together, puzzled no doubt, as I am. Also there is my mother's new pet, Eric, which seems odd but perhaps only because Lars, the boy drummer, is not joined to his hip for a change.

My entrance draws Ronnie's notice; he walks over to Kat, puts a hand on her shoulder, and points to me. "I'll go get him," he volunteers.

"Feeling better, I hope, girlie." Ronnie smiles as he passes. I give him a curt nod; one rescue does not make us best friends. Minutes later, he precedes a scowling Teppan into the Hall.

My father pauses, contemplates the group before him, locking eyes with each one of us. A slow, cautious smile brightens his handsome face. He walks directly to me, puts his arms around me, kisses my cheek.

He moves over to Meredith, whispers something in her ear and kisses her the same way. Braces her as she sways in recognition. Laughs as she glares at Kat, who nods, pointing to herself in acknowledgment of the truth.

Genevieve pulls away as he tries to kiss her. He steps in to whisper something all the same, and she relents, reluctantly lets him embrace her.

He startles Eric, his Swedish stand-in, seizing his hand and shaking it. Eric glances at my mother nervously. She dabs at her eyes with a lace handkerchief, teary and agitated; despite Gloria's efforts, inconsolable.

As if she has newly emerged from a shadow, I see her clearly, beneath the façade of Katarina Nilsson: Eugenie Roget Verlaine Herz, also known as Emilie de la Coeur and who knows how many other names. I see now that my mother is the one who has called this gathering, the one who has summoned me. Dear God, what is she doing?

She moves into the center of the space, struggling to maintain her composure.

*"Je t'aime, Stefan."* She loves him still, in spite of everything.

*"Ich liebe dich, Eugenie. Es tut mir lied."* An apology, how rare for him.

*"C'est trop tard."* Too late for him to repent, she apparently has decided, and too late to turn back.

He goes pale. In his astonishment, his smile deserts him. She steps to the side, and, starting with Eric, the rest queue up in front of my father, all aware now, as I am, what my mother intends. They form a straight line, purposely separating us.

*"Jag forkastar du,"* Eric declares. "I repudiate you, Teppan Nilsson, on behalf of myself and Zeke Segal, who, like me, cared for your wife more than you do." Eric goes to my mother; brings her hands to his lips, folds her into his arms.

Ronnie and Genevieve step forward. "We repudiate you, Sebastian de la Coeur," they pronounce, hands joined. Ronnie thrusts his chin at my father. "You know the reasons why, and I accept my own guilt as your accomplice. This is for Genevieve's Theo, too, whether you killed him or not. Save a spot onstage for me in hell."

"We'll slaughter them down there, boyo," my father says, and searches for me. I step around the queue and walk to his side, grasp his hand in mine. I won't let him go through the rest of this alone, not without some small comfort.

Ed moves up in line, gestures for Meredith to join him. She

looks frightened, then shocked when Ed presses a kiss to her cheek. "I repudiate you, Sebastian de la Coeur, while I, too, acknowledge my own guilt in your crimes. Still, I thank you for my daughter, Meredith, who you kept near me all these years and urged me to know. She is the best of what I'll remember."

"Meredith, sweetheart, anything you'd like to say?" my father asks, crushing my hand. "There must be . . ."

She slaps him, the blow imprinted for the merest second on his left cheek. "I repudiate you, Sebastian de Coeur, for making me betray the closest thing I've ever had to a sister, for ruining my marriages to two good men who loved me but could never compare to you, and now for ruining what Chloe has with Jackson. You're a selfish bastard, and you reap what you sow."

Gloria stumbles into the space Meredith vacates, unsteady, as if she's about to faint. Genevieve moves behind her, threads her fingers through her mother's. "Say it, it's all right," Gen counsels. "But if you can't, he'll know what you're thinking. You agreed to be here. We all agreed to be here."

I didn't. I wasn't consulted on this intervention. A conversation about Auguste Verlaine's death hardly qualifies as consent.

Gloria puts her arms around my father's neck, kisses his lips tenderly. "I repudiate you, Sebastian de la Coeur, for no longer being the fine man you used to be."

Leaving Eric's side, Katarina takes Gloria's hand in one of hers, Genevieve's in the other. She inclines her head toward me. "Speak if you wish to, Chloe. Unanimity is not necessary, but we may all feel better if we know we act as one."

Making them feel better is not my concern. This is about so much more than soothing their collective souls. Yet I stand before them, before him, immobilized. Indecision paralyzes me.

I could recuse myself from this vote on my father's corrupt character; abstain from enumerating his many crimes. Let the others' indictment go unchallenged, and the result will be the same.

If I do nothing, however, can I live with myself? What purpose do I serve here if I ignore my conscience and play the devoted daughter? Someone must testify to the suffering of Anya and Viktoria and the other women and their poor dead babies. Someone must speak for them, and for Esteban, and for my Guinevere.

Every eye in the room follows as, finally, I turn toward Teppan, the man who used to be the parent I adored. I stand on tiptoe, brace my hands on his shoulders. Kiss each of his cheeks. Raise my lips to his ear. Speak as softly as I can.

"The rest of them needn't hear this. This is between you and me, Daddy Bastian, like it's always been."

"Like it's always been. You know I love you, Clothilde."

"I love you, too, but I won't relive that scene at Zeke's cottage ever again. Promise me there will be no repeat?"

He puts his hands on my waist, squeezes gently; moves his thumbs higher, teases my ribcage just under my breasts. "I told you I felt nothing, I showed you."

He lies, even now, when everyone else has abandoned him.

He must realize Jackson and Ronnie described to me exactly what he displayed to them. Replaying those moments in my mind sickens me, but the disgust also energizes me. I close my eyes to the man holding me now and focus on the rapacious beast whose lust lifted me and a bed off the floor.

I push against his chest. "Take your hands off me, and look at me. Tell me the truth, Daddy."

He grips me tighter, dips his head down, his breath hot, compelling, against my ear. "We stood this close in Edinburgh. So close, remember?"

Fangs descend—mine—and the desire to break free beats back his desire to overwhelm me. "If that's your truth, you choose to deceive yourself," I hiss, a viper of his own creation. "I choose to call this repudiation."

I remove his hands from my person and run from the Hall, feeling simultaneously dirty and traitorous and nauseated. As

I rush for the grand staircase, racing for my second-floor bathroom before the contents of my stomach escape through my mouth, I hear my mother condemn the vampire she created, her one life.

*"Stefan, mon amour, je vous renie,"* she sobs. "I repudiate you for the reasons given by those here tonight, for the reasons I know too well, and for those you alone can know. Accept and appreciate your fate."

An anguished cry rises. Stained glass rains down; leaded pieces pelt me, ricocheting off stairs and floors as I run. Shards tear from sash and casement behind me, wooden sills ripping away with them.

When at last I make it to the toilet, I vomit, flush blood and bits of food away, the swirling water momentarily drowning out the sound of my father's lament.

A few seconds of peace, then the house quakes as he screams again.

*Chapter Ten*

## UPSTATE NEW YORK, DECEMBER 2011

Was it the blast of icy cold or the seam of eye-broiling sunlight that woke him? The pounding in his skull, a pounding particularly associated with fine old scotch? Did it matter? When he dug his phone out of his jeans, the plastic case having branded its rectangular shape onto his hip after he passed out, the time showed itself to be four minutes to eight. He had a noon flight out of JFK, at least a four-hour drive away, plus time for security check-in.

"Fuck, fucking idiot!" Fahey hollered, stepping down onto a spike of glass and slashing his left foot. There was glass everywhere. He picked his way over to his boots, found yesterday's socks stuffed inside, swabbed away the blood before putting them on. The French doors had shattered, as had the window on the adjacent wall. Snowflakes flitted through the broken panes, through the east-rising rays. A frigid breeze blew in, refreshing his half-dead brain cells, but instead of clean country air, he smelled something smoldering.

Fahey ran for the door that closed the music studio off from the rest of the Castle's third story. The knob was frozen, like the weather outside. He knelt, looked for a lock, found none; examined the hinges, to see how easily they could be dismantled and the door lifted, but there were no bolts to knock through.

He banged on the wood, shouted, "Fire!" His words bounced off with a force that knocked him onto his backside, onto another shard of glass.

"You could jump from the balcony and make it down with only a broken ankle or two, but I'm not inclined to allow you to exit that way either, so you may as well give up, Fahey. You're under compulsion. Logically, you know you should be able to get out of this room, but I've scrambled your wiring a bit, so you literally can't see the way clear."

On the piano bench near the French doors sat the man who built the Castle, a bottle of Sebastian de la Coeur's fine whisky in his right hand. He took a swig. "Helps the pain, but only just. That burning you smell is me, by the way. No need for panic, I assure you."

Panic, yes, that Fahey surely felt. He put a shoulder to the door, tried to break through. "I have a plane to catch. The BBC expects me in London so it can fire me. Happy?"

Another sip from the bottle, and Teppan Nilsson reached into the body of the baby grand, pulled out a revolver. "Actually, my friend Herr Glock and I intend to show the BBC just how valuable you are, for now at least." He glanced at the tall case clock in the corner, squinted at the hands through the broken glass of its face. "Three, three-and-a-half hours more at most. Despite the flurries, it looks like a fairly cloudless morning, which should cut down on roasting time considerably."

He unbuttoned his shirt, tore it off, trained the Glock on Fahey. "Let's call it three hours, definitely, so we need to start this party. Your phone, is it charged?"

"Go to hell," Fahey snapped, yet he was unable to resist checking the phone. "Charge should hold for a bit. Do you mean to have me call the ambulance as you shoot me?"

"I do mean to shoot you, but an ambulance, really? No flair for the dramatic, no wonder they want to fire your sorry ass."

Nilsson leaned in, got as close as possible without moving away from the piano. "You, Jackson Fahey, beloved of my beloved little girl, are my exit strategy. You're a videographer, or at least you were before that nasty incident in Afghanistan. You shot Matins and Vespers' first show ever back in Barcelona; looked pretty good, too. No question you're the right man for this job, you always have a small camera in that bag of yours. How do you upload your videos anyway? To the cloud or via satellite?"

The man never ceased to amaze. Where was this leading?

"Cloud if it's for later broadcast, satellite for a live feed." The burning smell was intensifying, honing a putrid edge on the hangover- and anxiety-induced nausea Fahey battled. He wished Nilsson would get to the point. "What do you want recorded? Let's just do it so I can leave."

*"No leaving, just obeying. Got it? Don't make me tell you again, Fahey. I intend to make every bullet count."*

The words shimmered before his eyes; he could taste them. So this was compulsion. Fahey began to understand what blinded Meredith and Genevieve to Sebastian's presence in Nilsson, and what moved Anton Kirkpatrick to murder a stranger.

"A live satellite feed has to be prearranged," he heard himself explaining. "I can call someone, Skype her on my laptop. Let me get my backpack," Fahey gestured to a space near the far end of the piano, "and I'll have everything I need, the camera and my collapsible tripod. The video will look better; we'll be able to get a couple different angles—less talking head, more conversational."

*"You're the director, I'm just the star."*

Fahey eased to his feet, managed to avoid cutting his hands on the strewn glass. He retrieved his gear and backed up to the couch where he'd spent the night. He pulled the coffee table closer, set up the computer, called Madrid.

Amanda Witt's familiar face quickly appeared. "Jackson? You look terrible. Are you back in the UK?"

"I need a satellite link as soon as possible." Fahey repositioned himself next to the piano, turned the laptop so she could see them both. "I'm still at Castle de la Coeur. This is Teppan Nilsson." Nilsson waved the Glock at the screen. "He wants me to shoot a video and wants the BBC to broadcast it or he'll kill me. Do I have that right?"

Nilsson rose slowly from the piano bench, bent over Fahey's shoulder, pressed the muzzle of the gun to Fahey's temple. "Forgive his manners, BBC beauty. Jackson neglected to introduce *you* to *me*."

Her pale face stared back, and she swiftly shook off whatever shock had registered. She cleared her throat, squared her shoulders. "Amanda Witt, chief of the Madrid Bureau, BBC World Service. If you can give me a summary of what this live video will be about, Mr. Nilsson, I should be able to arrange a link via London within the hour. Will that be satisfactory?"

He checked the case clock, dipped the gun to Fahey's jaw. "No later than nine fifteen, Miss Witt. I have a statement to make, very important, life or death, you might say, for Fahey here and myself. Succinct enough?"

Amanda swallowed, nodded. "I'll call back as soon as I can. Jackson, take care."

Nilsson slammed the laptop's lid down. "Have you had her? She looks delectable."

*"Lie to me, and I will kill you. I don't really need you, do I, Fahey? Any idiot can shoot video with a phone."*

Fahey stood, stepped behind Nilsson; grabbed the bottle and swallowed a long, throat-scorching pull of the scotch. Hair of the dog, anything so he wouldn't piss himself right there and then, with that voice in his head, that stench wafting around him.

"I wanted to," he heard himself reply, his voice unexpectedly steady. "I think Amanda wanted to, as well, but she was my boss and my mentor for a very long time, and that was more important to both of us."

*"Pity, I was hoping to probe your memory of hot, sex-filled*

*hours with her. I suppose we'll have to rely now on her platonic affection for you."*

"She'll do this. What happened or not between us personally won't make a difference."

*"So righteous, Jackson, so dull. So glad Chloe and I are almost rid of you."*

Nilsson's face, his handsome mask, sagged with pain. He snatched back the bottle, drank deeply from it. "Really doesn't help at all, but what's it gonna do, kill me? Hah!" He reopened the laptop, circled his finger over the keyboard. "Why don't you call my sweet child, Fahey, assuming she's still talking to you? I'm on her shit list, God knows. Same deal as with Amanda, you did well just then: First, Chloe sees only you, then me with Glockie here."

Fahey called Chloe's number. No answer. "Keep trying," Nilsson ordered.

Fahey texted, asking her to Skype him. After his fifth message, her head popped up on the laptop's screen, but she was turned away, telling someone out of frame that there was more broken glass in the inner courtyard to deal with.

"Chloe, I need to talk to you. Urgently."

She twisted around, peered into her phone, scanned the details of the space behind him. "Are you in the music studio? You're supposed to be on your way to the airport."

"Morning, little one." Nilsson swung into view, holding the Glock to Fahey's throat. "Need you to do Daddy a favor, in spite of the big, bad repudiation your mother's imposed. Need you to call the state police and tell them I'm holding your boyfriend hostage at gunpoint. Tell them I want a million dollars in a Swiss account and a helicopter hovering over the field across the road no later than ten o'clock. Oh, and tell the news people outside to call their networks to get a piece of the live BBC feed Jackson has his gorgeous friend in Madrid setting up for us. Now wave bye-bye and get it done, sweetheart, Daddy's getting a little hot under the collar up here. Hell of an eastern exposure, great for watching the sunrise."

"Jackson . . ."

"Do it, Chloe," Nilsson interrupted, "or I kill him."

"Shut up this minute, and let Jackson speak!"

Nilsson shoved Fahey in front of the screen.

"He's suffering badly already; he's probably been in this sun for more than an hour. We're getting close to the point of no return here. Assume he means what he says, love."

"Am I? Your love?"

"Always," Fahey promised. Her eyes glistened, tears glowing red. "Please, sweetheart, do as he asks."

She put her hand over her heart. "For you. Always, only for you."

Nilsson pulled the laptop away, inserted himself into the picture. "Fucking touching, dear daughter. Now get down to business, or always will be of very short duration." He slammed the lid down, in anger or hurt or whatever was motivating this plan. Did it, Fahey wondered, include anyone leaving this room alive?

*"By the end of this day, two men will be dead, of that you can be sure. Until then, no more talk, just action."*

"This is me in action: I ask questions, you answer them," Fahey snarled, resisting the grip on his brain. "I get that the sun is savaging you somehow, but you're not bursting into flame. What is it doing, and what the hell is that smell?"

Nilsson sniffed. "I do hope that aroma doesn't get overpowering, I need you to be in top form, distracted only by the possibility I might shoot you. Let's see, what is the sun doing to me? Not barbecuing exactly, that would make me crispy on the outside, which I'm not. You could say I'm being cooked from the inside. The shell that is my body will hold up for a while as my organs are braising within, vampirism being about biochemistry, after all. And yes, it feels as disgusting as it sounds."

He shook his leg; something sloshed. "Who knew? I got only the standard-issue 'Never before noon shalt thou expose thyself to the rays of the rising sun' speech from my darling Eugenie. She was a sweet little bloodsucker back then, but only a few years into it, she didn't know the fine points. This vampire oral-history thing has its limitations, I had no idea this was how the sun would kill me."

"You're committing suicide?"

Nilsson winked. "Except this time, it's for real, and you're coming with me, live via TV and internet to the world, courtesy of the BBC. Performance of a lifetime, eh?"

The case clock tolled a quarter after eight. Nilsson winced, emptied the bottle, pointed to the liquor cabinet. "You know your way around my stash. Find us another bottle, Fahey."

*"Consider yourself very lucky there's another one in there to find. I hate to think how cranky I'll be once the alcohol ceases to anesthetize."*

* * * *

Complicit. Unbelievable that he could end up part of this scheme, after all he'd done to make things right. After all he'd tried to do to make up for the fact that he hadn't acted sooner on what Anton Kirkpatrick had told him at the prison, or that he'd known for months that Nilsson was actually Sebastian de la Coeur's latest version of himself and done nothing to push the authorities in that direction.

Nilsson lay on the leather couch, eyes closed; he yawned, stretched long legs in front of him. Fahey swore he heard something squish. His stomach did a somersault, and he forced down the foul taste rising in his throat.

Laughter rang in his head. *"You can't fix everything. I know you like to play the hero, Fahey, but remember I'm the knight here, defender of the kingdom, champion of the cause. Know your part or rue the day you forgot it!"*

What was Fahey's part here: A. Aim the camera; B. Document Nilsson's last stand; C. Explain same to an uncomprehending world afterward? Or A and B, but not C, because he'd be dead, as well?

Outside, dredging equipment roared, ready to dig and sift another day. Nilsson raised his head enough to take a new swig from the bottle, already down by about one-quarter. Would he be able to sit up straight, let alone stand, for the video?

"Repudiation, what did you mean by that?" Fahey asked, calculating what might be done to maximize his camera's audio capabilities to compensate for the noise of the machinery and the wind whistling in through the broken doors and windows. He scanned the music studio, lighted on an amplifier connected to Sebastian's electric bass over by the bookshelves, wheeled the amp over toward the piano, stretching the cord as taut as he could.

"Microphone?" he asked.

Nilsson opened his eyes. "Good idea." He pointed to a panel in the wall just past the window. "Tap on that, there's a closet behind it."

Fahey found some cables and began to jury-rig a sound system, moving equipment over toward the couch.

"No!" Nilsson's bark sounded weaker, though the Glock ensured his bite was fearsome still. "I need to stay close to the French doors. I want to be well done, not medium rare."

"You'll bleach out against the sunlight if we don't reposition you."

"Find another way," Nilsson growled.

Fahey knelt in front of his suitcase, fished out a black V-neck sweater. "Put this on, we're probably the same size."

Nilsson slipped it over his head, shook his white-blond hair back into place; drowned the resulting fit of coughing in another swallow of scotch. "Here's the thing about repudiation, Fahey," he gasped, struggling to catch his breath. "My wife, my friends, all have rejected me, cast me aside forever, with no possibility of redemption. If I didn't have a gun to your head, I guarantee you that Chloe, by her mother's decree, would not even have laid eyes on me."

The barrel of the Glock appeared in the viewfinder. He had

better visuals now, but Fahey couldn't rely on his improvised sound system. "Stop the dredging!" he texted Chloe. "Need things quiet!" He sensed rather than saw Nilsson next to him, reading over his shoulder. "You're good. You think of everything."

"I didn't think to stay out of this room. Bit of a lapse there, don't you think?"

Nilsson pushed past him to the French doors. The sun was streaming through the music studio now; no escaping it, no need to stand anywhere near them, Fahey realized, except for dramatic effect.

"My wife—my Eugenie, my Emilie, my Katarina—who gave me her one life, who should love me best, has declared me unlovable, and everyone else I love, even my baby, has endorsed her repudiation. Punishment most extreme, rendering my further existence a profoundly moot point."

Nilsson pointed the gun at his own temple. "Now that I've baked for a few hours, a bullet can pass right through. Turns out, there's no substance to me after all."

Fahey felt an odd swell of sympathy for the man, so immensely talented yet so amazingly flawed.

*"You're right, of course. I had the perfect life several times over, the perfect woman, and I threw it all away. I deserve this fate."*

"Don't expect me to act the judge."

"Don't be a fool and walk away from my little girl. She's the best thing that ever happened to you."

"It's true," Fahey agreed, "though I'm not sure you'll leave me much choice about walking away."

The clock tolled nine, clanging a small-scale version of the chimes at Westminster. Nilsson's eyes lit up, aglow from whatever fire raged inside him.

"It's time, Fahey. Shall we?"

* * * *

When the satellite linked up, when Amanda Witt transferred him over to the waiting broadcast team, Fahey donned a wireless earpiece now connected to the BBC via his laptop, which also would act as video monitor. Which theoretically meant he'd be able to witness his own death unfold, as well as Nilsson's. For his part in incriminating Chloe's father, perhaps he deserved this fate.

Nilsson's voice had departed his head. Whether he was too weak to maintain the compulsion or could focus only by disconnecting, Fahey didn't know. He'd have to keep the man on message. Their satellite window was twenty minutes and no more.

A helicopter had set down on the grass, observable through the French doors, its rotors stilled despite Nilsson's original command. On his laptop, Fahey watched as the BBC cameras offered a 360-degree view of the grounds around the Castle; saw a sharpshooter assume his position atop a police van. Law-enforcement officers thick-bodied in their bulletproof vests waited warily. In the space outside the music studio, whispered voices issued a command: "Do not antagonize; take both men alive if possible."

A minute before nine fifteen, Chloe texted that all was ready. That Ed Chestack had received confirmation of the money transfer to a Swiss account in Nilsson's name. That the helicopter was fully fueled. That she loved Fahey more than one life allowed.

Fahey gave BBC London his prompt, listened for his ten-second countdown. When the cue came, a strange calm settled over him; he was ready.

To his surprise, Teppan Nilsson, consummate performer, was not. Nilsson stared at the camera, his voice apparently lost, waving the Glock. A loaded weapon and stage fright made for a dangerous combination

*Get it done, Jackson.* He recognized the voice he'd heard that day in Afghanistan, his own voice telling him there was no one else to seize this moment. Fahey swiveled the video camera on its tripod, looked decisively into its lens.

"Hello, I'm Jackson Fahey. Normally, I cover the European Union and eurozone issues for the BBC from my base in Brussels, Belgium. Today, I am coming to you from Castle de la Coeur just west of Ithaca, New York, the storied home of the late Sebastian and Emilie de la Coeur. The couple, leaders of the renowned progressive-rock band Court of Cruelty, committed suicide earlier this year."

*Breathe, Jackson.* One breath, two, then a smooth turn of the camera back to his companion.

"With me today is Teppan Nilsson, co-founder of Matins and Vespers, a Stockholm, Sweden-based Court of Cruelty tribute band. Mr. Nilsson has a statement he'd like to make. If you're ready, Mr. Nilsson, our time is short."

"It is, isn't it?" Nilsson slurred. He pointed the Glock at the ceiling, firing a shot that bounced downward and off Fahey's left calf.

Voices screamed through Fahey's earpiece. The tactical police unit pounded at the door of the music studio. Vibrating through the wall: Chloe's preternaturally loud shriek insisting that they must not try to enter the room, not under any circumstances.

His daughter's intervention somehow therapeutic, Nilsson smiled, his confidence restored. He grabbed the camera, focused it on Fahey's bloodied jeans, then swiveled it until it showed the bullet that had hit Fahey, now embedded in the side of a bookcase.

"Oops, so sorry. How clumsy of me, such a messy start to my message. Jackson, tell everyone you're all right."

Son of a bitch. "I'm okay," Fahey replied, beating a fist against the bullet wound. "Stings quite a bit, but I think the bleeding has already stopped. Please continue, Mr. Nilsson."

Reeking of rotted meat, Nilsson repositioned the camera toward his own face.

"Yesterday, the London police lodged charges against me, accusing me of having ordered, in June, the death of art gallery owner Esteban Gronlund, a former member of Court of Cruelty and a longtime friend and confidant of Sebastian de la Coeur. For the record, I did, indeed, order Gronlund's death by raping and coercing the man who killed him, a bartender named Anthony Kirkpatrick. I did it, I confess."

Confession could be no good for the soul of a man who lacked one. Fahey had to keep things moving, or they'd lose the satellite link before Nilsson finished.

"Why, Mr. Nilsson, would you do such a thing to a man—two men, if you include Anthony Kirkpatrick—that there is absolutely no evidence you knew prior to that night in June?"

Nilsson leaned forward, facing the camera dead-on. "Because I am the second coming of Sebastian de la Coeur. Esteban Gronlund and Anthony Kirkpatrick were conspiring against my daughter, C.J. Hart. They had to be stopped."

Brilliant, tell an altered version of the truth, and it shall set you free. Just as Fahey thought he could almost admire Nilsson's brass, another shot fired and a bullet pierced his right bicep, traversed the muscle, and came out the other side.

"Jesus!" Fahey cried, the camera getting a good angle on the blood bursting from his arm.

"Cut the satellite feed!" a voice yelled.

"Cut that feed and I will blow Fahey's head off!" Nilsson warned. "It's just a nasty flesh wound. Tell them you'll be all right, Jackson." He inched the camera forward, onto the hole in the sleeve of Fahey's green sweater, blood coagulating around the frayed fabric.

"I apologize again for the interruption," Nilsson addressed the camera coolly, "but I can't emphasize enough how serious I am about killing Jackson Fahey if it proves necessary to accomplish my goal. My principal aim is to simply come clean and reveal that I am the man you once knew as Sebastian de la Coeur."

Fahey's arm was on fire, the bullet wound in a spot where it hurt terribly to move or keep still. He checked the video feed on the laptop, found it wanting, so he removed the camera from the tripod with his good left hand and pulled back to get more of Nilsson in the frame. In his ear, the director asked: "Is it true? Is Sebastian alive?"

"Of course not," Fahey whispered. "Can't you see the man is insane?" Viewers, he hoped, saw a lunatic bent on self-destruction.

Nilsson noticed Fahey studying him; he paused to catch his breath, seemingly oblivious to the gurgling sound the air made as it entered and exited his lungs.

"When my true identity was revealed to me, I skipped my band's April memorial to the de la Coeurs in Barcelona so I could race to the mothers of my four babies and assure them Sebastian lived on." Nilsson sucked in more oxygen, required several breaths before he was able to continue. "I was not aware that each rendezvous with Viktoria Tolaj, Anya Morina, and the others was being videotaped. I could not know those videos would become an internet sensation, that I would become known as the Lethal Lover.

"When my babies died in the womb, one after the other, it cost me my sanity. I paid to have their mothers murdered immediately, and their bodies and those of my children disposed of in a remote corner of Sebastian and Emilie's estate in the Czech Republic."

Nilsson stopped, steadied himself against the edge of the piano. "I did not think. I acted rashly and ignobly," he said slowly, raising the Glock to his forehead. "I deserve to die; those women did not."

Some primal instinct seized Fahey, obliterating the pain in his leg and arm, hurtling him at Nilsson, the camera flying from his hand. He was intent on knocking the Glock away. Intent on eliminating any possibility others might watch Nilsson die.

With his injured leg, Fahey kicked at the coffee table, toppling the laptop. Out of the corner of his eye, he registered that all that flashed on the video feed was the now-bloodstained rug on the floor of the music studio.

Nilsson's reflexes were slower, but still sharp. As Fahey's body crashed into him, he aimed and fired.

A bullet struck Fahey square in the kneecap, he heard the bone shatter. Fahey went down in a heap, pulling the microphone and cables to the floor with him.

No horrifying video, no horrifying audio, the satellite feed went silent as he fell.

*"I said two men would be dead by the end of this day. I didn't say which two,"* a feeble voice whispered to Fahey. *"Sebastian is gone for good. So is Teppan."*

As his skull hit the floor, Fahey heard another gunshot. Felt the cold wetness of Teppan Nilsson's blood splash across his face. Felt an acid etching its way across his skin. Felt a pull down, down into blackness.

* * * *

He did not see police break down the music studio's door and push through to confirm Nilsson was dead. Did not see medics rush past the police, to confirm he was not. Eventually, Fahey could make out their efforts to get through the broken glass, the fractured furniture, the pooled blood. He felt them lift his body onto something rigid, carry it away from the odor of decay that enveloped Nilsson's corpse, out of the blistering sun, out of that place where immortal met mortality.

After a short distance, he felt them set him down; felt a cool hand around one of his, and a soft kiss.

Heard a prayer of thanks he knew was Chloe's, a cry of grief he knew was Katarina's, a call ahead to the hospital warning of one dead, one injured with three gunshot wounds plus head trauma and possibly burns.

Heard the buzz of radios, the blare of sirens, the ping of

monitors, the slice of scissors removing his clothes. Felt the searing blaze of his knee being moved, the icy cold of disinfectant swabbed over his wounds, the settling of a sheet over his exposed skin, the pinch of a needle in his undamaged arm, the whoosh of a drug through his veins.

Then no more, just a warm, welcoming void.

*Chapter Eleven*

# LONDON, FEBRUARY 2012

Aspect Ratio shimmers, its windows aglow in white and red mini-lights that shine like sugar on a Valentine's Day confection. Glass crystals in the same colors sparkle over the buffet and dance floor set up in the storefront next door, which we have leased as permanent event space.

Tastefully, joyfully, my gallery has been transformed into a most romantic spot to be married. I could never have envisioned it quite this way, a mere rectangle reimagined as this idyllic setting for two lives to be joined, but Meredith, sister of my heart, did. She's had experience, she knows how to plan a stylish way to say the vows, just isn't so strong on the making-them-stick part. As if anyone knows for certain the formula for love everlasting.

The groom is handsome in his black tuxedo, surrounded by family: siblings, parents, and cousins who ought to be weary from travel, but instead are buoyed by their happiness for him. The bride is lovely in a column of ivory silk, a design straight out of Old Hollywood.

The consummate planner has planned it all so precisely, so wonderfully. A flute and small organ play the opening notes of Pachelbel's *Canon in D*, just as my parents might have.

"Happy Birthday, C.J." Meredith hugs me so tightly I'm afraid she'll squeeze me out of my dress.

"Happy Wedding Day, Mer." I hug back, wiping tears away. "I've told Benjamin he'd better be good to you or he'll get to meet my inner monster."

She laughs, rushes to take her dad's arm, and they glide down the makeshift aisle. I take Ben's brother's arm and follow. Sitting to either side of the white runner on which we walk are the people Meredith does her best to love: her mother, a cold shadow of her warm, vivid daughter; Ed, the biological father she's getting to know in a new way; Gloria, the woman who pretty much raised us both; and Tweedle-Dee and Tweedle-Dum, Dan Grainger and Kevin Todd, who tried so hard to make her happy but let her go when they realized they couldn't. At the end of the third row: Jackson's parents, Michael and Maureen Fahey, who have become Meredith's friends, grateful for her support of their damaged son.

Of Jackson, there is no sign, though Meredith said she expected him. Did he notify her he'd be a no-show, or will she feel the disappointment of his absence? Just as I do. Just as well. It might have been awkward, the two of us here at a wedding that isn't ours.

The vows are earnest and unrehearsed. Meredith and Ben are completely in this moment, unafraid to voice what is in their hearts.

Ben pledges to cherish the woman Meredith is today and will be tomorrow; promises he will stand always beside her, to lift her when she stumbles and rise with her when she soars. His deep, strong voice almost fails him as he states proudly that he intends to honor her and love her faithfully for as long as they live.

Meredith apologizes to her ex-spouses for failing to love herself enough, and promises Ben that she knows she is worthy of him and his love. She pledges her devotion, her fidelity and her support, for richer and poorer, for better and worse, in sickness and health, till death parts them.

"And even after, I will cherish you," she says, winking at me through bright tears. She knows now, of course, what I am, what Sebastian and Emilie were. Helping Jackson bring my father to cosmic justice seems at last to have exorcised Sebastian's demons from her.

The Anglican priest, an art-school friend of Ben's from Accra, clasps her hands around Ben's and Meredith's, wishes them a bright future filled with joy and, if they want, happy and healthy children. She pronounces them man and wife; they kiss, and the guests applaud appreciatively. Grainger and Todd whoop loudly, confusing their wives and Ben's visiting relatives from Ghana. Maybe they've exorcised a few demons of their own.

We march back down the aisle and into the adjacent party hall to the strains of the Beatles. Love is, indeed, all we need. We've declared this place, this day, Court of Cruelty-free. *Court of Calamity,* as Daphne, the third member of our Aspect Ratio team, has taken to calling my parents' old band. No calamities today, Meredith has decreed, only happy thoughts. I wonder if she'll share her meds with me, just this once.

A chamber ensemble plays something by Mozart as hands are shaken, cheeks are kissed, backs patted. Ed's wife, a woman I've met maybe one other time in the decades I've known her husband, joins the receiving line and stands next to him wearing a genuine smile. Even Meredith's parents seem authentically happy, actually seem human in a way I've never observed before. Meredith always preferred my family to hers, something that never needed explaining despite all my issues with Emilie and Sebastian. We were strange, yes, but never bloodless.

As the crowd gravitates toward tables and the buffet line, the bride sidles up to me and hands me a flute filled with golden bubbly. "Drink this, it's sparkling pear cider and super-delicious. Our African guests mostly don't indulge, so Ben and I will hit the champagne later."

I sip, as ordered. "Hmm, tasty, and you, Meredith Grainger-Todd, prove your brilliance once again. Wait, are you *still* Meredith Grainger-Todd?"

She pinches my arm. “Lord, yes, haven’t we had enough people with multiple identities? I am who I am, and Benjamin doesn’t mind in the least. I freak his family out anyway, what’s one more thing? Now, mingle, sweetie, I must spend time with my husband. How great does that sound?”

I arch an eyebrow at my now-thrice-married pal. Meredith sticks out her tongue, shouts, “Cut me a break, will you, C.J.,” as she saunters over to her new best friend, looking gorgeous and gleeful.

“You heard the bride, mingle.” Gloria sips from her glass of real champagne. “Dan and Kevin’s wives are very nice, and they know hardly anyone. I did my best to explain who was who on the flight over from New York.”

“I’ve never been much for mingling. Never was good at all those social graces Emilie tried to instill in me.”

“Nonsense, you were a most polite child. Your teachers used to send reports back praising your deportment.”

“Had them fooled, didn’t I?”

She gathers me close. “I know this is hard for you, but I also know you’ll never let Meredith and Ben see it. If you need me, just give me a sign. Meanwhile, I think I’ll go fill a plate. The food smells wonderful.”

I hear her parting shot through strains of violin and viola: “Don’t forget to eat something!” Old habits, etc. I am a bit hungry. I force myself to consume actual food every day now. Among other things, it reminds me I’m still somewhat human.

Before I move toward the buffet, Jackson’s parents approach. Even if we hadn’t met at the hospital in Ithaca, I would have recognized them, his red hair and smiling green eyes, her dark hair and facial features so much like her son’s. Michael Fahey extends his hand, shakes mine; Maureen Fahey kisses my cheek, squeezes both my hands lightly.

“It’s so good to see you, Chloe, it’s been too long,” she says. “We were so delighted to receive Meredith’s invitation. This gallery is such a magical place for a wedding.”

"All Meredith's doing. I arrived back in London only yesterday." A disclaimer, but for them or for me?

Michael Fahey asks whether he can get us anything from the bar, anything to avoid an uncomfortable discussion of their son and our possible non-relationship. I don't know what they understand to be the status of affairs between Jackson and me; Lord knows, I don't know how to describe it. Maureen asks for a white wine; I raise my still-full flute of cider, and he slips away.

"This must be awkward for you, Maureen. I'm sorry."

"You mustn't apologize; these things take time to sort themselves out. Jackson had planned to be here, but the BBC called day before yesterday and asked whether he'd be willing to do a turn as part-time TV news presenter. He had to get back to the flat in Brussels, get settled in and up to speed. He goes on air tomorrow."

An anchor job. His face must be healed, but did that mean he wasn't ready for field reporting, or perhaps that they didn't want him doing it anymore?

She can tell what I'm thinking. "It's just temporary, they've told him, they were shorthanded and knew he was ready to return to work a few hours each week. I suppose they thought this would be a way to ease him back in, and I can't say I disagree. He can continue physical therapy on his days off."

"He's getting around all right?"

Her cheeks flushed, she waves her hand in front of her face. "Oh, yes, of course, the new knee is working famously; he just needs to build up strength. The doctors have suggested bicycling—they don't want him running—and Brussels is a very good place to cycle. He's optimistic, really, about everything. I believe he's in a good place."

Michael Fahey comes back with their drinks; she takes her cue. "I believe my husband needs to be fed about now. Before I forget . . ." She reaches into her purse and pulls out an envelope. "This is from Jackson. I understand it's your birthday today."

I force a smile to my lips. "February 19, might be an Aquarius, might be a Pisces, depends who you ask."

"Happy day then," she says, and pecks my cheek, leaving me with a greeting or something from her son I'm afraid to open, but also afraid not to. The time for cowardice is long past, the time for bravery long overdue. I slide my fingernail under the seal and read.

*Happy Birthday, Chloe,*

*I hope you're doing well. I think of you often.*

*I'm sure you've figured out by now that this recovery of mine can't be rushed, it happens on its own terms, at its own speed. But I finally return to work Monday. I'm getting there; I hope you are too.*

*Love,*

*Jackson*

I fold the note into my palm, drain my glass to head for the bridal table, but I crush the flute before I've taken a step. A flash of pain distracts me from the urge to smash something else, long enough to get me out of the gallery, out to the sidewalk, across the street where I can get some air and breathe.

From this vantage, Aspect Ratio, all that I've built here, looks more beautiful than ever. I am home here, I remind myself. Second chances are rare, this one doubly precious because it has come at such great cost. I force myself to reflect on each loss.

Why, then, am I still standing here, an anachronism on the corner of a small city block, dressed in red silk and pearls, feeling like an outsider again—or more to the point, still? Lifting the hem of my dress so it doesn't get dirty, I walk back to my gallery, back inside to the wedding, to my friends, to my frustrating, confounding world.

* * * *

Sixty days on since the vampire apocalypse, it continues to

consume my life. We were well into January before the plywood had been replaced with clear glass on most of the Castle's windows. Boards remain where the stained glass had been. Thanks to Sebastian's photography, each of those windows had been documented, so we have a guide for recreating them. All we need is the cash; the insurance company has finally agreed to pay, and we await the check. Seems the Castle is on a fault line, and Sebastian had taken out earthquake insurance. His cries of despair registered as seismic events, for which I am only retrospectively grateful.

My father had some redeeming qualities after all. By laying both Sebastian de la Coeur and Teppan Nilsson to rest, he closed the book on Gippel & Co.'s various investigations. The dredging equipment pulled out the next day, though I will spend as-yet-undetermined amounts to re-landscape the lake area.

Our assets are decidedly less liquid than they used to be. I have spent the last two weeks in Prague, sacking my parents' estate there for artwork and furnishings I can turn over as quick sales. Some smaller pieces traveled to London on the plane with me; a few more crates are due to arrive at the gallery shortly. Benjamin and I have scheduled a show tentatively called *Bohemian Legacy* for late March, which means we'll have only about three weeks to install it after he and Meredith return from their honeymoon in Kauai. Which means I have only two weeks to establish a design for the exhibition and an internal logic for the layout.

My mother and I have decided—or rather, I have decided and she has not objected—that the Prague house must be sold. It seems to hold little sentimental value for her, and she needs money to live on while she figures out her next move. Matins and Vespers is, at best, a hobby rather than an occupation; the band was only a temporary strategy anyway, a plan hatched back when suicide was only make-believe and a connection to my ongoing existence needed to be maintained. I'll have to work through Chestack to market the de la Coeurs' Czech homestead and find a buyer; we sort of agreed tonight that we'd get together to discuss business before he heads back to the States.

Once the bride and groom leave for the airport and the guests disperse to their hotels and the caterers clean up, I change out of my red bridesmaid's dress, ditch the red strappy sandals, and put on black yoga pants, a long purple sweater, and flats. The gown, a couture strapless-with-peplum number, stares down at me from inside its garment bag, hanging from the hook on the back of my office door. I bought it in Prague and paid way too much for it. All I have to do is sell three paintings to recoup; probably faster to just sell the dress.

Bills of lading, insurance vouchers, and assorted ephemera related to my income-versus-outflow issues sit piled on the desk before me, daring me to ignore them, when the front buzzer sounds. I walk through the darkened exhibit space, peer around the blinds on the door to see Ed standing there, still in his tux.

I open but don't unchain the door. "Did you forget something?"

"I was too restless to turn in when my wife did, so I checked email. Found something you and I should talk about."

I let him in, reset the security alarm, and guide him back to the office.

"Quiet like this." He looks around almost reverently. "It seems so strange to be in this place without them. Aspect Ratio *was* Esteban and, though not as much, was Sebastian too. Must be six years since I've been here, but I have pleasant memories of this place, positive, creative memories. Sebastian always came back to the Castle brimming with energy and new ideas, worthwhile ideas for investments and improvements to the winery. The art seemed to fire his business cylinders, if that makes any sense."

I understand completely. "It reminds me of Sebastian at his best and brings out the best creative instincts in me. I loved the place as soon as I saw it. Taking over this gallery is the best thing I've ever done."

I point to a chair, and he sits. "Drink? There's some champagne in the fridge and some vodka."

"I noticed you didn't drink anything tonight but that pear stuff Meredith was pushing."

"She decided that if she had to drink it, I did too. Really wasn't bad, and the rest of you got more champagne as a result. Win-win."

He nods skeptically, lays eyes on my dress hanging on the door. "You looked lovely tonight, Chloe. Red's a good color for you, nice change from your usual black. Interesting design, too, with that winding thing around the waistline. Slimming, not that you've ever had to worry about that."

What's really on his mind? Ed without an agenda is not a person I'm familiar with.

"Never realized you paid so much attention to my wardrobe, or to anything else that didn't have to do with my parents' money, so maybe you ought to tell me why you're here, beyond the reminiscing, that is."

Perceptive guy, he knows I'm on to him, but he's enjoying the game too much to let it go just yet.

"I was here the night Esteban and Sebastian first met Jackson Fahey and decided he was the one for you. I watched Esteban chat him up, watched Sebastian pretend to ignore him. Didn't think anything of it at the time, it was never much use to speculate about what Sebastian was up to. Eventually, he made his aims abundantly clear."

Abundantly and decidedly unsubtly, I have no doubt. "So this email you got was about Jackson? Has the BBC sued us or something?"

He gets up, walks to the mini-fridge, pulls out the lemon vodka. "I think I will have something. One for you, too?"

"No, thanks. I was hoping to get some work done before heading back to my flat, and it's getting late."

He pours himself a few fingers' worth, settles back into his chair. "Down to business then. The broker in Prague emailed an offer on the Czech estate."

"Didn't the broker just put out feelers, to see if the price was on the mark?"

Ed sips the vodka, grimacing at the taste. "Exactly, and before a full business day passed, our guy says, he'd already been approached with a deal. The prospective buyer can't devote the due-diligence time until mid to late May, so he's offering a binder to keep the house off the market in the meantime."

"Thus tying our hands for three months."

Ed stands and paces the very short length of my office. "That's where this gets weird. The buyer is giving us $2 million outright as a sign of good faith, to show he won't blow off a final deal in hopes we lower the price, though I'm sure he'd like that. He knows we need the cash badly and knows we need to unload the Czech place to get it, which gives him leverage, yet the offer is more than generous."

"It's not like our problems haven't been in the news." *Sit down already*, I want to compel Ed as he begins a new circuit of the room. "Who is he, some Russian oligarch with a passion for the Cruel?"

Chestack runs his hands through his hair, looks exhausted and something I wouldn't have expected, apprehensive. "That would make sense, some hard-headed dude from Moscow deciding he wants to own Sebastian and Emilie's Eastern Bloc pleasure palace as an expensive souvenir of the Cold War. This buyer doesn't add up so neatly, though. Even the name makes me suspicious."

Taking suspicious to a whole new level, even for Ed. "The name? Really?"

"According to the paperwork, the legal buyer would be a Swiss architectural-fittings company founded in Zurich in 1910, Gregor Zwilling GmBH. *Gregor Zwilling*, get it?"

My German isn't fluent, but I understand this one. "Gregor, the twin. So what?"

He massages his left temple. "Your father was a twin, and his brother's name was Gregor."

Stefan Herz, the man who became Sebastian de la Coeur, was one of a matched pair? "How do you know this? Daddy never talked about his family. All I know is what I've read in that dusty old Bible he left me."

"Must have been forty years ago, not long after I met him. I mentioned I had a twin sister, and Sebastian told me he had a fraternal twin; that he was born four minutes before his brother and that's why he got to study music while his twin ended up apprenticed to a blacksmith or ironmonger, something like that." Ed starts a third lap around the space. "Apparently, Gregor died on the job. His forge sparked a blaze that flamed out of control and took out the whole building and a few others besides."

I grab his wrist as he passes behind me. "My parents met in the 1860s, when Stefan was in his early thirties. When did Gregor die?"

"About a half-dozen years after Stefan left with Eugenie for good, maybe the early 1870s." Ed shakes me off, finally sits and downs the rest of his drink. "Sebastian said his youngest sister wrote him about Gregor's death. She told him that their mother was devastated, and that their siblings blamed him. He didn't say why."

I reach for a stapler and pound it on the desk like a gavel. "Counselor, unless you have evidence that someone is out to get us, I suggest we consider this offer on its merits. It's money in our quickly draining bank accounts."

In surrender, he raises his hands. "Other than *agita* about this thing I can't explain away, I have no evidence. I'll examine the financials, make sure all the terms are agreeable, and if still it meets your approval we'll sign your little bit of Old Bohemia over to Christoph Zwilling."

"He is?"

"CEO of the company, great-great-grandson of the founder. You want to get the ball rolling; he's the one we roll it to." Ed looks like he wants nothing more than to sleep. "Man, that vodka went right to my head."

"Let's get you a cab," I suggest, pulling his bulk to his feet. He extricates himself from my hold, walks out to the exhibit space and waits for me to disengage the alarm.

"This sounds too good to be true, Chloe. Talk to your mother, see what she knows about Gregor Herz, and Gregor Zwilling, for that matter."

"Katarina, the elusive? Haven't seen or heard from her since the week after my father's death. Oh, except for a text replying to my question about selling the Prague house. She was simply eloquent in her indifference: *'Fine.'* "

"Emilie de la Coeur is dead, and Kat can't stop you legally if this what you want to do. I'm just saying some caution might be in order."

"Why? I lose another bit of bad karma. No more worrying whether Interpol will find more corpses there."

Ed shakes his head. "Ronnie denies there are, and if anyone knows where Sebastian's bodies are buried, it's him."

"Such a comfort." I look forward to escorting my attorney through Aspect Ratio's front door for the second time tonight.

"I don't trust Ronnie any more than you do, so, yes, the sooner we dispose of the place, the better. In the meantime, though, until I can learn more about this Christoph Zwilling, don't worry about your checkbook. Listen to your gut."

Will do. Proven liars, probable liars, and potential liars are old news here. Keeping my wits about me has become a survival skill.

* * * *

It's something like three o'clock in the morning when my phone rings, startling me out of whatever fugue state I've entered while trying to read property assessments badly translated from Czech to English via a computer program run by the twenty-year-old aspiring model working in the Prague real estate office listing Castle de la Coeur Europe. I've lost track of the going rate per square foot in korunas much less dollars. For all I know, we could be giving the place away at $20 million.

By the time I locate my phone—hidden beneath the multipage printout of a document Ed has forwarded—the call has gone to voicemail. The number is one I recognize, and it frightens the hell out of me. Why so late? What can he want? My finger itches to launch a return call, but I wait for the message, force patience into the spot where impulse wants to prevail.

*"Juliette, I'm sorry I missed your birthday. I planned to call before midnight, but I fell asleep. Long day trying to settle back into my flat in Brussels; unpacking, buying groceries, et cetera. But you had the wedding. I'm sure you're wiped out, as well. No need to call me back, my mother gave you my note, I'm sure."*

I punch in Jackson's number; wait to hear his voice sounding good again, strong again.

"Hi," he says. "I wasn't sure if you had your mobile on."

"It was buried under some stuff on my desk."

He laughs, a rich rumble that rises from his throat like melted chocolate, all smooth and delicious. "Miss Hart, please tell me you're not working on your birthday."

"Technically, Mr. Fahey, it's no longer my birthday and, technically, I'm not working, just tying up a few loose ends. I hear you're about to be back on-air, doing an anchor spot."

"Yes, the mid-morning-to-mid-afternoon presenter," he replies, maybe a bit too enthusiastically. "High audience, so the pressure's on for me to be my brilliant, handsome self. Thank God for those expensive Park Avenue plastic surgeons."

Meredith tells me they were worth every penny I paid them, that Jackson has only a tiny scar beneath his right eye.

He goes quiet, as if at a loss what to say next. We haven't spoken in more than seven weeks, since he regained consciousness after the first surgery on his face to remove scar tissue from the burns. Powder burns from Teppan's Glock, the doctors said, but Jackson and I know it was something else, some toxic emission from the body that had been my father's.

That first day, Jackson couldn't talk, swathed in bandages. The second and third and fourth days, it seemed he couldn't stop reliving the memory of those last minutes, when Teppan's blood washed over his skin, corroding it. The doctors tried to keep him relaxed, with anti-anxiety meds Jackson refused to take. By the fifth day, he was calmer, with more post-op issues than post-traumatic stress, but one thing was obvious: He couldn't talk to me; couldn't bear to see me without cycling into some spiral of dismay and distress, disintegrating from the man who existed before that sun-drenched morning in the music studio into the one who woke in an emergency room with flesh hanging off his cheekbone and a knee joint that would never function again.

So I stayed away, and the days became weeks, then the weeks, months. The short drive to the hospital in Ithaca became a trans-Atlantic flight to England, now a flight to Brussels. Nothing has spanned that time or distance, and here we are, with no words, though there is so much to say.

"Jackson, it's late, I can tell you're exhausted. Call me in a few days, after you're back at work, I'll want all the details."

"I'm sorry, love."

"What is there to apologize for?"

"Only everything."

"You didn't kill him, my father killed himself. No absolution necessary, and even if it were, haven't you atoned enough?"

"I set everything in motion. I drove him to it."

"We all did, my mother most especially, but also me."

"No," he insists. "You were a victim."

Only I wasn't, a fine point he can't seem to comprehend. I didn't do what I did to avenge myself; my father committed no crime against me.

"I adored him my whole life, but I condemned him for what

he had become. I stood by and watched him die and almost take you with him. There's plenty of guilt to go around, plenty for us to dwell on forever and let it tear us to pieces. Kat and you and I, Jackson, we have to let it go. We all just have to let it go."

He coughs through what I know to be a sob, and my heart breaks. This is why he can't see me, can't bear to be anywhere near me.

"Sweetheart, you have to get ready for your new job."

"Am I? Your sweetheart?" he interrupts, echoing my words to him on the phone that morning in the music studio, before hell closed in on him.

"Always," I promise. "Longer."

He breathes in, out, inhales, holds it, holds it, exhales, a cadence that seems to soothe him.

"I'm okay," he whispers after several repetitions, though I am unconvinced. "Goodnight, birthday girl."

I switch off my phone, my personal battery too drained to contemplate another call like that tonight. Not that he'll call again. I can only imagine how much courage this one took.

I find my shoes under the desk, step into them and head for the storage room at the rear of the gallery. I slide a painting to one side, finger onto the keypad the combination that opens the wall safe, reach in for the two velvet boxes I brought back from the Castle last month.

The smaller one, of course, holds my pendant; the larger one, his. I slip mine around my neck, grasp Jackson's and place it against my heart, feeling the burn as the ruby ignites under my touch. I wish for pleasant dreams for him, for peace of mind, if such a thing is possible.

He will sleep soundly tonight, at the very least. I doubt I will.

Grabbing my coat and purse, my dress and the wheeled suitcase with the rest of my wedding wardrobe, I switch off the lights, switch on the security alarm, and walk home.

* * * *

He's left the hallway light on again. Its incandescence casts a yellow glow over his naked form, sprawled on my couch, Maureen Fahey's afghan spread across his midsection. There's something blasphemous about it, Will's body instead of her son's being warmed by her handiwork, but I can't get hung up on that. I have to accept that Will may be my real future and a life with Jackson mere fantasy. If that turns out to be true, I have to move past the consequences of my father's last hours to a place where there is no guilt, where I can be content with the person I am. The person who dragged Will into the miasma and now depends on him against all good sense and sense of fairness. More guilt there for me. Yet free of Teppan's compulsion, Will continues to stand by me and nourish me. I exert no power over him; no one forces him to love me, he just does. Honestly, I don't know how I could have gotten through the last two months without him.

I squeeze onto the edge of the sofa, place a hand on his thigh. His eyes open, take a minute to focus. "Mmm, hi, baby. Nice wedding?"

Kneading the taut muscle, I rest my head against his leg. "Beautiful wedding. Beautiful bride, handsome groom, a fairy tale come true." I bite down hard into a vein, suck at him ravenously, longer than I probably need to. After a few minutes, I ease off, let his blood redistribute itself, eventually feel his erection prod my shoulder for attention.

"No handsome prince for you, just a handsome frog." Will moans, enervated by the sexual imprint my mouth leaves behind. "You didn't text that you wanted me to stay away tonight. Oh, man, thank God you didn't."

"As if a text is all it would take to get rid of you."

He pulls away a little, out of reach of my tongue, my lips. "As if you'd prefer to be out there hunting. I was your first hunt, and I'm still your first. I'll be your last if you'll let me, but you already know that. And this is where you promise me, again, that this is the last time we have this conversation."

Makes it sound like we're an old married couple, fighting the same fights.

"I could compel you to stay away," I threaten, for the thousandth time. "You're ruining your life."

He tickles my nose with his cock. "If you were going to compel me to stay away, you'd have done it already, weeks ago, in New York or in Prague, but you didn't."

"You should be in Edinburgh," I protest, again for the thousandth time, though with less conviction than I might have before Jackson's call tonight. "You'll lose everything you've worked for."

He shoots me his usual disbelieving scowl. "Such a beautiful nag. I brew the damn beer, and my trust fund underwrites the operation, which, by the way, is on track to show a nice profit again this year. When I'm there at the brewpub, I'm working eighteen, nineteen hours a day. No one begrudges me a few days away with the mysterious girlfriend they never get to meet, even though everyone knows it's you because of that Christmas punch Fahey threw. No one minds a bit except the mysterious girlfriend herself. Good thing I have an abundance of self-esteem. One of us has to recognize that, right this minute and for as long as you need me, this is where I'm supposed to be, skin-to-skin with you."

Will pulls me up onto his chest, gives me a bruising kiss. He unzips my jacket, pushes it off my shoulders, wraps a hand around my right breast and squeezes. "Admit it: You love it when I get all domineering on you. Makes you feel like less of a vampire bitch."

"I don't love you, Will. A vampire bitch is exactly what I am." To prove my point, I bite his lower lip until I draw blood and sip the red bubble that rises.

He bites back. "You're not in love with me, so what? You like me just fine."

His hands reach for the hem of my sweater; he inches it up my body, stopping as he does to tease gently across my stomach. He slides his fingers past the waistband of my pants, eases them down until I can kick free of them, spreads my legs and lifts me onto him, pushes into the slickness, thrusts high and hard.

"If it's me or Fahey, he wins every time, I get that. But damn, Chloe, if he gives up the fight, you'll need more than compulsion to keep me away."

Will tugs a breast from my lacy red bra, sucks it into his mouth as I ride him, as he gives as good as he gets. He's always good to me, driven by nothing more than a desire to be with me. He really doesn't give a damn about the vampire crap.

If only there weren't that other guy.

* * * *

By the time Chestack's plane takes off for New York three days later, the deal with Gregor Zwilling GmbH has been sealed. Christoph Zwilling has ninety days to wrap up his other pressing business before acquiring my parents' Czech home-away-from-home so he can use its trim pieces and mantels and gargoyles and gates and grates as templates for his plaster and wood and metal reproductions. I have ninety days to clear out anything not attached to the structures that I want to keep or sell off.

The $2 million has been deposited, money for repairing the Castle and the grounds, for undoing the damage Teppan wrought. Dare I take an unanxious breath? Dare I believe that someday this last year will be just a sad coda to many happy childhood memories of my Daddy Bastian?

At Aspect Ratio, crates from an earlier Prague shipment stand empty, their contents strewn everywhere as Daphne and I catalog them, piece by meticulously recorded piece. She's channeling Meredith, cautioning me to lift with my knees, fetching me juice and healthy snacks, as though good nutrition can distract me from becoming too preoccupied with the daunting task ahead.

Over the next ninety days, the real heavy lifting will be my travel-and-transport schedule. I figure I'll need to make a trip a month in March, April, and early May to get the rest of the sellable stuff at the Czech property inventoried and readied for shipment. I must calculate how many more shipping containers I'll need, how many packers and how much packing material, how much storage space I'll need here in the UK once the goods land. Also the taxes and tariffs and other red tape Ed can manage inefficiently at best from Ithaca, given that the number of containers will be uncertain until it isn't. So much easier to deal with the British bureaucracy in London from London.

On the plus side, for the art conservator that still breathes within me, there are those old tapestries at the Prague house that need tending to, something to keep me busy when I'm not de-Crueling the premises, setting up the *Bohemian Legacy* exhibit, and trying generally to create order out of this chaos.

Something to keep me out of trouble after there's no more of this chaos to contend with and before a new round begins. Because there's always a new round.

In response to the sixth or seventh text I've sent informing my mother about the deal on the house—she's ignored all Chestack's texts and calls, he claims—and asking what, if anything, she wants me to set aside for her, she deigns to write only this much:

*Aside from the tapestries, I care nothing for what remains at the Prague house. Honor it, or trash it, with my blessing. I know you'll want to keep something of your father's. I have my good memories of him to hold onto. Matins and Vespers has signed on at Casa Cruella for a first anniversary tribute concert to Sebastian and Emilie. Barcelona is lovely in April, remember?*

If the name Gregor Zwilling troubles her at all, if it gives her the same pause it still gives Ed, Katarina doesn't say. Maybe she doesn't care, or if she does, maybe she's ignoring it as one more potentially unsettling association with her late husband.

Have I become the world's biggest worrier? I'm actually concerned for my mother. This is the first time in her life she's been alone, even allowing for the sturdy, handsome Swede who seldom leaves her side. Truth is, loyal, faithful Eric is as temporary an attachment for her as Will is for me, as Jackson would be. Much as I hate to admit it, we're not that different, she and I, even our ways of dealing with our sorrow are pretty similar: We run away, and try to lose ourselves in men who refuse to see how bad we are for them.

Kat's right about one thing: Barcelona is lovely in the spring. Will Matins and Vespers end there, where it began, after the last chords have been played? Will she seize the new beginning that, after 150 years or so, she's more than due?

In another century and a half, will I be just like her?

*Chapter Twelve*

# BRUSSELS, APRIL 2012

All his dreams began like this, though they ended differently each night: He was in a lush garden filled with flowers and fragrance, sitting on a bench, when a little girl ran up to him and settled on the grass at his feet and showed him her dolls, a prince and a princess.

A tiny child with shiny, dark-brown curls, about four years old or maybe five, he didn't know for sure, all he had were nephews, all tall for their age as he had been. This sprite had laughing eyes, but he couldn't say what color they were, he never remembered. She told him her dolls' names—they were never the same from dream to dream—and she babbled some story about what the prince and the princess had done that day, what they had eaten for lunch, what her cat looked like: gray and tan and white with an "M" on its forehead; she knew her letters and wanted to know if he did, too.

With each successive dream, scenes were more vivid, colors brighter, sounds clearer. Last night, the child had offered him a taste of her ice cream. It was vanilla, clean, sweet vanilla; he felt it cold on his tongue. At the end of every dream—he now knew the end was coming when he asked the little girl her name—he got a bit more of an answer.

"You know what my name is, you're my daddy," she'd always

say.

"Is your name Guinevere?" he'd always ask.

"No, she was your baby who died," she'd explain. "I'm your other baby. I didn't die, you know that, silly."

He didn't, truly.

Most nights, the little girl would giggle and scamper away, and he'd follow her into a maze, losing her in the leafy labyrinth, never learning what to call her. So he was caught by surprise this night: She wore sparkles on her shoes that fell off as she skipped along, leaving a twinkling trail to guide him. He hurried to catch up, and when she saw him she stopped and smiled and ran into his arms.

"You found me! I can tell you my name now if you still want to know."

He hugged her tightly. "I do, please tell me."

"My name is Avalon Fahey, but you call me Ava, you and Mommy. Now you remember, don't you?" She kissed his scarred cheek, and in her eyes this time he saw an enchanting green: Chloe's eyes.

He jerked awake and bolted upright; a cold sweat spread across his forehead and trickled down from his hairline to his jaw as he shivered. A hand touched his back, and he pulled away, startled.

Amanda turned on the light so he could see her, recognize her. "The dream again? You're more agitated tonight."

"The dream again," he confirmed and lay down next to her. Amanda put her head on his chest, listened to his pounding heart. He curled his arm around her, pulled her closer.

"Avalon. You shouted that just before you woke. Is that a place or a person?"

He closed his eyes, conjured his dream daughter's face. "Definitely a person, the little girl; maybe the place where I see her, too, I don't know." He kissed Amanda's forehead, tightened his arms around her. It felt good not to be alone, good to tell someone what he saw when he slept.

Amanda hummed softly, puffs of her breath warm on his

skin. Witt's *Symphony in BBC Major*, they called it in Madrid: Humming meant she was thinking hard.

Fahey was hard, but not from thinking. If he had been thinking, if she had been thinking, they wouldn't be naked together now, after a long weekend of scratching an itch they'd left so long unscratched. She'd come to Brussels for an all-Europe bureau chiefs' summit with the executive director. She'd stayed behind after the others had headed for the airport or train station and invited him to dinner, two old work friends getting together to catch up. Lord, he'd needed to get laid though, to burn off the restlessness that had built inside him, that couldn't be exhausted simply by pushing his body further at the gym, through the limits his doctors had set. He felt strong. He needed to move. He needed to do. Amanda had called, and hadn't she known exactly what kind of doing would do the trick.

Thus had she discovered the dream. Just like someone else he knew, it seemed Amanda didn't sleep after sex but watched him, listened to him. He stroked her breast now, plucked at her nipple, though he couldn't say whether she'd noticed, so intent was she on the puzzle, humming something that sounded like Court of Cruelty's song "Wisdom." Then again, maybe everything sounded like the Cruel to him. Maybe he'd never get that music out of his brain, or the smell of Teppan Nilsson slowly cooking in the sun.

"Allegorically, it makes sense, Jackson: The little girl is Avalon, and this garden you see in your dream is Avalon, too, like King Arthur's resting place, where everything is peaceful. She lives in your paradise."

A tear formed at the edge of the eye closest to her, and he pushed it away before Amanda could see it. He refused to cry in front of her.

"She told me her name was Avalon Fahey and that her Mommy and I called her Ava. What the hell does that mean, when she explicitly tells me she isn't the baby Chloe and I lost, repeatedly tells me she isn't Guinevere? What am I supposed to divine from this bloody dream? It's been like this for two months, night after night, Mandy, it's unrelenting."

She pushed up on her elbow, wiped from his cheek the remnant of a second tear. "It's not unpleasant, though, or not altogether so. Last night, you looked very calm to me. Sometimes, you looked happy, actually."

It was true, the dream wasn't disturbing, just perplexing. He slept fairly well most nights, in spite of it. "What's your diagnosis, Doctor Witt?"

"How long since you talked to Chloe?"

"Middle of February, on her birthday. The dream started that night."

"Has it occurred to you that if you called her again, the dream might go away?"

He was afraid of that very thing, but he wasn't going to admit it to Amanda. He had little enough dignity left as it was. She had seen what happened at the Castle that morning, however remotely; had watched Nilsson point the muzzle of a Glock at Fahey's head, manipulate him into stage-directing the big hostage scene for the worldwide television audience, then proceed to blow up his knee.

"I think this is based in some unresolved feelings you have about Chloe's miscarriage. You never addressed them because of what happened with Teppan Nilsson so soon after. Maybe this dream is your subconscious forcing you to face your grief."

He kissed her, teased her lips open to let him inside. He didn't want to deal with grief anymore; he wanted to remember what it felt like to be a man. Enough with reminders of the things he'd never reclaim from those terrible days in New York. He wanted to rejoice in his renewed strength, in his vigorously living body as it did what vigorously living bodies did together. He wanted physical sensation, not psychoanalysis.

Amanda broke off the kiss and made him look at her. "I know you needed to get back on the horse, you took a bad, bad fall, but it's been four months since you were in that room with

Nilsson. You've conquered your injuries, and your anxieties about work and, well, about sex, quite stupendously. Isn't it time you tackled the rest?"

He threw a long leg over her, trapped her against the mattress, but she was right. Time to face his demons. "Where do I start?"

"Find your way back to Chloe. Being here with you has been lovely, but it's just for now. She's the one you walked through hell for, I watched you do it. The gossip blogs say she's been shuttling between London and Prague, cleaning out her parents' home there, preparing it for an imminent sale, though she also had a big exhibit open last month at her gallery. Wherever she is, go after her."

He released Amanda from the snug prison of his body, suddenly wanting very much a woman who wasn't lying naked in his bed. Amanda pouted, just for effect.

"This means I'll never be reassigned to Madrid, doesn't it?"

"Well, you might, but not by me. I've been reassigned to Berlin, remember?" She shivered, pulled the blanket up and over her. "In thirty days, both of us will be stuck up here in the drearier climes of Europe's central latitudes. No going back for us, not to the old days."

He'd known that for quite a while; this merely made official the fact that his Brussels gig was going to have a long run. While he'd been working the anchor desk, he'd actually missed covering those fusty debates about fiscal austerity and profligate government spending in Greece. He had leapt at the chance to return to reporting, even if it meant afternoons with the leaders of the European Union and their finance ministers and the International Monetary Fund, being fed a steady diet of political economics.

So much for the dream he'd had of running away to sunny Spain with Chloe and their baby. In his new dream, though, a little girl still called him Daddy. Fahey wrapped himself around Amanda and the warmth she was willing to give him only for what remained of the weekend. He willed himself to sleep so he and Avalon could visit again.

* * * *

His eyes had barely adjusted to the dimly lit Barcelona nightclub when he heard his name shouted.

"Jackson Fahey! You have returned to us for this commemorative event! Consort of Sebastian and Emilie's princess, we drink to your newfound health!"

Vassals by the dozens, men in all black, women in short pink tops and short black skirts, rose from their seats and raised their glasses, hailing him like a hero back from the battlefield. The battle part of it was true enough, he supposed, even if the consort role was no longer his. The bartender waved Fahey over, a just-pulled pint of Catalan brew spilling over in its eagerness to reach him. He shook the man's hand, quaffed a quarter of the beer down, and accepted the applause.

Who knew he'd be the opening act at this first-anniversary tribute to the much-beloved de la Coeurs, one now actually dead, one as yet undetectable, and one—Christ, did he even know whether she'd show up? It was worth a shot, Fahey figured. He'd already spent two weeks failing to find her; she was never in London when he was, never in Prague when that seemed a possibility. If not here at Casa Cruella tonight, a year after they'd first met, then where? Every cell in his body was ablaze, as if the ruby pendant he'd mislaid somewhere at the Castle could still brand him with its mysterious heat, luring him back to Barcelona, back to this God-forsaken little temple to the Court of Cruelty, at this particular moment.

It wasn't as if it hadn't happened before, being drawn by the pendant into the drama of a lifetime.

Matins and Vespers' first set was at ten o'clock. By nine, the club was full to bursting, heavy metal screeching in the background. Waitresses flattened themselves against the walls to circulate with drink orders. Fahey parked himself on a stool near the service bar. Several of the girls stopped to kiss him hello, swearing to him in Spanish that they remembered him from last year. More likely, they remembered him from TV coverage of Teppan Nilsson's Christmastime adventure in hostage-taking. He happily locked lips with each for a minute, what the hell.

A decided non-vassal, or maybe just some guy who'd come straight from work, grabbed the stool next to him and laughed as Fahey smooched a quintet of concertgoers, dressed in black fishnets and Camelot Barbie pink and black, who chanted his name until each one had been bussed. When Fahey spun back to the bar, a fresh pint awaited him courtesy of the gentleman to his left.

*"Muchas gracias"*

*"De nada,"* the gentleman replied, though his accent suggested no innate connection to the Spanish language. He extended a hand. "My English is, fortunately, much better than my Spanish. I'm Chris."

"Jackson here, but you probably worked that out. Never expected a reception like this. Last year, I covered the show. This year, I'm hoping to knock back a few beers, actually listen to the tunes, and relax." Relaxing would, of course, be impossible until Chloe revealed herself, or didn't.

Chris pointed to the too-large amps positioned on the small stage. "The Cruel were not known for mellow music, likewise Matins and Vespers. Ear-bleeding sounds, I like tunes loud and mean."

Big fan evidently, the absence of medieval leather notwithstanding. He got up close to Fahey, leaned in. "You might even say 'Born to Slay the King' was written for me. Someone else beat me to it, and my mission was blown."

The guy was film-star handsome. "What are you," Fahey asked, "a professional assassin?"

"Something like that."

Not a subject Fahey was going to pursue, not tonight. "Maybe you'll get lucky and the band will rock your song. They've improved a lot since the show just after Sebastian and Emilie's deaths."

Chris's eyes darkened, from deep brown to almost black; Fahey tried not to stare. "How good can they be without Teppan Nilsson? Surely he was the soul of this band?"

Its corrupt, stained soul, but Fahey opted to keep that opinion to himself. Though Nilsson had taken permanent leave of his band mates, they could soldier on indefinitely without him, screaming through "Slay the King" and all the rest of the songs every vassal on earth could sing from memory. Eric had improved on bass and organ, was these days a more-than-passable impersonator of the great Sebastian de la Coeur. Katarina's private tutelage was paying off in more ways than one.

As if she'd been reading his mind, Kat appeared at Fahey's elbow, spun his stool around to face her, kissed him hard on the lips. "Darling boy," she said frostily, "how good it is to see you again, standing straight, walking tall." She ran her thumb along his scar. "So pretty. Thank goodness you took absolutely all the time you needed to recover. How vexing you are, though, making us wait ages for your official resurrection."

A verbal flaying, however subtle, was the least he deserved. Fahey kissed the air next to Kat's cheeks. "You're looking well. How have you been since, you know, that day?"

"Too polite for a man my husband almost killed, don't you agree, sir?" Chris looked her up and down and arched a provocative eyebrow. Kat laughed, a glittery, shimmery sound that surely seduced its way from her throat straight to the man's crotch. Her arm curled away from Fahey's waist, and she offered her hand to the stranger on the next barstool. Chris kissed her knuckles; Fahey swore he heard her gasp as if she'd been shocked. Electricity crackled through the space between them, Fahey felt it buzz through his hair, across his skin.

"I must get backstage before Eric comes looking for me," she said breathlessly, talking to Fahey but looking at Chris, "you know how jealous he becomes. So nice to meet you . . ."

"Chris," Fahey said.

"Christoph, if you prefer a more formal introduction," the object of her momentary desire offered. "I hope that I may call you Katarina. My condolences on the death of your husband."

She nodded demurely, lowering her eyes, but Fahey saw them heat through the contact lenses she wore from a cool blue to a torrid indigo. It was clear she had tapped into some new wavelength before she turned and walked backstage, a languid sway to her hips as she moved, one more intentional than Fahey remembered seeing before. The woman had picked up the scent, had the prey in her sights.

"She's fabulous, incredibly beautiful." Chris seemed astonished to realize as much, his eyes continuing to follow Kat until she stepped out of sight. "Do you know her well?"

Well enough for her husband to try to kill him, Fahey mused, but the real Kat? Hardly at all, not even her daughter knew what went on inside that very old, very young-looking head.

"I've known her about a year," Fahey said. "You two seemed to get on well."

"This Eric? Who is he?"

"Band mate-plus, you might say, he's been with Kat since I met her. She and Teppan had an unconventional marriage, from what I could tell."

Chris looked in the direction Katarina had gone. "We connected, she and I. I intend to connect further."

More intimately, and Eric be damned, it wasn't hard to read between those lines. Fahey guessed Chris liked his sex as loud and mean as his music.

The Hammond B-3 obliged and roared to life onstage. Casa Cruella's lights went even dimmer, though that seemed barely possible. Behind the drum kit, Lars crashed his cymbals to call the crowd to attention.

Chris gestured to the barkeep, who produced a bottle of scotch and two glasses before drifting away toward others clamoring for alcohol enough to raise the musical dead. Chris poured two fingers for Fahey, two for himself, and raised his glass. “To Katarina!” he toasted, and then, with a harsh rasp Fahey was sure he hadn’t imagined, “To Emilie!”

Recognition went both ways, it seemed to Fahey, no longer certain whom to think of as the predator and whom the prey. Kat, he suspected, would not gracefully be denied what she wanted. His new drinking friend seemed similarly strong-willed, understandable if you bought his assassin line.

He considered his companion as the club’s owner took the stage and prattled on about Barcelona’s special place in the kingdom of the Cruel. Chris was in his late thirties, Fahey estimated: muscular, broad-shouldered, tall, a familiar type. Just what Kat liked in her men.

Aware he was under scrutiny, Chris lifted the bottle to ask, then decided Fahey needed another drink, correctly so. He poured two fingers’ more for each of them.

“To Sebastian, but not those who would be like him, mere pretenders to the throne,” Chris mocked as Eric took the stage, bass guitar slung around him.

Fahey felt his throat close, as if someone was pressing a fist to his windpipe. He scrambled to his feet, as if that would help. He wouldn’t have drunk to Sebastian, that bastard son of a bitch, anyway, but he hadn’t counted on discovering that he couldn’t even if he tried. Do not panic, he commanded himself: Breathe in, breathe out. Before he even saw her, Chloe’s presence ignited his blood, her fire kindling his anxiety.

A pink spotlight bathed the stage. She and Kat walked into its glow, hand in hand. The crowd went nuts. Fahey sat down hard on his stool again, fearing he might pass out.

Dressed in tonight’s uniform, a hot-pink top, microscopic black skirt and black boots up to there, her ruby pendant reflecting the light, Chloe looked positively gorgeous—and undeniably pregnant.

Fahey shut his eyes, waited for the spell to pass. When he

opened them, nothing had changed: The club was quaking; the applause was deafening, or maybe that was just his heart thundering. She sat at the piano and played the opening notes of "Cri de Coeur," her body slim in profile except for the roundness of an unborn child.

Chloe was pregnant again? Fahey's fists clenched at the thought of Will Baumann in her bed. It had to have been Baumann creating an apparently thriving life within her so soon after they'd lost Guinevere. She would have turned to him after Fahey turned away. She had to feed, had to survive, pleasure for pleasure.

On the second verse, Katarina joined the song, her flute soaring. Lost in the music, she looked so like her daughter that Fahey couldn't believe he was the only one who saw the resemblance, who saw through the blue contacts to Emilie's malachite-green eyes, passed on to Chloe, the eyes he had fallen in love with.

The same green eyes he now saw night after night in his dream, on the miniature version of Chloe who called him Daddy.

*"I'm your other baby, I didn't die."*

Not pregnant again . . . pregnant still. More than one life.

"Are you feeling ill? You look terrible," Chris, Christoph, his wingman, slid another drink his way.

"Need some air, that's all." Fahey rushed for the club's exit, pressed his forehead against the cold stone of the outer wall, banged his dense skull against it.

So stupid, he should have known. Avalon, his little dream girl, had been trying to tell him for months.

* * * *

Five minutes into a forty-minute set. That gave him thirty-five minutes to pull it together. He could have called Chloe at any time in the last two weeks, could have confirmed which city she was in, arranged to meet her. But he hadn't wanted to risk it, hadn't wanted to give her the chance to say no. Which he deserved, after all those months of burrowing first into a hole of pain, then into a hole of fear, when she was bearing their baby and the other burdens that horrific sun-grilled morning had heaped on her. Regular bulletins to Meredith at his hospitals had relayed Chloe's descriptions of the army of glaziers needed to repair the Castle's windows, the orange-shrouded fumigation teams that fogged the music studio, the renovators who tore out the rug and the hardwood floor, tossed the upholstered furniture, painted and repainted until the only smell left was that of water-based, semi-gloss eggshell white.

The mess had fallen to Chloe to fix, yet she had thought to send Meredith back to England with him on a private jet, to deliver him into his parents' tender care and to his doctors, with very emphatic instructions that they were to do anything necessary to make him whole again. She had seen to everything: the investigating police; the insistent press; the cleanup; their child; and him, best of all. Proof of her love was everywhere.

Fahey bummed a cigarette from guys smoking on the sidewalk outside Casa Cruella, inhaled the nicotine blast until it burned; took more than a few hits of the weed they were passing around, too, which settled his stomach. Christ, he couldn't think how long it had been since his lungs were filled to bursting, the way his brain felt now that he saw his future laid before him. Every possibility was open to him, every question now had myriad potential solutions, but fundamentally what he wanted was to spend his finite life with the woman at that piano and their sweet baby girl.

Thirty minutes into the forty-minute set, he saluted his street-corner comrades adios and went back inside to reintroduce himself to his fate.

His eyes re-acclimated to Casa Cruella's shadows, and he spotted Chloe moving through the crowd, kissing any number of cheeks, being embraced by any number of strangers; just what she hated, the daughter-of-the-realm thing she'd told her father she'd never do again. Maybe it was different now that Teppan was gone, or maybe she wanted Fahey to find her here; he had to believe that. He stationed himself near the door, at the farthest point from the stage, and waited for her to take a seat at the bar. He watched her wrap herself back into Chloe Hart and throw off the Clothilde de la Coeur persona. She smiled at the bartender, said something that made him laugh, swiveled toward him so she could hear better, facing away from the masses and Fahey.

Slipping past as many people as he could as quickly as he could, he finally stood behind her. Immediately, she knew he was there: Her shoulders tensed, her spine stiffened.

*"Por favor,"* he signaled the barkeep, a beer for him and a Virgin Mary for the lovely mother of his child.

*"El es el padre?"* the barkeep asked.

*"Si,"* she replied. "Now, what was his name?"

Fahey lowered his mouth to her ear, blew lightly, bit the lobe. "My name is Bond, Blood Bond." He reached around her waist, set his hands lightly on her stomach. "This is Avalon Fahey, our daughter."

"You've given *this* baby a name?"

"No, I thought you did."

She leaned back against his chest. "Not after Guinevere. I didn't want to jinx this one."

Fahey kissed the top of her head, stroked her belly. "She's strong, our Ava, and smart, and looks just like her mother. I see her when I sleep. She brought me here, and I'm not leaving tonight without both of you."

Chloe covered his hands with hers. "What are you talking about?"

"Never mind. I'm deranged, crazy in love. How long have you known about her?"

Twisting so she could see his face, she placed warm fingers on his scar, ran their tips along its length; lowered her hands to his thigh, then to his new knee, caressing it through his jeans. "Since the day you and Meredith left for London. When she texted me before takeoff, I was miserable and weepy and my breasts were tender and I was hungry for actual food even though I wanted to vomit, the way I had felt with Guinevere. I went back to the midwife, and on the ultrasound, there she was: two arms; two legs; one strong heartbeat. The measurements confirmed I was four months' along. Same pregnancy, still due in June."

"Twins, then?"

"Fraternal, apparently they run in my father's family. She must have been tucked up behind Guinevere, hiding."

Fahey leaned in and kissed Chloe hard, starved for her. When he finally lifted his lips, she bit them, dipped her tongue into the blood that bubbled up, walked her fingers up his leg, circling them around his eager cock. Fahey wanted to carry her out of this very crowded club to the nearest place where he could make love to her, far away from the prying eyes of the vassals surrounding them. Already, people had noticed him and the Cruel's fair princess. He had a more private, more intimate reunion in mind.

Swells from the musical organ rescued them from curious stares. Eric swiped the microphone stand and growled his way into the final song of the set, "Born to Slay the King." Fahey scanned the front of the house, looking for the self-proclaimed assassin. Chris was perched near the edge of the stage, watching Kat gyrate with a pink-and black-ribboned tambourine, beating it against her hip as she slithered like a python around Eric, anointing his cheek with her tongue as she ascended, stroking his chest and thighs as she wound herself down his body and up again.

Vassals went wild, chanting, "Kat! Kat! Kat!" until it drowned out the music.

"If Emilie were here, she'd be appalled." Chloe was kneeling on her barstool for a better view.

"Get down, you're seven months' pregnant!"

She put her arms around his neck, to reassure him, Fahey

supposed, and for good measure nipped him and lapped up a bubble of blood. “Intoxicating, my love. I’ve missed you so much.”

Witch, she was weaving her magic, casting a spell on him again. Fahey shut his eyes, willed his loins to behave, wanted her never to stop. When something shifted Chloe’s attention away, an icy cold replaced the warmth of her body. Her eyes riveted on Chris, whose eyes were riveted on her mother. Kat did a bump-and-grind to the rhythm of her late husband’s paean to violent revolution. She strutted her stuff to the corner of the stage, selling the song to one man alone.

“Who is that?” Chloe rocked the stool.

Matins and Vespers fired a musical volley, unleashing the bone-crushing force of Lars’s drums and the strident wail of an electric guitar to end the song and the set. Chris opened his arms wide. Kat dived off the stage into his embrace, plastering her lips onto his, wrapping her legs around his waist.

Chloe dug fingernails into Fahey’s flesh. He slipped his arms under her knees and lifted her, sat on the barstool and lowered her onto his lap. His eyes caught a flash of silver as Eric hurled Kat’s flute at Chris’s head. Chris caught the instrument in one hand, his teeth bright against the darkness of the club, their gleam bouncing off the metal. A feral smile, like that of a wolf beholding his dinner.

“The light is disturbed around them.” Chloe’s eyes fixed on her mother and her new beau, whom Kat was now restraining from leaping onto the stage in pursuit of her old beau; Eric would have been wolf chow otherwise. Fahey calculated the men as evenly matched inch for inch, pound for pound, but that vicious grin put the odds dramatically in Chris’s favor.

“The light, that’s what concerns you?”

“It distorts as it bends around that man, the same way it does with Kat. The same way it bent around my father, and bends around me when I look in the mirror. The human eye doesn’t detect it; non-digital cameras can’t compensate for it.”

Something here was distorted, but Fahey was sure light had nothing to do with it; more like frustration and jealousy and blind rage. Lars and another big Swede dragged Eric backstage, kicking and vowing to kill the bastard who'd swept Kat out from under him, as if she'd ever been truly his. Drunken vassals, slowly comprehending there would be no second set, screamed their displeasure and rushed the stage, fists thrust up, demanding that their cover charge be refunded. A medieval riot seemed a distinct possibility, lacking only lit torches and pitchforks. Casa Cruella's owner stood on a table, mobile phone incongruously in his gauntleted hand, beseeching help from the Barcelona police, gesticulating wildly to the bartender to bring up the house lights.

A second angry wave surged forward from the back of the club, strewing chairs across the floor. Chloe slipped off Fahey's lap, tugged on his arm, pulling him to his feet.

"What the hell did Kat just start?" she shouted over a din made worse by the Spanish death-metal rock now vibrating off the walls. "She couldn't just lie low, God forbid."

Maybe, Fahey mused, there was no lying low after you'd lost someone you'd loved for a century and a half, especially when you were the one who'd made him want to die. At the bar's far corner, Kat and Chris melded to each other, his hand on her breast, her tongue no doubt down his throat, oblivious to the pandemonium around them.

"Unbelievable. She's lost her mind." Chloe reached for the leather jacket she'd draped over the bar. She fished out a fistful of euro, waved them at the bartender, tossed them his way. "That man is a vampire, Jackson. I've seen only three people with that aura around them: Sebastian and Emilie and me. Who *is* he?"

"He made a point of introducing himself to Kat as Christoph, but he didn't give a last name. Unless he was faking it, he's not local. Knows enough Spanish to order a drink, but not much more."

"Christoph Zwilling, I'd bet the Castle on it. Damn it,

Chestack was right. He said something smelled rank about this deal. Why didn't I listen to him?"

"What deal, and who the hell is Christoph Zwilling?"

"I've made a very pricey bargain with that devil: He's buying my parents' estate outside Prague."

Slaying the king by buying his house and seducing his wife? Is that what this was?

In his head, Fahey heard Chloe shriek. Something pink fluttered, and he shifted his gaze to where Kat straddled Chris's lap, her skirt hiked up so high as to be barely visible; her body moving in rhythm with the body part now inside it. It was only a matter of seconds before they became a sex video gone viral, as phone cameras documented the madness around them.

"Kill the lights! Kill all of them!" Chloe roared at the bartender, who dashed to flip switches behind him, casting Casa Cruella into gloom. Only the emergency exit lamps remained lit, rendering the black-red glow of Chloe's eyes all the more fearsome. Several brawling patrons swiftly backed away, recognizing danger.

Didn't faze Fahey, he'd seen far worse from the de la Coeurs. He reeled Chloe in close, kissed her gently, burned by the rage radiating from her. "Hated doing that, didn't you?" he whispered, running his tongue over his tender lip, the pain ebbing. "Would have been so much easier to wash your hands of your mother."

Against him, Chloe felt brittle, as if her fury would shake her apart. He hugged her all the more tightly.

"Emilie was a proper nineteenth-century noblewoman. That woman over there?" Chloe hissed. "I don't know *who* she is."

Fahey tipped her chin up, so he could look into her green-again eyes. "Maybe this is her way of burying your father."

"Then Christoph Zwilling will be her next mistake."

Chloe pushed Fahey off, her outrage louder than the bass line blaring through the near-darkness. "I've spent the last year cleaning up my parents' messes. I'm done."

Through the vassal throng she rushed, toward the glow of the streetlight at the top of the stairs, climbing so quickly Fahey lost sight of her. He raced up the steps two at a time and guessed she'd go left, toward the hotel where he'd first seen her a year ago, wearing that red wig, disguised as someone who wasn't Clothilde de la Coeur, the person she'd tried to shed a long time ago.

Except Sebastian and Emilie were her destiny, and she'd never be comfortably free of them. Neither would he. Loving Chloe meant embracing that unsettling truth.

Six blocks later, he caught up with her. She was standing in the rain in front of the hotel, dripping wet. She'd already waited months for him to make up his mind.

"Stay with me. Stay with us," she said, and stepped inside, letting the door slam behind her.

He made a sign of the cross and followed.

## Court of Cruelty Discography (LPs/CDs)

*Born to Slay the King* (acoustic, 1975)
*Miserere Nobis* (1976)
*Children's Crusade* (two discs, 1977)
*Peasants' Faire* (live, 1978)
*For My Liege, My Life* (greatest hits, 1979)
*As Albion Mourns* (1980)
*Heir Presumptive* (1981)
*Fiefdom of the Feral* (1982)
*Corpus Incorruptus* (1983)
*Gifts of the Holy Ghost* (1984)
*Auto Da Fe* (live, 1985)
*Heir Apparent* (1986)
*Circles of Hell* (1987)
*Maiden's Madrigal* (1988)
*Blood Sacrifice* (1990)
*The Rack* (1992)
*Monarch's Kiss* (live, 1994)
*Plague of Fools* (1995)
*Knights Errant* (1996)
*Communion of Saints,*
*Commingling of Sinners* (last studio album, 1997)

## Noteworthy songs

"Born to Slay the King"
"Bride Price"
"Croix de Guerre" / "Cri de Coeur"
"Faithless Servant"
"Fear of the Lord"
"Feudal/Futile"
"Fortitude"
"Inquisition"
"Lady Anna's Disgrace"
"Piety"
"Plague of Fools"
"Sanctifying Grace"
"Slaughter of the Innocents"
"Wifely Duties"

## ABOUT THE AUTHOR

**Joanne McLaughlin** has worked at newspapers and news websites in Philadelphia, upstate New York and northeastern Ohio, involved in articles on everything from politics and murder, to sports and interior design, to fashion and financial markets, to Pulitzer Prize-finalist architecture criticism. As vice president of a musicians-management firm and record company, she applied her creative talents to publicizing blues artists and producing and promoting their work. A Penn State graduate with a grown musician/schoolteacher son, she lives in suburban Philadelphia. Learn more at joannemclaughlin.net.

**Email:** joannemclaughlinwrites@gmail.com
**Twitter:** @joannemclaugh
**Facebook:** Joanne McLaughlin Writes

**Also By Author:** "Never Before Noon," Vampires of the Court of Cruelty Book One (2016, Eternal Press, an imprint of Caliburn Press); "Peppina's Sweetheart" (2015, Kindle Direct); "Grass and Granite" (2015, Kindle Direct)

www.ingramcontent.com/pod-product-compliance
Lightning Source LLC
Chambersburg PA
CBHW052022240626
47153CB00006B/1919
*9781732585218*